nt of his
rimal

ly. But

around
body,
and
So

him that

st. The

ire.

at
night. Why you let ther   knew
I was innocent."

Other titles by Rita Herron

RITA HERRON

LAST KISS *Goodbye*

HQN™

ISBN-13: 978-0-373-77102-8
ISBN-10:   0-373-77102-9

LAST KISS GOODBYE

This edition published by arrangement with Harlequin Books S.A.

® and TM are trademarks of the publisher. Trademarks indicated with ® are registered in the United States Patent and Trademark Office, the Canadian Trade Marks Office and in other countries.

www.HQNBooks.com

Printed in U.S.A.

Dear Reader,

Having grown up in the rural South, where local legends, folklore and superstitions abound, add flavor to small-town life and make the town come alive, I developed an affinity for using those elements in my own storytelling.

There are also Southern scenes that paint such vivid parts of rural life in my mind that I had to use those, as well. For example, the trailer parks (mobile home parks) where some of my own family live. The junkyards sprinkled throughout the countryside where old cars, buses, trucks are left, their parts sold off. And of course, the kudzu vines that grow out of control and take over the dilapidated barns and rotting wooden houses.

In this latest romantic suspense, *Last Kiss Goodbye,* I tried to paint those pictures for you by way of the legends and myths in the fictitious small town of Kudzu Hollow, Georgia.

When I first began, one thought stuck out in my mind—I knew I wanted the heroine to have witnessed her parents' murder when she was a child, and that the only thing she remembered about that horrific night was kissing her mother goodbye. That gave me my title.

Of course, for a Rita Herron heart-pounding romantic suspense story, I had to add a strong sense of family, emotional turmoil, murder and small-town secrets, along with a sizzling romance between two wounded souls who desperately need each other!

With this book, I've also included guidelines for you and your book club (if you belong to one) to aid you in discussing the story and the metaphors I've used.

I hope you enjoy!

Sincerely,

Rita

To George Scott, my favorite, fantastic bookseller—thanks for all your support, and for helping to make my single-title romantic suspense debut, A BREATH AWAY, a success!

LAST
KISS
Goodbye

PROLOGUE

"MOMMY!" EIGHT-YEAR-OLD Ivy Stanton stared at the blood on her hands in horror. There was so much of it. All over her. Her mother. The floor.

"Ivy, Jesus, look what you've done!" Her daddy's gray eyes seared her like fire pokers. Outside the wind howled, rattling the windowpanes and metal of their trailer. The Christmas tree lights blinked, flashing a rainbow of colors across the room.

"She's dead," her daddy said, "and it's all your fault."

Ivy shook her head in denial, but he shoved her blood-soaked hands toward her face, and she started to cry. Then she looked down at the knife on the floor. And her mother's lifeless body sprawled across the carpet. Her pretty brown eyes stared up at the ceiling, icy now.

No! Her mama couldn't be dead. If Ivy just kissed her, she'd wake up. Then she'd smile and hug Ivy and tell her everything was going to be all right. That tomorrow they'd finish decorating the Christmas tree and wrap the presents.

Ivy pressed her lips against her mama's cheek, but it was so cold and stiff, she shivered.

Then her father yanked her up by the arm. "You're poison, Ivy. You've ruined this family."

"No!" She struggled against him, but he shoved her so close to her mother, Ivy saw the whites of her mama's bulging eyes. Ivy's stomach cramped, and she coughed, choking. All that blood. So red.

No, not red. The color faded. Just yucky brown.

Even the colored Christmas lights disappeared, turned to black dots before her eyes.

He snagged her hair and flung her backward. Pain exploded in her head as she hit the wall. She scrambled to her knees, tried to run toward the door, but he lunged after her, grabbed her ankle and twisted it so hard she thought she heard it snap. She cried out and kicked at his hands until she was free. A bolt of thunder jolted the trailer, shaking it as if a tornado was coming. Two of her mama's ceramic Santa Clauses crashed to the floor.

Ivy crawled across the glass, felt shards stab her palms. She had to save the Santas. Save them for when her mama came back.

Her daddy reached for her again. No. No time to get the glass Santas. She had to escape.

She grabbed the cloth Santa instead, the new one her mama had just sewed from felt scraps. Clutching it, Ivy vaulted up and out the trailer door. Her ankle throbbed as she hobbled down the wooden steps and darted toward the junkyard. Her father chased her, his screech echoing over the wind. Tree limbs reached like claws above her in the shadows. Lightning flashed in jagged patterns.

It was dark, and she could barely see. She tripped

over a tire rim. A stabbing pain shot through her ankle and leg, and she had to heave for air. But she forced herself up, fighting the wind. It was so strong it hurled her forward. Rain began to splatter down, mud squishing inside her sneakers. Behind her, her father shouted a curse. His bad knee slowed him down.

Her chest ached as she dashed through the rows of broken-down cars. Ones people didn't want anymore.

Just like her daddy didn't want her.

He'd told her so dozens of times.

Ivy's legs gave way again, and she collapsed on the soggy ground. The Santa flew from her hands. Mud soaked her clothes, splashed her face.

Then someone grabbed her from behind.

Flailing, she yelled and kicked.

"Stop fighting me, dammit."

He released her, and she scrambled away on her knees. It wasn't her father. Bad-boy Matt Mahoney was standing in the shadows. He stood motionless, his chin jutting up, a pair of ragged jeans hanging off his hips. He was soaked with rain and smelled like car grease. And he was so muscular and big he could stomp her into the ground. His black eyes tracked her as if she was an ant he wanted to kill.

"Dammit to hell, Ivy." He launched forward with one giant step, picked her up, then the Santa, and carried her toward a rusty van. Kudzu vines covered the roof and dangled over the windows, blocking all light.

Ivy shuddered. It was pitch-black. She knew the

nasty things men did to women in the dark. Had heard her daddy and mama. And those other men from Red Row.

Knew what bad boys like Matt wanted.

He opened the door, then shoved her on the bench seat in the back. With one hand, he untied the bandanna from around his head and wiped at the blood on her mouth. She couldn't breathe. He was going to choke her just like the kudzu choked the wildflowers in the yard.

Suddenly he yanked a knife from his pocket. The blade shimmered in the dark as he ripped away the front seat cover. His expression changed as he gently spread it over her. Then he pushed the cloth Santa back into her hands. "Shh, no one can see you in here," he murmured softly. "It's a good place to hide. Rest now, little Ivy."

She searched his big black eyes. She knew what he saw. She was covered in mud and leaves and blood. A bad girl just like her daddy said.

She willed away the memory. Told herself it wasn't true. Her mama hadn't died. She would come back tomorrow. Glue the Santas together. Pick Ivy up and kiss her again. And this time her mama's lips would be warm.

Ivy's head spun, and the bloody red color faded to brown again. She didn't want to remember. To see the red. Not ever again.

No, she had to forget....

She closed her eyes, dragging the makeshift blanket over her head to shut out the night and the grisly images.

CHAPTER ONE

Fifteen years later

"DON'T GO BACK to Kudzu Hollow, Ivy. Please. I'm begging you, it's too dangerous. There's nothing but evil and death in that town."

Ivy squeezed her adopted mother's hand, then bent to kiss her cheek, her cool leathery skin reminding her of the time she'd kissed her birth mother goodbye.

The day she'd died.

In fact that kiss was the last thing Ivy remembered about that horrible night. That and the terrified cries echoing in her head. Her mother's. Her own. She couldn't be sure which. Or maybe it was both, all mingled together, haunting her in the night.

Miss Nellie wheezed, cutting into Ivy's morbid thoughts. Her adopted mother was close to death now, too. She'd suddenly taken ill a few days ago, and had gone downhill fast. She claimed she'd made peace with her maker, but Ivy wasn't so sure. Sometimes she saw doubt, worry, secrets in Miss Nellie's eyes. Secrets the woman refused to share.

Secrets that told her Miss Nellie had a dark side.

"I have to go back, Miss Nellie," she said in a low whisper. "I…I've been having nightmares. Panic attacks." *And sometimes I see images from the past in the night, monsters that can't be real. Cries and whispers of death. Screams of ghosts and spirits crying out for salvation. And I'm lost in the middle….*

Miss Nellie's hand trembled as she lifted it to brush a strand of hair from Ivy's cheek. "Forget about the past, dear. You have to let it go."

"How can I?" Fading sunlight dappled the patchwork quilt in gold and created a halo around Miss Nellie's face. Ivy stood and faced the bedroom window, the scents of illness and dust surrounding her. She hated to lose Miss Nellie, but the elderly woman had looked so pale and her cheeks were sallow. The doctors weren't certain what had caused her illness, but they'd said she wouldn't make it another week, much less to Christmas.

Christmas—the Santas…

Ivy shuddered and fought against the fear that gnawed at her at the thought of the upcoming holidays, with all the twinkling lights, festive ornaments and decorations. Snowmen and reindeer, and of course, the Santas. Those Santas were the only thing she had left of her mother. Dozens of them. Soft ones sculpted from fine red-and-white velvet, with tiny black boots and belts and long cottony beards. Crystal and homemade crafted Santas with glass eyes and painted smiles. Wooden ones carved from bark and painted in a folk art style. Ivy kept them boxed up, though, couldn't bear to look at them.

Just as she couldn't look at Miss Nellie now.

She'd always felt Miss Nellie held something back, some part of herself she kept at a distance from Ivy. She knew it had to do with Nellie losing her own son when he was small, but her foster mother refused to talk about him or even show Ivy pictures.

A sob built in Ivy's throat. Miss Nellie was all she had. Another reason she wanted answers. When Miss Nellie passed, she'd take her secrets with her to the grave. Just as Ivy's parents had.

And Miss Nellie had secrets.

"Please tell me what you meant in the journal, Miss Nellie. How did you come to get me?"

"That journal was private, you shouldn't have been snooping." Miss Nellie clammed up abruptly, her thin lips pinched and almost blue as she turned her head away.

"I didn't mean to snoop, Miss Nellie, but I need to know."

"All that matters is that God wanted me to raise you. And I got you out of Kudzu Hollow. That town is tainted, I tell you," Miss Nellie warned. "There's evil there. I knew it when I lived there. And I've seen the papers, heard stories on the news over the years. Ever since your folks was murdered, bad things have been happening. Livestock and animals attacking one another. Children dying before their time. Folks rising from the grave. Men becoming animals. Teenagers turning against their folks that raised them."

Miss Nellie was superstitious. It was the way of the people of Appalachia. But Ivy couldn't argue. She'd seen the stories, too, had read the papers. Every few years, always after a bout of bad thunderstorms and rain, the entire town seemed to go crazy. Crime spiked to a high. There had been several killings.

Even more odd was the fact that very few people ever left the town—alive, anyway. And the ones who'd lost loved ones seemed trapped by the old legends. Either that or they were held there by the spirits of the dead, who supposedly roamed the graveyard on the side of the mountain.

"No town or person is all bad," Ivy said, clinging to her optimistic nature. "There has to be some good there, too."

Miss Nellie's expression softened slightly. "You're so naive, Ivy. You always try to find good in everything. But there ain't no good there. Just ghosts and the devil." The old woman coughed and reached for her oxygen mask, inhaled a deep breath, then continued in a wheezing voice. "I used to hear the children chant when they were skipping rope.

'Evil in the kudzu
devil in the men
Death in the hollow
again and again.'

And it's true. People are afraid to stay. Afraid to leave."

Ivy shivered. She'd been so afraid to return.

But those old fears were keeping her from having a sane life. From being with a man. From loving.

Even the colors hadn't returned. The fall leaves outside had already started changing, but all she would see were brown and hints of yellow. There was no red. Even oranges appeared a muddy color.

She crossed the room to Miss Nellie's bed and sat down beside her in the hard wooden chair. "If you don't want me to go back, then tell me the truth about the night my parents died."

Miss Nellie's face turned ashen. "The only thing you need to know is that they locked up the killer. None of them Mahoney boys were ever any account."

Ivy bit her bottom lip, her stomach knotting. Matt Mahoney hadn't been all bad. She wasn't sure how she knew that, but she did.

So why had everyone been so quick to blame him? She'd written him letters to find out, but he'd never responded. And six months ago, she'd drummed up enough courage to drive to the prison to hear his side, but he'd refused her visit.

The past few months, the local paper had featured articles on a lawyer named Willis who was writing a book on old cases and corruption in small-town politics. He'd managed to clear prisoners who'd been falsely arrested, citing new evidence based on advances in DNA testing. He was working on Matt's case now.

What if they'd convicted the wrong man for her parents' murders? Matt had been sixteen at the time. Why would he have killed her folks? That question had haunted her for years now.

That and the fact that if he was innocent, Matt had spent fifteen years in jail for a crime he hadn't committed.

All because she'd been too much of a coward to remember the events of that night.

Six weeks later

MATT MAHONEY HAD SPENT the last fifteen years in jail for a murder he hadn't committed. And someone was going to pay for the way he'd been wronged.

Thank God Abram Willis had taken an interest in his case. Willis had chosen to devote half of his practice to cold case files, to "the Innocents," as he referred to them. Men and women falsely imprisoned.

And he'd been digging into Matt's case for months now. Today would tell if he'd been successful.

Matt glanced at the lawyer and hoped he'd presented the case effectively, that he'd crossed all his t's and dotted all the i's. The judge had reviewed the evidence and called them to reconvene for his decision.

Willis fidgeted with his tie, then adjusted his wire-rims. The damn lawyer looked as nervous as Matt felt. Except Matt's future was on the line here.

What was left of it.

The bailiff called the court to order, and the judge slammed down the gavel, then cleared his throat. Tufts of white hair stood up on the back of his balding head, making him look almost approachable. But his lack of expression during the hours Willis had presented the case made Matt wonder. And the steady gaze that he settled on Matt at that moment added to the mounting tension in the courtroom. Matt glanced at the sunlight streaming through the window, aching to step outside and bask in it. This judge was the only thing standing between him and freedom. He could almost taste the fresh air, smell the grass and leaves, feel the heat beating on his face and back.

But if he didn't win today, he would go back inside.

Back to the dismal existence and that damn cell block that had become his life.

The judge cleared his throat. "After studying the evidence collected fifteen years ago, and after reviewing the current DNA evidence supplied, the court agrees that a mistake was made in this case. I'm ruling to overturn your conviction." His expression turned grave. "The court offers its deepest apologies to you, Mr. Mahoney, but also issues you a warning. We're trying to right a wrong here today. Remember that, and don't use your incarceration as an excuse to make trouble."

Matt exhaled slowly, the burning ache of disbelief rolling through him. Had he really heard the judge correctly? After all this time, was he ruling in Matt's favor?

"You are free to go, Mr. Mahoney. With the court's regrets, of course."

He pounded the gavel, ending the session, and Willis jumped up and slapped Matt on the back in congratulations. A deputy stepped forward and removed the ankle bracelet. Matt stood immobile, breathless, as the metal fell away. He couldn't believe it. He was free. Free to walk out the door for the first time in fifteen years. Free to go anywhere he wanted without a guard breathing down his shoulder, without handcuffs and chains around his ankles. Free to go to bed at night without another man watching him, or worrying that he might never live to see freedom.

But if the judge thought he'd righted the wrong just by releasing him, he was a damn idiot.

Matt had lost fifteen years of his life.

And someone had to answer for that. The town of Kudzu Hollow. Ivy Stanton.

And the person responsible for the Stanton slayings. The real killer had to be punished this time. And Matt would make certain that happened.

Even if it killed him.

"I KNOW YOU'RE STILL grieving over Miss Nellie's death, Ivy," George Riddon said. "And I want to help you if you'd let me."

Ivy stared at her partner at *Southern Scrapbooks*, the magazine she'd birthed with the help of her own savings and George's funding, and bit her lip. She'd thought George had stopped by her house to talk business. But so far, his visit had seemed personal. He'd been pushing her to date him for months now, had hinted that he wanted more.

Much more than she could give.

"I'm sorry, George, but it's just too soon."

He slid his hands around her arms and held her still when she would have walked away. "Listen, I want you, Ivy. I've been patient, but a man can only wait so long. We would be really good together. All you need to do is give us a chance."

She froze, the note of anger in his voice spiking her own. "No one is asking you to wait."

A fierce look flashed in his hazel eyes. Eyes before that had always been kind and businesslike. "What are you saying? That you won't ever…that you can't see me that way? Is it my age?"

"No, of course not. You're not that much older than me." Ivy simply couldn't see any man that way. She wished she could.

Sometimes she was so lonely.

He released her abruptly and snapped open the September layout she'd completed on Southern romantic rendezvous. "Look at all these places. Maybe if we took a trip together we could kindle the fire between us."

She glanced down at the rows of pictures she'd scrapbooked for the magazine. Idyllic, charming bed-and-breakfasts in the mountains, the Grand Ole Opry Hotel in Nashville, a cozy inn on the river in New Orleans, the Chattanooga Choo-choo. A deep sadness washed over her. When she'd photographed and finished the layout, she had imagined herself there, walking hand in hand with a lover, making love as the river rushed over rocks nearby. She longed for a companion in life. But as much as she'd tried, she couldn't imagine that person as George.

"Please just let it go." She sighed. "I have too much on my mind right now."

His jaw tightened as he ran a hand over his sandy-blond beard. "I'm beginning to think you're a cold fish. That you use your past as an excuse so you won't have to get close to anyone."

Ivy glared at him. Granted, she hadn't made a lot of friends, but she wasn't a cold fish. She needed order to keep the demons at bay. The endless patterns of her day, the routines, the sameness kept her sane and safe.

Get up at seven. Shower. Go to the office. Hit the gym after work for a three-mile run around the track to help her sleep at night. Dinner. Reading. Tea. Bed. Then start it all over the next day, a vicious circle where she was never moving forward, just in a circle like the track.

Sometimes the routines kept the nightmares away. And when those nightmares left her, erotic dreams filled her sleeping hours. Dreams of being touched, loved, caressed by an anonymous dark-haired man. He seemed familiar, but she couldn't quite see his face or discern his features.

If or when she gave her body to a man, he had to be someone she really wanted to be with, a man who made her feel alive and special. A man who moved emotions inside her. A man she could trust enough to share her secrets.

That man wasn't George.

"I'm sorry." He sighed, looking frustrated but resigned. "I know you're still troubled over Miss Nellie's diary. But if you don't get over it, Ivy, this magazine is going to fall apart because you're not focused."

She swallowed hard. The magazine was her baby, the only thing she'd ever put her heart into. Failure was not an option.

"What *do* you have planned for the October

issue?" George asked. "The deadlines are approaching."

"I was thinking about featuring Appalachian folklore and ghost stories. That would fit with the Halloween theme."

He plucked at his beard again as he chewed over the idea. "That could work. Do you have a specific place in mind?"

"Kudzu Hollow."

He frowned. "I thought Miss Nellie convinced you not to go back there."

The television droned in the background, but Ivy froze, momentarily caught off guard when a special news segment flashed on the screen. Abram Willis, the lawyer who'd been working on Matt Mahoney's case, appeared in front of a massive stone, columned structure, a flock of reporters on his heels. The courthouse in Nashville.

A tall man with thinning hair and a tanning-bed-bronzed complexion stopped in front of the lawyer, blocking his exit. "This is Don Rivers reporting to you from C & N News. We have a live interview with Abram Willis, the nationally acclaimed attorney, currently fighting to free falsely accused prisoners."

"Ivy—"

"Shh." She pushed past George and turned up the volume, her eyes glued to the set, her adrenaline churning. The distinguished attorney paused to address the group, absentmindedly straightening his tie, which matched his streaked gray hair. But it was the man beside him who captured Ivy's attention.

Well over six feet tall with jet-black hair, and eyes so dark brown they looked black. His powerful body exuded pure raw masculinity, as well as bitterness and anger. The scar that zigzagged down his left cheek added an air of brutality that bordered on frightening. But something about his darkness drew her, made her wonder if he really was the hard, cold man he appeared on the surface. Pain radiated from his body, and his eyes held such deep sadness that Ivy literally trembled with compassion.

For a fleeting second, another image passed through the far recesses of her brain, the image of Matt Mahoney as a teenager. He'd been fierce, angry, frightening. But all the teenage girls had wanted him, had whispered about the girls he'd taken in the back of his daddy's '75 Chevy.

Now he looked exhausted, half-dead from defeat. Yet a small spark lit his eyes—relief at his sudden and unexpected freedom.

"Mr. Willis, is it true that the court overturned the ruling on Mr. Mahoney's murder conviction?" Rivers asked. "That he spent fifteen years in jail for a crime that evidence now proves he didn't commit?"

Willis nodded, puffing up his chest as he straightened his suit jacket, but Matt averted his face as if shying away from the camera. "That's correct," the attorney said. "Justice has finally been served. Mr. Mahoney has been cleared of charges and has been pardoned."

The reporter shoved a microphone in Matt's face. "Mr. Mahoney, tell us how it feels to be free."

"What are you going to do now?" another reporter shouted.

A chorus of others followed. "Are you receiving monetary retribution for the past fifteen years?"

"Are you going home?"

"If you didn't kill that family, do you know who did?"

Ivy pressed her hand to her mouth, waiting for his answer. But Matt scowled at the camera, pushed the microphone away with an angry swipe of his hand and stalked through the crowd without responding.

"What the hell is it, Ivy?" George said, sliding his hand to her waist. "You act like you've seen a ghost."

She gestured toward the screen with a shaky hand, the black hole of her past threatening to swallow her. "That's the man who was convicted of killing my parents."

MATT INHALED THE CRISP fall air as he walked away from the courthouse, barely noting that the smells of grass, honeysuckle and clean air that he'd craved were missing, that the city with its concrete buildings and sidewalks had destroyed those things, just as prison had decimated his dignity. Goddamn bloodsucking reporters. He'd half wanted to use them as a tool to vent his case, since they'd sure as hell done a number on him years ago. But he wouldn't give them the satisfaction.

And what could he say?

That he was bitter. That he hated the system that had failed him. That he despised the citizens who still stared at him as if he was guilty. That he wished he had a nice home to go to. Someone waiting on him. A family. A loving wife or lover. Anyone who cared about him. A future.

He didn't.

In fact, going home meant facing the very people who'd condemned him. The neighbors and family who'd gossiped about his family, testified against his character, thrown him away and forgotten about him.

The ones who believed he was a murderer.

But he would face them, anyway. Because some-one in Kudzu Hollow knew the truth about the Stanton slayings and had allowed him to take the fall.

One last glance at the columns of the courthouse and its stately presence, and he remembered all he'd learned in prison. Laws varied, depending on a person's financial status. For the poor, the old adage "innocent until proven guilty" didn't matter one iota. In fact, it was the opposite—you were guilty from the beginning, and nothing you said made a damn bit of difference. From the moment the sheriff had slapped handcuffs on him, Matt had been labeled a killer. Not one person in Kudzu Hollow had spoken up to defend him.

Then in prison…hell, everyone screamed they were innocent. He'd had a hard time telling the dif-ference himself. He'd met men bad to the bone, some meaner and more depraved than he'd ever imagined. But other innocents like him, convicted by bad cops, seedy lawyers, piss-poor judges and shoddy crime scene techs, filled the cells, too.

Trouble was, once the prisoners were all thrown in there together, fighting for survival took priority.

And they all became animals.

Sweat beaded his forehead at the memory of the acts he'd committed in the name of survival.

His life would never be the same. He'd lost his youth, and for a while his chance for an education, although the last few years he'd pulled himself together and had been studying the law. One day soon, he'd obtain his license and take the bar exam. Become a respectable citizen and prove to the world that it had been wrong about him. Maybe he'd even work with Willis to help free other innocents.

Matt's chest squeezed, though, as he climbed into the lawyer's black Cadillac. Now only one thing drove him—bittersweet revenge on the man responsible.

If only he knew his identity.

That fateful night raced back as Willis drove through Nashville, Matt's mind wandering back in time as the sea of cars and traffic noises swirled around him.

Fifteen years ago, he'd been up to no good, stealing tires from the junkyard, when he'd spotted that little Stanton girl running for her life. Hell, he'd felt sorry for the kid. They'd both grown up in the trailer park that backed up to the junkyard. He knew the kind of life she had. Had heard folks in town gossiping that her mother liked the men, that if she wasn't married she'd be shacked up in one of Talulah's Red Row trailers making money on her back. And some said that she did spend her days there with her legs spread wide, entertaining customer after customer while her old man sold car parts and pedaled junk for a living. And Matt had finally learned that was true, although he wasn't proud of the way he'd found out.

Old man Stanton had beat his wife. They were white trash just like his family. Ivy had been such a puny little thing, with bundles of curly blond hair and those big green eyes that he hated to think of her big-bellied father taking his fists to her. The poor kid didn't have enough meat or muscle on her to fend off a spider, much less a drunk, two-hundred-pound, pissed old fart who wreaked of whiskey and a bad temper.

When Matt had seen all that blood on her hands and shirt, the devil had climbed inside him. He'd wanted to kill her bastard daddy. Teach him to pound on somebody his own size. And he had gone to the trailer, the one with the torn, yellowed curtains, the broken-down swing set and the beer cans smashed against the porch.

But he hadn't killed anyone.

No, her mother had been dead when he arrived. A vicious slaying, as if animals had been at it. Matt had damn near lost his dinner seeing all the blood on the floor, like a fucking river. And her daddy had been found later, buried beneath the kudzu, his body slashed and bloody, his face carved as if an animal had ripped him apart.

Not that Matt's pleas of innocence had mattered.

The sheriff had found his boot prints, his damn *fingerprints* on the doorknob, and he'd been rail-roaded to jail for the crime, anyway.

Craving fresh air, and suddenly claustrophobic as prison memories assaulted him, Matt cranked down the window, uncaring that the air that assaulted him was tainted with smog and exhaust fumes. It spelled freedom.

He was thirty-one now. Thirty-one with nowhere to go, nothing to do, and not a soul in the world who gave a damn that he was out. Thirty-one and so damn scarred inside and out that no sane woman would ever want him.

All because he'd had a tender streak for a little girl who hadn't bothered to show up at his trial and defend him.

Damn fool. That's what he was. What he'd always been.

But never again.

The sun warmed his face as Willis wove through the heavy rush hour traffic. Matt dragged his mind from the depths of despair where he'd lived for so long, and tried to soak up the changes in the city. New businesses and skyscrapers had cropped up on every corner, rising toward the heavens. Car horns and humming motors of SUVs and minivans whizzing by bombarded him, as did the loud machinery on a construction site. The sight of modern vehicles, the styles so different from fifteen years ago, reminded him of all that he'd missed.

"How about a motel on the outskirts of the city?" Willis asked. "There's a used car lot across the street, and a motor vehicle place a few blocks away so you can renew your driver's license tomorrow."

Matt nodded. "Sounds good." Willis pulled into a

Motel 6 and cut the engine. Matt turned to him, forever grateful. "Thank you for all you did for me, Abram."

A smile lifted the older man's lips. "Just don't make me regret it."

Matt's gaze met his, and he nodded. He just hoped he could keep that promise.

Willis handed him an envelope. "Here's some cash from your account and a credit card. I'll let you know when the state compensation comes in. It won't be near enough, but it should help you get started."

Matt accepted the envelope. "Thanks again." He shook Abram's hand, then climbed out, smiling at the fact that he could step outside alone. Then he went inside and registered. A few minutes later, he walked across the street to the Wal-Mart, bought a couple of pairs of jeans and T-shirts, along with some toiletries—all mundane tasks that felt so liberating. Like a kid, excitement stirred inside him as he stopped at the Burger King and ordered a couple of Whoppers and fries. He grabbed the bag, inhaling the smell of fast food with a grin, then walked to the convenience store on the corner, bought a six-pack of beer and headed back to the motel for his celebration.

He had to go back to Kudzu Hollow and face his demons soon, but not tonight.

Tonight he'd celebrate his freedom. Tomorrow he'd renew his driver's license, buy a car and a used computer, then locate Ivy Stanton. And when he found her, he'd surprise her with a little visit.

Unlike the day the police had questioned her about her parents' murders, this time she wouldn't claim she didn't know what had happened.

This time, she'd damn well do some talking.

ARTHUR BOLES WAVED his son into his office with a glare, popped an antacid tablet into his mouth and released a string of expletives. "Dammit, Crandall, I've paid you a small fortune to keep that Mahoney boy in jail. How did you let that confounded fool Willis get him free?"

"Listen, calm down, Arthur," his attorney screeched over the telephone line. "I did everything I could. By all rights, the boy should have been paroled years ago."

"But you managed to keep that from happening, so why couldn't you stop this disaster?"

"I've used up all my favors and jeopardized my own reputation for you," Crandall snapped. "Now I'm through, Arthur. Through doing your dirty work for you, through putting myself on the line. I fully intend to salvage my career and wash my hands of the whole mess."

Arthur ran a palm over his thinning hair, watching as his son, A.J., paced the room like a caged animal. The boy was nervous. Hell, they all were.

"You can't walk away from me now, Crandall."

"I can and I will," the lawyer snapped. "And if you dare try to use what I've done to blackmail me, I will expose you and your son."

Crandall slammed down the phone, and Arthur cursed again, then raked a hand across his desk, sending papers flying in fury. Crandall wouldn't reveal a damn word. Arthur would see to that.

"Dad," A.J. said in a worried voice as he paused, jerked open the liquor cabinet and grabbed a fifth of bourbon. Tipping up the bottle, he drank straight from it like a heathen, the brown liquid dribbling down his chin. Just as he had fifteen years ago. The night the trouble had started.

"What in the hell are we going to do?" A.J. swiped a hand over his mouth. "Mahoney's out. And you know the first place he'll come."

Traces of desperation and fear lined A.J.'s face, suddenly aging his son another ten years. Arthur's own panic gripped his chest like a vise, but he stalked toward A.J., took the bottle from his hand. "I'll take care of things. Don't worry."

A.J. relaxed slightly, but remnants of memories lingered in his eyes. The same ones that troubled Arthur. They both had made mistakes fifteen years ago. But they'd survived this long without anyone knowing.

And those mistakes would go with them to their graves.

Even if Arthur had to kill Crandall and Mahoney to keep them buried.

IVY HAD BEEN ALONE FOR SO LONG.

His dark eyes skated over her, and her body tingled in response. She wasn't a cold fish. No, she craved his touch. Could not get enough.

His shaggy black hair nudged his collar, the desire in his dark eyes nearly bringing her to her knees. *She reached for him, but he shook her hand away and made her wait. With one finger he flicked the buttons on her shirt free, the corner of his mouth twitching as he peeled it from her shoulders. Cool air brushed her skin, and her nipples budded beneath the flimsy lace of her bra. A hot look of hunger colored his irises, but he still didn't move to kiss her. He simply stood stone still, watching her chest rise and fall as he slid her panties down her thighs. She stepped out of them, suddenly feeling shy.*

But the hiss of his breath was so erotic that all shyness fled.

He smiled, then cupped one hand behind her neck, lowered his mouth and claimed hers. Her heart pounded as he tasted and explored, teased her lips apart and thrust his tongue inside. Then he trailed kisses down her neck and lower, to her breasts. Pleasure rippled through her. She had been waiting all her life for this moment. For his touch. His lips. His hands.

His fingers slid along her spine, over the curve of her hips, then lower to her blond curls that were already wet from wanting him. A groan erupted from his throat as he pulled back and looked at her. A fierce need glimmered in his eyes, making her ache to strip him and touch him all over.

But when she reached for him, he drifted away, swallowed by the darkness....

IVY JERKED AWAKE, panting and sweating, the sheets twisted around her legs and arms where she'd rolled from side to side as waves of erotic satisfaction splintered through her. She wasn't the cold fish George had accused her of being. She was starved for love, for a man's comfort, for his touches and kisses.

And the man in her dreams...this time she had seen his face.

And that face had belonged to the man who'd been imprisoned for killing her parents—Matt Mahoney.

God. She dropped her head into her hands, trembling. Matt Mahoney was not a man she would ever have sex with. Not a man who would want her.

The dark coldness of the room closed around her, suffocating her. The screams of terror suddenly exploded in her head again, and her heart pounded. A monster's face replaced Matt's, and she saw the blood. Brown, not red. Floating like a river around her mother's body. A wail lodged in Ivy's throat as the smell of death bombarded her. She had to run but her legs wouldn't move. The silent voices screeched in her ears.

Run like the wind. Run from the monster or he'll get you again.

Just as she had fifteen years ago. Anything to escape the horror.

Or he would kill her, too. And there would be no tomorrow.

TOMORROW WAS THE beginning of another bad day. The beginning of the end for some in Kudzu Hollow.

For years now, the dark cloud, as Lady Bella Rue

called it, had hovered about the small mountain community, floating away only occasionally, only long enough to give the locals a momentary reprieve. But before hope could be rekindled, the cloud returned with a vengeance to dump more sorrow and misfortune on the town.

Lady Bella Rue gathered her shawl around her trembling shoulders, fighting the wind as she walked outside and descended the steps to her root cellar. Storm clouds brewed above, the smell of rain and trouble filling her nostrils, a streak of lightning splintering off the mountain ridges. Thunder followed like an unwelcome guest announcing its arrival.

The frizzled hen she kept in the yard scratched at the ground, a reminder of the West African legends. She had learned from the best. And she had visited the crossroads and prayed to the devil for nine days and nights to strengthen her powers.

But she did not practice evil sorcery, as the locals said. Neither was she a lady of darkness as the kids had taunted when they'd dubbed her Lady Bella Rue years ago. No she desperately wanted to save the town.

Thunder rumbled again, growing louder, and the impending pain and fear of what was to come pierced her heart, settling so deeply in her bones that she could almost feel the brittle edges poking through her paper-thin skin. Folks whispered that the evil had started the day the Stanton family had been murdered. Others thought that Lady Bella Rue was the cause. That she had killed her own child and cast a wretched spell on the town years ago, beginning a vicious cycle of family members turning on one another.

But they were wrong.

The gods and goddesses of the rivers, mountains and land were angry at the people, and fought the devil at every turn. Just as she did.

And the ones who'd lost family over the years were trapped here, just as she was herself. Forced to listen to her baby's cry at night as it echoed in the wind from the tangled vines of the kudzu. As long as she was alive, she would visit her son's grave and pray for his spirit.

She touched the red flannel charm bag she kept tucked inside her blouse, hoping the mixture of Jerusalem bean, devil's shoestring, High John the Conqueror root, bloodroot, snakeroot and Adam and Eve root would be strong enough to stave off the evil when the rain came. After all, how could she protect the town if she was dead herself?

Methodically, she gathered the roots and ingredients for the protection spell she hoped would help stave off the dangers. She would need eggs, candles, sulfur and chimney dust. She also needed graveyard dust, so she climbed the steps from the root cellar and headed toward her son's grave. There, she would pray and chant and maybe be able to see the future. If she knew the man who brought danger this time, the man already possessed, perhaps she could make a spell to strip the devil from his soul before the killing began.

If not, God help them all. More would die.

And Satan would win again.

CHAPTER TWO

KILLING CAME EASY for some.

And some were punished for it.

But not him.

He had escaped. But his soul was weak, and he craved another just as he craved the satisfaction of sex from the women he took to his bed. The one beside him flicked her tongue across his belly, and his muscles clenched. She had power over him now, but only because he'd allowed her the momentary privilege. Her breath bathed his skin, and he tunneled his fingers through her hair, pushing her head south.

Now he had the power, and she would do as he said.

And she would never tell anyone about their rendezvous.

Since Matt Mahoney's release, people might ask questions. Maybe look into the past.

A new investigation or anyone snooping around would be a problem.

Oblivious to his thoughts, the whore glided her hands over his stomach and stroked his erection as she flicked her tongue along his length. He relinquished himself to the pleasure as she captured him in her mouth. One stroke. Two. Her tongue worked magic.

Energized now, he jerked her up to straddle him, then slid his hands along her spine, angling her hips so he could sink himself into her. She scraped his chest with bloodred nails and released a low moan, then lowered her tits and brushed his mouth with her nipples. He licked the pointed tips, suckled her like a baby, watched her throw her head back in wild abandon. Her cries lit a fire inside him, and he thrust harder, then flipped her on the bed and climbed above her, shoving her hands up and hammering into her. She dragged her legs up, her stiletto heels dangling as she raised her lush hips to meet him.

He closed his eyes and stripped away her face. Saw another woman's instead.

Blond hair. Sparkling, innocent green eyes. Lips begging for him to fuck. Her voice telling him no. Her eyes screaming in terror.

Release splintered through him, mind-boggling in intensity. He pumped harder, groaning as the woman below him dug her sharp heels into his buttocks and cried out her own pleasure.

"God, baby…"

His chest was dewy, his arms shaking as he opened his eyes. But the face that he'd imagined with his climax had disappeared. The whorish, made-up woman had replaced her. Mascara streaked her eyes, and her ruby-red lips had faded to a dull smudged pink.

They would be pale blue in death. Icy cold. Not smiling.

The mere thought gave him pleasure.

And his cock stiffened again.

He took her once more, this time flattening her on her stomach, with her face stuffed into the pillow. She was helpless. Begging him to stop. Begging him to continue. Her gasp as he shoved himself up her was his undoing, and he imagined his hands sliding around her throat, choking her.

> One kiss. Two kisses. Three kisses.
> Sigh.
> Four kisses. Five kisses. Six kisses.
> Cry.
> Seven kisses. Eight kisses. Nine kisses.
> Die.
> One last kiss
> and then goodbye.

For a brief second, he thought he'd done it. Plunged the knife into her. Watched the life spill from her. Then the blackness faded, and he found himself lying on his back as he had so many times in the past.

She raised up and kissed his neck. "Honey, anytime you want a little fun, you call Chantel."

He nodded, threw a hand over his forehead, panting as she stood, picked up her red teddy and slid it on. The past fifteen years he had had his share of women, but none as gorgeous as Chantel.

Well, there was one....

His first. But no one knew.

The door slammed as Chantel left, and he sat up, grabbed the half-full bottle of bourbon from his nightstand and took a swig, the woman already forgotten.

More important matters to attend to now. He had seen the news report, watched Mahoney being released from prison, recognized the fury in his expression. Mahoney wanted revenge. Wanted answers. Wanted the real killer behind bars.

His stomach knotted. All that he'd worked so hard to attain the last few years might slip through his fingers if the truth was revealed. That truth had to remain hidden.

Sweat soaked his body now, and he guzzled the brown whiskey, his mind searching for a plan. What if Mahoney returned to Kudzu Hollow asking questions? What if he discovered the truth about that night fifteen years ago?

Ivy Stanton's face flashed in his head. She had been so little then, just a scrawny, knock-kneed kid with a gap-toothed, crooked smile. But now she was a woman.

His sex stirred again just thinking about Lily Stanton. Would Ivy be as tasty as her mother had been?

He cursed himself, fighting the desperate urge to find out. He couldn't think with his dick right now. His future might be in trouble.

And he'd do whatever necessary to make sure it didn't explode in his face.

IT TOOK MATT A WEEK to start acclimating into the world, renew his license, buy an SUV and track down Ivy Stanton. Apparently she worked at a small magazine called *Southern Scrapbooks,* a publication that showcased regional and small-town folklore, sites, restaurants, entertainment venues and other unique attractions, especially mysteries or oddities associated with small Southern towns.

As he knocked on the door to her home in downtown Chattanooga, he studied the Victorian house she'd rented near the river. The scenic, homey-looking place robbed his breath for a minute. A fall wreath made of fake leaves decorated the door, while a bird feeder swayed in the breeze in a nearby dogwood tree. White wicker rocking chairs flanked the doorway, and a chaise sat kitty-cornered beside a tea table, as if inviting someone to lounge for a lazy afternoon with a glass of sweet iced tea beneath the twirling ceiling fans on the porch.

Bitterness swelled inside him.

The beauty around him once again reminded him of the life he'd been denied. Latching onto his anger, he knocked on the door a second time, but no one answered. Irritated, he climbed back in his car and drove toward the magazine office. It was only a few blocks away, a nondescript, small building that was much older than Ivy's house, tucked in a historic area that held many small businesses.

Five minutes later, he sucked in his breath as he strode into the office. A hum of voices swirled from a back room. In the outer area, a rail-thin brunette leaned over a table studying what seemed to be a photograph layout of restaurants and cafés.

He cleared his throat. "Excuse me, but where can I find Iv—Ann Ivy?"

The woman pursed her lips and glanced at him, and he was grateful he hadn't completely slipped and used her name instead of the pseudonym she'd adopted for the magazine.

"She's not here. I'm Miss Evans. Can I help you?"

"I really need to talk to Miss Ivy myself," Matt said. "When will she be back?"

"I'm not sure. She went out of town to research a story."

He chewed the inside of his cheek. "She contacted me about an upcoming issue, and I need to discuss some layouts with her."

The woman's cell phone rang, and she glanced at it, then back up, looking harried. "Listen, I'm really busy—"

"If you can just tell me where she went, I'll track her down."

"She's on assignment. Some little Appalachian town called Kudzu Hollow." Miss Evans reached in her pocket and handed him a business card. "Here's her cell number."

He pasted on a phony grin, then thanked her and left, his stomach churning.

Ivy had gone back to Kudzu Hollow. That was the last place he'd expected to find her. Why had she returned home now? And why would she do a story on the town?

Unless she'd seen the reports of his release...

Had she actually returned to talk to him?

Or did she believe he was guilty? If so, was she trying to find a way to put him back in prison?

His chest tightened at the mere thought. He'd die before he'd go back inside.

An hour and a half later, he was coasting up the highway toward eastern Tennessee, growing nearer and nearer his destination. A few phone calls, and he'd discovered Ivy had rented a cabin on the mountain. He'd reserved a cabin beside her.

Horns blared, a siren wailed in the distance and rap music pounded through the speakers of the black pickup in front of him. An eighteen-wheeler nearly cut Matt off, boxing him in next to a cement truck.

His claustrophobia mounted.

One day the real killer would know what it was like to lie in a cramped, six-by-six cell and piss in a pot in front of strangers. He would know what it was like to suffer.

To lose everyone he cared about. His entire future.

Yes, Matt Mahoney had been innocent when he'd gone to jail.

But he wasn't innocent any longer.

Now he would finally confront Ivy Stanton and force her to admit the truth about what had happened that night. Find out why the hell she hadn't spoken up years ago and defended him.

Then he'd make her pay for keeping quiet.

THE VOICES WOULDN'T BE quiet.

And the color red was back.

But only in Ivy's dreams.

They had become more frequent since she'd seen that newscast of Matt Mahoney's release. And even more intense since she'd come to Kudzu Hollow the week before. Nightmares of blood and screams, of that last kiss goodbye, the cold unbending skin of her mother's lips, the eyes wide open in death...

Ivy shivered, willing away the vivid images as she clutched the metal fence surrounding the junkyard, but the photos and article chronicling her parents' brutal murders remained etched in her mind forever.

There was no turning back now. She'd come here for answers and she couldn't leave until she had them. The only way for her to move forward in her life was to travel backward in time.

She'd spent the last week incognito, using her pseudonym, Ann Ivy, so the locals around Kudzu Hollow wouldn't know her true identity. She'd driven the countryside and town taking photographs and studying the people. Soon, maybe she'd gather enough nerve to approach the locals about her parents' murders.

And to visit their graves.

But one step at a time.

Having finally gotten up the courage to stop by the junkyard today, she studied the landscape. Rusted and stripped vehicles of all sizes and models filled the overgrown yard, everything from Corvettes to pickups and broken-down school buses that had transported their last group of kids. Weeds choked the land, and kudzu climbed like snakes up the broken windows, over tires and hubcaps and scattered car parts. Tall trees dropped dead leaves, adding a layer of brown and gold to the dilapidated site, a reminder that winter was on its way. Winter and death.

Ivy tried to banish her anxiety, then imagined her father working the lot, selling off parts as needed, trying to rebuild an engine in the station wagon he'd kept, huddling with a cigarette as he swiped at grease on his coveralls. That brief memory seemed to stir the pungent air with the scent of those filterless Camels he liked so much, the smell of his booze, the sound of his angry booming voice as his boots pounded on the squeaky floor of the trailer.

She shuddered and clutched her jacket around her, willing other memories to follow, but the door slammed shut with a vicious slap, and there was nothing but emptiness. And the sense that she had run from the trailer to the junkyard more than once. Taken solace in the rusted old cars. Pretended they weren't broken, that they could magically transport her far away from her miserable home.

Frustrated, she yanked her gaze sideways, beyond the junkyard to the trailer park where she'd lived. Weeds choked the brown grass, and the trailers were faded and rusted, although families still dwelled in some of the same single- and double-wide mobile homes that had stood for twenty years. A few new ones had been added, she noted, although the rain had washed mud and leaves onto the aluminum sides, aging them automatically. Several small children in ratty jackets and jeans played chase in the yards just as she had probably done, and two neighborhood women sat on a sagging porch, chatting. Tricycles and plastic bats and toys littered the ground, and a couple of stray cats slept beside a double-wide while a mangy dog scrounged for food in the overflowing garbage.

Although the scenery seemed familiar, Ivy couldn't remember anything about that fatal night her parents died.

Except that last kiss goodbye.

Suddenly another image returned, this one more disturbing. She had been running through the junkyard, had fallen in the mud. A big boy suddenly appeared, piercing her with his dark brown eyes. Bad-boy Matt Mahoney. He reached for her, and she froze in terror, the world spinning and spinning until she spiraled downward into a black abyss of nothingness. The tunnel of darkness sucked her into its vortex, and the memory crashed to a halt.

The familiar rush of renewed panic that had started after Miss Nellie's death squeezed Ivy's chest again. The accompanying light-headedness, the flash of white dots before her eyes, the inability to breathe—she couldn't control it. A sudden gust of wind rattled the power lines, and gray, mottled storm clouds rolled over the tops of the ridges. Rain splattered the earth, the howling wind blowing leaves and debris across the brown grass. Tree branches swayed with its force, lightning zigzagged across the turbulent sky, illuminating the jagged peaks, which rose like a fortress guarding the town's secrets. The earth suddenly rumbled, and the ground shook beneath her feet.

Her heart pounded. What was that noise? An earthquake maybe? A tornado?

Or the ghosts of the people who had died in the town, the ghosts that Miss Nellie had warned her about? The spirits that wandered the junkyard, trapped beneath the kudzu, begging to escape...

NIGHT HAD SET IN by the time Matt reached the mountains. Although the majestic scenery and fresh fall air was a welcome reprieve from the city, a storm brewed on the horizon. Thunderclouds rumbled across the sky, and lightning flashed above the treetops. As he neared the hollow, rain slashed the Pathfinder, drilling the ground. It was almost as if Satan had sent this storm to remind him of that awful last night he'd spent in Kudzu Hollow.

A glutton for punishment, he drove toward the trailer park, unable to face the town just yet. The graveyard for cars still sat in the same location, but weeds and kudzu had overtaken the place. Apparently, no one had kept up Roy Stanton's business.

Sweat rolled down Matt's neck as he bounced over the ruts in the road and neared his old home. His mother's parting words echoed in his mind: *I'm so ashamed of you, Matt. Your brothers are thugs, and I knew you wasn't any good, but I never thought you'd be a killer.*

She hadn't believed him innocent any more than the locals had. Her lack of faith had cut him to the core.

Determined to show her the papers exonerating him, he veered into the parking lot and stopped in front of his old homestead. Weeds filled the yard, and what little grass was left was patchy, with mud holes big enough for a small kid to get mired in. Rust stains colored the silver aluminum, a broken windowpane marked the front, and red mud caked the steps to the stoop. What had he expected? For his mother to have inherited some money and be living in a mansion?

For her to have hung a Welcome Home banner out for him?

He cut the engine, inhaled a deep breath, grabbed the papers and climbed out. Ducking against the downpour, he ran up the rickety steps and knocked. His heart pounded as he waited. But no one answered.

He knocked again, then glanced sideways. Someone nudged the front window curtain back slightly. His mother, years older, and now fully white-haired, with prominent wrinkles around her mouth, peered through the opening. When she saw him, her gray eyes widened in fear.

"Go away, boy. I don't want you bothering me."

Pain shot through his chest. "Come on, Mom. Let me in. It's Matt."

"I told you to go away. I don't want trouble."

He waved the papers like a white flag, begging the enemy for a truce. "But I'm free. Just read this. The judge cleared me, and these papers prove it. I told you I was innocent."

A moment of hesitation followed, then his mother shook her bony finger at him. "I said go away, or I'll call the sheriff. I don't have sons anymore. They're all dead to me."

Her words slammed into him with a force worse than the punches he'd taken in prison.

Gritting his teeth, he jogged down the steps, grief digging at his throat. Rain sluiced off him as he plowed through the mud to the Pathfinder. When he got inside, he buried his head in his hands, desolation and shame searing him like a hot poker. He'd hoped like hell that at least his mother would believe him now. But the papers hadn't changed her opinion.

Which meant the rest of the people in town probably hadn't changed theirs, either.

A SUDDEN MOMENT of déjà vu struck Ivy. Had it been raining the night her parents died? Her stomach knotted, the onset of another attack imminent. Beneath the wind, she detected a cry echoing from the hills, but the sound might have been her own thready voice trilling out a prayer to the heavens.

Whirling around, she ran toward her car, shivering and eager to return to the cabin she'd rented. Darkness descended quickly, the shadows stealing daylight and reminding her that night would soon trap her.

And so would her nightmares—the blood, the screams, the mangled bodies.

She cranked up the defogger, squinting through the blinding rain as she drove around the mountain and into Kudzu Hollow. The town seemed tiny to her after living in Chattanooga for the last few years. The park, the brick storefronts, sheriff's office and small diner were reminiscent of a Norman Rockwell painting. At first glance, the town appeared to be the perfect place to raise a family. And the cabin on the creek where she was staying would be a romantic spot for a young couple to honeymoon.

But Miss Nellie had been right. The rumors about the ghosts and the killings destroyed any romanticism. Whispers of death floated from beneath the green leafy kudzu vines that crawled along walls and the ground. Locals claimed that nothing could kill the kudzu. It was parasitic, killing its own host. Just as the people couldn't destroy the evil here, or force the ghosts to move on to another realm. Just as the evil drew the devil to the town and the families killed their own.

A flashing sign for a local pub named Ole Peculiar drew her eye, but she headed to The Rattlesnake Diner on the next block instead. Determined to learn more about the locals, she veered into the graveled parking lot, climbed out and rushed up the steps, shaking water from her hair as she entered.

A short, sturdy, middle-aged waitress wearing a colorful dress, white apron and a name tag that read *Daisy,* approached her, her short gray curls framing a tired face. "Hello again, Miss Ann. You back to take more pictures?"

Ivy smiled. "Not at the moment. I'm starving."

Daisy removed the pencil tucked in her brown bouffant hair. "Well, what'll it be, honey? Rattlesnake stew?"

Ivy swallowed. She'd thought the dish a legend, but apparently the cook, Boone, an old-timer who'd lived in the mountains for decades, had inherited the recipe from his grandmother. "A bowl of your vegetable soup. And sweet iced tea, please."

Daisy nodded, then waddled away, and Ivy twisted her hands together as she studied the handmade arts and crafts along one wall. Local artisans' paintings, photographs and jewelry decorated the café in an artful arrangement, with price tags attached. Photographs and sketches of local scenery included valleys and gorges in the mountain, a little white chapel at the top of a cliff, the creek behind her cabin, a water wheel, then one of the junkyard. A charcoal sketch of Rattlesnake Mountain hung in the center, the etchings of the natural indentations that resembled a nest of rattlesnakes along the stone surface, sent a chill up her spine.

According to her research, the originators of the folklore and black magic in the area had been birthed by a small group of witches who believed that the rocks, mountains, trees and rivers were all inhabited by spirits—spirits that never knew human form. Rattlesnake Mountain once held pits of rattlesnakes that the practitioners of hoodoo and voodoo used for their evil spells. The sorcerers were given a Christian name, then a secret name, that was used only for black magic purposes.

Daisy delivered the soup. "Here you go, sweetie."

"Thanks. This looks delicious."

"You still working on the scrapbook on the town?" Daisy asked.

Ivy nodded and sipped her iced tea. "Yes."

"My daughter and I are making a scrapbook of my grandbaby. We're even thinking of starting a scrapbooking club."

"Really?" Ivy smiled. "My mother used to belong

to one of those." At least her adopted mother, Miss
Nellie, had. That club and the popularity of scrapbooking had actually triggered her idea for the
magazine.

"You see that chapel?" Daisy pointed to the photograph on the wall. "The locals call it the Chapel
of Forever. It's where Hughie and I got married.
Legend says that if you marry in that chapel, your
marriage will last through eternity."

Ivy made a mental note to add that bit of folklore
to her magazine feature article. "Do you know when
or how the legend got started?"

"No, but I'll check around and see if someone
else does. Maybe Miss Gussy. She's been around
longer than me."

The bell on the door tinkled, and they both glanced
up as an odd, elderly woman stepped inside. Dressed
in all black, in a long skirt that nearly touched the
floor, a hat and veil that half covered her wrinkled
face, and army boots with thick socks rolled over the
edges, she was almost spooky. Two other ladies whispered and gave her a wide berth as they left. Two teenagers got up and hurried toward the door. Another
woman followed the eccentric lady in, the polar
opposite in appearance. Platinum-blond hair formed
a pile of curls on top of her head, gaudy costume
jewelry adorned every finger and a skintight, bloodred
dress dipped low enough to reveal massive cleavage
that a man could get lost in. Shiny white, knee-high
boots hugged her killer legs and completed the outfit.

"I cannot believe the two of them have the nerve
to show up here," Daisy said.

Ivy frowned. "Who are they?"

"The one in the red, that's Talulah. She's the head mistress down on Red Row."

"Red Row?"

Daisy leaned closer. "The row of trailers where all her prostitutes live. A seedy place that no decent citizen would ever visit."

But the men probably kept them in business, Ivy thought, as the two women moved to the rear and grabbed a booth, ignoring the stares and blatant whispers.

"And the other woman?"

"Lady Bella Rue. She calls herself a root doctor. Folks say she's a lady of darkness, that she's connected to the moon, the spirits and the devil himself. Even killed her own boy, though no one could prove it."

Ivy sipped her tea, her curiosity spiked.

"I think folks around here were just too scared of her to pursue it," Daisy continued. "They say she's a *seer* to boot."

"You mean she can see the future?"

Daisy nodded. "Some people think she cast a spell on the town—that's what brings all the evil when it rains. The kudzu sparkles yellow sometimes, then other times has this metallic blue-green mist rising from it. Folks say Lady Bella Rue's tears of guilt turn the kudzu those odd colors, or maybe it's devil's breath." Daisy hesitated long enough to inhale a breath. "Better stay away from her. If you anger her, she might put a hex on you. Once she does, bad luck and death will follow you the rest of your life."

Ivy's hand trembled as she placed her glass on the table. Bad luck and death had already been a part of her life, and had brought her here now.

A strained silence fell across the room, the rain pounding the roof accentuating the tension. It was almost as if the townspeople sensed winter and death were imminent. That these two women's presence in town represented a bad omen.

A middle-aged lady at the next table waved Daisy over to her side. Ivy ate her soup while she listened. "I heard that Mahoney boy has been released."

Daisy refilled their tea, ice clinking. "Some fancy lawyer got him out. I just hope he doesn't come back to town and stir up trouble."

"Land sakes alive. We breathed a lot easier when he was in jail. We'll have to go back to locking our doors at night."

"You're right. We don't need his kind around," another woman said. "Although I thought he did us a service when he killed those Stantons. The woman was a slut. I heard she worked for Talulah on Red Row."

Ivy clenched her hands in her lap, anger knifing through her. Her mother had not been a slut! She'd loved Ivy. Had brushed her hair and played dolls with her and collected Santa Clauses. She'd strung glittery Christmas lights all around the trailer and tried to make it pretty. They'd even baked home-made sugar cookies and strung popcorn for the tree they'd cut down in the woods.

She had not deserved to die.

And what about Matt Mahoney? Had he deserved to go to jail for murder?

Not according to Abram Willis and the judge who'd released him...

ARTHUR BOLES BURIED his face behind the local newspaper and sipped his coffee, unable to focus on the words on the printed page for studying the young woman talking to Daisy. Ivy Stanton.

He would have recognized her anywhere. After all, he'd kept tabs on her all these years that she'd lived with Nellie. Years during which he had worried that she would remember something, that she'd return to Kudzu Hollow, see his face and spill her guts about that night. Years where he wished he'd silenced her already.

Years where he'd thought of her mother's lush wanton body, the way Lily Stanton had taken him into her nest and given him pleasure without asking for anything but money. God, he'd missed her over the years. Missed her lips touching his, her mouth closing around his cock, the sight of her spreading herself for him to bury his length in. Missed the way her tits had swayed when she rode him, and the way she'd use her tongue to make him come. And the way her eyes had gone all melting and soft when he'd returned the pleasure.

Not that there hadn't been replacements. Red Row still stood to serve its customers. The anonymity was an important part of the business. And if one of the whores did decide to talk, well, hell, he'd shut her up like he had the others.

And how ironic. Talulah, that old root doctor and

Ivy Stanton all in one room together. All held the secrets to his past. Maybe the key to his future.

All expendable...

But he still couldn't help himself from staring at Ivy Stanton all grown up. She'd turned into a beautiful, seductive woman. Not in the same bold, untamed way her mama had, for an air of innocence surrounded her. A naivete her mother had never possessed. Oh, maybe she had once, but she'd lost it long before he'd come along. Lily had not been lily-white. She had even taken the innocence of others and been proud of it. Young boys ripe for a woman's body had come to her, and she had taught them well.

His cock swelled, and he rubbed it beneath the table, grateful it was dark and he'd taken a booth in the back corner. He could almost taste the sweetness of Ivy Stanton, the unbridled passion she had yet to discover. The fear and tension radiating from her slender body. The feel of those silky blond curls tickling his bare belly.

Maybe he would toy with Ivy a little. See if she did remember him. And just as her mother had taken the innocence of the young men in town, his son for one, he'd steal that innocence from her daughter....

UNEASY WITH THE CLIMATE in the diner, Ivy paid her bill and rushed outside, tugging her raincoat around her. Suddenly aware of the shadows, she darted toward her car, climbed in, locked the door and started the engine. The fine hairs at the nape of her neck prickled.

Someone was watching her.

Rattled, Ivy checked the street and sidewalks for strangers, but here everyone was a stranger. A lone figure clad in a black hooded sweatshirt stood beneath the awning of the pub, smoking a cigarette. Was he watching her?

She pulled onto Main Street, then drove through town, slowing as the rain intensified. Bright lights nearly blinded her from behind as a car suddenly raced up on her tail. She tensed, checking the mirror, and glanced around the darkened street. In Chattanooga, she sometimes sensed she was being followed, but had finally chalked her uneasiness up to Miss Nellie's constant paranoia.

Here no one knew her real identity. At least she didn't think so.

Just to be safe, she turned down a side street, then another, driving as if she'd entered a maze. Finally, the headlights disappeared, and she sighed in relief. Through the blurred, foggy windshield, she checked the storefronts as she passed, choosing several to photograph for her scrapbook layout. The dollar store, arts and crafts store and antique shop would be perfect for the spread. Halloween ghosts, skeletons, spiders, ghouls and goblins filled the windows. A few Thanksgiving pieces also appeared. And through the glass, a nearly life-size Santa was lit up, waving.

The old familiar grief clawed at her throat, and she headed out of town toward the cabin.

A car appeared behind her again, then moved closer, so fast and close that its bumper skimmed hers. Ivy gasped, grappling for control of the Jetta, then sped up. Instead of slowing, the driver gunned his engine, swerved around her, then sideswiped her car, knocking her into a spin. Tires squealed and the car skidded, metal scraping metal as she hit the guardrail and careened toward the embankment.

MATT DOWNSHIFTED as he drove the slick, winding road toward Cliff's Cabins. Next to the trailer park, a new subdivision of log homes had been built on the mountainside. The primitive landscaping, natural pine islands and spacious backyards looked inviting against the ridges. So far the new development was the only hint of progress in the sleepy town.

His hands tightened around the steering wheel as his last night in town flashed though his mind. Ivy had been terrified of him, of her father. How would she react when he confronted her? Would she cower away from him as if he were an animal? Scream and run? Call him a murderer?

The sign for the cabins dangled precariously from a lopsided wooden pole, blowing in the wind, and he veered onto the unpaved road that led to the rental units. A mile from the turn-off, he parked in the graveled lot, hurried inside the office and retrieved the key. The frail man at the desk glanced up at him over bifocals, but said nothing. Either he was so old or blind he didn't recognize Matt, or he didn't care. Back in his SUV, Matt backed up and circled the cabins, his gaze tracking the numbers: 32A—his; 32B—Ivy Stanton's.

He parked, sat and stared at the cabin through the

fog, his heart racing with anticipation. Should he knock on her door tonight? Force a confrontation?

An engine suddenly rumbled down the drive, and he glanced in the rearview mirror, as bright lights pierced the night. A black Jetta swerved, spitting gravel, then lurched to a stop in front of 32B. The lights flickered off, and he had to blink to adjust his vision. A woman gripped the steering wheel, then leaned her head forward, her shoulders shaking. He frowned. Something was wrong. The driver's side of the car had been dented.

He swallowed, debating whether to offer her help, but the door swung open and the breath froze in his lungs. Ivy Stanton.

As if she'd gathered her control, she climbed out, the wind whipping a long denim skirt around her ankles, the rain beating at her face as she braced herself against the elements and ran toward the cabin. His gaze skimmed over her profile, his gut clenching. She was petite, maybe five-three, and slender. Cornsilk blond hair cascaded down her back and shoulders and shifted upward, caught in the breeze, the wet strands clinging to her cheeks just as they had fifteen years ago. And just as he remembered her as a child, she was pale-skinned and delicate. But instead of a small child, she'd morphed into a beautiful woman. And so damn sexy. Soaked, her cotton top clung to curves that begged for a man's hands. Her nipples tightened beneath the thin fabric, highlighted by the lightning.

It had been a long damn time since he'd been with a woman.

Although he had had invitations from some of his

prison buddies' sisters and friends. Another strange group of prison groupies, women infatuated by inmates, wrote them letters, offering conjugal visits. He'd even succumbed to his basic needs and accepted a few offers.

But that raw sex had left him unsatisfied and feeling dirty.

Hell, he wasn't sure he'd know what to do with a real woman, a nice one….

Matt cursed. Confronting Ivy was first on his list, being attracted to her, dead last.

As if she suddenly sensed his presence, halfway to the cabin, she pivoted in the darkness, her eyelashes fluttering over cheeks made rosy from the chill of the storm. Their gazes locked, and the eyes that had bewitched him as a child completely mesmerized him now. In them, he saw fear, pain and an emptiness that he felt mirrored in his own troubled soul.

Hell.

His body hardened again, the need to protect her as he had years ago building inside him, as intense as the thunder roaring above. But this time he ignored it.

The bitter memory of being dragged to the jail and imprisoned for her parents' murders surfaced, stifling the lust mounting in his loins, and he jerked his gaze away.

She suddenly broke into a sprint, unlocked the cabin and slammed the door shut. Had she recognized him? Known he'd come here after her? Was she as frightened of him as she had been that night he'd rescued her?

He muttered a curse, telling himself it didn't matter.

Ivy Stanton had been trouble fifteen years ago. A needy little kid. He'd been nice to her and look what had happened. He'd ended up in jail, his life destroyed.

But she wasn't a needy little girl anymore. No, dammit, she was a stunning woman, one who had messed with his libido in ten seconds flat. Which meant she would be more trouble than before. No telling what would happen if he got involved with her now.

He glanced down at the clothes he'd bought at Wal-Mart. Even though they were clean, he reeked of foul prison odors. Dirt, sweat and the stench of urine permeated his soul.

His resolve clicked back in, obliterating any sympathy he had for Ivy. He didn't give a damn why she'd returned, or that his body craved a woman right now, that it had reacted to her. It was time she told the truth about that night.

And before he left this hellhole of a town, he'd make sure she did—no matter what it cost either one of them.

HE STOOD BY THE STREAM in back of Cliff's Cabins, his all-weather coat tucked around him, rain dripping from the brim of his hat, gushing down as hard and fast as the icy water rushing over the rocks. Kudzu climbed along the embankment, killing wild-flowers, crawling toward the pines like snakes. The rain would only make the plant grow faster. Faster and faster until it claimed everything in sight.

This damn rain brought all the problems again—the violence, the worry, the memories....

It had all started the night of the Stanton slayings.

And now little Ivy Stanton was back.

He should have killed her fifteen years ago. Had been furious at his slip in judgment in letting her go. Had waited each day with his heart in his throat, afraid she'd remember.

Had slept only the nights he'd talked to Nellie and learned she hadn't.

But now she'd returned. And so had that Mahoney boy.

Holy Mother of God. He'd done everything in his power to see that he stayed in jail. And Nellie and he had done everything possible to make sure Ivy's mind remained a blank. That she never contacted Mahoney.

But what would happen if she saw the ex-con in town?

Or *him?*

He scratched his chin and glanced back at Ivy's cabin. He could almost see the bluish-green tint surrounding the kudzu that the locals claimed were spirits. Almost hear the voices of the ghosts crying out in the night.

But the Appalachian folktales didn't worry him. The dead were already gone. Lost forever. Let them walk the grounds and haunt the town.

The live ones still posed the problem.

He flicked his lighter, lit the cigarette, cupping his

hand around the flame so the wind didn't blow it out until he'd inhaled a few drags. Smoke curled toward the sky, a halo of hazy white against the night.

Damn shame to have to kill a pretty girl like Ivy.

But he'd do anything to protect his secrets. If he didn't, things would spiral out of control again. He was sure of it.

What would Ivy think when she saw the message he'd left inside her cabin?

A deep laugh rumbled in his chest as he pictured her horrified face. Her childhood image had taunted him for years. Had threatened to ruin his life.

But little Ivy Stanton wasn't a child anymore. That meant he *could* kill her this time. He wouldn't freeze up and let guilt rule his actions.

And Matt Mahoney would be the perfect person to pin the crime on. After all, the ex-con had a rap sheet. A motive. And no one in Kudzu Hollow would be surprised that the joint had only made him meaner.

Yes, they'd be glad to rid themselves of Mahoney.

Then Kudzu Hollow could go back to normal.

As normal as it could get.

After all, *he* couldn't control the rain. And when it came, fate played its own nasty game and filled the town with evil.

CHAPTER THREE

IVY SLAMMED THE DOOR to the cabin, the fine hairs on the back of her neck standing on end as she slid the curtain aside and peered out the corner of the rain-lashed window. A tree branch scraped the glass, wind rattled the pane and she nearly jumped out of her skin. She hadn't seen the driver or the make of the vehicle that had sideswiped her, but she had stopped, and the man who owned the gas station had rushed to check on her. Unfortunately, he hadn't seen anything helpful, either. Still, for insurance purposes, she'd driven to the sheriff's department, met the deputy and filed a report. He'd muttered something about the weather making teenagers do crazy things. But she wasn't at all sure teenagers had been driving the car.

And now someone had been sitting in that SUV outside her cabin. Someone who'd been watching her.

Someone who meant her harm.

She'd sensed an aura of anger when she'd met his eyes through the window. Was he the same man who'd intentionally sideswiped her earlier? The person who'd been following her in Chattanooga for the last few weeks? And if so, what did he want? Why would someone wish to hurt her?

Fog coated the windows, the darkness cloaking the room adding to her nervousness. The scents of pine floors, dust and cleaning solution wafted around her, and a spider spun an intricate web in the corner to trap its prey.

Why did Ivy feel that someone might be spinning a web to trap her?

Her chest tightened. She'd varied the routines. Broken the patterns. Ventured to a new place.

And now the ominous threat of danger ate at her nerves.

Hoping the man had gone, she glanced again at the SUV, but it remained. She tried to remember if she'd seen it earlier, maybe in town. It looked black, although with her color blindness she never could be quite sure. The windows were tinted. Nothing else distinguishable.

Shivering, she grabbed the afghan off the couch and wrapped it around her shoulders, trying to warm herself and stop the trembling. What if the man came after her tonight?

A flash of lightning illuminated the room, and she startled, her breath catching. The familiar stirring of another panic attack teetered on the surface, and she forced herself to take steady, deep breaths as she rubbed her hands up and down her arms. Just because Miss Nellie had filled her head with superstitious stories didn't mean they were real. And just because a man was parked near her cabin didn't mean he intended to harm her.

Suddenly, the door of the SUV swung open, and a giant emerged, silhouetted in shadows, rain drenching his face and body. He had to be at least six-four, with the broadest shoulders she'd ever seen, dark shaggy hair and stark features that gave him a wolfish look. Another bolt of lightning highlighted his profile, and she gasped at the jagged scar on his left cheek. Matt Mahoney.

She recognized him from the television newscast.

He stalked slowly across the muddy ground, and she gripped the window ledge for support. But a few feet from her cabin, he veered off toward the neighboring one. Her breath gushed out in relief, and she raked her trembling hand through her hair in frantic movements.

He must be staying in the cabin beside her. Dear Lord, did he know *she* was here? Had he been waiting for her to return, to go inside?

Forcing herself away from the window, she flipped on the lamp, then let out a bloodcurdling scream. Jagged bold letters were scrawled on the wall: Leave Town Or Die.

Although the words looked brown to her, a dark, thick substance smeared the knotty pine walls.

Another shudder rippled through her as the stench enveloped her, and she screamed again in horror. The warning had been written in blood, and a dead chicken lay on the bed below it, its body and feathers bloody and mangled.

MATT FROZE, silently telling himself he'd imagined the scream from the cabin next door, that the shrill sound had been the wind blowing.

But he glanced at Ivy's cabin, anyway, and a

sense of foreboding washed over him. If she had cried out, he was the last person to help her. He had his own agenda this go-around, and it sure as hell didn't include rescuing her ass again. Even if it was the prettiest piece he'd seen in years.

No, his boots remained firmly planted on the ground.

But his conscience kicked in.

If the real killer still lived in town, he'd be nervous about Ivy's return. Just as he wouldn't be thrilled to see *him*.

What if he was in there now? What if he attacked Ivy....

Muttering a curse, limbs tight with agitation, Matt stalked through the mud to her cabin, then pounded on the door. A mixture of emotions pummeled him—dread, excitement, the need for revenge. After all these years, he'd finally meet her face-to-face, look into those eyes and watch her reaction to him in person. Several tense seconds passed and he knocked again, but Ivy didn't answer. The pounding storm filled the air with foreboding.

Christ.

Various ugly scenarios roared through his head. Ivy being raped and murdered. Her throat slashed like her mother's had been. Blood covering the goddamn floor.

Even as he assured himself Ivy was fine, that he had imagined her cry for help, his hand snaked forward to reach for the doorknob. He wouldn't sleep unless he knew she was safe. Besides, if a murder occurred in the cabin next to him, he'd probably wind up in jail once more, taking the fall.

He couldn't be locked behind bars. Not ever again.

Self-preservation kicked in, and he halted just before his hand closed on the knob. His fingerprints had landed him in trouble the first time. He wouldn't make the same mistake. Instead, he dragged his shirttail from his jeans, wrapped it around his hand and clutched the doorknob.

Slowly, he pushed open the wooden door, the rusty hinges squeaking. Ivy cried out again, then flung herself against the sofa, clenching the back. He raised his hand to calm her, at the same time searching the dimly lit room for an intruder.

"Wh-what do you want?" Ivy whispered.

"Is someone here?"

"No…"

He jerked his head toward her with a frown. She was cowering from him. Then her gaze flashed sideways quickly, as if to search for something to protect herself, and his temper spiked.

"You don't remember me, Ivy?"

Those big green eyes that had tugged at him when she was little did a number on him now. They snatched at his sanity and resolve. She was afraid of him. Her reaction shouldn't bother him, but it cut him like a knife.

He knew he looked like hell. His hair was too long and he needed a shave. Scarred as he was, he probably looked downright scary. The past few days, little kids had stared at him on the street. Women had yanked their heads away. Old ladies had whispered and rushed past as if he were some hideous beast.

Ivy's fingers dug into the upholstery. "Yes, I saw you on the news. You're Matt Mahoney."

He balled his hands into fists. Her gaze followed the movement, and she backed up another step. She thought he intended to hit her, he realized. Then he remembered her old man beating on her and her mama, and understood her reaction.

"I heard you scream," he said in a gruff voice. "I came to see if you were all right." Her gaze flashed sideways again, and he followed the movement.

"What the hell?" His gut tightened at the sight of the bloody warning on the wall. Then he saw the dead animal and cursed.

"You were outside in that SUV, watching me." Her voice rose in hysteria. "You've been following me, haven't you? You were in Chattanooga, too. And now this…"

He narrowed his eyes. "I didn't do this, Ivy. And I haven't been following you." Not technically, anyway.

She flinched as lightning illuminated the room, and he found himself wanting to turn his head to spare her from seeing his scar. But he forced himself to remain immobile, his gaze pinning her in place. It was her fault he'd ended up in jail. Her fault he'd been convicted.

She needed to face the reality of what her silence had cost him. The brutality he'd suffered because he'd helped her.

And she needed to give him some answers.

IVY CLUNG TO THE AFGHAN, the anger and bitterness in Matt Mahoney's body language stealing her breath. He'd been tough back when she'd known him, but just a teenager looking for trouble and a good time.

Now, he seemed hard. Cold. Aged and bitter. Prison had probably done that to him. She tried not to think about the horrors he must have endured inside. She'd read stories, seen articles, news reports....

She'd wanted to think that he'd survived.

But the icy bleakness in his eyes told a different story. Still physically fit, he stood tall and proud, though, like a warrior prepared for battle. The long gash on his cheek appeared even more stark in real life, but the rest of his body was sculpted like an athlete's. His muscular arms were defined, and he didn't have a fat cell anywhere that she could see. And in spite of his shaggy wet hair, the scar and his brooding expression, he was more masculine, sexier, than she'd ever imagined.

But his soul was completely black. It had been destroyed.

She offered a tentative smile, but a warning flashed in his eyes.

A warning she would definitely heed.

Maybe he had left the bloody message and chicken as a sick idea of revenge.

"I was watching you outside," he snarled, "but I didn't write that threat or kill that chicken, Ivy. Unlike your father, my style is not to terrorize women." He cut his eyes toward the wall, then started toward her, his fists still clenched, his long arms swinging by his side.

Reacting on autopilot, from memories Ivy thought she'd long ago forgotten, she threw up a hand. "Stop. Let's talk."

He didn't stop, though. He kept coming, his heavy boots hammering the wood floor, his husky, angry breathing rattling the tension-laden air. She frantically searched for a weapon. Glanced at the phone, gauging whether or not she could reach it.

His gaze fell to it, and he gestured toward the handset. His hand was steady. Scarred, too, with large knuckles, his fingernails short and blunt. "You going to call the sheriff, or am I?"

Her pulse clamored in her throat. "You really want me to phone the sheriff?"

"Hell, no," Matt muttered. "The law is the last damn thing I want to see my first night in town. But if someone's threatening you, you have to inform the cops."

He was right. She grabbed the phone and punched 911. Seconds later, an operator's voice echoed over the line, and Ivy explained the situation.

"I'll send Sheriff Boles right over," the operator said. "Are you sure you're all right, miss?"

Ivy squeezed the phone so tightly her fingers grew numb. No, she wasn't sure. Matt Mahoney's steely look had started her heart pounding.

"Miss?"

"Y-yes, just send the sheriff."

"All right. Hang tight."

Ivy's hands trembled as she placed the handset back into the cradle. "The sheriff's on his way."

Matt grimaced. "It looks like someone doesn't want you in town, Ivy."

Her frayed nerves shattered at his blunt tone. "But no one here knows my real identity."

A deep sarcastic chuckle rumbled from his chest. "Apparently someone does."

She shuddered. He was right. The sideswipe incident earlier suddenly took on a more dire meaning. But who had figured out her identity? And why would they want to run her out of town?

Matt cleared his throat. "I imagine they won't be too happy to see me, either."

She bit her lip, a million questions racing through her mind. "Why did you come back?"

"Why do you think?"

He stepped closer, so close she inhaled the scent of soap, something clean and fresh like Irish Spring. But another more woodsy odor radiated from him, as well, all primal male. A muscle ticked in his jaw as he waited for her reply. But she couldn't find her voice.

"I came to see you," he finally said in a gruff voice.

"Me?" Her voice quivered. "But…why?"

He lifted his big hand and twirled a damp strand of hair around his finger. Tension radiated from every pore in his body, the heat between them igniting a mixture of fear and excitement in her belly. He had the darkest, deepest eyes she'd ever seen. Brown. No, black. He looked so lost and angry. So alone.

The way she'd felt so many times.

His pain drew her. She suddenly wanted to wipe it from his eyes. Assure him that life wasn't all evil.

Miss Nellie would say she was a sucker.

That erotic dream floated back. Matt Mahoney kissing her. Stripping off her clothes. Touching her in secret places. Eliciting feelings she'd never felt before. Making her come alive.

A bold and sexy look flared in his eyes. Hunger. Lust. The urgent need of a man to take what he wanted.

She backed away, frightened by the potency of that desire. Half wanting it, half terrified of the desperate need that accompanied it.

He chuckled sardonically. "Don't worry, Ivy, I'm not going to attack you." Still, he moved closer again, until he was only a breath away, until his masculine scent trapped her like honey did a fly. With a soft sigh, he traced a finger down the side of her cheek, and her skin tingled.

"I've been waiting a long time for us to meet face-to-face, so you could explain why you didn't tell everyone what happened that night," he said in a husky voice. "Why you let them throw me in a cell to rot for the rest of my life when you knew I was innocent?"

MATT STEELED HIMSELF AGAINST the pain that flashed on Ivy's face. He had every right to be angry. To confront her. After all, he'd waited fifteen damn years to do so. Half a lifetime, during which his life had disintegrated, where he'd been shunned and cast aside. But he hadn't banked on the fact that frightening Ivy would carve a pit of guilt in his belly. Make him feel like the low-down criminal everyone thought him to be.

Or that the sudden attraction he felt for her might be reflected in her own expressive eyes.

No, he'd imagined her reaction. Been so desperate for a woman that he'd twisted fear into desire. Ivy was too young, too beautiful, too innocent for a man like him.

She licked her lips and his throat went dry.

"I...I'm sorry, Matt."

"Sorry?" he hissed. "Sorry doesn't make up for prison, Ivy."

"I know." Her eyes flickered with regret, and he silently cursed, wishing he could drag his gaze away from her soft, luscious-looking mouth. The other half of him wanted to kiss her. Taste those sweet pink lips. Swirl his tongue inside and watch her fall apart in his arms.

Damn. Ivy was not a little girl anymore. And he wanted her with a vengeance.

Yet, just as they had fifteen years ago, emotions moved inside him, careening around like he was on a free fall ride. A gut instinct to protect her rifled through him. Even if it meant protecting her from him.

Only Ivy did that to him. Made him think. Feel. Want things he couldn't have. Dreams he couldn't afford to acknowledge.

"I don't remember what happened that night, Matt," she said in a low, strained voice. "I...that's the reason I came back here. I need to remember."

He flattened his mouth in a thin line. Wanted to tell her he didn't believe her. But the truth radiated in her tortured eyes.

Disturbed by his reaction to her, he dragged his gaze away. Scanned the room. Saw a dingy-looking, cloth Santa perched on top of the faded wooden dresser. Memories crashed back. Ivy clinging to a Santa doll that night. Dropping it in the mud. Him picking it up and carrying her, trying to shield her against the rain.

His gut clenched as another memory followed. One he'd forgotten. Ivy in town, stopping to give half of her peanut butter sandwich to a homeless blind man begging on the street. Her clothes had been hanging off of her, her shoes ratty. She'd barely had enough to eat herself. But she'd been kind to the old man.

A siren wailed from outside, and Matt swallowed, every nerve in his body bunched tight. She'd seen him looking at the Santa, and her face had turned ashen. Had she really blocked out memories of that night?

The siren grew louder. His first instinct urged him to flee as fast as he could. But running would only make him look guilty, just as hiding out the night of the Stantons' slaying had.

Good God. How had he landed himself into this mess his first night back in Kudzu Hollow?

A pounding on the door brought reality back, and Ivy rushed to answer it.

A.J. Boles, his teenage buddy, stood in the doorway, wearing a sheriff's uniform, rain dripping off the brim of his hat. Matt couldn't have been more surprised if his own sorry-assed daddy had returned to welcome him home.

A.J. had been a hellion in their day, had liked vandalizing cars, playing with fire, drinking and women. Yeah, he'd especially liked women. He'd even bragged about screwing the married ones, choosing who to bang just because he hated their rich husbands. A.J.'s own daddy had been pretty well-off, was some big shot real estate developer. Matt had never understood their relationship, only known that A.J. and his old man hadn't gotten along.

Like he and his own old man hadn't, but for different reasons.

"Sheriff Boles. You're Ann Ivy?"

Ivy nodded, glanced sideways and met Matt's gaze, silently asking if he'd reveal her real identity.

But Matt remained silent, hidden by the shadows studying his former friend. The cocky attitude remained as A.J. skimmed his eyes over Ivy, mentally undressing her.

Matt clenched his fists, that protective instinct swelling inside him again.

No, A.J. hadn't changed. He still liked women. Was a taker. Then again, all the women had liked him, and had given it up pretty easily.

But the idea of him taking anything from Ivy roused Matt's anger.

Reining in the control he'd mastered in prison, he forced himself to tamp down his temper. A.J.'s sandy-blond hair had gotten darker. His lean body had filled out, and he'd grown an inch or two, putting him around five-eleven.

"What's the problem, ma'am?" A.J. asked.

Ivy waved him in. "Come on inside, and I'll show you."

Three steps in, A.J. finally noticed Matt. He froze, thumbs in his belt loops, feet spread wide.

"Holy hell, if it isn't Matt Mahoney. I heard you got released."

"Word spreads fast."

A.J.'s gaze shot toward the wall, and his eyes widened as he spotted the blood-smeared writing and dead animal. "Shit." He turned to Ivy. "When did this happen?"

"It was like that when I arrived here tonight."

A.J. quickly glanced at Matt, his eyebrows raised as if waiting on an explanation. Matt squared his shoulders, searched for the old familiar connection between him and his buddy, felt tension knot his neck at A.J.'s assessment. He'd had fifteen years of being stared at with suspicion, as if he was a rabid dog that preyed on children. As if he deserved to die.

He hadn't expected it from A.J.

"Mahoney?" A.J. finally asked.

Disappointment assaulted Matt at the silent implication. He'd hoped that his friend would remember old alliances. After all, they'd fished together. Set off stink bombs in the girls' locker room so they could watch them run outside in their underwear. Hidden in the closet with nude girlie magazines and laughed at the raunchy jokes. And they'd taken their first trip to Red Row together, another bonding of sorts.

Then Matt had ended up in jail, and A.J. had wound up sheriff.

Strange how the world went around.

"Matt's staying next door. I screamed and he came to check on me," Ivy answered for him.

"You two are here together?" A.J. asked in an incredulous voice.

"No," Matt cut in before Ivy could bother.

A.J. scowled. "We don't want trouble around here, Mahoney."

Matt shrugged, feigning nonchalance. "Who says I'm here to cause trouble?"

"Why else would you have come back?"

Matt grinned. "To see my old friends, of course."

A.J. didn't take the bait. "When did you get to town?"

"Tonight," Matt said, meeting A.J.'s glare head-on. "Just a few hours ago."

"You're here one day and now this?" A.J. gestured toward the bloody writing, then shifted on the balls of his feet. "Do you have any idea who did this, ma'am?"

Ivy shook her head. "No…"

"Why would someone want to hurt you?" A.J. asked.

"I don't know," Ivy said quietly.

A.J. hesitated, then turned on that charming smile. The ladies' man was back. "If you don't tell me the truth, I can't help you."

A heartbeat of silence stretched through the room. The question stood in the air—should she confess the truth about her identity? Could she trust the sheriff to keep her secret?

Could he help her if she didn't?

Matt refrained from offering advice. He didn't trust anyone in this town. Including her.

And A.J. wanted Ivy. That much was evident, at least to him. But he couldn't tell her that. After all, her personal life was none of his business.

"My real name is Ivy Stanton," she said. "I came here under the pen name I use in my magazine."

Realization quickly flared in A.J.'s eyes. "I see. So no one else in Kudzu Hollow knows who you really are?"

"Not that I know of. And I'd like to keep it that way for a while."

"Probably wise. It's a small town. Gossip spreads fast."

Matt grimaced. And friendships died quickly.

A.J. frowned. "How long have you been in town, Miss Stanton?"

"About a week."

He gestured around the cabin. "Is there anything missing?"

Ivy bit her lip. "I…I haven't really checked."

"Look around and see." A.J. strode back to the door and checked the lock, while Ivy began to search the room. "There's no sign of forced entry. Did you leave the cabin unlocked?"

"No."

Matt assessed the cabin, too, watching A.J. Essentially, the rental unit consisted of one big room, sparsely furnished. An iron bed dominated the center, with an old-fashioned quilt in green and rose covering it. A simple pine dresser sat in one corner, a desk in the opposite. A breakfast bar separated the small kitchen nook from the den. Across from the bed a small sitting area held a sofa and chair situated around a ceiling-high stone fireplace. Built-in bookshelves held a few paperback novels, a small TV set and a stereo. The floors were made of heart of pine, the walls the same, making the room dark and cozy. Except the "present" Ivy had received had destroyed the relaxing atmosphere.

"I don't see anything missing," she said after checking the closet.

A.J. took a quick run through the cabin. "The window's open in the bathroom. My guess is that's how the guy got in and out."

Ivy sighed. "I…I don't know if this is related or not, but in town earlier, a car sideswiped me after I left the diner. I…thought it was just some teenagers, or maybe a drunk leaving the bar."

Matt's instincts roared to life. Twice in one night, something strange had happened to Ivy. Someone definitely knew her identity, and didn't want her here.

A.J, gently stroked her arm as if to comfort her. "Are you all right? Were you hurt?"

Ivy pulled away. "I'm fine, but the driver damaged my car."

"Did you get the make of the vehicle or see anyone inside?" A.J. asked.

"No, it all happened so fast. The windows were tinted, and it was raining," Ivy whispered. "I did file a report with your deputy for insurance purposes."

"So you had to give your name?" Matt asked.

Ivy twitched, shifting uncomfortably, but nodded.

Matt gestured toward the wall, irritated that A.J. was so close to Ivy, although he had no idea why it irked him so. "Are you going to collect blood samples to have tested?"

A.J.'s mouth twisted. "Yeah. And I'll take some pictures, too."

"Do you send them away to a crime lab?" Matt asked.

A.J. grunted. "Are you questioning my abilities as a law enforcement agent, Matt?"

"No," he replied. "But proper testing is crucial. After all, faulty DNA evidence sent *me* to jail."

"Is that right?" A.J. asked with an eyebrow raise.

Matt's cold gaze met his former friend's. "If you don't believe me, you can look at the transcripts. And hell, test my damn blood. It won't match that smear on the wall."

"Don't worry. I will."

Matt glared at him. Was this the way he'd be treated the rest of his life?

Every time a crime took place, no matter how petty, the cops would suspect him first.

IVY DIDN'T UNDERSTAND the dynamics, but tension simmered in the air as the sheriff retrieved his camera and a crime scene kit from the car. Tension between her and Matt. And between him and the sheriff.

"I'm going to call the owner of the cabins," Matt said. "He should know about this."

"She'll need another room," A.J. said. "This is a crime scene now."

Ivy nodded. Still shaken, she slumped into the rocking chair in the corner and watched as the sheriff photographed the wall, then took a sample of the blood, and dusted the wall, doorknobs, the bathroom windowsill, even the phone for fingerprints.

Matt remained silent, having perched on one of the bar stools as if he intended to supervise A.J.'s investigation. Miss Nellie's warning echoed back: *Don't go to Kudzu Hollow. It's too dangerous.*

It was dangerous only if someone still had secrets. If the person who'd really killed her parents had gotten away with it and didn't want her back.

Which meant Matt was innocent, as the judge had decreed.

Ivy massaged her temple where a headache pulsed. Finally, just as the sheriff finished the fingerprinting, Cliff appeared. He looked haggard and upset at the sight of the blood on the wall. When he saw the chicken's head, he staggered on his feet. Matt caught him.

"Are you okay?" Matt asked.

Ivy fanned the man's face and rushed to get him a glass of water.

"I ain't had no trouble out here before," Cliff said in a weak voice. "What's going on now?"

"I don't know," Sheriff Boles replied. "Some prankster kids may have vandalized the room just to stir up trouble. You know how this weather affects them."

The old man nodded. "I should have moved away from here when my Gertie died. But I couldn't bear to leave her."

"Cliff, I need to move to another cabin," Ivy said.

"Good Lord, yes. I wouldn't feel right you staying here." He rubbed a freckled hand over his chin, but his color was improving. "I'll get a cleaning crew to take care of this mess." He stood, composing himself. "Let me unlock the cabin on the other side of Mr. Mahoney. I'll leave the key inside."

Ivy thanked him and walked him to the door, worried about the man's health. He was too old for such a shock, but he assured her that he was fine as he toddled outside.

Sheriff Boles's cell phone jangled, and he flipped it open. "Boles here." He hesitated. "Yeah. Jesus. I'll be right there."

The sheriff stopped beside Ivy and placed a hand on her shoulder. "Call me if anything else strange happens, Ivy. That's what I'm here for, to protect the citizens." He removed a business card from his pocket and handed it to her. "My home phone number's on there as well as my cell."

"Thanks, Sheriff. I appreciate your concern."

Matt followed the sheriff to the door with a frown. "What's wrong, A.J.? What was that call about?"

A.J. hesitated. "It's started again."

"What's started again?" Ivy asked.

"The trouble. A fight broke out with some teens in front of one of the gas stations. And there's been a murder out near the junkyard." The sheriff leveled his gaze at Matt, an insinuation in his eyes. "You weren't out there earlier, were you?"

Matt's jaw tightened. "I dropped by to see my mother, but that's the only place I stopped."

"And how did it go? Was she glad to see you, Matt?"

His shoulders stiffened. "Yeah, she welcomed me with open arms." Sarcasm laced his voice and anguish radiated from him, stirring Ivy's compassion.

The sheriff stared at Matt for a long minute, eyes locked. "You didn't have a run-in with anyone else while you were out there?"

Matt's expression turned lethal. "No. Who was murdered?"

"I'm not at liberty to divulge the victim's identity. We have to notify the next of kin." Sheriff Boles turned back to Ivy with a smile. "Like I said, call me if you have any more problems, Miss Stanton, day or night. And if I were you, I'd keep my doors locked." He tugged his hat lower on his head, then opened the door, the wind hurling rain inside. "In fact, if I were the two of you, I'd get out of town. There's nothing for either one of you here anymore. Nothing but trouble."

Ivy barely suppressed a shudder. In the next second, she wondered if his comment had been a threat instead of a warning.

As soon as A.J. left, a strained silence engulfed the room. The air was charged with tension, the accusations A.J. had posed lingering, leaving the rancid smell of suspicion. Did A.J. really think Matt had committed murder the first night he was back? What had happened to make his buddy distrust him?

"I can't believe someone knows who I am," Ivy said in a strained voice. "But that is blood, isn't it?"

He narrowed his eyes. "Yes, what did you think it was?"

"I…wasn't sure." She paused, heat staining her cheeks. "I…don't see red anymore. The color red. Not since that night."

The reality of her words slammed into him. He'd heard she'd been traumatized, had blacked out her memories. But she'd blocked out colors, as well? Maybe that explained her drab clothing. A woman like her should be dressed in pretty bright colors, not denim or brown.

His earlier need to seek vengeance against her vanished, shame replacing his anger. "Let's get you moved. Go ahead and pack your things."

Ivy licked her lips. "You don't have to come with me, Matt."

He banked his own emotions. "I want to make sure you get safely situated inside."

Her gaze locked with his, fear still lingering. But something else—a different kind of emotion—flickered in her eyes. Regret? Surprise? Gratitude?

She didn't want to be alone. Any fool could see that. Although she was desperately trying to put up a brave front, she was terrified. Who could blame her? The bloody message on the wall and dead animal turned his stomach, and he'd seen worse shit in the pen. Things he would never discuss.

That stupid macho part of him wanted to rescue her again. Wipe the fear off her face. Hold her until she stopped shaking.

They reached for her suitcase at the same time. Her hand touched his, sending a shard of desire straight through him. She had the softest skin he'd ever felt. The most tender touch. And those hands were fine-boned, with long slender fingers. He wanted to twine her fingers in his, bring them to his lips, kiss the soft pads of each one, then feel them on his skin. Stroking. Teasing. Touching. Loving.

Yes, she had the hands of an angel.

But those hands shouldn't be touched by a man's dirty ones.

Not by his hands, especially. Hands that had done things he wasn't proud of.

Hands that had shaken the devil's more than once—hands that knew what it was like to murder.

THE DEVIL HAD GOTTEN INTO him. That was the only explanation.

Tommy Werth stared at his hands, turning the palms over to study the bruises and scratches, remembering the first time he'd taken the notion to kill.

The idea had started in his mind years ago, but he'd put it on hold, like a phone call he didn't want to answer. But the urge had grown stronger lately, that phone ringing incessantly, urging him to follow through. So often that the need had finally possessed him, possessed his body, as if someone else's soul had slipped inside him.

Whispering the things he had to do. Telling him it was all right. Urging him to choke his mama. That she deserved it.

Suggesting ways he could pull it off and not get caught.

Leave her out in the old junkyard. Hide her beneath the kudzu with the other ghosts of people long gone. Let the snakes and rats destroy any evidence he might have left behind.

So that's what he'd done.

Squeezed the breath out of her. Watched her eyes pop wide open in shock and terror.

He'd let her know that he was in charge now. That her reign as dictator had ended. He no longer had to listen to her mind-numbing chatter. To her bitching and ranting. Calling him weak. Ridiculing him because he had stupid allergies. Hoarding money from him while she blew all their cash on stupid garage sale finds, and that home shopping channel where she bought those ridiculous little trinkets. Ceramic kitty cats and frogs to sit around and collect dust. Hell, he'd dump them all in the trash tomorrow.

Yes, he was free now. Free from his mother.

A laugh rumbled in his chest as he let himself inside the house. He kicked off his boots, not bothering to wipe the mud off before traipsing across the white linoleum. She wouldn't be here to fuss at him in the morning.

Or ever again, for that matter.

Adrenaline pumped through him as he grabbed a beer from the fridge, opened it and took a long swig. She couldn't tell him not to drink anymore, either. Or what to eat or where to go or who he could hang out with.

No, he was free of the old witch. Finally.

He yanked his T-shirt over his head as he walked to the den, tossed it on the sofa and turned on the tube, settling the remote on MTV. The loud, heavy metal music rocked through him as the cold beer settled in his belly.

His mother's face floated into his mind again, and he smiled, adrenaline surging through him as he remembered the sight of her panicked expression. The first moment she realized he was going to kill her. Then the sound of her last breath, whistling out with her life, growing weaker, more feeble. The rain dripping down her cheeks like teardrops. The kudzu vine he'd wrapped around her neck until he'd choked the life from her.

She would never scream at him again. Or call him a worthless ass or cuss him for being lazy and stupid. Because he had outsmarted her.

Yes, he had just kissed his mother goodbye, along with all his problems.

He cranked up the TV volume a little louder and strummed his imaginary electric guitar, keeping perfect time with the rhythm. Tomorrow he'd call his buddies and arrange a party to celebrate. Tell Trash to bring over some pot.

Now the old biddy was dust in the wind, he could really start living.

For a brief second, he remembered the spooky legends about the ghosts in the hollow. Imagined his mom's skeletal face floating toward him. Saw her bones sticking out, the skin peeling away as she rotted. The worms and maggots feeding on her. The bony remainders of her fingers digging through the dirt, pawing upward through the vines and dirt to grab him.

He threw his head back and laughed. Good thing he didn't believe in all that shit, or else he wouldn't sleep tonight for fear she'd return and haunt him.

CHAPTER FOUR

A.J. MET HIS DEPUTY, Jimmy Pritchard, at the junk-yard, his irritation mounting as he spotted Lady Bella Rue hovering close by, kneeling on the damp ground, sprinkling one of her weird concoctions around the edges of the oak tree, chanting as if she could commune with the devil. Though the rain had slackened, the sky was dark as Hades, the ground drenched and soggy. The stench of the chicken houses nearby, and a dead animal probably trapped below that kudzu, nearly knocked him on his ass.

But so far, he hadn't found a dead body.

The old biddy seemed oblivious as to his arrival, which only proved that she was as a crazy as a loon, just like everyone said. He wanted to order her to leave town and bother someone else. But he was almost as unnerved by her as the children who ran from her and taunted her, calling her evil. Besides, he had enough problems to deal with now that Matt Mahoney and Ivy Stanton were back in town.

Geez. He thought he'd squashed the guilt years ago. That the past was the past. But seeing Mahoney and Ivy Stanton today resurrected bad memories and the fear of being caught in his lies.

The old woman paused and looked up at him from beneath her veil, her gnarled bony fingers powdery with whatever substance she was spreading around. His stomach knotted as he strode toward her, the ancient language she spoke in her chants a reminder of the old childhood rhymes about the evil in the town.

> Death in the hollow,
> Sin in the well.
> Blood on my fingers,
> Going to hell.

Her eyes looked like two flat crystals piercing through him as if she could see inside his soul. He was scared shitless of what she might find. His weaknesses. Flaws. The lies. The secret fantasies.

And what if she decided to cast one of her wicked spells on him? He'd heard of her magic, that she'd made her own husband's dick shrivel up and nearly fall off because she'd found him cheating on her with one of the ladies from Red Row. Then she'd gone crazy and killed her own kid....

"What's this all about?" he asked his deputy. "I thought you said there was a murder."

His deputy cut a withering glance toward Lady Bella Rue. "She says there has been."

Holy Mother of God. "Lady Bella Rue?"

"Yes," she said in that small voice. "The body's trapped in the kudzu."

He jerked the flashlight around. The junkyard was at least three miles across. Kudzu snaked all around the old vehicles, stretching across the hollow and up the mountainside as if it owned the town.

"Did you witness the murder, Lady Bella Rue?"

She pressed a hand to the rag knotted around her neck and murmured a Hail Mary. He refused to ask the significance of the knots.

"Not exactly. But I know she's there."

More of her hocus-pocus. "Listen, if you didn't see someone hurt, or witness a crime, then why did you drag us out here tonight?"

"She's there," Lady Bella Rue insisted, pointing toward the pit of kudzu. "Just look for yourself. I can see her fingers poking up through the leaves."

A.J. glanced at his deputy and barely suppressed a rude comment. Pritchard shrugged but remained a safe distance from the odd old woman.

"Just look!" she trilled, as if they were both incompetent imbeciles.

He grunted in frustration, but swung the flashlight along the edge of the junkyard closest to them, then dragged it at an angle across one square foot at a time. The wind howled behind him. A yellowish mist rose from the leaves like fireflies. Spooky as hell. About five hundred feet from them, the weeds rustled. Was it the wind? Leaves settling from the heavy rain?

A ghost, maybe?

His heart thumped faster as he walked along the edge of the junkyard, peering through the tangled vines with the flashlight beam. Flies buzzed around him. The smell of rotting vegetation grew more intense. A worm slithered across a rusted tire, then curled onto a wet leaf.

Then he saw it. Long pointed fingers poking up through the brush.

Jesus Christ. Lady Bella Rue was right. It was a woman's hand.

And judging from her outstretched fingers, she'd probably been struggling to escape, but she'd been trapped beneath the kudzu, left to die.

IVY THREW THINGS INTO her suitcase, ducked into the bathroom and gathered her toiletries. Part of her was grateful for Matt's masculine presence, another part felt unsettled as he watched her pack her personal items. An electric current had passed between them when she'd first looked into his eyes, an attraction she had never felt for another man. The desire to know him on a more intimate level plucked at her nerves, making them ping like an out of tune harp that had not been played in a long time.

But a sexual attraction was ridiculous considering their past. *That* was what bound them together— the horrible night her parents had died. The answers that needed to be found were locked somewhere in her mind. And she had to gather the courage to search for them, not let this warning tonight deter her from accomplishing her goal. Because she could not give herself to any man until she felt whole. Alive. Not the dead shell of a person she'd been her entire life.

She couldn't resort to the patterns, the routines, the grays and blacks and browns.

"Are you almost ready?" Matt asked in a gruff voice.

She nodded, once again drawn by the pain in his eyes. The intense hunger radiating from him shook her to the core. At the same time, that raw masculinity frightened her. Matt obviously harbored a grudge, and for all intents and purposes, should hate her. But instead, she'd felt a protective aura about him, as if he wouldn't allow any harm to come to her.

She jammed her toothbrush and comb into the cosmetic bag, then carried it to the door and set the bag beside her suitcase while she stuffed her laptop into its case. The notes on the town she'd accumulated so far went next, along with her camera.

"You really are writing a story on Kudzu Hollow?" Matt asked.

"How did you know that?"

He twisted his mouth as if he realized he'd just been caught in a lie. "I went to Chattanooga, to your office, to look for you."

Her breath caught. "How did you find out where I lived? I don't use my real name."

"The Internet."

If he had found her so quickly, the person who'd killed her parents could, too. He might already be in Kudzu Hollow looking for her. And he might have left that warning....

"Why come to me, Matt?" She grabbed her camera bag and laptop bag and slung them over her shoulder, anxious to leave the room. When she reached for her suitcase and cosmetic bag, he hauled them up instead.

"I told you already. I wanted to know why you hadn't come forward to tell the police what happened that night."

"You thought all these years that I remembered and that I didn't speak up?" She swallowed, searching his face. "Why would I do that?"

He shrugged. "I...don't know. Because you were too scared. Maybe you knew the killer and was afraid of him. I realize going to Chattanooga didn't make sense. But nothing made sense at the time."

She paused at the door, the room suddenly too warm. "But it does. If I saw the person who killed my parents, Matt, I probably *was* scared. The therapist I saw afterward said I was traumatized and repressed my memories."

Matt nodded, and they walked outside. The rain had dwindled slightly, although the wind shook the trees, spraying the ground and cabin. A fine mist drizzled down from the porch awning, but she ignored it and followed Matt past his cabin to the one on the opposite side. Shuffling her bags into one hand as he opened the door, he flipped on the lamp, throwing a dim, watery light across the room. Basically, the cabin was identical to her other one, only the quilt design varied, and a photo of a hawk hung above the bed.

Matt placed her bags on the floor, then folded his arms across his chest.

"Would you like some coffee or tea?" Ivy asked

as she put down her own bags, suddenly anxious about being alone.

"Coffee sounds good."

She nodded, rummaged in her bag for the few food items she'd brought. Finding the can of coffee, she spooned grounds into the coffeemaker, added water and hit the on button. Trying to calm herself with the mundane chore, she found mugs inside the pine cabinet.

"Have you learned anything while you've been here?" Matt asked.

She shook her head. "Nothing concrete. Basically, I've been doing background research for my article. Taking pictures of the countryside and local sites. Learning about the legends."

"Have you driven out to the trailer park yet?"

She poured them both some coffee and squeezed her own mug between her hands, remembering the eerie feeling that had overcome her earlier.

"No, but I stopped by the junkyard. It looks the same, only more grown over, choked by weeds and kudzu."

Matt cleared his throat, his voice level, but his eyes spoke volumes. He wanted answers. "Did being at the junkyard jog your memory?"

She bit her lip, then forced herself to meet his intense gaze. "I remembered playing in the cars as a child. Pretending to drive them, imagining they were magical, that they could take me far away."

"You don't remember running through the junkyard that night? Falling in the mud?"

She blinked, her hand trembling. "That really happened?"

His throat worked as he swallowed. "Yes."

"You were there?" she whispered.

"Yes."

"You came out of nowhere," she said softly. "You scared me to death."

"You thought I was going to hurt you."

Her chest squeezed as he absentmindedly stroked the scar on his cheek. "But you picked me up and carried me to that van."

More pain flashed on his face. Memories of the ordeal that had followed? His arrest, conviction? Years in jail…

"I'm so sorry, Matt. I…want to remember everything that happened. I wish I could have kept you out of jail and made the real killer pay."

"Do you?" His harsh voice sliced through the quiet. "Then you believe I am innocent?"

She brushed a strand of hair from her cheek with a shaky finger. "The evidence said you are."

"But a jury convicted me fifteen years ago."

"Are you trying to make me pay, Matt? Make me feel guilty?"

He averted his gaze, a muscle ticking in his jaw as his expression hardened. "No."

"You saved me that night. I…I should be thanking you." She started to reach out and touch his arm, force him to feel her regret, to understand that she believed in his innocence, that she wasn't frightened of him.

But that would be a lie.

Not that she feared he was a killer, but he made

her feel things she'd never felt. Made her ache to comfort him and feel his arms around her. Tempted her to tear down her own protective walls.

But those walls kept her safe. Kept the demons at bay.

"I do want to find the real killer," Ivy said softly.

His shoulders tensed as he moved closer. Their gazes locked, tension thrumming between them. He lifted his hand, rubbed a finger along her cheek, and his voice grew husky, "Even if it puts you in danger, Ivy?"

She considered his question. Her instincts urged her to run. But she'd been running all her life. Matt's past had been destroyed because of her fears. The scars rested on his face. In his eyes. Ones hidden deep inside.

"Yes," she said softly. "Even if it puts me in danger."

"What if it means finding out that the person who killed your parents was someone you knew and trusted?"

He was right again. "The therapist I saw in Chattanooga warned me that was a possibility."

"And?"

"And I'm here, aren't I?" Ivy pressed a hand over his, the heat of his strong fingers scorching hers. "I'm not running any longer, Matt. We both deserve some answers."

IVY'S ADMISSION HAUNTED MATT, taunting him with what-ifs. What if they'd met under different circumstances? What if he wasn't a scarred ex-con whose soul had died in the war in prison?

Hatred had filled his mind for so long he didn't know if he could actually relinquish the emotion. But when he looked into Ivy's captivating eyes, he had the urge to do just that.

No, he lived for revenge.

He dropped his hand from her cheek, his body simmering with heat as he tried to tear his gaze away from her. Those eyes were so green he felt as if he'd looked into a sea of emerald glass. After facing ugliness for fifteen years, he found the sight captivating. She was so damn beautiful, fragile, innocent.

For a moment, his anger faded and another emotion replaced it—raw, unadulterated lust. And then she touched him…a gentle touch. Tender. Erotic. More seductive than she could have imagined.

He'd never been touched like that in his life. Not as if someone actually gave a damn about him.

You've been in prison for fifteen years. Of course you're going to experience lust. Your choices in women haven't exactly been stellar babes.

"Matt? What do you remember about that night?" Ivy asked.

Her question forced him to take a reality check. He was scarred and rough. She was light and tender. They didn't even belong in the same room.

God, he'd wanted to forget that night for so long that he'd almost blocked out the details himself. But he couldn't. Every detail might count. He had to retrace his steps. Hers.

"I was stealing hubcaps from the junkyard," he said, ashamed to admit he had been committing a crime.

She didn't speak, simply sipped her coffee and studied him. "Were you alone?"

He frowned, scrunching his face. "Yes. I...A.J. was supposed to meet me, but he canceled at the last minute. Said something more important came up."

"You think he chickened out?"

"I think he was screwing some girl." Maybe one of the ladies from Red Row, but Matt decided to spare Ivy that tidbit.

"So, you were there to take some hubcaps?"

He nodded. "I'd just turned sixteen. Like every adolescent boy, I wanted a car, but my mother couldn't afford it. She had this junker that I intended to fix up. Thought at least then I'd have a ride."

Ivy's eyes flickered with something that looked like sympathy, and he wished he hadn't tried to justify his actions. He didn't want her sympathy or pity. He simply wanted answers. The truth.

"My first car was a fixer-upper, too," she said softly, then stopped abruptly. "I'm sorry. I...that was cruel."

"Don't apologize, Ivy. You didn't have any more control over what happened than I did."

"Yes, I did, Matt. If I hadn't been such a coward, if I remembered seeing my parents' murderer, and identified the killer, you wouldn't have been convicted."

He couldn't argue, but didn't want her beating herself up. Not anymore. "Try to remember now, Ivy."

She sighed and ran a hand through her tangled wet hair, then closed her eyes as if painting a mental picture of the events of that night. "You picked me up and carried me to the van. You even saved the cloth Santa I dropped in the mud."

"I was in the junkyard when I heard you crying," he said gruffly. "You were running and crying like the devil was chasing you, like you were scared out of your mind."

This time shame reddened her face as she looked at him. "You knew my father was abusive?"

Matt stared at her for a long moment. "Yes, Ivy. No kid should be treated like he treated you."

"My dad called me poison." Ivy traced a finger around the top of her mug. "I used to hate my name because of that."

"God. What a bastard."

She almost smiled at his comment. "Yes, he was," she confessed. "It took me a long time to realize that it wasn't my fault he had a temper."

"No, some men are just born mean." His mother had said that about Matt. Then he'd gotten arrested and gone to jail and proven her right.

"So he was chasing you?" he asked.

She looked down into the coffee as if the mug held the answers, but continued to frown.

"I don't know for sure if Daddy was chasing me or if it was someone else. I have recurring nightmares. It's always night, black outside, raining. Someone's after me, a monster, but I can't see his face."

"The man who killed your parents," he said quietly. "You don't *want* to see his face."

"But I do," she insisted. "I have to. I know your life has been a nightmare these past few years, but, in a way, I locked myself in my own prison, too. I...can't sleep at night. I can't be close to anyone. I...I'm suffering from panic attacks."

Guilt warred with his need for vengeance. An image of Ivy haunted by demons followed, tearing him up inside. "Then we should stop now. Talking about it will only bring the nightmares back."

She shook her head, that false bravado flashing on her face. "No, tell me the rest, Matt. I have to know, to see this through." She paused, emotion glittering in her eyes, but then she squared her shoulders and lifted her chin. "You went to my house after you tucked me into the van?"

He nodded. She must have read the police reports. "I was mad," he admitted in a low voice. "A real hellion back then. Thought I'd teach your father a lesson. Teach him to beat on someone his own size."

Her head jerked up as if she was surprised that he'd gone to her father to defend her. Had any man ever protected her? Taken care of her? Loved her or held her and tried to wipe that sadness from her? Matt wanted to, and he'd just reconnected with her again.

"When I arrived at your house," he said, "I...saw your mother lying on the floor. There was blood everywhere. She was...already dead."

"And my father?"

"I never saw him," Matt admitted.

"So he could have killed my mother," Ivy whispered.

"That's what I thought at first," he admitted. "I

figured he was still around, but if he was, he had a knife, so I decided to get my tail out of there."

"But if he killed my mother," Ivy said, "then who killed him?"

Matt grimaced. He'd asked himself the same question a thousand times. Ivy's mother had had lovers. He didn't know if Ivy knew that fact, and he didn't want to be the one to tell her.

But he had to consider the possibility that maybe one of her lovers had avenged her murder by killing the old man.

Matt had to think logically here. No, a john wouldn't kill her old man to avenge her death. It had to be a man who'd cared for her. A man who'd gotten serious about Lily.

Or what if it was the other way around? What if Lily Stanton had been looking for a way out of her life with her abusive husband? Perhaps she fell for one of her lovers and wanted him to help her escape. Some of the customers who visited Red Row were prominent citizens, married men who didn't want their visits advertised, either because of their wives or their careers. She might have been desperate, threatened to expose the man's identity, and he killed her to keep her from divulging the truth.

Either way, identifying Lily's lovers might lead them to her murderer.

CHAPTER FIVE

A.J. HAD TO FIND this woman's killer. He wiped sweat from his brow as the crime scene unit photographed the area, then whacked the kudzu from around her neck to free her. He had wanted to process the crime himself, but had decided to call for the crime unit on this one. Besides, wading into the knee-high snake pit of kudzu and rusted cars was not his idea of a good time.

He liked crime work to a point. But he drew the line at rats gnawing on him. And the equipment he had in the Kudzu Hollow sheriff's office was not the most updated. But he would do his job. Find the killer. Put him behind bars.

Atone for the past. He'd been doing that for the last fifteen years. All because of one stupid mistake he'd made as a kid.

Lady Bella Rue shook her head as the men lifted the body, placed it on a stretcher and carried it to the embankment. "That's Dora Leigh Werth."

A.J. nodded. His deputy, Jimmy, had latched onto one of the female crime techs and was soaking up the details as she methodically searched for evidence. Plucking a feather from the kudzu here, a piece of torn clothing there, she bagged it for forensics and trace—a needle-in-a-haystack task that hopefully might lead to a clue. Then again, there was no telling how long some of the debris in the junkyard had been here.

A.J. had scoured the area for footprints and signs the killer might have left before the CSI unit arrived, but found little. A few dog paw prints. Trash. Beer bottles tossed into the kudzu. The junkyard drew teens who wanted a quiet place to sneak a drink or smoke weed. Sometimes the boys parked here with dates, using the spooky tales and atmosphere to entice their girlfriends into a make-out session.

He had used the same routine when he was young. But then the trouble had begun....

"Tell me again why you were here," he asked Lady Bella Rue.

She gripped the string of knots around her neck and whispered another Hail Mary. "I came to spread a protective spell over the land," she said simply. "I sensed something evil was about to happen around the junkyard."

"You lost your son near here, didn't you?"

Beneath the black hat, her face paled. And Lady Bella Rue was not a pale woman. Her skin had once been a glossy shade of caramel, a mixture of her black and white heritage that had fed the gossip vine for years—just who were her daddy and mama? Some said her mama had come from Africa, had been a witch doctor in the old country. Others claimed she worked out of Red Row. Others suggested she had been spawned by the devil.

"He fell off a cliff on this side of the mountain when he was only three," she said in a low voice. "He wandered away from me while I was picking roots."

Or she had pushed him. A.J. knew the rumors.

"How well did you know Dora Leigh Werth?"

"As well as I know everyone around here," Lady Bella Rue said with a bark of laughter. "You know, Sheriff, that half the town is afraid of me. Talulah is my only real friend, though, I do what I can to protect the others, anyway."

Yeah, she was a real saint and he was a fucking virgin. "And why do you do that if you don't like the people in town?"

"I pity those with closed minds."

Or maybe she thought she could atone for killing her son. He stared down at her hunched figure, the gnarled hands of a conjurer. "How do I know that you didn't kill this woman? That the spells you claim protect people haven't been causing havoc all these years?"

Her cackling laughter echoed off the mountain. "I am not that powerful, Sheriff Boles. And what purpose would it serve me to kill this innocent woman?"

"I don't know. Maybe she knew something about you that you didn't want revealed."

"People think I killed my own boy. They already call me a witch, the devil's child. What worse could they possibly say about me?"

He shrugged. He had no answer to that question. "Sometimes people don't have a motive. They just snap and turn evil."

Her head tilted beneath the veil. "You would know that, wouldn't you?"

He didn't like the eerie way she seemed to look into people, as if she could read their minds, see inside their souls. "I've seen a lot on the job over the past few years," he admitted.

She clucked sarcastically, as if she knew he was hiding sinister secrets himself, and he kicked at the muddy ground.

"Look at me, Sheriff," Lady Bella Rue said. "Dora Leigh was a hefty woman. My arthritic hands don't have the strength to strangle her, much less drag her out in that field of kudzu and bury her beneath it."

"But you have strength in your black magic?"

She adjusted her hat, looking nervous. "I dabble."

"And who says she was strangled?" A.J. asked, his eyes slanting toward her. "The coroner hasn't revealed anything about her cause of death yet."

"Actually she was stabbed first. But that didn't kill her. I saw the vines being wrapped around her neck, choking the life out of her," she whispered.

He chewed the inside of his cheek. If she had used black magic to murder the woman, it would be hard to prove. Even A.J. didn't like to admit he believed in the gift, because the power of magic was in believing. And he knew for a fact that Lady Bella Rue kept all sorts of eerie hoodoo items at her place. Gourds. Roots and herbs. Rattlesnake skin. Bones of animals. Chicken heads. Poisons. Some of the kids even claimed she had fingers from humans, but he had no proof. Yet.

She angled her veiled head toward him. "So you believe my spells and charms work?"

He stared beyond her to the woods, refusing to back down. "I think you live on the dark side of life. That you try your hand at black magic. That you have secrets, Lady Bella Rue."

"Everyone has secrets," she said with conviction. "But yours will be revealed, Sheriff Boles. Then everyone will know the truth about you."

His gut tightened as anger bled through him. What if the old woman was right?

No…he couldn't let the past catch up with him. He was sheriff now, respected by the town.

He'd do whatever necessary to protect his reputation.

"WHAT ARE YOU HIDING from me?" Ivy asked as Matt literally closed down in front of her.

"Nothing."

She didn't believe him. "Matt, what else happened that night? After you saw my mother's body, what did you do?"

He finished his coffee and poured another cup, stalling. "I ran," he said, disgust riddling his voice. "I thought your old man, or the killer, whoever it was, might still be around."

"Did you hear anyone in the house?"

He shook his head. "No. For the past fifteen years, I've retraced that night a thousand times in my head to check if I missed something. But I don't remember hearing or seeing anyone else. And when

I got away safe, I wasn't about to call the cops. I figured I'd get fingered for the crime."

Which was exactly what had happened.

Ivy dropped her eyes back to her coffee. "Then they found my dad later that night in the junkyard, with a kitchen knife in his back?"

Matt nodded, his dark eyes hooded. "And the cops found my fingerprints on the doorknob. Apparently, I'd stepped in blood, too, which was on the bottom of my boots, along with mud from the junkyard, where I'd seen you earlier. The case was a slam dunk."

"What about your lawyer? Didn't he argue that you had no motive?"

"My lawyer was some young, overworked, smart-ass kid doing a stint for the D.A. He was living off of his daddy's fat wad of money and didn't give a rat's ass about whether or not I was innocent or guilty. All he wanted to do was finish his assignment, work for his old man and buy a Mercedes." Matt sighed. "Besides, I was pretty stupid. Instead of going home and telling my mother what I'd witnessed so she could have backed me in court and provided me with an alibi, I tried to find A.J."

"And?"

"And he wasn't home. In fact, nobody was at his house. So I hid out in the junkyard all night."

Ivy rubbed a hand over her forehead. "All night. You mean in one of the cars?"

He nodded, but stared at his boots. "In that old Impala near where I left you."

Her throat ached so badly she couldn't swallow. "You came back to check on me?"

"I…figured you might have seen your mama's killer." He rammed a hand through his hair, leaving the shaggy ends in a mess. "I thought the killer might come looking for you, too."

Emotions fluttered through Ivy. He had returned to protect her. To make sure she was safe. And when he'd needed her, she'd retreated into her own silent world of denial.

She started to reach out to offer him a comforting hand, but he stiffened, his shoulders rigid. "I don't want your sympathy or pity, Ivy. I was a stupid kid then. If I hadn't been up to no good, stealing hubcaps that night, I wouldn't have been in the junkyard at all."

"And you wouldn't have saved me. Then you wouldn't have gotten in trouble."

"I didn't mean to imply you were at fault."

"It's the truth, Matt. You must have hated me all these years."

He hesitated, his voice rattling with emotions when he finally spoke. "I don't hate you."

Ivy's heart splintered. Her cowardice had hurt him so much. God. She couldn't ever go back to running.

"Neither one of us was at fault," he said, "but someone did kill your parents and they've gone free all this time."

"Someone who knows why we both returned to Kudzu Hollow." Which explained the message to her. It also meant Matt would be in danger.

Her mind ticked over possible reasons why someone would have wanted to kill her parents. They hadn't had money. In fact, they'd fought about it all the time....

If her father had killed her mother and she'd witnessed it, it made sense that Ivy had been traumatized enough to repress the memory.

But if her father stabbed her mother, then who had killed him? Someone who cared for her mom?

But whom? From what Ivy remembered, her mother hadn't had many friends. She had worked at the local pub for a short time as a waitress, but her father had put an end to that. Ivy recalled that bitter argument because it had turned into a physical fight. Her mother had cried and cried, claiming that she wanted the tips, that it was the best money in town, the only way she could afford to save a penny.

And she had wanted to save money, Ivy remembered. At night, she'd tell Ivy stories of faraway places. Show her pictures of cities she wanted them to visit. Of big fancy houses and shopping centers, and schools. Even colleges that she dreamed of Ivy attending. Tall massive stone structures with architecture that resembled castles from a fairyland.

"See those pretty green vines growing on that building?" she had said.

Ivy had stared in awe at the photos. "It looks like a castle, Mommy. Like something a queen would live in."

"It's not a house," her mother had explained. "It's an Ivy League university." She had hugged Ivy into the circle of her arms then and traced her finger over the beautiful green vines crawling up the stone structures. "That's the reason I named you Ivy. Because

one day I want you to attend an Ivy League school.
Then you can make something of yourself, be important. Not like your mama and daddy."

Tears pressed against Ivy's eyelids as she recalled
her mother's words. Lily had loved her and would
still be with her if someone hadn't brutally stolen her
life.

"Ivy?" Worry tinged Matt's voice. "Are you all
right?"

"I'm fine." She placed her empty coffee mug on
the counter, inhaling sharply. "I'm just tired. It's
been a long day."

He nodded. "Then I'll go. Let you get some
sleep."

Ivy nodded, as well, but she didn't turn around.
She wasn't sure she would sleep. Not with memories
of that bloody message and dead chicken taunting
her. Not knowing that someone might try to harm her.

And that Matt might be in danger, too.

MATT ORDERED HIMSELF to leave. Being in the same
room with Ivy disturbed his equilibrium. Resurrected his protective instincts. Made him want to
hold her and erase the fear from her eyes. Made him
want other things he couldn't have. A kiss. A touch.
A night with her in his arms.

But he had a mission and nothing would deter him.
Especially a woman. Still, Ivy looked so lost he could
hardly drag himself away. Traces of guilt and helpless-
ness had echoed in her voice. And fear lingered in her
eyes as well as the memory of that gruesome threat.

Restless energy pounding through him, he laid a

hand on her shoulder and gently turned her to face him. Her creamy skin looked ashen. "Ivy? Did you remember something else?"

She shook her head. "Not about that night. Just…little things about my mother. The reason she named me Ivy."

He smiled. "For those deep green eyes of yours."

"No. Because she wanted me to attend an Ivy League college. She said my eyes were the same color as the ivy."

His throat tightened. In spite of the fact that she'd frequented Red Row, Lily had loved Ivy. Had Lily been working to save money to help her daughter escape the life she'd been saddled with? She should have found another way, a life that hadn't been so dangerous.

"But my father called me Poison Ivy," Ivy whispered, a bleak note in her voice. "He said I was poison to his marriage."

Anger sent a blade of pain through Matt. "Like I said earlier, Ivy, your father was a bastard."

She bit down on her lip, and the soft glow from the lamp across the room cast her beautiful face in an angelic glow. Matt wondered what she saw when she looked at him. The scar on his face? The animal he'd become in the pen?

The filth, the fights, the unspeakable acts…

He wished he could will away his past. He ached to kiss her, almost tipped up her chin and claimed that soft mouth for his own. Let her tenderness soothe his blemished soul.

But he couldn't. He had killed. Not her father or

mother. But since then, he had taken lives. In dirty ways he never wanted her to know about.

"Do you think you can sleep?" he asked gruffly.

She hesitated. "I…don't know. But we both need to try. Tomorrow…tomorrow I want to talk to some people in town."

"Maybe you should heed that warning and leave, Ivy. It's dangerous for you to ask questions."

"I can't leave," she whispered. "The nightmares follow me everywhere I go."

God, he understood about nightmares. He might be out of prison, but the sins he'd committed inside would dog him forever. The very reason he slept with the window open. With a knife. With his face toward the door.

Never turn your back or you might be attacked. Or worse…

Ivy reached up and traced a finger along the edge of his scar, and his breath hissed between clenched teeth. Emotions crowded his chest— anger begging for release, but a tenderness tugged at him, too, one he hadn't felt in so long he thought that side of him had died.

"Does it hurt?" she whispered.

Every damn minute of every day, he wanted to say. But pain had become his friend, reminding him he was alive. Still, her concern touched him, made the pain recede momentarily. The back of his throat burned. Jesus Christ, he felt as if he might actually get choked up. Big ugly tough men like him did not get emotional. They learned to channel their feelings into productive ones like anger. Revenge.

So he lied.

"No."

She stroked his cheek again, and moistened her lips with her tongue, drawing his eyes to the erotic movement. Heat engulfed his body. Need and hunger speared through him, a craving to be closer to her that nearly made his knees buckle.

He had to walk away before he made a fool of himself. There was no changing the man he'd become, a bitter fighter, not a lover.

And while he'd do his damnedest to keep her safe, loving her in any way was not an option.

TOMMY WERTH'S TEMPLES throbbed as if a hammer were beating against his skull. His stomach cramped in response, and he thought for a minute he was going to puke. Throwing off the covers, he tried to sit up, but the room swayed. He was so dizzy he flopped back down, but that movement sent his stomach into another spin cycle. The pounding grew louder, and through the blurry haze of his mind, he realized someone was really banging at the door.

Yanking his boxers up and tugging his Metallica T-shirt down over his growling belly, he scrubbed a hand over his face, peered through bleary eyes at the clock. It was the middle of the night. Who the fuck was bothering him? One of his buddies…

No, Trash and Ace would just crawl through the window.

The hammering sound continued. He cursed again. The only way to stop the noise was to answer the damn door. Head threatening to explode, he stood, grabbed the door edge for support, then wobbled through his dark bedroom. He fumbled for the switch, then flipped on a lamp and winced as bright light pierced his eyes. He blinked furiously, then lurched forward and leaned against the door. "Who is it?"

"Sheriff Boles, Tommy. I need to talk to you."

Panic zinged through him. Shit. Shit. Shit. What the hell was the sheriff doing here?

The night before rolled through his mind like a movie trailer. He'd come home and gotten drunk. All that beer. Man, it had been good. But what had happened before?

Geez…his mother.

No. No. No. They couldn't have found her yet. He'd buried her too deep. He had to calm down. Act cool.

"Tommy, open up," the loud voice boomed. "Now."

The sheriff's commanding voice intensified the pain in Tommy's head. He had to run. Get away. But where could he hide? The cellar? The attic?

No, hiding would make him look guilty. Maybe they hadn't found the old hag, after all. Maybe they were only looking for her. But who would have reported her missing? She didn't have many friends.

"Tommy, open the door or I'm going to open it."

No time to run. To think. To escape. Had to face him. Lie if he had to.

He fidgeted with the doorknob, then yanked at the wood. It was swollen from the rain, but finally screeched open. "Sorry, Sheriff, I was asleep."

His bleary eyes latched onto the sheriff's badge, and he took a step back, staggering slightly.

"You okay, Tommy? You don't look so well."

"I…got the flu or something."

"Or something." The sheriff stepped inside, sniffed, then glared down at him. "What you have is a hangover."

Tommy shrugged and clutched at his stomach. "Yeah, well, I'm nearly eighteen."

"You're sixteen and underage," Sheriff Boles stated.

"Look, Sheriff, it's not like I'm out driving or anything. I wasn't bothering anyone here in my own house."

"Have you been here all night?"

Was he trying to trip him up? "Yeah." Tommy gestured toward his mother's fancy white couch, littered with bags of chips, a half-eaten frozen pizza he'd fixed, and a dozen empty beer cans that smelled sour. "My mom was out, so I had a little party."

"By yourself?"

Once again panic clawed at his stomach, but he refused to puke in front of this man, who would probably laugh his ass off. Tommy had heard the sheriff could drink almost anyone in the town under the table at the Ole Peculiar.

Stupid. Stupid. Stupid. Why hadn't he called someone over last night? Then he would at least have an alibi.

"Were you alone, Tommy?"

"Yeah." He swallowed down the bile in his throat. Better not say too much. Keep quiet or he'd give something away.

"What were you celebrating?" the sheriff asked.

Tommy shifted on his feet, rubbed a hand over the emblem on his T-shirt. "Listen, Sheriff, give me a break. I'm sure you knocked back a few when you were my age, too, didn't you?"

Boles's thick mouth flattened at that comment. Score one for Tommy.

"What'd you stop by for?" he asked. "Did you need to see my mother?"

Sheriff Boles's eyes turned somber, his mouth thinning into a flat line. "Actually, that's the reason I'm here. I have some bad news for you, Tommy."

Tommy braced himself to act dutifully shocked and upset.

"We found your mother's body." Boles hesitated, looking grim. "I'm afraid she's dead."

The memory of the blood squirting from her body flashed back, like ketchup spewing from a broken bottle. Other moments of the night before bombarded him. Her shrill scream that had pierced the black night. The smell of her urinating on herself.

His mouth fought a smile, but his stomach protested. Maybe it wouldn't be such a bad idea if he got sick in front of the sheriff. It might be a nice touch. Make him appear to be the grieving, shocked son. Somebody who gave a damn.

He made a choking sound, half crying, half sick, then ran to the bathroom, dropped down and emptied his stomach. The sheriff's boots clattered on the cold linoleum floor. Seconds later, he appeared, doused a washcloth in cold water and handed it to Tommy.

Sweat poured off his face and neck, and his hands were shaking. He even managed to choke out a few tears. Then he accepted the cloth, leaned over the toilet again, pressed it over his face and moaned.

Behind the washcloth, he finally allowed himself to smile. He was a pretty good actor, if he did say so himself.

IVY TRIED TO SHUT OUT the images of blood and violence, but they taunted her, anyway, following her into the shadows of night as she prepared for bed. She still didn't have a good read on Sheriff Boles. One minute he'd acted friendly to her, the next he'd practically told her to heed that bloody warning.

She slipped on a long-sleeved nightshirt, still shivering from the chill in the room. The old-fashioned, brown paneled walls added another layer of darkness to the cabin, and the wind howled through the wooden cracks like an injured wild animal. If it wasn't so late, she'd turn on the gas logs in the fireplace to warm the room, but going to bed with them burning didn't seem like a wise idea. These cabins had been built years ago; the aging wood and faded carpet testified to the fact that things might be in disrepair.

Not willing to take a chance, she grabbed an extra blanket from the closet, tugged on wool socks and set the teakettle on the stove. Better keep to the rituals.

Tea. Read a few minutes. Listen to some soft jazz music. Then maybe she would fall asleep sometime before morning.

The tea made, she brought her laptop to bed, then decided to do a little more research on the town and its history to wind down.

Curious, she accessed the local paper's archives, starting with her parents' deaths. A photo of her had appeared in one of the papers, clinging to that muddy Santa, her clothes hanging on her skinny young body, as a social worker carted her away.

Eight-year-old Ivy Stanton, thought to have possibly witnessed the brutal murder of her parents, is temporarily placed in foster care. Sources report that she has undergone a psychiatric evaluation. Doctors report that if she did witness the murders, she's repressed the memories. Whether or not she will ever recall the events of that night remains a mystery.

Ivy pulled the photos of the crime scene she'd managed to obtain from an investigator from her briefcase. She had seen the photos but never really studied them before. The stark, black-and-white pictures showed her mother's dead, bloody body sprawled on the cheap linoleum floor of their trailer. Her hand had been outstretched as if reaching for something. Maybe for Ivy. Maybe for a weapon to defend herself. Or for help.

Blood had pooled around her head and chest, a river of brown that had spread under the table. Her head lay at an odd angle, her dress was tattered and shoved up around her knees, and one high heel was missing. Her mother had always liked shoes, especially heels. Ivy had loved playing dress-up in them, wobbling and trying to walk like a model.

She forced herself to read the article, nearly choking as the reporter hinted that her mother might have been killed by a jealous lover. He'd also alluded to the fact that she had once been a waitress at the local honky-tonk and that the men liked her.

The gossip in town echoed in Ivy's head—*that Stanton woman was a slut.*

Ivy chewed her lip. Had her mother had a lover?

She certainly was beautiful. Her golden hair matched Ivy's, although her mother had been taller and full-figured. And her eyes were brown, like hot cocoa, Ivy remembered, not green. She'd been warm and laughing—that is, when her husband hadn't been around.

No, her mother hadn't been a slut. She couldn't have been. She stayed home with Ivy, met her at the school bus every day, baked homemade chocolate chip cookies for her in the afternoon and helped her with her homework.

An animal growled outside, and Ivy rose and peered through the window into the woods. Tall trees swayed, sending rain splattering on the muddy ground, leaves and twigs. A small pinpoint of light moved behind a tree—maybe from a cigarette or lighter? The growl of the animal grew louder. Closer. A mountain lion? Or a bear, maybe? Did they inhabit this part of Appalachia? Did they come this close to the cabins?

The light moved again, and panic slammed into her. Was the person who'd left that bloody message out there, watching her from the woods?

CHAPTER SIX

MATT TOSSED AND TURNED, unable to sleep for thinking about Ivy. Wondering if she was okay. If she'd been too shaken to rest.

Dammit. He wasn't supposed to worry about her. He had only one purpose here in town and that was to find the person who'd framed him for murder. Once that individual was punished, Matt would leave this godforsaken town forever.

Throwing the covers aside, he walked to the table and spread out the transcript files of his trial. He slumped down and read through the pages again, searching for any clue as to how he could have saved himself. His lawyer hadn't committed any serious infractions; he simply hadn't built a defense. He definitely should have put Matt on the stand, but he'd reasoned that Matt's angry attitude would hurt his case. Maybe he'd been right.

Or maybe someone on that jury would have seen through to the frightened boy underneath the tough facade.

Hell, it didn't matter. What was done was done. All that mattered now was righting that wrong. And exacting revenge. Matt had to harness the drive that had helped him survive prison.

Turning back to the task, he studied the list of witnesses for the prosecution. Randy Putnam, the owner of the local hardware store back then, had testified that he'd caught Matt trying to lift a tool set once. The principal at the high school had added that he'd been truant, had caused fights in school, had an explosive temper and was rebellious toward adults. Old man Dayton had testified that he'd seen Matt stealing car parts from the junkyard, which the D.A. had gladly used to crucify him. The entire case hinged on suppositions that Matt had gotten caught stealing and had killed Stanton. Of course, he'd waffled slightly on Matt's motive for killing Mrs. Stanton.

But his own mother had erased any lingering doubt about his guilt when she'd admitted on the stand that he'd fought with his father all the time. That he'd beaten him with a bat once. And another time, he'd challenged him with a pocketknife.

He *had* hit the old man, but only to stop him from beating on his mother. But had she mentioned that detail? No. The woman had covered for his old man's ass so many times Matt had lost count. Then his father had run off and left her high and dry, with nothing.

During the trial, Matt had heard gossip that some people thought he might have even killed his old man. But Matt had been eleven when his father had left town. Although if Jerry Mahoney had stayed around and continued his abusive ways, Matt probably would have murdered him. Then he would have ended up in jail, anyway. But at least he would have had the satisfaction of killing the bastard first.

You have killed since.

But only in self-defense.

Did it really matter? He had taken another man's life....

Sweat beaded on his forehead and trickled down his face. He swiped at the moisture, desperate to wipe away the ugly memories, as well. The sheriff then, Larry Lumbar, had described the bloody scene at Ivy's trailer and displayed samples of fingerprints matching Matt's. His boot prints were shown, as well. Matt had no alibi. A.J. had claimed he'd been home with his daddy. Matt's mother had admitted that he hadn't come home all night.

No other suspects were even considered. No one had thought to investigate the Stantons' personal lives. The couple had had no money to steal, so robbery couldn't have been a motive.

Only meanness could, Lumbar had stated. Meanness that came from the likes of out-of-control teenagers like Matt. The sheriff had even commented that he'd never had kids for fear they'd turn out like Matt.

Matt frowned. If he had a son, would the child turn out to be a hellion like he had been? Matt shook off the ridiculous thought, wondering where it had come from. He'd long ago given up illusions of marriage or a family. Maybe aggression did run in the family. Maybe the Mahoney genes were completely skewed with violent tendencies.

No, the best he could hope for was a good job, to become a lawyer.

Weary and frustrated, he stood and paced across the cold room. Tomorrow he'd start probing around town. Find out who might have had a motive for killing the Stantons.

He'd talk to Ivy. See if she remembered anything else.

He crossed the small, dusty room and glanced through the fog-coated window toward her cabin. The image of her frightened green eyes haunted him. The way she'd cowered from him one minute, then touched his cheek so gently the next. Was she sleeping peacefully in the cabin next door? Or was she haunted by nightmares just as he was?

Ivy thought remembering them would make them go away.

But would it, or would it only put her in more danger?

SHE WAS RUNNING through the graveyard, weaving in and out of the maze of tall tombstones. Blood streaked one stone monument, words scrawled in brown letters that said death was coming. The monster was right behind her. Clawing at her feet. Trying to drag her down into the ground. The earth opened up in front of her, an empty black hole. Two hands reached for her, pulling at her ankles….

She screamed and pumped her legs harder. Her muscles cramped. A shrill sound pierced the air. Mutilated chickens dropped from the sky in front of her. A skeleton rolled across the ground, brittle bones turned to ashes. Empty eye sockets stared.

Her mother's...

No...

Then her father ran toward her, his hands stretched out, fists waving. But this time she held a knife. He panted, coming closer, the scent of his foul breath on her face. She lifted the knife and plunged it into his chest....

IVY JERKED AWAKE, TREMBLING and hugging the covers to her as she searched the shadow-filled room. Had she heard a scream, or had it been her own? And in her dream...had she killed her father?

Could that be possible? She'd only been eight, but still...

The piercing sound filled the room again, and she realized it was her cell phone. George Riddon had called right when she'd gotten in bed, but she'd let her voice mail pick it up. But she couldn't keep avoiding him. They had to discuss work. "Hello?"

"Ivy?"

"George?"

"Yeah, it's me. I...wanted to see if you were okay. You didn't answer your phone last night."

"I'm sorry, George. I was so tired I collapsed into bed."

"Ivy, what's going on?" He sounded agitated now. "You're not sleeping well again, are you? Did you have another nightmare?"

"Yes," she admitted as she ran fingers through

her tangled hair, trying to unwind the knots. "But I'm fine now."

"You want to talk about it?" His tone softened from businesslike to personal.

"No. I...I'm okay." She had to change the subject, steer them back to a safer topic—work. "I've gathered some notes on a few of the legends. I'll e-mail them to you when we hang up. And I've already snapped some photographs for the spread."

"Great. Are you about ready to wrap it up and come home?"

"No. I want to get photos of the hollow itself, and there's a small church called the Chapel of Forever I intend to include. An interesting lady named Lady Bella Rue lives on the outskirts of town. Everyone says she practices hoodoo. Let me talk to her, and I can add a special segment on black magic."

"Sounds like the piece is coming along. When do you think you'll be back in Chattanooga?"

Ivy stood and walked to the window, then pushed the curtain aside and peered through the glass. Darkness still bathed the woods, a storm filling the sky with mottled gray clouds. The bloody warning registered in her mind again, then Matt Mahoney's troubled eyes. The scar on his face. The invisible ones that he couldn't hide.

"I don't know, George. Maybe another week."

"That long? Gosh, Ivy, I miss you. I could come and help so you can finish sooner."

In the distance, sunlight fought to break through the clouds. But more rain rolled above the mountain-tops. "George, I thought I explained that I need to be alone here so I can deal with my past. And there are stories about evil happening when it rains. I might be able to do something with that."

A long tense silence followed, but Ivy was too busy watching Matt walk outside his cabin to fill it with chatter. He was shirtless, his broad chest peppered with dark hair, the muscles in his arms enormous. He scratched at his chin where thick beard stubble grew, and glanced at her cabin. For a moment, she felt as if he was looking at her, as if he saw her in her nightgown through the window. Her skin tingled and burned, a warm feeling pooling in her stomach as if he'd touched her.

"Listen," George said, sounding concerned as he broke the quiet, "I wouldn't be in the way. I only want to help you, be with you, Ivy."

Guilt at the way she'd put him off surfaced, but she glanced at Matt again and tamped it down. She'd never misled George. "No, George, I really need to do this by myself. Please try to understand."

"Let me support you, be a friend. That's all I'm asking for now."

But he did want more, and they both knew it. Undertones of the truth reverberated in the hurt tone in his voice.

"I wish you could let the past go," he finally murmured. "I don't want to see you suffer anymore, Ivy. It hurts me to watch you in pain."

More guilt assailed her. But George needed to accept that a romantic relationship between them was never going to happen. And if he continued to push her, she might have to sever their business relationship, as well.

EILEEN MAHONEY WAS ABOUT to go out of her mind, and now her oldest boy was back to tip her over the edge the rest of the way. She put a kettle on for coffee, then hurried to the bathroom for her morning rituals. The day she'd seen that TV broadcast of her son being released, she'd known there would be hell to pay. She'd fretted for a whole week, expecting him at every turn. And sure enough, on that seventh day, he'd come knocking on the door, waving that piece of paper just like he was somebody she ought to listen to.

As if he hadn't shamed her enough fifteen years ago.

As if she hadn't sacrificed her heart, her soul and sanity already to try and save him.

But in the end, nothing had made a difference.

Now he had to show his sorry face and stir up trouble again. What had happened to her young'uns to make 'em all turn out so rotten? First, Matt being mean as a snake when he was little, fighting with his daddy ever whichaway and that. Then getting arrested for stealing. Then getting locked up for butchering the Stantons. It was a wonder he hadn't knocked up some poor girl and left Eileen with a bastard grandbaby to raise.

And her other two—Benji and Robbie... Land sakes alive, they had about done her in. She'd thought that when Benji got accused of killing that kid and disappeared, the Lord would spare her any more pain. And when Robbie had joined the service, she'd actually believed one of her boys might do her proud. Then he'd gone missing… AWOL, they said.

It was a wonder she wasn't in the crazy house, like old Miss Mazy, who pulled all her hair out when her boy turned bad and shot his sister last year.

Another month of rain.

Lord help, would it ever stop?

She swiped a washcloth across her face, nearly jumping out of her skin when she heard a knock on the front door. What if he'd come back again? She might have to call the law.

Hands shaking like Ms. Hattie once did with the palsy, she tugged her tattered housecoat around her shoulders, then peered out the window. No way would she open the door to the likes of her son, not when she was alone. But the sheriff's patrol car sat in her drive, pretty as you please. Maybe he'd come to tell her that he'd locked Matt back up again, and she wouldn't have to worry about him for another few years. By then, she'd probably be in her grave, anyway. God willing, she was ready anytime. But she didn't want the rest of the town gossiping that her boy had killed her.

"I know'd that mean Matt Mahoney would murder her one day," Ms. Hattie would say.

"How'd he do it? Butcher knife?" someone else would ask.

"Heard tell he locked her in the trunk of the car, drove it in the kudzu pit and left her there to suffocate."

No, sirree. The Mahoneys had fed the town grapevine plenty as it was. And there were still some secrets they didn't know. Some they never would....

The knock sounded again, and she rolled her shoulders to ease the knot of tension as she tottered to the front door and unlocked it. Mercy, her knees were killing her this morning. That rain drove her arthritis plumb crazy.

"Morning, Mrs. Mahoney."

Sheriff Boles tipped his hat, and she smirked. He acted like he was important these days, but she remembered when he'd been nothin' but trouble hisself.

"I hate to bother you so early, but I have to ask you a couple of questions."

She held him at the door, refusing him entrance. It wasn't proper, her not being dressed. She wasn't like those whores down on Red Row. "If this is about that boy of mine, I know he's back in town."

"Then he did drive out here last night?"

She nodded, clutching her housecoat to her neck. "Why? Did he do something again?"

The sheriff shrugged and glanced across the front yard. "What time was he here?"

"About dark. But I didn't let him in."

"Do you know where he was going when he left?"

She shook her head. "What's going on, A.J.?"

He tilted his head, his hat shading his eyes. She'd

never quite trusted A.J. Back in high school, all the no-account boys had worn their hats pulled down to hide their eyes 'cause they was stoned. A.J. still wore his hat thataway.

"Dora Leigh Werth was murdered last night. We found her body in the junkyard, under the kudzu."

Eileen swallowed, fingernails clasping the house-coat again. "I know'd when he come back they'd be trouble. But why in God's name would he kill old Dora Leigh?"

"I TOLD YOU, I HAD no reason to kill Dora Leigh Werth," Matt said. Although he wasn't surprised to find A.J. on his doorstep at breakfast, already wielding accusations. "I didn't even know the woman."

"Then how can you explain the fact that she was murdered last night, only hours after you arrived back in town?" A.J. asked. "And she was stabbed in the back with a kitchen knife. Then strangled by the kudzu and left in the junkyard."

Just like Ivy's father, Roy Stanton.

A.J. didn't even have to say it. Matt heard the implication.

"Hell if I know. There have been other murders in Kudzu Hollow since I've been in jail, and I didn't commit them."

"But this one is too similar to the one you…to the Stanton killings."

It was too late. A.J. had said it. Matt would always be a murderer to his mother, to the town. But he'd thought his one-time best friend honestly believed him.

"Dammit, A.J." He dropped his head forward, rubbing his neck to calm his raging temper. He refused to let A.J. see how much his deception hurt. Matt was a grown man now. He hadn't had any friends in forever. He didn't need one now.

"Maybe someone murdered her to set me up again. The same person who left that bloody message and chicken on Ivy's pillow." He paced, his boots pounding the wooden floor of the cabin. He felt like a caged animal. He could not be locked up again like a savage. Not for another crime he hadn't committed. He'd rather die first.

"I'd be a fool to come here and kill someone my first night in town," Matt continued. "You think I want to go back to jail?"

"I don't know." A.J. narrowed his eyes, grasping. "Maybe you don't know how to handle being out. I've heard of it happening. Some guys like the security. Prison gives them a free place to live, food. They don't have to work."

Fury heated Matt's veins. "Well, I'm not one of them, A.J. I didn't deserve to go to jail fifteen years ago, but let me tell you, it was hell. Pure hell. Every damn day, I dreamed about freedom. About what I was missing. About the things we talked about doing. The girls we wanted to date. The cars we planned to drive. I may not have had big career dreams, but I sure as hell didn't intend to live my life in the state pen being turned into some kind of…" He couldn't say it.

Shame seared through him.

He thought he saw pain flash in A.J.'s eyes.

"I thought you were my friend back then," Matt said. "I came looking for you that night to tell you what happened, but I couldn't find you anywhere."

"I was at home—"

"The hell you were. I know for a fact that's a lie. I came by—"

"I was drunk." A.J. sucked in a harsh breath. "I passed out in the backyard, in the garage."

Matt stared at the corner of A.J.'s eye. It was twitching. It used to do that when he lied.

Was he lying now? And if so, why?

IVY SPOTTED THE SHERIFF'S car at Matt's cabin, and worry nagged at her. Why was he visiting so early? Had he discovered the identity of the person who'd threatened her? If so, why wouldn't he have come to her?

Then again, before he'd left he'd received a call about a murder. Maybe that explained his visit.

Fear coated her throat as she swallowed. Surely he didn't think Matt had ridden into town and killed someone last night?

Not the Matt who had phoned the sheriff when he'd seen the terror in her eyes. Not the young boy who'd carried her to safety in the junkyard fifteen years ago. Not the one who'd slept in the car next to her to protect her.

She hadn't defended him fifteen years ago, but she had to now.

Furious, she shrugged on a raincoat over her denim skirt and blouse, then braced herself against the wind as she crossed the damp grass toward Matt's cabin. The two men had stepped outside onto the porch. Matt's gaze latched onto hers, his eyes shooting over her, questioning. Sheriff Boles stared blatantly, tilting his hat so she could see his raised eyebrows. A flicker of male interest appeared in his eyes and sent a shiver through her.

"Good morning, Miss Stanton."

"Is it?"

His mouth twitched sideways. "Not really, but I was trying to be pleasant."

"Did you find out anything about the intruder in my cabin last night?"

"Haven't talked to forensics yet. I'll let you know when I do."

Matt cleared his throat. He'd shaved, showered and dressed in jeans and a white shirt that contrasted with his dark skin and hair. But she remembered him bare chested and her cheeks reddened.

"What's going on here?" Ivy asked.

"The sheriff was just leaving," Matt said in a cold voice.

"I came to question Matt about Dora Leigh Werth, the woman we found murdered in the junkyard last night."

"I don't know her," Ivy said.

"And I explained that I don't know the woman, either," Matt said, a hint of steel in his voice.

The sheriff jammed his thumbs in his belt loops. "She has a teenage son. He was pretty torn up."

"That's a shame," Ivy said. "Do you have any leads?"

"I'm working on it." The sheriff cut his eyes toward Matt, who stiffened, his lips pressing into a thin line. "I told you to leave town last night, but now you'd better stick around."

"You can't possibly think that Matt killed her?" Ivy asked. "Because he was innocent fifteen years ago. In fact, Matt picked me up and carried me to a van to hide out, then he stayed in the car next to me to protect me."

A.J. rocked back on his heels. "You remember what happened that night?"

"I'm starting to," Ivy said, forcing a strength into her voice that she didn't feel. "And before I leave, I hope to remember the rest."

A long, tense second ticked by. "Then see me when you do," Sheriff Boles said. "I'll make certain the killer is punished."

Ivy nodded, although the menacing look in the lawman's eyes sent another wave of icy chills down her spine.

The sheriff turned and stalked toward his police car, and Matt swung her around. "Ivy, I don't need anyone fighting my battles for me. And you shouldn't go around confessing that you remember things. It's too dangerous."

"I...simply told the truth."

Matt's jaw tightened. "I'm not sure you can trust A.J."

"You think A.J. might be involved? That he knows something about my parents' murders?"

Matt shrugged. "He's changed."

"You two were good friends when you were teenagers, weren't you?" Ivy asked softly.

He nodded, and she could almost read his thoughts. He and A.J. weren't friends anymore. Now Matt had no friends.

"Just don't go announcing that your memory is returning. If the killer is still around, he may come after you."

She flinched. Matt was right about the danger. But he was wrong about not having any friends. She would be his friend if he would let her.

"Then we'd better figure out who killed my parents, Matt, because I'm not backing down or running away this time."

CHAPTER SEVEN

THEY HAD TO FIND her parents' murderer.

Ivy had made the statement as if he and she were working together.

And she'd defended him in front of A.J. Not a very smart move, but still, Matt had to admit her belief in him stirred emotions that he hadn't felt in a long time. Hope. Admiration. Arousal.

But she had to face reality.

"Ivy, it's too dangerous for you to poke around. Please leave town and let me handle this."

A softness flickered in her eyes, but the shadows remained. "I realize you're trying to protect me, just like you did back then, Matt, but I'm not afraid."

He gripped her arm. "You should be after last night. Someone meant to scare you."

She nodded, but didn't cower away from him as she had the first moment she'd spotted him. "I have to follow this through, Matt. I can't move on with my life until I settle things in the past. Until I make it up to you."

"God, Ivy, you don't owe me anything. You were just a kid when your parents were murdered."

"But I'm not a kid anymore."

Man, she had that right. She was all grown up. Talented. Smart. Beautiful. Filled out in all the right places. And she was gutsy and had courage.

Dammit. He wanted her so badly he could practically taste the sweet saltiness of her skin. And he could feel her fingers triggering sparks of awareness through his lifeless body.

Their gazes locked, and heat rippled between them in waves, like the embers of a fire flickering into flame. Then she licked her lips and lifted her hand to his scarred cheek again, and he was lost.

He lowered his head and claimed her mouth, a fierce hunger rising in him from the depths of his soul. He had never tasted a woman who ignited such desire. Never had a woman's lips felt so soft and supple. Never had he ached to bury himself inside a woman so deeply that he physically hurt from having to restrain himself.

She gently slid her hand into his hair, and her mouth moved beneath his. A low, throaty sound floated from her as he cupped her face with his hands. Loving her was so easy. *Not* loving her would be the problem.

He didn't have the strength to walk away just yet, though. Instead, he caressed her cheeks with his fingers as he deepened the kiss, nibbled on her luscious lower lip, then trailed one hand down her back, over the sweet curve of her hip, and dragged her closer to his body. As her breasts pressed against his chest, his sex throbbed, straining toward her.

A storm cloud rumbled above, and the raindrops splattering his head finally registered. What was he

doing? Practically mauling Ivy outside, where anyone could see. About to take her on the ground like
some damn animal.

That's what you were in the pen....

He wrenched himself away, then forced himself
to look into her eyes. She'd be terrified, sickened
maybe. She might even run.

But a hazy glow of excitement pinkened her
cheeks, and her green eyes had turned to emeralds,
shimmering with desire. Her chest rose and fell,
her breathing uneven. He was breathless himself,
couldn't remember the last time he'd really kissed
a woman. Even in the pen, on those rare occasions
he'd enjoyed a conjugal visit, the coupling had
been raw sex. Physical release. No kissing or tender
touching. Just desperation. Not this emotional,
urgent, erotic play of lips on lips, skin against skin.
The kind that filled the empty void that had eaten
away his soul for years.

He wanted to kiss her again. To carry her inside,
lay her on the bed and make long, slow love to her.

But raindrops dotted her face and hair, the sky
looked ominous and Ivy was in danger.

"I'm sorry—"

She pressed her fingers to his lips. "Don't. I'm not."

He didn't understand her. But he clasped her hand
in his, stroked the pads of her fingers. "Ivy, I didn't
kill your parents, but I'm not a good guy, either. I've
done things—"

"Shh. It doesn't matter."

He swallowed hard, wishing that were true. But
the past had shaped him into a man who didn't

deserve her. Had changed him forever. And although he had found tenderness in the moment, he wasn't a tender man. The rage and ugliness had settled just below the surface, and sometimes erupted, and he couldn't control it. Like the caged animal he'd become inside the pen, that beast fought for escape.

Ivy had seen her share of beasts when she was a kid. He wouldn't expose her to his temper, too.

His heart pounded as he dragged his gaze from her lips. "I'm going to town."

She dug her fingernails into his bicep to keep him from fully pulling away. "I'll go with you, Matt."

He shook his head. "No, I won't put you in danger. Not any more than you already are."

"But—"

He pinned her with a warning look and slowly extracted her fingers from his arm. "No, Ivy."

She bit her lip again, glanced toward the woods. "Then I'll work on my article. I need to finish my research for the magazine."

He studied her face, wondering why she'd kissed him. Not that it mattered. They'd both gotten caught up in the moment. She'd been shaken by last night's events. He'd been shaken by…her.

They'd both needed a little comfort.

It couldn't happen again. Because he had killed before. And he wouldn't hesitate to do so again if he found out who had framed him.

Or if someone tried to hurt Ivy.

MATT STALKED TO HIS CABIN, and Ivy ran inside to escape the rain, but her lips still tingled from his kiss. Erotic sensations had flooded her the minute he'd pulled her up against him. If he hadn't put some distance between them, she wouldn't have been able to stop herself from asking him to come inside. And then...what?

Where could they possibly go from here? A romantic relationship was out of the question. Matt harbored bitterness and sought revenge, while she carried the trauma of her past around her as if it were a shield. She had used her miserable childhood to keep from getting close to anyone. She couldn't forge a bond, then have someone else she loved ripped from her arms as her mother had been. And Ivy couldn't look at a male and not think about the violent man her father had been.

But Matt wasn't violent...at least not toward her.

How did she really know? He'd admitted he'd done things he wasn't proud of. And she'd heard stories about prison life.

George, on the other hand, was exactly the type of man she should be interested in. He was stable. A businessman. Safe.

He didn't trigger any of the emotions that Matt evoked. Didn't make her nervous or frightened. Didn't make her body tingle with a need that she didn't quite understand, but that made her want to beg for more of his touches.

Yes, George was safe.

And Matt wasn't.

But she wanted him, anyway.

Forcing herself to ban the kiss from her mind, she reviewed the police reports on her parents' murder, then retrieved all the articles she could find on Kudzu Hollow the past few years. Although the other crimes weren't connected, the folklore about the evil aura surrounding the town intrigued her, and would add an atmospheric layer to her article.

She skimmed several stories about the town, noting the fact that for the past ten years, during heavy rains, crimes escalated. Two murders had occurred the first year, three the next, two the following, with a string of other random crimes added to the list. Several cases involved teens. Two had murdered their parents. A fourteen-year-old boy had stabbed his older brother to death. And a cheerleader had killed her best friend, supposedly because she'd bumped her from the captain's spot. Town officials had even built a separate wing on the jail to house juveniles, so they would be separated from adult prisoners.

Another bizarre string of incidents had occurred. Animals turned up dead. Chickens were slaughtered. Places in the woods where bonfires had been set indicated ritualistic acts had been committed there. A pit full of burned rattlesnakes had been found at the foot of Rattlesnake Mountain. Some locals suspected a satanic cult had sprung up in the area. Some blamed Lady Bella Rue for bringing black magic to Kudzu Hollow, claiming she'd cursed the town because of the children's tauntings. The Baptist church touted that Talulah and the girls from Red Row were the source of sin. They'd even tried to run them out of town.

Fueled with renewed energy, Ivy grabbed her

camera bag, shrugged on her raincoat and headed outside to her car. She wanted to visit Lady Bella Rue and learn more about the root doctor. If she was really a seer, then she might have some insight into these murders, as well as Ivy's parents' deaths.

"DAD, IVY SAYS SHE'S starting to remember that night."

Arthur Boles stopped dead in his tracks in his home office and stared at his son, wishing like hell they'd both left town years ago. But he'd thought leaving might draw suspicion to him and A.J. And he'd had investments to protect.

His son, for one.

Their secrets, for another.

A.J. was his biggest asset, his biggest liability, all rolled into one.

Arthur poured himself a cup of strong coffee and gripped the mug with a shaky hand. "What exactly did she say?"

A.J. slumped onto the sofa, dropped his head in his hands and massaged his temple. "That Mahoney found her running in the junkyard that night. That he picked her up and carried her to a van, where she hid out all night."

"That's where they found her, right?"

A.J. nodded, his face a sick yellow. "She said that Mahoney stayed in the car next to her to protect her." Sweat trickled down A.J.'s jaw. "What if Matt—"

"Shut up," Arthur barked. "The evidence proved that Mahoney was at the scene, and you know it.

After the murder, he probably went back and hid in the junkyard so the sheriff couldn't find him."

A.J. stood, walked over to the bar and reached for the Scotch, but Arthur barred him with an outstretched hand. "It's not even noon, A.J. What are you thinking? You can't show up in uniform drunk when you have an image to uphold."

"That image may be falling apart, Dad." A.J.'s hand trembled, obviously itching for the bottle, as he pushed aside his father's arm. "There was another murder last night. Dora Leigh Werth. Found her body in the junkyard. Stabbed. Strangled by the kudzu."

"Just like Stanton?"

"Yeah. And if Matt didn't do it, and I don't think he did, then someone else did. But it makes me nervous having Matt back. He's going to ask questions."

"Hell, don't you think I know that?" Arthur tried to think, but agitation sliced into his brain like a knife. He'd had to save his son's butt too many times to count.

"You weren't drinking last night, were you?"

A.J. cut his gaze toward his father. "After the murder…geesh, I had to have something to calm me down. Ever since the Stanton slayings, and Matt going to jail, I've felt trapped in this town. It's killing me."

"*You've* been trapped?" Arthur gripped A.J. by the shirt, rage knotting every muscle in his body. "You think I wanted to stay here in this little podunk mountain town all these years?"

"You have your business." A.J. eyed the liquor

like a starved animal. "I had plans, but now I'm stuck. And I'm the one who has to deal with the evil in this town. I'm sick of it."

Arthur sighed. The evil. Another part of the ugly puzzle. Even his son didn't know the whole story. Arthur had to instigate damage control. "All right, so you knocked back a few drinks last night. At home?"

A.J. glanced at the painting on the wall above the mantel. "At the Ole Peculiar."

Great. An alibi if he needed it. Then again, witnesses would report that their sheriff had been inebriated. "Then what did you do?"

"Nothing."

Arthur growled. He'd always known when his son was lying—his voice changed. Hell, A.J. couldn't even make eye contact. "Don't lie to me, boy. You took a trip to Red Row, didn't you?"

Guilt flashed in A.J.'s bleary eyes, and Arthur slammed a fist on his desk. The Waterford crystal paperweight slid sideways with the force. "Goddammit, A.J. When will you ever learn?" Arthur didn't wait for a response. He knew the answer: never.

Furious, he stormed from the room, grabbed his raincoat and hat, and headed to see Talulah. On the way, he had a phone call to make. One he dreaded.

His friend wouldn't be happy that Ivy was remembering, not at all….

That meant hell to pay for him. Especially if Ivy revealed the truth.

MATT SPENT HALF THE afternoon researching the town and the crimes that had occurred the past few years. He hadn't known exactly what he was looking for, but had a hunch that the events might be tied to his past. Late afternoon shadows painted a murky gray across the land as he drove by the junkyard, his mind soaring back fifteen years to the night he'd found Ivy running. She'd said she wasn't sure her father had been chasing her. Matt had assumed that was who she'd been running from. But what if someone else had been chasing her? What if her father had already been dead?

The more he contemplated the various scenarios, the more convinced he was that the answers might be found at Red Row. With Lily Stanton's lovers.

Rain slashed his windshield as he drove by the kudzu-covered cars and the trailer park. His hands tightened around the steering wheel as he passed his mother's trailer, then he pressed the gas, sped up and drove by Ivy's old homestead. The mobile home, a 1960s model, had slid off its coasters, the windows were boarded up, and what was left of the white paint had faded, creating a cross between mildew-yellow and puke-green.

In his mind, he saw Ivy's mother's face, stone-cold white, with all that blood spilled around her on the crusty linoleum floor. Who had done such a brutal thing to her?

Someone with a personal grudge…

Had she been blackmailing one of her customers?

A mixture of emotions flowed through him as he made his way toward the back of the mobile home park, to Red Row. Excitement that he might find answers here. Dread that someone might discover that he had visited the hooker corner of the trailer park before. Not to question the girls, but as a paying customer.

Hell, half the boys in town had lost their virginity to women of the red light district. Why should Kudzu Hollow be any different than anywhere else?

A flash of black caught his eyes and grabbed his attention. A black Mercedes parked in front of Talulah's trailer. Glittery lights adorned the window frames of her place, and a red, heart-shaped wreath greeted visitors. A sign with Talulah's name boldly painted on it hung beside the door, as if she meant to advertise her position as head mistress of Red Row.

His gaze landed back on the expensive sedan. Damn. It was the middle of the morning. He hadn't expected her to be entertaining a john now. And in reality, he'd assumed Talulah had retired herself from the lineup. Must be a high payer or a long-time regular.

Curious as to her visitor's identity, Matt drove past Talulah's, then turned around at the end of the drive and parked several car lengths down, facing the row of trailers.

Fifteen minutes later, impatience gnawed at him as he watched the doorway. Finally, Talulah's trailer door opened, and a gray-haired man with a slight paunch stepped onto the stoop. Matt squinted, waiting until the man turned so he could see his face. Shock bolted through him.

It had been fifteen years, and he was older and had beefed up, but Matt was damn certain the man was A.J.'s father.

Arthur Boles Senior had always been a pompous ass. He'd made money in real estate, had driven a fancy car and snubbed his nose at the trailer trash crowd. Funny that he didn't mind supporting Talulah's business. Just how long had Mr. Boles been one of Talulah's customers?

An uneasy feeling slithered through Matt as his mind ticked away with speculations. Arthur Boles was exactly the kind of man who wouldn't want his goings-on made public. Fifteen years ago, he'd been on the verge of success and had been cutthroat in his business dealings. Had he been cutthroat in personal matters, as well—enough to kill Lily Stanton if she'd threatened to reveal that he frequented Red Row?

TALULAH SHUDDERED as she watched Arthur climb into his Mercedes. Once upon a time, she'd actually harbored a crush on the real estate guru, but time had changed all that. He had been good to her financially all these years, however. For that she was grateful. He had kept her from having to stay on her back. And in exchange, she had accepted his money and guarded his precious secrets.

The wind blew raindrops on her face and she sighed, hating the bad weather and the trouble it always brought. It slowed down business, too. And sometimes the men got cranky, even rough with her girls, and she had to step in to protect them. She rubbed her thigh, where a scar still remained from one especially violent episode.

Lily Stanton's pretty face slipped into her mind,

and Talulah shuddered again as she reached for the doorknob to go back inside. But a car door slammed nearby, and she looked up, wondering if Arthur was back.

Instead, a younger man—handsome even with that jagged scar on his cheek—walked toward her. His tall, muscular frame sent excitement skittering through her. It had been a long time since she'd experienced a younger man's touch. Maybe she'd handle this hunk herself, just for old time's sake. God, he was so dark and sexy looking, she might not even charge him.

He climbed the steps, his gaze latching onto hers, and her stomach suddenly fluttered as recognition dawned.

"Matthew Mahoney. I should have known you'd come calling."

His mouth tilted up slightly, the only sign of a reaction. Otherwise, he appeared to be a mass of controlled emotion and muscles.

"Come on in, darlin'. What can Talulah do for you?" She slid her hand around his arm and pulled him inside, suddenly wishing she'd taken the time to tidy up her place. And wishing she'd donned a little more makeup to camouflage her age lines. "It's been forever, darling. I bet you need some good loving."

Matt's jaw tightened as he extracted her hand from his arm. "I didn't come here for sex, Talulah."

Her eyes widened. Was she so old now and un-inviting that she was doomed to have a parade of men all day who just wanted to talk? Insulted, she dropped her voice to a purr. "But I know you haven't married. And prison had to be lonely."

His expression went from emotionless to stone-cold angry. "*Lonely* doesn't begin to describe the hell I've been through."

"I know, you poor baby." She stroked his arm again, patted his cheek lovingly. "But Talulah will make you feel better."

"Talulah, really, I'm not here for sex."

Okay, if he didn't want her, she could at least make some money off of him. He had to be horny. "I have some new girls, young ones, ripe for loving. They'll do whatever you fancy."

For a brief second, his eyes sparked as if he was tempted. Then he shook his head, dismissing the suggestion. "I want to talk, Talulah. Seriously, this is important."

God, what was wrong with men these days? They had sex thrown in their faces and they denied Talulah. Had she really lost all her appeal? Or had the joint turned him into a freak? Maybe a homo.

"I did not kill Lily Stanton or her husband," Matt said, "but I think I have an idea who did."

She gasped, hating this kind of talk. Lady Bella Rue was her friend, but tolerating her friend's constant barrage about the evil taxed her to the hilt. She preferred the lighter side of life, the exhilaration from living and having good sex. After all, sex added years to a person's life, and Talulah wanted to stay young.

And if he was here, thinking she knew anything about that night, if he wanted answers…

"Who?" she croaked, already planning her lies.

"One of Lily's lovers." He hesitated, then folded his massive arms across his broad chest. "I need to know everyone Lily slept with, if one of her lovers or johns was serious about her, or if she might have been blackmailing a client."

Talulah's heart stuttered. How could she answer that question, plus protect her girls and her customers at the same time? No, Matt didn't understand the kind of betrayal he was asking of her. And the danger in her talking…

If her girls and clients couldn't count on her discretion, her confidence, then her entire foundation would fall apart. And if her male customers thought she'd spilled their secrets, they'd completely shut down her business.

Laughter bubbled in her throat. What would Kudzu Hollow do without her services? She kept the men alive and sane. And if she shut down, she'd have to go back to begging, lying on her back all day, start over from scratch.

Although if it came down to it, *she* could blackmail someone, she thought suddenly. But that was too damn dangerous.

Still, she knew half the town's dirty little secrets. And if the shit hit the fan about what had happened years ago, and she needed out, she'd do whatever necessary to survive. Even open Pandora's box and let the secrets spill out.

But for now…Talulah had to play innocent.

A wicked laugh caught in her throat. As innocent as the day she was born, and the woman who had spawned her…

CHAPTER EIGHT

IVY SQUINTED THROUGH the steamy windshield, struggling against the wind and rain as her car bounced over the ruts in the dirt drive. She'd spent most of the morning and afternoon researching more of the local legends, but now evening approached, and she was determined to see Lady Bella Rue before nightfall. Even if the old woman did have her spooked.

Her shanty sat back in the woods, shrouded by trees that robbed it of light, the rotting wooden sides so black they looked as if they'd been painted with soot. Smoke spiraled in puffy waves from the chimney top against the gray sky, casting a haze over the run-down house. Scrawny chickens scratched for food in a small pen; mud holes the size of basketballs dotted the yard like small ponds. On the sagging front porch sat an old washing machine topped with a collection of gourds. A feathered hat encircled with beads hung on the front door, and an assortment of dried roots, berries and snakeskins framed the doorway.

As Ivy climbed out of her car, the wet ground sucked at her feet, and the sound of voices chanting from the woods nearby echoed from the shadows of the trees. She pivoted to see a group of teenagers tossing rocks toward the windows, so enthralled by their taunting that they were oblivious to the rain or her arrival. She tugged her rain hood over her head and stepped carefully through the sludge, noting the various feathered animal parts hanging above one window. A wolf that had been stuffed but looked real guarded the front door.

A rock hit the pane, and glass burst and shattered. Laughter rippled from the teenagers as the chanting grew louder.

> "Witch in the old shack,
> Magic in the air,
> Cooking up evil
> With bones and hair.
>
> Fingers and toes
> She eats all day.
> Boys and girls
> She loves to slay."

Angry and worried they might hurt the old lady, Ivy turned and yelled at them to leave.

A big boy in sagging pants and a black hooded sweatshirt tossed another rock at the porch. "You go in there, lady, and she'll eat you, too!"

"She might cook you in her big pot," another boy shouted.

A girl wearing scruffy jeans cupped her hands around her mouth and yelled, "Or throw you off a mountain ridge like she did her kid."

"Or she might cast a spell on you and make snakes grow in your belly!" another boy called.

"Go home and leave her alone, or I'll call the sheriff," Ivy shouted back.

The door suddenly screeched open, and Lady Bella Rue's frail body appeared, her eyes two dark, empty sockets. "Come on in before they hit you with one of them rocks."

Ivy climbed the rickety steps and ducked her head beneath the doorway, blinking to adjust her eyes as she entered the dimly lit room. The ceiling was low, the wood floors aged, with threadbare braided rugs scattered on top. A long, battered kitchen worktable occupied most of the cramped space. Fire crackled in the fireplace, steam rose from a large black pot on the stove and the smell of something indistinguishable filled the air. Ivy shivered slightly, wondering about the rancid odor, but tried to ignore it as Lady Bella Rue took her coat.

"I hope you don't mind me stopping by without calling first," Ivy said.

The woman waved off her concern with a gnarled hand. "I knew you were coming."

"You did?"

She nodded, and Ivy wondered if she truly was a seer. Taking a deep breath, Ivy scanned the remainder of the small combination kitchen-living room. A tall oak pie safe sat against one wall, overflowing with jars of various herbs, roots and other ingredients. More gourds held roots and herbs, as well as snakeskins, feathers, cloth pouches, dead toads and small bags that resembled the charms she'd seen in the New Age shops in Chattanooga. A large jar labeled Graveyard Dust sat on the mantel beside another that read Bones.

"Would you like a cup of tea?"

For a brief second, Ivy hesitated, her mind jolting back to the teenagers' chants, but she refused to allow a few silly rhymes to spook her. This wasn't a Hansel and Gretel story; it was real life, and Lady Bella Rue was not going to cook her in her cauldron.

"Don't worry, dear. It's all fresh roots and natural stuff that I use." A tiny smile tilted the corners of Lady Bella Rue's mouth as if she'd read Ivy's thoughts. "Quite healthy, I might add."

Ivy smiled and forced herself to relax, although a mouse skittered behind a cabinet in the corner and her skin crawled. "Tea would be nice. It's so miserable outside."

Lady Bella Rue pointed to a wooden, ladder-back chair, and Ivy settled into it. A black cat with three legs lay curled in the rocking chair situated by the fire. Three more cats, one gray and the other two black, had sprawled on the braided rug, and a stuffed raccoon and stuffed mountain lion held a place by the hearth.

At least inside, the drilling rain drowned out the sound of the teens' vicious chants. "Do those kids bother you often?"

Lady Bella Rue clucked her teeth. "Every now and then. I don't let them get to me, though. Sticks and stones, you know…" She tacked a piece of heavy plastic over the shattered window to keep out the rain, then removed the teakettle, poured hot water into two cups and tottered over and placed them on the table. "Once you've had real grief in your life, buried your own husband and son, nothing else can hurt you."

A well of sadness pitted the woman's eyes, but Ivy also saw ageless wisdom reflected from the depths, too.

"Then again, dear," Lady Bella Rue said gently, "you understand about grieving and loss, don't you?"

Ivy nodded, cupping her hands around the hot tea to warm them. Oddly, even with the strange collection of bones, animal feathers and God knew what else, she felt safe here with this woman. Maybe safer than she'd ever been in her life.

Except when Matt had held her.

Matt…her parents' murders—the reason for her visit.

"There is evil in the town, as the children say," Lady Bella Rue said in a low voice. "It's been following you, child."

"Yes. I ran away from it years ago, and I can't do that now."

"You are beginning to remember, am I right?"

"Little bits of my past. But that night…not as much as I want to."

"There will be pain when you do," she said.

Ivy's stomach clenched. She was afraid of what she would discover. "It will be worth it to know the truth, though." To free Matt. To free herself. No more nightmares. No more being locked into the patterns.

"Ahh, sometimes the truth can kill you."

Ivy's gaze shot upward. In Lady Bella Rue's eyes, she read concern, not a threat.

"Did you know my mother?" she asked softly.

The older woman fiddled with the beads around her neck, then touched a pouch tucked inside her blouse. "Not well, but I knew of her."

"Did she have friends? Anyone she was close to? Another woman? A man, maybe?"

"Your mother loved you very much, my dear." An odd look passed across her face. "She wanted you to have a better life than she had."

"I know." Ivy confided about the photographs of the Ivy League schools.

"She thought she had found a way out for herself, for you."

"You mean away from my father?"

"Yes, and a way to make enough money so you could have the life she wanted."

"How?" Ivy sipped her tea. "Was she planning to leave my dad? Did she get a job somewhere?"

The old woman slid her wrinkled hand over Ivy's and squeezed gently. "I do not have all the answers, child. I cannot see everything. But I do know that your mother trusted someone. She thought he was the answer to all her problems."

"Who was it?"

"I don't know his name. But this man that she trusted—he was the one who killed her."

"COME ON, TALULAH. YOU know I didn't kill Lily," Matt said. "Who are you protecting?"

Talulah ran her ruby-red nails along the seam of her flimsy, white satin robe. "I can't disclose my clients' names, Matthew, or my customers would never come back." She pursed her thick red lips into a pout. "And I'm not just here for talking."

Frustration knotted Matt's neck, but he removed his wallet and tossed three twenties on the table. "Did Lily ever speak about any man in particular?"

Talulah stuffed the money into her massive cleavage, intentionally leaning over to attract Matt's attention. He did look—he couldn't help it—but God help him, his body didn't even twitch.

Not like it had with Ivy, and he'd only kissed her.

Damn. He had to forget about that kiss.

"I can't give you a name," Talulah said, "but she was excited, making plans to leave Kudzu Hollow. Some big real estate broker from Atlanta wanted to buy a lot of land, all of the junkyard property and more."

Matt frowned. A.J.'s father had been involved in real estate for years. Did he know the man?

The fact that Arthur Boles had just visited Talulah triggered an entirely different thought pattern now—what if he had been involved with Lily? Or what if he'd introduced the real estate agent to her, or had arranged the deal himself?

"Did the sale go through?" Matt asked.

Talulah shrugged, one side of her robe sliding down to reveal her pale shoulder. "Must not have. The junkyard's still there."

"But there is a new subdivision nearby. Maybe she sold only part of the land."

Talulah rolled her eyes, then checked the polish on her nails, looking bored. "I don't talk business with my people. Didn't back then, either."

"No pillow talk?"

A wicked smile curled her painted lips. "Well, if they want to talk, I listen. But business stuff goes in one ear and out the next."

He didn't buy her story for a minute. Talulah was not the fluffy dumb blonde she portrayed to the world. She might have snitched business tips from her johns and made her own fortune off of them.

"I heard Ivy Stanton is back in town," Talulah said, taking him off guard with the change in subject.

"Who told you that?"

"News travels fast around here, Matt."

And he'd bet Talulah knew more about the people in this town than anyone, even their own families. Hell, Ivy had filed that police report. The deputy or A.J. or even a secretary at the courthouse or jail could have revealed her identity.

"Have you seen her?" Talulah asked.

Matt nodded.

"What does she look like now?" The woman's expression turned almost wistful. "Is she as beautiful as her mother?"

More so, Matt wanted to say. But she wasn't a hooker. No, Ivy was innocent and trusting and…nothing like Lily Stanton.

Instead he simply nodded. "Someone threatened her already and warned her to leave town."

Talulah averted her gaze. "Maybe she should listen. For the past few years, this town has known nothing but death and evil. There was another murder last night. Poor Dora Leigh Werth."

"Maybe it's time to end the cycle," Matt said. "And the only way to do that is for everyone to stop keeping secrets. Find out what's really going on around here."

"So, you intend to tell Ivy about her mother and Red Row?"

His insides twisted. The last thing he wanted to do was hurt Ivy. "Maybe I can find the answers on my own without her discovering her mother's indiscretions."

She tilted her head in thought. "If you're so determined to stir up trouble and dig around, the best place to go is the Ole Peculiar. Buck, the owner, has been around forever. His son helps him out now, serves as bartender."

"Nemo is a bartender?" In high school, he'd been a big football jock looking toward a scholarship.

"Yes, it was sad. His senior year, he and two of his buddies were joyriding and had an accident on Rattlesnake Mountain. Didn't think Nemo would make it, but he survived." She crossed herself. "He has a limp and some brain damage, though. Took him months before he could even talk again."

Matt frowned. So Nemo had received a bum wrap in life, as well. Even worse than Matt—at least his own mind and body were intact.

Talulah was right. If he wanted to find out which men frequented Red Row, and who had been regulars in the past, the best place to pick up that kind of information was at the Ole Peculiar.

"Thanks, Talulah." He stood, leaned over and dropped a kiss on her cheek.

She grinned, ran her fingers up along the nape of his neck and pulled him down to plant a juicy one on his mouth. "If you want anything else, just come back to Talulah, sugar."

He smiled, turned and walked out the door, then wiped the lipstick off his lips with his handkerchief. After fifteen years of doing without sex on a regular basis, he should have accepted her offer. Hell, he should have jumped at it. Gotten screwed, then asked the questions.

Unfortunately, that kiss from Ivy taunted him. Her sweet taste. Those soft luscious lips. She was the only female he wanted to crawl into bed with and get naked.

But she was the one woman he couldn't have.

Stewing over the reasons, he climbed into his Pathfinder and headed toward town, steering the SUV through the trailer park one more time. Like a glutton for punishment, he slowed when he spotted a faded tan Chevy sitting in front of his mother's trailer.

He wondered who the car belonged to, then saw the license plate, and his gut clenched. The personalized tag read BOSS. He muttered a curse. He knew that tag. The car belonged to Lumbar, the former sheriff who'd locked Matt away for a crime he hadn't committed.

Why the hell was he visiting Matt's mother?

LADY BELLA RUE HANDED Ivy the small pouch. "Hang this mojo around your neck and it will protect you." She removed another one from her pocket. "And dig a hole under the front steps of the place where you're staying. This will help ward off the evil and danger."

Ivy accepted the homemade charms, wrinkling her nose at the strong odor of the one intended to be buried. "What's in here?"

"Oh, just a little graveyard dust, High John the Conqueror root, eel skin, crushed bones and steel dust. It's soaked in urine." Lady Bella Rue lapsed into a discussion of the old voodoo customs and spells used for protection purposes.

"Do you mind if I include you in my article?" Ivy asked. "I think readers would be interested in the information about hoodoo and root doctoring."

The old woman folded her hands. "I am not afraid to admit my beliefs and customs, but neither do I want strangers knocking on my door asking for potions or mocking me."

"I won't use your name," Ivy explained. "And are you a seer, as they say in town?"

"Sometimes I have 'feelings' about things," she said admittedly, a mysterious, somber tone. "But if you believe the town gossip, you would think I am to blame for the evil here. That I cast spells to put snakes and worms inside of people to drive them insane. That I cause children to turn against their parents." She flattened her gnarled hands over her chest. "But I am not the devil. Evil grows in the kudzu and the trees. It fills the air and the souls when people breathe."

Lady Bella Rue gathered Ivy's hands in hers.

"You are in grave danger, child. Be careful or you will succumb to the evil here this time."

"What evil? Who wants to hurt me, Lady Bella Rue?"

"I am not sure. But death is knocking at your door, and if you do not watch your back, if you trust the wrong person, you won't leave Kudzu Hollow alive. Death will claim you as it did your mother."

TOMMY WERTH SAW his mother's ghostly face everywhere he went. Her mouth wide open with a scream, her bulging eyes, the horror in her face. And her hand trying to claw up toward heaven as she'd choked and died.

His own hands shaking, he jammed the crack pipe into his jeans pocket and strode through the woods. The last hint of daylight slid behind the storm clouds, shrouding the forest in murky shadows. Dammit. He didn't know why he was so spooked, but ever since the sheriff had shown up at his door this morning, he'd had the uncanny sense that his mother's ghost was whispering down his neck. Following him. Trying to drive him crazy enough to spill his guts about killing her. Maybe she was so mean she'd escaped hell to come back and haunt him. Maybe she was a witch like that old Lady Bella Rue. He could see the root doctor's cabin from the woods where the cult had staked out for the night, knew the kids had stolen one of the chickens and some of her graveyard dust for tonight's sacrificial ceremonies.

The bonfire flickered, the bright orange-and-yellow flames shooting toward the treetops where the river cult had decided to hold their ritual. The sound of the water racing over rocks mingled with the noises of animals scurrying through the wet leaves, and the chants that echoed from the embankment. He grinned and broke into the clearing. For a second, he stood in awe of the other kids who'd gathered.

All had painted their faces black and wore black clothing, although a few had added feathery head-dresses and beads. He paused and knelt, blackening his own face. Doing so offered them anonymity if a stranger spotted them. The group had decided to adopt the practices of the original Santerians and Rastafarians. Someone had brought a goat and chicken to sacrifice, one boy in dreadlocks threw himself into the water, shouting that he was pos-sessed now by the river water, and several girls danced around the fire half-naked, their bodies gleaming with oils and paint. The scent of pot floated from the circle, drawing Tommy closer.

He joined the crowd, accepted a joint from one of his friends and inhaled, swallowing the smoke. The acrid burn in his throat sent a rush to his head, erasing the image of his mother's face. Another toke and a mind-blowing buzz hit him. This was some strong-as-shit stuff. Must be from Ace's stash. He'd started growing it himself two years ago, and supplied the group with it weekly.

His buddy Clete, aka Trash, clapped him on the back. "Come on, man, join in."

They'd all adopted nicknames to add secrecy to the group. His was Snake.

"We're going to cut the chicken's head off now," Ace said.

Tommy inhaled another hit, the haze of the drug making his legs wobble. The chicken clucked and pecked at the ground. Trash reached out and tried to grab it, but it strutted away from the fire in a flurry, and he chased it. Seconds later, they held it down as it squawked and flapped, trying to escape. With a grin, Ace raised the hatchet up to whack off its head. Several of the girls broke into a chant.

> "Blood for the master
> Feed our souls.
> Straight to the devil
> On the burning coals."

Near the edge of the river, one of the girls suddenly screamed bloody murder. Ace paused, hatchet midair, and chaos broke out as the group ran toward her.

"Jesus! Look! Oh, my God, it's a skeleton!"

"It's a grave. Someone buried a body here!" the girl shouted.

Tommy followed the group, his heart pumping like crazy. Had they really found a body?

Trash released the chicken, ran to the woods, then dropped to the ground.

Tommy and Ace pushed to the front, watching as Trash dug away the wet dirt and leaves with his hands, slinging debris against the trees and everyone's shoes. First a skull appeared. The eye sockets, nose, mouth. Next came the arms—skinny remnants

of what was left of them. Then ribs void of skin.
Tommy's stomach lurched. Bugs had eaten away the
flesh. Age and maggots had feasted on dry skin that
had rotted and peeled away from the bone.

"Stop digging!" someone shouted.

"I'm gonna barf!"

"Man, those bones are gross!"

"Oh, God, look at his face. How long's he been
in the ground?"

"Who killed him?"

"Who do you think it was?"

Tommy suddenly saw his mother's face hovering
above the rotting bones and flesh. A rustle of leaves
jerked his eyes toward the woods. Someone was out
there. Watching them. And if whoever it was reported this to the police, they'd probably all get in
trouble. The sheriff would question them. Tommy
sure as hell didn't need that.

No way could he give the cops a reason to grill
him.

Nerves pinched his neck. He'd find the person
spying on them and make sure he stayed quiet.
Even if Tommy had to kill him and put him in the
ground himself.

IVY STARED AT THE SCENE in horror—kids dressed
in black, their faces and bodies blackened with
paint. A bloody goat lay dead by the river. Fire
crackled, flames rippling upward toward the treetops, too close for comfort. Too close to Lady
Bella's Rue's wooden shanty.

The smell of marijuana engulfed her, thick and

pungent, mingling with the scent of burning wood and smoke. Ivy's eyes watered and her throat burned.

Had those kids just said they'd found a body?

She had to tell someone. Report what they were doing.

Suddenly the underbrush rustled, and a youth shot through the woods racing toward her. The leafy shadows of the trees hid her, but he seemed to sense exactly where she stood. The stupidity of venturing into the forest alone slammed into her. But she'd seen the fire and had worried that it would spread to Lady Bella Rue's place.

Dear Lord, she had to get out of here. Ivy clenched her purse strap, reached inside for her cell phone, then backed away.

"I know you're watching," he said in a low ominous voice. "And I'm going to find you and shut you up."

Panicking, Ivy raced back through the woods toward her car. She had to call the sheriff. No, Matt. Tell him what was happening. Protect Lady Bella Rue.

Briars stabbed her legs, tree branches clawed at her thighs and her hair caught on a low branch. She yelped and had to stop to yank it free.

Voices echoed in her head. *Hurry, Ivy. Run. Run like the wind. Daddy's going to get you. And so is the monster who killed your mama.*

Her heart tripped in her chest, and she heaved for air. She lurched forward and stumbled over a rotting stump. A hand clamped around her wrist. Fingernails dug into her skin. He had her now.

And judging from the feral look in his glazed eyes, he was going to kill her.

KILLING IVY MIGHT BE the only answer. The only way out.

But he had to think. Do it right. So nobody would know.

If he lost courage this time, everything he'd worked so hard for all these years would come crashing down. And all of it would have been for nothing.

He closed his eyes. Saw an image of her soft green eyes looking up at him. Heard her wispy voice crying out that night so long ago. Saw the rise of her chest with her breath. The pale white of her throat.

More recent images of Ivy replaced those of her as a child. The throat he'd wanted to kiss. The mouth he'd wanted to possess.

His body twitched with anger. And arousal.

His hands tightened around the phone, and he slammed it down. Dammit, he should have gotten rid of her years ago. Shouldn't have let her get to him.

He paced, restless, scraping his hand through his hair. And even now…now when he had no choice, he still wanted her. Wanted her alive. Wanted to have her just one time. Feel her lie beneath him. Touch her skin. Have her open to him while he slid inside her.

Make her come just like he had her mother.

But time had run out.

It was too late for that. Just like it was too late for Ivy…

CHAPTER NINE

THE FACT THAT LUMBAR, the man who'd arrested him and put him in jail, was visiting Matt's mother gnawed at Matt on the short drive into town. For a brief second, he'd entertained the idea of stopping and confronting the two of them together, but sanity had grabbed hold of his balls and yanked hard. For all he knew, his mother had called Lumbar to inform him of Matt's visit. Except that Lumbar wasn't sheriff now, A.J. was.

So why had the man been at his mother's?

Stewing over the possibility that the two of them had a personal relationship turned his stomach. Maybe Lumbar intended to try to put Matt back in jail. He had wasted no time in slamming the cuffs on Matt years ago, and railroading him off to prison.

Sweat beaded his neck as another possibility registered. What if Lumbar had pinned the crime on Matt because he'd known Lily Stanton? Lumbar might have been one of her clients. As sheriff, he sure as hell wouldn't have wanted anyone to know he was getting his kicks on Red Row. If Lily had decided to blackmail him, maybe he'd lost his temper, killed her and Stanton, then used Matt as an easy patsy.

No one had suspected Lumbar, especially with the circumstantial evidence against Matt and his history of being a troublemaker.

Adrenaline surged through his veins. He had to dig deeper, find out if Lumbar had visited Lily. For a brief second, he thought about Ivy, wondered what she was doing, was tempted to go back to the cabin and check on her. But if he did, he'd want to kiss her again, but that would only make him want another kiss and another.

No, he'd shared his last kiss with Ivy.

The wooden sign for the Ole Peculiar swayed in the wind as he swerved into the parking lot, killed the engine and climbed out. This being Friday night, the lot was full. Country music wafted from the place, cutting into the howling wind. Thick cigarette smoke mingled with the fresh air and scents of rain and mildew as he opened the wooden door.

Locals overflowed the red padded booths and bar stools. Beer bottles and mugs clinked, laughter flowed, and in the back corner a jukebox blared out tunes, while a rowdy pool game drew onlookers. Matt didn't expect to know anyone, but he did recognize Buck Potts, the owner, and his son, Nemo. Matt wove through the crowd and dropped onto a bar stool.

"W-what do…you want?" Nemo asked, his stutter an indication of his impairment since his accident.

"A beer. Whatever you've got on draft is fine."

Nemo squinted as if he thought he recognized Matt, then reached for a mug. Buck shouldered his

way through the crowd to stand beside his son, as
if he needed protection. "What are you doing in
here, Mahoney?"

Matt forced himself not to react, although Buck's
distrust rankled him. "Enjoying Friday night, just
like everyone else."

"We don't want trouble," Buck snarled. "Me and
my boy don't need it."

"I just want a beer and some answers."

Buck dried a mug with one hand while cutting
Matt a suspicious look. "Then ask what you want
and get out of here."

Matt accepted the beer from Nemo, thanked him,
then leaned forward, elbows braced on the bar. "I
want to know about Lily Stanton."

Buck scrubbed a scarred hand over his chin.
"What makes you think I'd know anything about
her?"

"You've been running this place for years. Guys
mouth off after a few rounds."

"No one has been bragging about a murder, if
that's what you mean."

"How about bragging about sleeping with her?"

The man threw his head back and laughed, his
belly jiggling. "That was a long time ago. What does
it have to do with anything now?"

"Just a hunch," Matt said with a shrug. "Tell me
who liked her back then."

Buck polished the counter with a cloth. "Half the
men in this bar slept with her."

Matt grimaced. "Did anyone mention that she'd
grown too attached to him? That she wanted more?"

A frown drew Buck's thick eyebrows into a solid line. "No."

"Anyone hint that she might be blackmailing him?"

Buck worked his mouth from side to side. "Don't recall anyone talking about blackmail."

"How about Sheriff Lumbar? Did he frequent Red Row?"

Buck shifted his eyes toward the door, looking nervous. "He didn't want folks to know, but yeah, I seen him there a few times."

"With Lily?"

"I don't know which one of Talulah's girls he liked. But if I had to guess, I'd say Lily was one of them."

Matt nodded. He'd have a conversation with the former sheriff, maybe push Talulah again.

"I heard Lily's daughter's back in town," Buck said. "Is she anything like her mother?"

Matt swallowed, his hand tightening around the beer mug at the lascivious look in Buck's eyes. "No. And she doesn't know what her mother did, and it had better stay that way."

Buck shot him a curious look, but Matt flashed him another warning, letting him know that Ivy was off-limits.

HE WAS GOING TO KILL HER.

Ivy kicked and fought back, but the boy wrenched her hands behind her, threw her down on the ground and crawled on top of her, pinning her face in the wet leaves. She screamed and bucked, trying to jab him with her elbow, but his weight had knocked the breath from her, and she couldn't move.

"Get off of me!" Ivy shouted.

"Shut up, you bitch. You shouldn't be nosing around out here."

"Let me go!"

She kicked out again, but her legs met air. He slid his hands around her neck, his fingers digging into her flesh, cutting off her windpipe. She tried to scream, but he pinched her harder, digging into the column of her throat. She gagged and clawed at the ground in mindless panic, desperately searching for a rock, a stick, anything to fend him off. Finally she latched onto a stick and tried to swing it high enough to jab his eyes. But he cursed and choked her so hard she bit her tongue and tasted blood.

Suddenly something else rustled the trees and leaves behind her. Dear God, maybe it was one of the other kids. Maybe they'd stop him. A low growl echoed behind her, and the boy's grip loosened slightly. Her heart slammed ninety miles an hour in her chest as she tried to take advantage of the moment and move. But his knees dug into her again, sending shards of pain throughout her lower back and numbing her legs.

"Be still," he mumbled. "There's a fuckin' wolf stalking us."

Ivy wheezed out a breath, spitting blood onto the muddy ground as the boy released her and stood.

"That's it, fellow, don't attack." His shaky voice vibrated with fear. "Just trot on your way."

Ivy rolled sideways to see the massive animal

behind her. A thick gray pelt gleamed, his eyes two yellow orbs shining in the darkness. He growled and bared his jagged teeth. She forced herself not to make any sudden movements, either. If the wolf was hungry, he might attack her. But instead of stalking toward her the wolf paused beside her, and tilted his head, looking right at her. For a moment, a sense of peace washed over her as if they'd connected, as if he actually meant to protect her.

Then he snarled, flashing his fangs and leaped toward the boy. Twigs snapped, leaves rustled. Abandoning caution, the youth took off in a sprint. The wolf growled and chased him through the woods. Ivy levered herself up and ran toward her car.

Seconds later, she climbed inside her Jetta, started the engine and sped toward town. She had to find the sheriff, tell him what the kids were doing. What if they hurt Lady Bella Rue? Or what if they set the woods on fire and it spread?

Still panting, she whipped the car over the pot-holes, speeding past the junkyard toward the jail, then the diner in town, then the Ole Peculiar. Her heart tripped when she spotted Matt's Pathfinder in the parking lot.

Not bothering to question her sanity, she jerked the car into the lot, fumbled with her keys and purse, then climbed out and darted toward the door. A thick fog of smoke encompassed her as she entered, blurring her vision, and her eyes watered as she searched the room. Several men turned to stare, and a chair scraped across the wooden floor. Tim McGraw's voice crooned in the background, and the sound of pool balls clanging together mingled with conversation and laughter.

Heaving for control, she staggered forward, but her legs buckled and she nearly slid on the sticky floor.

"Damn," a husky voice muttered, "if it ain't Lily Stanton all over again." A beefy man suddenly rose from his chair and grabbed her.

In the next second, Matt's voice echoed over the din of confusion. "Let her go."

She clung to Matt's arms, hanging on to him as if she'd collapse if he released her.

He shook her slightly. "What in the hell are you doing here, Ivy?"

It was so dark and smoky she could barely see his face, but anger glittered in his eyes.

"I...had to see you," she choked out. Tears suddenly burned her eyes and trickled down her cheeks. "Matt, someone tried to kill me."

"WHAT?" MATT'S hands tightened around her as he dragged her outside. Watery light from a street-lamp illuminated her face, but shadows filled her eyes and her breathing sounded erratic. "What happened? Are you hurt?"

"I went out to Lady Bella Rue's," Ivy blurted. "And when I left, I saw a fire by the river, so I walked a few feet into the woods to see—"

"You went into the woods alone?" he barked. "What were you thinking, Ivy? For God's sake, someone threatened you yesterday."

"It was just a bunch of kids with a campfire. I was

worried they'd let it get out of hand and the trees would catch on fire and spread to Lady Bella Rue's house…."

Matt exhaled, struggling to control his temper as he noticed the blood dotting Ivy's forehead. He reached up to touch it, slid her hair away from her forehead and examined the scrape. Dirt and leaves clung to her long, tangled tresses, and mud caked her cheek and clothes.

"Then what happened?"

"A group of teenagers, all dressed in black hooded sweatshirts, with their faces and hands painted black, had gathered in the woods around a big bonfire. It looked like they belonged to a cult of some kind. They…killed a goat…and put its bloody carcass beside the river. They were about to cut off a chicken's head, and…they were chanting and smoking weed, and oh, God…then they said something about a body." Her voice cracked again. "Then he saw me."

The fear that had clawed at Matt's chest mounted, snatching the air from his lungs. "Who saw you? What body?"

"One of the boys. He chased me into the woods and tried to strangle me." She inhaled sharply. "I think they were digging up a body. Or…maybe they buried someone."

Unable to help himself, Matt yanked her closer and wrapped his arms around her. Fear and anger warred with the need for vengeance against the person who'd hurt her. She felt small and so damn feminine that his heart raced, a dozen emotions pummeling him at the same time.

"Matt…" She clutched at his chest, her tears soaking his shirt. He stroked her back, murmuring soft words of comfort, hating the way her slender frame trembled, and despising the boy who'd frightened her.

Finally, her breathing steadied and her tears subsided. Her eyes turned luminous in the darkness as she stared up at him.

He wiped a fresh tear from her face with the pad of his thumb, then tilted her chin up to examine her injuries. The pale skin of her throat looked red, bruises already forming deep purple-and-yellow marks around her neck. Emotions crowded his chest. He'd sworn to protect her, yet she'd almost died tonight.

"We're going to report this to the sheriff," Matt said in a thick voice. "And from now on, Ivy, you don't go anywhere in this town without me."

MATT REMAINED A PILLAR of strength as Ivy leaned into him. He helped her to his SUV and drove to the jail, then ushered her inside, his arm still protectively encircling her.

The sheriff jerked his head up from his desk, a surprised look dawning. "Mahoney. Miss Stanton."

"I wasn't sure you'd be here on a Friday night," Matt said.

"I'm never off-duty, not during a murder investigation."

Matt nodded. "Ivy has something to tell you."

Ivy glanced into Matt's eyes for encouragement, then accepted the wooden chair across from the sheriff, and a glass of water.

"What's going on?" Sheriff Boles asked.

Ivy reiterated the story she'd shared with Matt, her trembling subsiding slightly at Matt's calm demeanor. He remained behind her chair, one hand on her shoulder, a comforting gesture that kept her from falling apart as she recounted the details of the attack.

"If this wolf hadn't scared the boy off…he would have strangled me."

The sheriff frowned, his tone skeptical. "A wolf?"

"Yes."

"Odd. Don't see many of them around here."

Ivy remembered the stuffed one on Lady Bella Rue's porch and bit her lip. The big animal had looked exactly like that stuffed creature, the same size… No. Lady Bella Rue might be a root doctor, but she couldn't perform magic. And she couldn't conjure a live animal from a dead one. No one could.

"Did you get a look at the boy's face?"

Ivy shook her head, racking her brain for any detail that might help. "The hood completely covered his face and hair, and like I said, he'd blackened his skin with paint."

"Was he tall? Thin? Heavy?"

"Taller than me, about five-eight maybe. And he was muscular but wiry. He had long limbs and…strong hands."

"You said there was a whole group of them?"

"Yes." Ivy twisted her fingers together. "They appeared to be performing rituals, maybe sacrificing animals. Some of them were chanting around the fire."

"And you smelled weed?"

"Yes."

Sheriff Boles's boots hit the floor with a resounding thud. "Guess I'd better check it out. I've suspected some of the teens around here might be hanging out by the river, up to no good, but haven't been able to pin anything on them yet."

"They've done this sort of thing before?" Matt asked.

The sheriff nodded. "I've found bloody towels, a few decapitated chickens, a pit of snakes once, and they've disturbed the graveyard a couple of times. Always when we have one of these rainy spells." He holstered his gun. "But so far, no one's actually caught them in the act. Although I do have a couple of boys in the back now. Caught them vandalizing."

Ivy wrestled with her nerves as she stood. "So he didn't want me to report him, that's why he tried to kill me?"

"Probably. Do you think you can lead me to the spot where they met?"

She nodded.

Matt cleared his throat. "It could be dangerous, A.J. Do you think it's smart to take Ivy out there?"

Ivy reached for his arm to calm him. "It's all right, Matt. I'm worried about Lady Bella Rue. I have to do this."

Matt cut her a sharp look, tension vibrating between them. "Then I'm going with you."

Ivy didn't argue. Revisiting the place where she'd almost died had her pulse pounding. And the prospect of going into the woods alone at night with

Matt's old friend, even if he was the sheriff, made her even more nervous. Behind that uniform and badge lurked a sinister side just waiting to surface.

Ivy didn't want to be around when he finally unleashed it.

TWENTY MINUTES LATER, MATT gritted his teeth as he, A.J. and Deputy Pritchard followed Ivy through the cold, dark woods. Mud from the wet ground kept clumping on his boots. Night sounds of skittering animals, rustling trees and the river rushing over rocks filled the stony silence.

"Here's the clearing where they built the campfire," Ivy said, stopping beneath an alcove of trees. The remnants of the fire still lingered, smoke billowing upward. The pungent odor of pot filled the air, mingling with charred wood and dead animals.

"They're all gone," she exclaimed. "But there were dozens of them, I swear it."

"The kid who attacked you must have made it back and warned the others." A.J. walked over to a pile of rocks, grimaced and shook his head. Matt followed him and saw the blood, then the carcass of the goat that had been slaughtered. Below, on a rocky ledge, he spotted two chickens, both decapitated, along with a cluster of something that looked like bones.

"Damn kids in this town aren't anything but trouble," A.J. grumbled.

Just like the two of them had been, Matt thought, but refrained from comment.

A few beer cans littered the ground, along with a beaded necklace and several feathers. A.J. had brought some evidence bags, so he collected them, then turned to Ivy. "Maybe we'll get some prints. If I can ID one of the pricks, maybe he'll give up the name of your attacker."

She wrapped her arms around her waist, and Matt moved up behind her. He wanted more evidence, something concrete to tie to the rotten little bastard. "Where were you when he attacked you, Ivy?"

She bit her lip, then pointed toward the woods, near where they'd entered.

A.J. gestured to his deputy. "Keep looking around here. I'll check this out."

As they made their way through the heavy brush, Matt searched for footprints or traces of evidence the boy might have left behind. A few feet later, he noticed indentions in the ground where the leaves and dirt had been disturbed.

"That's where he knocked me down," Ivy said in a low voice.

A.J. shone a flashlight on the area while Matt knelt and examined the spot. He noticed a scrap of fabric caught in a branch, and A.J. plucked it out and slid it into a paper bag.

"That looks like it came from the boy's sweatshirt," Ivy said.

A.J. nodded. "I'll have it checked, Ivy, but since the school colors are gold and black, half the kids in this town own black sweatshirts like this. Are you sure you didn't see anything else? You didn't recognize anyone? Hear a name, maybe?"

"No. And I don't know any of the kids in town," Ivy answered.

"Sheriff, come here!" Deputy Pritchard shouted.

A.J. sprinted back toward the river, and Matt took Ivy's hand and raced behind him.

"What is it?" A.J. asked as they broke through the clearing again.

"Take a look for yourself." Pritchard pointed to the dirt at the edge of the woods.

The three of them joined the deputy, and Matt's stomach clenched.

"Oh, my God!" Ivy rasped. "They did find a body."

"Yeah." Pritchard grunted. "And the poor bastard's been here a while."

Ivy stared at it in shock as Matt tugged her against him. Rotting skin had disintegrated from the bone, bugs having feasted on the flesh. What was left of the body looked brown and gray, just brittle bone.

A.J. reached for his cell phone. "I'll call a crime scene unit and the medical examiner."

"Come on," Matt said softly. "I'll take you back to your cabin, Ivy."

She nodded against his chest. "But my car—"

"We'll get it later."

Tension hovered in the air as they hurried to his Pathfinder, climbed inside and drove toward Cliff's Cabins.

Who was buried there by the river? Matt wondered. Had the kids known the corpse was there, or had they just happened upon it during their cult ceremony?

An image of Ivy almost dying flashed back, and panic slithered through his limbs. He wanted to take her into his arms. Wanted to hold her all night. Remind himself that they were both still alive.

Hell, he wanted to make love to her. He had from the first moment he'd laid eyes on her again.

But what did Ivy want?

HE WANTED IVY. But he couldn't have her.

Frustration ate at him. The trouble was escalating. Ivy and Mahoney were getting closer, and there was nothing that he could do to stop them, short of murder.

Sweat beaded on his forehead, tension knotted his muscles as he neared Red Row. If he couldn't have Ivy...

Chantel would be good. Yes, she would do.

No. He couldn't get too close to any one hooker. Money talked. And these girls wanted to make a dime any way they could. Scruples be damned. They'd open their legs for one man one minute, their mouths the next—and not just for sex. They'd talk for the right price.

And no one could know that he was in Kudzu Hollow.

Especially Ivy or Matt Mahoney.

Damn man.

He'd taken up with Ivy as if he owned her. And she looked at him as if he had hung the moon and her safety rested on his shoulders.

A chuckle rumbled in his chest at the irony. She was not safe with Mahoney. In fact, just the opposite. Hooking up with him had put her in more danger.

Both would have to be disposed of.

He would take care of them later. First he needed to release his tension before he exploded. He parked at Red Row, and five minutes later, sprawled restlessly in bed with a redhead with tits the size of melons. As the woman touched him, began to pleasure him, his mind drifted to Ivy. She was so beautiful. Pale skin. Delicate lips. Golden silky hair. Just like her mother.

The redhead's fingernails scraped over the bare flesh of his belly and his body quivered. "What's wrong, hon? You seem distracted."

Dammit, his penis had softened. He silently chided himself for mentally losing ground. Couldn't let this slut think he was incapable of meeting her demands.

Could she meet his?

He flipped her over to her stomach, threaded the silk cords around her wrists and tied her to the bedposts. She moaned and complained, tugging at the bindings, but the minute his tongue licked its way down her back and over her buttocks, she shivered. Deciding to test her, he pulled away and reached for her ankles, to tie them, as well. She struggled playfully, but fear echoed in her voice when she moaned.

Just the way he liked it.

He smiled and crawled above her, feathering his fingers along her inner thighs but avoiding her sensitive spot until she begged for more. Then he rammed himself inside her, and let the fantasies begin as he took his pleasure.

One kiss. Two kisses. Three kisses.
Sigh.
Four kisses. Five kisses. Six kisses.
Cry.
Seven kisses. Eight kisses. Nine kisses.
Die.
One last kiss
and then goodbye.

CHAPTER TEN

IVY TRIED TO BANISH the image of the bones sticking through dirt and leaves as she opened the door to her cabin. "Whose body do you think was buried by the river?"

"I don't know," Matt replied. "From the size of the hands, it was probably a man."

"Who would bury someone like that without even giving them a proper ceremony?"

"Someone who wanted to hide the fact that the man was dead," Matt said matter-of-factly.

Ivy halted and flipped on the lamp, realization dawning. "You mean he was murdered?"

Matt shrugged, although a hint of anger—or worry?—still darkened his expression. "Probably."

Fear clenched her insides, but she schooled her reaction as she moved quietly to the stove, filled the teakettle with water and placed it on the burner. *Remember the routines, the patterns. The walls. Keep yourself safe, Ivy.*

"Lady Bella Rue and Miss Nellie were right about this town," she whispered.

"Who is Miss Nellie?"

"The woman who raised me after my parents

died." Ivy removed two teacups and the sweetener, then offered one to Matt, but he shook his head. She hadn't really pictured him as a tea drinker, so brewed a pot of coffee.

"Is she a relative?"

Ivy shook her head. "She lived in Kudzu Hollow and knew of my family. She'd lost a child of her own when he was little, and thought the two of us should be together. But she took me to Chattanooga so I could escape my past." Only she never had escaped.

Matt frowned. "You were close?"

Ivy contemplated how to answer without sounding callous. "Not really. She was always nice to me, but I felt as if she was holding something back." Her heart mostly. "She…wasn't very affectionate." Guilt pressed against her conscience. "That sounds very ungrateful of me, doesn't it? The woman gave me a home. No telling where I would have wound up without her."

"Having a place to live is a long stretch from having a real home."

Pain flickered in Matt's eyes, and Ivy ached for him. Prison had been a shelter, but certainly no home. And even before prison, he hadn't had an easy life. And when he was finally released, even his best friend still treated him like a criminal. Judging from his sarcastic comment about his mother, she hadn't welcomed him, either.

Matt plucked a leaf from her hair, and a tingle of awareness slid though her, warming her from the chill she'd felt since the attack. He had been protective and kind to her, and that last kiss taunted her.

The feel of his lips against hers. The tender way he'd held her.

But he was only being a friend, hoping she could help clear him.

The teakettle whistled, shattering the moment. "I…think I'll take a hot bath. Clean off the dirt and leaves."

He inched forward. His gaze met hers, and the raw masculine look in his eyes sent another shiver through her.

"Are you all right, Ivy?"

Unexpected moisture pooled in her eyes, and she nodded. But she refused to break down again. Matt had already done so much for her.

And what had she done for him except add to his trouble?

He swept a strand of her hair away from her face and traced a finger over her cheek. "Go get your bath, Ivy. I'll be waiting when you're finished."

"You don't have to stay, Matt. I'm fine now."

His mouth tightened, his feral look daring her to argue. "I want to stay."

She wanted that, too. She couldn't deny it any more than she could deny the heat rippling between them. But there was more than heat. She was falling in love with him. Matt was tough, had seen the darkest dregs of society in prison, yet his touch remained so gentle that she ached for more of it, for the feel of his fingertips along her nerve endings.

She couldn't ask for more from him, though, or get accustomed to having him in her life.

No. Ivy had been alone forever, and would be

once again, when she and Matt discovered her parents' murderer.

Afraid she might give in to the temptation to drop her defenses and allow Matt closer, she poured her tea, then escaped to the bathroom. But as she stripped off her dirty clothes and slipped into the warm bubbles, fingers of need and desire coursed through her. She closed her eyes and imagined Matt touching her, gliding his hands against her sensitive skin, stirring passions and pleasures that she'd never experienced before with a man.

Pleasures that only he could give her.

AS THE BATHROOM DOOR closed, separating him from Ivy, Matt felt the invisible barrier between them being erected again. Ivy was cautious. Had been hurt. Didn't let anyone close. He knew that without asking. And he didn't want to hurt her.

But God help him, he wanted her.

An image of her taunted him—Ivy removing her clothes, her naked body glistening with moisture, her nipples peaking and begging for his lips, her arms drawing him into her embrace, her legs spreading for him....

His sex hardened, the ache that rolled through him creating an emotional need as strong as his physical response. He wanted her so badly he could taste her. Could almost feel her skin beneath his fingertips. Her feminine body pulsing as he slid inside her.

But reality whistled as sharp and jarring as that damn teakettle had. Ivy had just been mauled and nearly strangled. Remnants of fear had rimmed her beautiful eyes, the leftover horror of seeing that skeleton lingering in the shadows. He could not act on his needs tonight.

His stomach growled, reminding him of another kind of hunger that he hadn't bothered to satisfy lately. When had he last eaten? When had Ivy?

Determined to be a gentleman instead of exploring the heat that had ignited between them, he knocked gently on the door. "Ivy, I'm going to drop by the diner and pick up some supper for us. Will you be okay for a few minutes?"

"Yes, I'm fine," she called.

"I'll secure all the doors and windows before I go. Don't answer them for anyone."

"I'm okay, Matt, really."

For a brief second, he leaned against the door, listening to the splash of water. Every cell in his body burned, urging him to open the door and join her. But thankfully, the rational side of his brain throttled that more basic nature. "My cell number is on the table. I should be back in ten minutes. Call me if you need me."

She agreed, and he checked the windows and doors, then rushed outside. More rain hovered on the horizon, the swirling wind and dark clouds a reminder that there was no relief in sight. He glanced back at the cabin, searching the perimeter with his gaze before he drove away. Anxious about being away from Ivy, he phoned the diner and ordered two of the daily specials to go. Barbecue and Brunswick stew. He hoped to hell Ivy wasn't a vegetarian, and realized he should have asked. There were a lot of things he didn't know about her. Her favorite food. Favorite color. The type of music she listened to. All trivial things that he wanted to explore. All personal...

But the more he knew about Ivy, the more he liked her.

And the more he wanted her.

FANTASIES OF MAKING LOVE with Matt played through Ivy's mind, igniting a maelstrom of need. How could she want something from him that she'd never even considered with another man?

Because you're letting down your defenses. Remember, your heart is involved. Protect it.

The revelation shattered her fantasies, just as the chill of the bathwater hit her. All her life, she'd closed herself off from others, the pain of losing her parents the catalyst for locking herself in a self-imposed prison. Miss Nellie had maintained the same type of distance, probably due to her own traumatic loss. The two of them had been perfect together, coexisting but never really forging a close enough bond that it would destroy them when they parted.

Ivy didn't want to feel this way about Matt. Didn't welcome the gut-wrenching pain she would experience when he left her. And he would leave. Everyone she'd ever loved had left....

But she felt helpless to stop the need building inside her.

Maybe if she wasn't so frightened of what she

would find in her past, she could have a future. But what about Matt? Would he even consider building a life with someone who'd stood silently by while he suffered in prison? How could he possibly want to be with such a coward?

Trembling, Ivy climbed from the tub, dried off, donned a thick terry-cloth robe and combed her tangled hair. The bruises on her neck looked stark in the mirror. Another image replaced hers: her mother's face. Her bruised cheek. A swollen eye. A fractured wrist.

Ivy closed her eyes, shutting out those pictures and focusing on the good memories.

Her mother singing softly to her at night, promising that they would have a better life. She'd sounded so convincing.

Ivy opened her eyes, contemplating the possibilities. Maybe her mother had planned to leave her father. If he'd discovered her intentions, he would have lost his temper. Maybe killed her. But who had murdered *him?*

Matt had mentioned that someone had wanted to buy the property by the junkyard. Had her mother planned to use that money to escape with her and start a new life? Something nagged at the back of her mind, but she couldn't quite pinpoint what was bothering her.

Her cell phone rang, a jarring sound that caused her to jump. It was probably Matt calling to check on her. He'd been so protective.

She dug the mobile unit from her purse and checked the number. George.

Sighing, and half-tempted to not respond, she stared at the number. But she couldn't keep avoiding him, not with her business at stake.

"Hi, George."

"Ivy, my God, I thought you weren't going to answer again."

His frantic voice surprised her. "What's wrong?"

"I saw the news report. They found a body in Kudzu Hollow. There's a cult of kids there performing sacrificial rituals. And another woman was murdered." He wheezed a shaky breath. "That place sounds dangerous."

"I'm fine, George. I'm faxing over some photos and my notes on Lady Bella Rue."

"Ivy," George said softly. "You have enough for the piece. Please come home. I'm worried about your safety."

She gritted her teeth, wishing she could return his feelings, but Matt's face filled her mind and heart, not George's. "I'll come back in a few days. I…still have some things to resolve here. And I want to visit my old homestead."

"The place where your parents were killed?" he asked in an incredulous voice. "Jesus Christ, Ivy, you don't need to do that. You have a life here in Chattanooga. And I care about you."

"I appreciate your concern, George, but I can't leave now. Not yet." Refusing to wait for a reply, and unwilling to argue further, she disconnected.

The phone trilled a second later. Feeling guilty, and expecting George to have redialed, she hit the button. "George—"

"Hello, Ivy."

She froze at the sound of a man's voice—a strangely familiar one. Husky. Low. Hoarse. Muffled.

"I warned you, Ivy."

In the background, music trilled: "Here Comes Santa Claus…." The hair on the back of her neck prickled, the image of the broken Santas flashing back. "Who is this?"

"You should have listened. Now I have no choice but to take care of you the way I did your mother." A nasty laugh echoed over the phone just before the line went silent.

MATT KEPT HIS HEAD DOWN as he paid for the food, well aware that every pair of eyes in the diner pierced his back. Whispers and echoes of disbelief and distrust fed the charged atmosphere. Talk of the body the sheriff had uncovered and the murder of Dora Leigh Werth had everyone bordering on hysteria.

"Heard there's a cult of devil worshipers down by the river," someone whispered.

"Poor Dora Leigh's boy. Wonder who'll take care of him? Just awful the way his mama was murdered."

"And what do you think about that body Sheriff Boles found in the woods?"

"I don't know, but it all started when that Stanton girl and Mahoney boy came back to town."

"Sheriff ought to run 'em both out of Kudzu Hollow."

196   LAST KISS GOODBYE

Anger knotted Matt's insides. He was tempted to remind them that their own children were up to evil, but he managed to rein in his temper. Reacting would only blacken his own bad reputation.

Lady Bella Rue and Talulah were seated in the corner, the old root doctor's fingers worrying the mojo around her neck, while Talulah smiled and fluttered her fingers in a wave.

Great. All he needed to feed the rumor mill more was for the locals to think he was fanning the covers at Red Row.

And if that talk reached Ivy?

A frisson of unease tightened his gut. He didn't like leaving her alone for a minute, not in this god-forsaken town.

His boots pounded on the wooden floor as he crossed the room, and just as he reached for the doorknob, the door sprang open. His mother stood beneath the awning, beside the former sheriff, Lumbar.

Her mouth flopped open, her eyes widening in fear. Lumbar pressed a protective hand to her waist, and Matt followed the movement. Of all the con-founded surprises! His mother *was* seeing Larry Lumbar. For a moment, Matt was so shocked his legs wobbled.

"Maybe we'd better leave," his mother whispered.

Lumbar grunted. "He's the one going to leave."

"As a matter of fact, I am," Matt said, finally recovering, although old hurts and pains knifed through him. "I didn't realize you were friends with the man who put me in jail."

She swayed and clutched Lumbar's arm. "I didn't expect you to be here."

"It's a public place, why shouldn't I be?" he growled.

"Stay away from your mother," Lumbar barked. "You may have been released from prison, but we all know you're no good. Soon you'll be back in the pen with the animals where you belong."

Emotions pummeled Matt. Anger. Hatred. The thirst for vengeance.

But he'd learned one thing while caged up—how to control that temper. Bottle it for later.

It was the only way he'd survived on the inside. And now it seemed the only way he'd survive on the outside. Because if he unleashed his fists on Lumbar, he wouldn't stop until he'd killed the man, and then he *would* end up incarcerated again.

His cell phone trilled, and he flipped it open, his glare still fixed on Lumbar.

"Matt?"

"Ivy, what is it?"

"Someone just called and…threatened me."

Panic pumped through Matt, and he pushed past Lumbar, out the door. "I'm on my way. Lock the doors and don't open them for anyone but me, Ivy." He sprinted toward his SUV, jumped inside and started the engine. His heart pounded as he sped toward the cabin.

IVY PACED BACK AND FORTH across the small room, stewing over the man's warning, trying to place his voice, figure out if she knew him. That song haunted her. He had to have known about her mother's collection.

What had his exact words been? "I'll take care of you just like I did your mother."

If he had killed her mom, then that meant her father hadn't. Ivy sighed and clutched her robe around her neck. Relief spilled through her. At least she didn't have to go through life thinking that one of her parents had murdered the other.

A small consolation for a life without a family.

Something scraped against the window. In the back, a noise reverberated against the thin wood of the cabin. Ivy jumped, certain someone was outside. What if he broke in before Matt arrived?

She needed a weapon. Her mind raced as she visually swept the room. She grabbed the fire poker, ready to use it if she needed to.

Tires squealed, and she ran to the window and peered outside, praying it was Matt, not the caller. The fog and rain made visibility difficult, but when the car lights flicked off, she recognized the SUV. Relief poured through her and she dropped the poker.

As soon as Ivy opened the door, Matt dragged her into his arms.

"God, Ivy, are you okay?"

She nodded against his chest. The leather of his jacket felt cold from the wind, but the warmth of his body found hers, and she nestled closer as he stroked her back. His breathing sounded choppy, his chest rising and falling against hers. The scents of rain, fear and need enveloped her.

"Thank you for coming, Matt. I didn't know what to do."

Slowly, he threaded one hand behind her head into her damp hair and pulled away, searching her eyes.

"Tell me exactly what he said."

Ivy grappled for control and cleared her throat. "He said that he'd warned me, that he was going to take care of me just like he did my mother. And that music was playing in the background...."

Matt's eyes narrowed. "What music?"

"'Here Comes Santa Claus.' Don't you see, Matt? He knew about my mother's collection of Santas. And he practically admitted that he killed her." She hesitated. "That means my father didn't."

Matt clasped her hands, seeming to understand the significance of her comment. "Did you read the caller's number?"

"It was an unknown again."

"He's probably calling from a throwaway cell. Makes it nearly impossible to trace."

"What are we going to do now?" Ivy asked.

Matt caressed her cheek with his hand, but his gaze strayed to her neck, to the bruises from the boy's fingers, and anger tightened his jaw.

"We'll find out who it is. But for now, you need some rest. This has been a harrowing day for you."

"I'm just glad you're here, Matt. I...don't want to be alone."

"You won't be," he whispered. "I'm staying with you."

Their gazes locked, questions standing between

them. Heat surfaced. The need to touch Matt nearly overwhelmed her.

Matt cleared his throat. "If he calls back, I'll answer."

"What if he tries to break in?" Ivy asked.

A muscle ticked in Matt's jaw. "Then I'll kill him."

The conviction in his cold statement shook Ivy to the core. But he was only trying to protect her.

"I don't want to cause you trouble, Matt. Maybe we should call the sheriff."

"I don't trust A.J., Ivy." His gaze bore into hers as he twirled a strand of her damp hair around his finger. "Do you trust me?"

Matt had just threatened to kill a man. She shouldn't trust him.

But he would never hurt her. At least not physically.

"Ivy?"

The pain and uncertainty in his voice tore her heart in two. She'd tried to maintain her walls, but somehow Matt had managed to scale them. She couldn't hurt him. Even if he broke her heart.

She cupped his jaw in her hands, unable to deny what she wanted. What she thought they both wanted.

"Yes, Matt, I trust you." With a whisper of a sigh, she rose on her tiptoes, pulled his face closer, pressed her lips to his and kissed him.

His mouth felt warm, and he tasted of coffee and man, a heady combination. The faint memory of the boy trying to strangle her threatened to shatter the moment, but adrenaline surged through Ivy, reminding her that she had almost died earlier. She didn't want to go to her grave without knowing how it felt to be close to Matt. And doing without the splendor of his kiss would be like dying.

MATT CLOSED HIS EYES, sinking every raging emotion into the kiss. Vying for tenderness slowed him only slightly. He wanted Ivy, had to know she was safe and alive in his arms. God, he'd almost lost her tonight. And now another threat…

A moan reverberated from her throat, and a surge of white-hot excitement shot through him. He ran his hands over her silky hair, drew her closer, probed her lips apart with his tongue and tasted the inside of her mouth. She was warm and sweet and delicious, like honey. His heart pounded, his body pulsing with raw desire, and he ran his hands down her shoulders, lowered his mouth to nibble at her neck, the sensitive lobe of her ear, then beyond her collarbone to tug the edges of her robe apart with his teeth. She sighed and dropped her head back, offering him deeper access, and he opened her robe, his chest tightening at the sight of her bare breasts. Pink rosebud nipples strained toward him. He cupped her glorious mounds in his hands, savoring the weight of them.

Her nipples tightened, and his mouth watered.

Reminding himself that this was Ivy, he lowered his head, then pressed tender kisses along the curve of her breasts, slowly inching his way toward her nipple. She groaned and her legs buckled, so he braced her with his other hand, still flicking his tongue southward until he drew her nipple into his mouth.

"Oh, Matt…" She shoved her hands into his hair. The thrill of her offering nearly undid him. He suckled her deeply, aching to throw her down and ravage her, but she tasted so sweet and was so beautiful that he ordered himself to fight the animal within him.

She wriggled her hips restlessly, and he moved to the other breast, feasting on it until she panted against him, whispering his name in a breathless sigh. "Matt…"

He raised his head and searched her glazed eyes, smiled at the haze of satisfaction and desire lighting them.

Then he lifted her, carried her to the bed and laid her gently on the sheets. Her robe parted, and he glimpsed heaven between her slender thighs. God, she was so perfect.

"Ivy, we should stop now. I don't want to take advantage of you."

"Please, Matt, don't torture me, then stop like that."

"You deserve more than this, Ivy," he said in a gruff voice. "You're frightened, vulnerable. I'm… an ex-con."

"You're the man I want to be with tonight. And prison was a mistake."

But it was still very much a part of him. The ugliness. The things he'd done.

He couldn't touch Ivy with that ugliness.

A sudden memory of his first night in prison gripped him, and he shuddered. Sweat exploded on his face and his stomach heaved.

Shame washed over him and he spun away, trying desperately to banish the images. He'd only been a kid. Some of the brutes inside had decided to teach him a lesson. Break him in…

Matt's lungs suddenly closed, and he choked on the bile rising to his throat.

"Matt…"

The present faded, blending into the past. The beatings. The…other. It had only been one night, and then he'd learned how to fight dirty….

But he couldn't forget it. Couldn't tell Ivy.

"I…I'm sorry, Ivy."

Pain and grief stabbing at him, he yanked himself away from her, strode toward the door, then flung it open. He gasped for fresh air as he slammed the door behind him. But he couldn't leave Ivy alone.

He couldn't go back inside and make love to her, either.

CHAPTER ELEVEN

THE COLDNESS THAT SWEPT over Ivy kept her immobile for several seconds after Matt left the cabin, a coldness that had nothing to do with the hailing rain and heavy winds beating against the cabin. What had just happened? One minute she and Matt had been kissing, and he'd touched her with such want and hunger that she'd almost come apart in his arms. The next minute, pain and anguish had overridden his desires, and he'd run away as if he couldn't stand to look at her.

The mood had changed as soon as she'd mentioned prison....

Did he still blame her for his conviction?

Aching from the loss, she gathered the robe around her and belted it, then slid off the bed, wondering what to do. She still wanted Matt. Craved his erotic touch. Her body burned from just thinking about the way his mouth had claimed her breasts. And she'd felt Matt's hard length pushing against her. Had seen the need in his eyes and heard the hiss of his breath as he'd prolonged the pleasure.

Confused, and worried that she had done something wrong, she pushed open the door and searched the darkness. The wind rattled the tree branches, spewing rain onto the porch. Through the murky gray surrounding her, she spotted Matt leaning over the porch rail in the corner, staring out into the darkness. His back was to her, and his head was down as if he was engaged in a silent emotional battle.

"Go back inside, Ivy."

His husky voice made her pause, but she needed to understand what had happened. If he blamed her or hated her, she could live with it. Or she'd try to make it up to him. Whatever.

But she couldn't stand the chasm between them.

"Matt…" She walked toward him, reaching out her hand as she neared him, but drew back when he barked her name again.

"I said go back inside."

"No." Grateful that her voice remained steady, she continued. "Not until you explain why you pulled away from me."

He made a growling sound deep in his throat. Did he think he was going to scare her off?

"I…did I do something wrong, Matt?" Sadness laced her voice, but she couldn't help it. Finally, she'd felt safe with someone, had opened herself up to have a relationship, at least physically, and he had deserted her.

Matt dropped his head forward, a heavy sigh escaping. "God, no, Ivy. Don't think that."

She laid her hand on his shoulder, stroked the knotted muscle at his neck. So much tension. He stiffened, then swung around. The anguish in his eyes trapped the air in her lungs.

"What's wrong, Matt?" she whispered. "Please tell me. Let me help you."

"I won't talk about it," he said.

"I hurt you somehow. Just tell me what I did and I'll fix it."

"It's not you, Ivy. Jesus, you're perfect."

Confusion blurred her head. "Perfect?" Her bitter laugh filled the air. "I'm hardly perfect, Matt. I blanked out half my childhood. I haven't been able to let a man near me until you touched me. One guy...even called me a cold fish."

"Bastard." Matt couldn't hide his anger. "You're no cold fish, Ivy. I...you know that now or you wouldn't have responded to me the way you did a few moments ago."

"You're right. I did respond. I wanted you, Matt, and I thought you wanted me. The moment, in there—it was so wonderful."

He closed his eyes, speaking between clenched teeth. "That's just it. It was perfect. You're so good, so beautiful. And..." He opened his eyes then, a resigned, lost expression darkening them. "And I'm not, Ivy. I didn't kill your parents, but I'm no saint, either." He lifted his hand and pointed to his cheek. "That scar is only the beginning."

Her heart cracked open and bled. "If you think a scar makes a difference, makes you less handsome, then you don't see the man I see, Matt."

"It's worse, Ivy. There are things you don't know...."

She cradled his hand in hers, felt it trembling, then rested it against her cheek. "I want to know. I'll listen, Matt. I'll understand whatever is it…."

"No," he growled. "You deserve something better. Someone not tainted by jail."

"But I want *you*, Matt, don't you get it?" She poured her feelings into her voice. "The good, the bad, the ugly."

"You can't mean that, Ivy." His voice rippled with harshness. "You wouldn't, not if you knew…"

"You asked me if I trusted you, Matt." She squeezed his hand, lowered it to her heart. "Now I want you to trust me."

He stared at her for a heartbeat of silence. Emotions warred in his eyes. He was wavering. But in the end, he lost the battle. Or she lost it, because a shutter closed over his face.

"Please just go to bed, Ivy."

Tears filled her eyes, but she did as he said. But just before she shut the door, she whispered, "I'll be waiting, Matt, whenever you're ready."

WHENEVER YOU'RE READY.

Hell, he'd never be ready to talk about prison. Or reveal to her how terrified he was of loving her and losing her.

He had grown accustomed to pain. To darkness. But he had no idea how to deal with this sudden sweet tenderness in his life. With Ivy. Any second, he might snap and do something to break the trust she'd given him so freely. Any second he'd disappoint her, just as he had his mother.

And himself.

He'd sworn not to break in prison, not to… No, he would *not* think about jail. The violence. The beating. The…

His body shook with the effort it took to banish the memories. With the determination not to beg Ivy for a second chance. To accept her sweetness, crawl between her tender thighs and let her loving wash away the devil from his soul.

A wolf howled somewhere in the distance, and he stood on the porch for what seemed like forever, listening to its heart-wrenching loneliness. Ivy's words echoed in his head as the rain beat a staccato rhythm on the weathered wood, and the trees trembled violently from the storm. Overriding his willpower, black memories, heavy and thick, clouded his mind just as the gray clouds above had obliterated the sun the past few days. This fall storm would end one day, hopefully.

But the one in his head would rage on forever. There was no end to it, no rainbow around the corner, no sun waiting to burst through the darkness.

Only for just a moment, when he'd held Ivy in his arms, he'd felt the cloud lifting….

But it wasn't fair to expect her to repair his damaged soul or accept someone who would never be whole. For God's sake, he'd broken into a sweat, choking on his own memories when he was on the verge of making love to her. What woman would want a scarred man like that?

I want you, the good, the bad, the ugly.

But Ivy had no idea how deep the ugly ran.

Matt gripped the rail with an iron fist. He needed to go back in. They'd have the dinner he picked up. That's all they could share. His bones vibrated with fury and anguish as he turned his face up to the wind and rain. Just thinking about someone threatening her made his deep-seated anger surface. Her father. This anonymous man who'd phoned her. The other psychos he knew who lived among them.

Matt had to focus. Make sure she was safe. And find out who killed her parents.

Then he'd get out of her life, so she could go back to hers, where she belonged. Where she would forever be safe from men like him...

IVY SNUGGLED UNDER the covers with her favorite Santa, closed her eyes and made a wish—please make the storm stop. It sounded like monsters outside were beating on the windows and roof. They were trying to tear the house down. Trying to break in. Trying to get her.

The howl of the wind grew louder. Tree branches scraped against the glass panes, and twigs and limbs slapped the side of the house. Rain pinged on the roof, pounding so loudly she thought her eardrums might burst.

Her mother's laughter drifted through the haze. Soft. Tinkling. A beautiful sound that reminded Ivy she was safe. Music floated through the paper-thin walls, a guitar strumming softly. She wanted to crawl in bed with her mother.

She started to climb from bed, but a man's voice echoed from the other room, and she froze.

Daddy didn't like for her to get in bed with them. He always made her go back to her room. Laughed and said she was acting like a baby.

Ivy frowned and clenched the covers. Was her father home?

Earlier, he'd gone to the bars, carousing. Mama said he wouldn't be back until morning.

Ivy knew what that meant. Her father would get drunk. And hopefully he'd sleep it off before coming home. If he didn't, he'd probably lost at poker, and he'd be in a bad mood. His temper was like a volcano, explosive and hot. And he took it out on her mother.

Another clap of thunder shook the house. Ivy jumped off the bed, racing toward the door. The monsters were coming closer. They would snatch her this time.

Lightning streaked the room, and she clutched the Santa in one arm, then listened at the door. The man's voice drifted through the house. Deep. Husky.

No. Not her father's. Another man's voice.

But who was visiting her mama?

Curious, Ivy opened the door slightly, then tiptoed silently across the wooden floor, wincing when the boards squeaked. Better not let Mama know she was up. But she had to know the man's name.

One step more. Two. Three. She reached her mother's bedroom door.

Ivy held her breath and peeked through the crack. Her stomach flip-flopped. A tall man wearing nothing but his underwear stood beside the bed, and her mother...no, Ivy couldn't look.

But she had to. Had to see who was in there. Make sure it wasn't Daddy drunk again, going to hit her.

No, it wasn't Daddy. This man was bigger. His hair was lighter.

Why was the man half-naked? And why was he in her mama's bedroom?

The man suddenly crawled on top of the bed and pinned her mother down on the mattress like a wrestler. Her mother groaned and struggled to get away, and he started bouncing on top of her. No! He was going to hurt her! Ivy had to stop him!

She cried out and pushed at the door. She had to save her mama.

The man turned and gave her an icy look. Her mother yelled for the man to get off of her.

Ivy tried to make her legs move, but they were glued to the floor. Suddenly the man jumped off the bed and ran toward her....

IVY JERKED AWAKE, PANTING as she dug her hands into the covers, trembling all over. The dream...it had been real. A memory.

The door suddenly burst open, and Ivy screamed, expecting to see the man in her dream, the one who chased her. But Matt stalked toward her.

"What's wrong, Ivy?"

She searched his face, trying to remember that other man, but a black curtain shrouded his face, just as her memory had been blank for so long.

The mattress dipped as Matt sat down on the bed beside her. "What's wrong? I heard you cry out."

He stroked her arms, but his gaze scanned the room as if searching for an intruder. "Did that man call again?"

"No." She chewed on her lip, her heart racing. "I…had a nightmare. I think it was about the night my mother died."

Matt gripped her arms and forced her to face him. "Did you remember something?"

Confusion and anguish rippled through her. "There was a man at my house. A man in the bedroom with my mother."

A muscle ticked in Matt's jaw. "It wasn't your father?"

She shook her head. "No, Matt. My mother…I think the man was either raping her or…or he was her lover."

MATT RESISTED ADMITTING THAT the man might have been a customer. Better Ivy believe her mother had a lover, someone who really cared about her. But the blackmail scheme seemed equally plausible.

"Matt, maybe I saw my mother being attacked."

Matt's pulse clamored at the sound of fear and pain in Ivy's voice. "It's possible. It's also possible your mother had a boyfriend in town." He lowered his voice, stroking her arm, hoping to soften the blow. "After all, no one could have blamed her for wanting to escape your father."

Ivy nodded, hugging her knees to her chest and folding her arms over them. "I wish I could remember the man's face."

"How about his height? Or the color of his hair?"

Her gaze flew to his, eyes wide. "He was taller and bigger than my father. And his hair...I think it was lighter, but I don't remember the exact color."

"What about his age?"

She shook her head, her hair falling in a tangled curtain around her troubled face. "I don't know. I was so young.... Every man looks old and big to you when you're eight."

He smiled, remembering the way she'd cowered from him. "So I looked old to you?"

Ivy's mouth tilted slightly into a half smile. "Not that old. But...I'd heard things about you."

"I'm sure they weren't good."

"You did have a reputation as a bad boy, but all the teenage girls swooned over you."

He grunted. They certainly didn't anymore. They ran from his scarred face. Only Ivy hadn't backed away.

Her declaration echoed in his head, tugging at him, making him pull her closer. *I want you, Matt. The good, the bad, the ugly.*

No, he couldn't allow himself to believe that declaration. There were things she didn't know about him. And if she found out about Red Row...

She angled her head to look at him. Questions and need shimmered in her eyes. "It's late, Matt. You haven't slept at all."

Shadows streaked the room, but he embraced them, allowing them to hide his true emotions. "I...wanted to watch the cabin."

"You have to rest, too." She pulled at his arm, drew him down on the bed beside her. "Please, stay with me. I don't know if I can fall asleep again, I'm afraid I'll have another nightmare."

He stretched his arm beneath her and pulled her up against his chest, savoring the fresh scent of her shampooed hair and the scent that belonged to Ivy.

"I can't keep fighting my memories," she whispered. "I should go back to sleep and finish the dream. Maybe then I'd see the man's face."

Matt nodded and pulled her closer, toying with her hair as she nestled against him. If she could identify the killer, this whole mess would end, and Ivy could return to Chattanooga. Then he could make a life for himself, be somebody.

But as he held her in his arms and closed his eyes, he imagined life without Ivy, and the emptiness threatened to consume him.

With that realization, the familiar bitterness assaulted him. Who was he kidding? He might be out of prison, supposedly free now. But people still remembered him as bad-boy Mahoney. Some would always think he was guilty. Others would know that he'd been in jail and realize he'd done bad things while incarcerated. Even his own mother hated him.

Hell, he'd never be free of his past.

Ivy moaned softly and whispered his name in the darkness, then lifted a hand to brush her fingers gently against his cheek. Unable to help himself, he imagined a different world. Then he rolled toward her, inhaled her sweetness, buried his head in her hair and pretended that Ivy was his to keep. At least until morning.

ARTHUR BOLES LEFT Talulah's more satisfied than any man had a right to be. Tonight hadn't been fun—hell, it had been damn near exhilarating. Talulah had slapped him on the ass and told him to stop brooding and talking and give her a good time. His mouth watered just thinking about sliding into her hot wet pussy and watching her cheeks flame as he pounded into her.

He tried not to think about the fact that she was a whore and that she'd gotten paid to do it. All he wanted was to remember her hot lips sucking his dick until come had flowed down her mouth like warm milk. Then she'd lapped it up and climbed on top of him and taken him for the ride of his life.

She was special. At least to him. Hell, she kept him satisfied in a way no other woman ever had.

He tightened his belt, climbed into his Mercedes and headed toward his place for supplies, but adrenaline still surged through him from the past hour. The tawdry sex had done wonders for his nerves. Helped to calm his rattled cage. Helped him decide.

He'd known what he had to do all along, from the very moment Mahoney had been released. And with that Stanton girl back in town, too...

God help him, he just prayed he hadn't waited too long.

Yes, he'd played it damn smart by coming to

Talulah's tonight. She would provide him with the perfect alibi.

One not even his own son would dare to question.

Five minutes later, he'd stopped by his estate, loaded the trunk with supplies and headed toward Cliff's Cabins. Thankfully, the rain died, or else his plan might not work. Still, the wet pavement slowed him down as he wound around the mountain. The road was quiet tonight, the wind's whistle a lullaby, the lack of cars another good sign. Falling rocks tumbled down the embankment, three big stones bouncing off the side of his car. He cursed, hating the damage they'd do to his paint job. But a few tiny dents would be easy to fix and were a small hazard to pay compared to the price of not taking care of business tonight.

Tearing open a cigar with his teeth, he pressed the cigarette lighter, then puffed on the tip of his favorite Cuban brand until the tobacco lit up and the pungent taste filled his mouth. Five minutes later, he swerved into the drive for Cliff's Cabins, parked beneath an overhang and climbed out. Wet leaves fluttered down into his hair as he opened the trunk and grabbed the can of gasoline. Tonight he would end this ordeal once and for all. Cliff's Cabins had been built so long ago that hopefully, even wet, the logs would go up in seconds. Before Mahoney and Ivy Stanton knew it, they would be nothing but names in tomorrow's obituaries.

A final goodbye that would end the saga that had started fifteen years ago in this town.

Two kids who'd stumbled into the middle of something they didn't understand.

Two kids who had to die so he could protect the truth.

Ashes to ashes, dust to dust.

Kill them he must.

CHAPTER TWELVE

TOMMY DROVE TOWARD his friend Trash's house like a bat out of hell. Shit, he'd barely escaped that wolf alive. Where had the beast come from? And why hadn't it chased after that stupid woman instead of him?

He glanced down, shuddering at the sight of his shredded sweatshirt, and could still picture the wolf's teeth embedded in the black material. Then the damn thing had chomped at his tennis shoes. Tommy wiggled his foot, and pain shot through his big toe. One second longer and it would have been his entire foot in the animal's mouth. His goddamn foot—food for a freaking wolf!

He shuddered again, feeling sick. And if it hadn't eaten or mauled him to death, didn't wolves carry rabies or some shit like that?

The buzz he'd had from the pot had worn off, and his throat was so dry it felt as if he'd swallowed a half ton of gravel. His head pounded and his stomach growled. The only thing worse than the munchies without food was the d.t.'s, and the way his hands were shaking he was sure he had both. He needed another hit—bad.

But no…there was something worse. His head was clearing, and he remembered mouthing off to Trash about offing his mother. He slapped his hand over his forehead. Stupid. Stupid. Stupid. What kind of moron was he? What if Trash talked?

He'd watched enough *Law & Order* to know how the system worked. If that bitch from the woods told that asshole sheriff about their cult, and the sheriff found out Trash was involved, and the sheriff put pressure on Trash or offered him a deal…

God, why hadn't Tommy kept his damn mouth shut?

Panic clawed at him as he swung his Jeep toward Trash's street. He had to talk to his friend. Make sure he kept quiet.

Shaking like a leaf in the wind, he peered through the dark, saw Trash's new truck in the driveway and threw the Jeep into Park. What if Trash's mother was home?

She might smell the weed.

Sweat poured down his back, but he took a deep breath, opened a pack of Juicy Fruit and crammed a piece in his mouth. Jamming his ball cap over his eyes, he lumbered out, holding the side of the Jeep to steady himself before he climbed the steps. The garage light was on. Trash couldn't have been home long. The others had all scattered, too, like ants being chased from an anthill.

He checked the garage, but Trash's mother's car was not inside. A good sign. Now talk to Trash. Make sure he kept quiet.

Legs wobbling, Tommy climbed the steps, knocked

and waited. A second later, Trash opened the door. Soot and black paint still darkened his face and hands, and his clothes reeked of dope and the campfire.

"Your mom's not home?" Tommy asked. Trash was munching on a bag of barbecue potato chips.

"She's out with her girlfriends."

And Trash's dad had run off years ago.

"Come on in, man," Trash said. "I've been thinking about what you told me earlier."

Nerves pinged in Tommy's chest like bowling pins crashing and toppling down. "That's why I'm here."

He needed to coax his pal outside. Lure him somewhere. Tommy had a baseball bat in his car.

"Listen," Trash said, eyes still wired from the crack he'd snorted before Tommy had shown up. "You said it felt good to kill your mother?"

"You can't go talking about that," he exclaimed. "No one can know."

Trash gave him the coldest look Tommy had ever seen, as if the devil had jumped into his skin. "Then you have to do something for me."

"What?" Hell, he'd do anything.

"Help me kill my old lady." Trash's eyes lit up. He was wired now. "It'll be fun."

Tommy's mouth gaped. "You're serious?"

"As shit." Trash yanked him down the hall, then opened the basement door and rushed down the dark stairs. "Come on, we'll make a plan. Then we'll hide and wait until she gets home. And tonight, it's bye-bye, Mommy." Trash snapped his fingers. "We can even cut off some of her hair and use it in one of the rituals."

Tommy grinned. Maybe this was his way out. After all, if Trash killed his own mama he wouldn't rat *him* out. The first killing had come easy. What was one more?

MURDERED BODIES, BUG-EATEN SKIN, old women buried in the kudzu—when would it end?

A.J. staggered into his apartment and opened the cabinet, hoping he had another bottle of bourbon inside, but shit, no. He'd finished it off the night before. And Buck had actually thrown him out tonight, told him he'd call his daddy if he didn't call it a night.

Fucking loser bartender shouldn't be able to tell the sheriff what to do. A.J. would make sure the guy received a few extra parking tickets. Hell, he'd can his liquor license, but no sense cutting off his own nose to spite his face.

The buzz of alcohol from the Ole Peculiar still surged through his veins. He collapsed on the sofa and closed his eyes, but in his mind, he saw that bug-infested, half-eaten body, bones rotting in the dirt. He'd had to do something to banish that image. A.J. had never had a weak stomach, but over the years he'd developed an aversion to corpses. Probably because he'd seen so damn many in this town. Every time he turned around someone was killed.

Ivy Stanton's face flashed in his head, the sight of her pale cheeks as she'd described her attack, and his gut clenched. For her, he'd wanted to be a hero tonight. For the first time in a long time, he wished he could erase his past. Forget what had happened fifteen years ago.

Hadn't he paid enough penance for that night already?

Matt had already moved in on Ivy, though. A.J. had seen the look in his old friend's eyes—not just lust, either, like he'd have expected. But as if Matt actually cared about the woman.

Matt was an ex-con. What would a woman see in that? Not a future...

He closed his eyes again, imagining Matt going back to jail where he belonged, and Ivy turning to him for help. He'd be her savior.

That is, unless she remembered more...

Then, hell, what would he do? Call his daddy for help again?

His head rolled back, and exhaustion weighted his limbs. Seconds later, he fell into a fitful sleep. The years rolled away and he was at Red Row.

Lily had been the most beautiful of the hookers. Hell, today guys would call her a M.I.L.F.—a Mother I'd Like to Fuck.

She was just as beautiful naked as he'd thought she'd be, just as talented and sexy. His body burned just dreaming about her.

But then everything went blank.

He jerked awake, the telephone cutting into the stale silence in the room. He rubbed at his bleary face and frowned. Hell, what now?

He yanked up the phone. "Sheriff Boles." He leaned his head back, hoped he hadn't slurred his words.

"Sheriff, this is Lady Bella Rue."

A moan rumbled from his mouth. "What do you want?"

"There's something sinister happening tonight," she said in that spooky voice that grated on his nerves. "Danger is in the air. Another killing will take place. Maybe more than one."

He mentally called her a thousand names. "And where is this killing going to take place?"

"I…I can't be sure, but you must do something to prevent it."

Yeah, yeah. Like he could stop all this evil. "All right. Who's going to be murdered? And who's doing the killing?"

A long silence stretched out. "I can't tell you that, but I feel it in my bones. I see the darkness, hear the cries of death and terror—"

A.J. severed the line. The old kook needed to get a life or have her visions come through more clearly. A location, name, anything would help, not just these cryptic messages.

The telephone trilled again, and he picked it up, ready to tell her off. But a man's voice brought him up short.

"Sheriff, this is the medical examiner."

A.J. sat up straighter, blinking to focus. "What is it?"

"We identified that body you found near the river. You won't believe who it was."

A.J. swallowed. He had no earthly idea. "Who?"

"Jerry Mahoney."

A.J.'s buzz morphed into an adrenaline rush.

Everyone thought that Matt's father had run off years ago. No one had reported him dead.

No wonder. Because someone had killed him.

Had Matt done away with his father?

A.J. scrubbed his hand over his chin, hung up, then stumbled into the bathroom and splashed cold water on his face. This new information might solve his problems. Arresting Matt for killing his daddy would prevent him from snooping around and teaming up with Ivy.

Seconds later, A.J. ran out the door and called his father, to tell him how they could stop Mahoney in a way that didn't include violence. He had to make one more stop before Matt's. He'd drop by and inform Mrs. Mahoney that he'd found her old man.

He wondered if she'd cry over the bastard's body or if she'd throw a party.

IVY STARTED IT. FIRST JUST a lazy kiss on the neck. Next, her lips had brushed his chin. Then his scar. Then her fingers had tiptoed across his chest, plucking at his buttons.

Matt lay perfectly still, pretending sleep. Trying to resist. Praying she'd stop and fall asleep.

Praying she wouldn't.

Sugary-sweet touches floated across the hair dusting his torso. Her lips pressed into his throat. She whispered his name so softly it sounded like notes on a piano. And slowly, ever so erotically, her tongue found his ear.

He moaned silently. Or maybe it was out loud— who could tell? His heart beat like a drumroll, out of control. Sighing her name, he grabbed her hands to stop their torture, then rolled to face her. She lay on her side, a sultry smile on her lips as she looked into his eyes. He read the longing. The tenderness. The trust. And his heart shattered.

"I thought you were asleep," she whispered.

"I thought *you* were."

She smiled. "I couldn't sleep."

"And you think I could with you kissing me like that?"

She laughed, the first happy sound he'd ever heard from her, and his throat closed. Ivy was the type of woman who should always be laughing. Who should be happy.

But he couldn't give her joy. He had found the strength somehow to turn away from her before. He needed that resolve now.

But it deserted him, and he felt as weak as a newborn kitten. Starved for another kiss.

She seemed to sense the change, and her eyes turned molten. Desire and need flickered, as well as determination, a heady combination that sent heat bolting through him.

He cradled her face in his hands, stroked her hair from her cheek. The reservations he'd had earlier still whispered in his head, but he shut them out, like closing the door on an unwanted guest.

Even if he didn't deserve pleasure, Ivy did. He wouldn't deny her.

Still, he struggled to be a stand-up guy. "Ivy…we shouldn't do this."

"It's just us right now, Matt. No past. No tomorrow."

No ugly ghosts hiding in the closet to haunt them. But there were still secrets....

Emotions thickened his throat so he couldn't speak, but words weren't necessary. All he needed was to touch Ivy.

Praying he wouldn't hurt her, he traced a finger along her cheek, loving the smooth silkiness of her skin. He lowered his head and pulled her up to him, claiming her mouth with his own. Hunger surged through his bloodstream, the yearning so powerful he sighed into her mouth and thrust his tongue between her lips to taste her. She met his need with her own, deepening the kiss and spearing her hands along his shoulder blades. Downward they roamed, massaging his muscles, coaxing his response, urging him to move faster, to make love to her.

When she pushed at his shirt, he hissed between his teeth, then sat up and tore off the garment and flung it to the floor. His eyes met hers, and he saw his own passion reflected in the depths. Then he lowered his fingers to pluck at her nightshirt, slowly unbuttoning the pearl buttons, inhaling sharply as her bare breasts came into view. Seconds later, he cupped and kneaded her mounds, licking and kissing the soft peaks, biting at the rigid points until she writhed against him.

"God, Matt...I never knew I could feel like this."

"Like what, Ivy?"

"Like I'd die if I didn't get closer to a man. The burn, the ache. I want you so badly it hurts," she whispered.

Her soft admission fueled his hunger, and he

peeled off the gown until she lay naked beside him. His breath caught in his chest, and he could only stare at the beauty beside him.

"Matt?"

He pressed a soft kiss to her lips. "Please let me look."

A pure feminine smile curved her mouth, and she tenderly tunneled her fingers through his hair. "I want to see you, too."

"Later," he growled. For now, he drank in the sight of her breasts, heavy and full, glistening with moisture from his mouth. His eyes traced the curve of her hips, down to the thatch of yellow-blond curls at her thighs, and need flared so hot inside him that he thought he might burst. Slowly he lowered his head, licked and tasted her breasts, then traced a fiery path of kisses down her belly.

She threw her head back, moaned and clutched at his arms. "Matt, please…"

"Shh, baby, we've got all night. I don't want to hurry." He raised his head and looked at her as he spread her legs with his hands. "I've waited all my life for this."

Her cheeks flushed, and he pressed a quick kiss to her mouth, then pulled back and lowered his head to the heart of her. Ivy arched and groaned, fingers tightening around the sheets as he lifted her hips with his hands and plunged his tongue inside her. In. Out. A flick of his tongue across her damp center. Then he sucked her clit into his mouth and she went wild, bucking and crying out in pleasure as her body spasmed in ecstasy. His own desire and hunger heightened by her reaction, he plunged his tongue inside her again, using it as he would his sex, tasting her release and feeling the tremors of her body as she hugged him.

"Oh, Matt," Ivy whimpered. "I...want you." She yanked at his arms. "Here. Let me touch you, feel you, look at you."

Her softly muttered plea almost pushed him over the edge.

But he had only meant to give her pleasure. Not take his own.

She reached for his belt and his sex hardened, pulsing to be inside her. Her fingers brushed his belly, and he sucked in a breath and felt the first notch of his belt come undone just as his sanity and resolve shattered.

But something rattled outside, and he froze. The whistle of the wind? An animal? Or somebody? The sound broke the silence again, and he jerked upright. Was someone in the woods near the cabin?

Nerves on alert, reminding himself that Ivy was in danger, that a killer was after her and he was supposed to be protecting her, he pressed his hand over hers to stop the torture.

"Matt, what is it?"

"Shh." Body strung tight, he stood and stalked to the front door, glanced out the window. Thought he saw someone in the woods beyond.

A bright blue light twirled in the distance, and a siren wailed over the mountain. He rushed back to the doorway of the bedroom. "Get dressed."

"What is it?" Ivy asked in a choked voice.

"The cops," Matt said, as the squad car roared to a stop outside.

He refastened his belt, hurriedly pulled on his shirt, buttoning it up as he raced back to the front window and peered outside.

Déjà vu flooded him, and fifteen years rolled away like they'd never happened as he watched the sheriff stalking up the steps toward him.

IVY THREW ON A PAIR of jeans and a brown sweater, dragged a brush through her hair, her hands trembling as the knock sounded. Why would the cops come out to her place in the middle of the night?

"Maybe they found the boy who attacked me," she said.

Matt shot a skeptical look over his shoulder. "Then why the lights and siren?"

She clutched his arm, willing him to be calm as he opened the door.

Sheriff Boles stood on the porch, rain dripping off his hat, his look somber as he stared at Matt, then behind him to Ivy. "I checked next door and realized you weren't there, so I figured you'd be here. I need to talk to you, Mahoney."

"Sounds official, A.J." Matt stepped aside and allowed him entrance, but his body went stone-cold rigid.

"It is." The sheriff kicked dirt and leaves from his boots, but instead of entering, remained in the doorway. "Actually, I need you to ride down to the sheriff's office with me."

Matt folded his arms, his mouth set in a grim line. "What's this about, A.J.?"

"Did you find out who attacked me?" Ivy asked.

"Not yet, but I'm working on it," the sheriff said. "But we did learn the identity of the body in the woods by the river."

Ivy pressed a hand to her pounding heart. "Who was it?"

The sheriff angled his head toward Matt. "Your father."

Matt faltered, shifting slightly in shock, and Ivy clutched his arm.

"You found my father? Dead?" he asked in a hoarse voice.

"The coroner just called. The dental records prove it's Jerry Mahoney."

"Does my mother know?" Matt asked.

A.J. hooked his thumbs in his belt loops. "I stopped by and told her before I came here."

"How…did she take it?"

The sheriff cut his eyes away. "She seemed fine. Not surprised, really." Another suspicious look from the sheriff made Ivy realize the implication—he thought Matt's mother had covered for him, that he had killed his father.

A.J. tilted his head toward the door. "Come with me, Matt. I need you to answer some questions."

"You think I killed my old man?" he asked harshly.

"I don't know," the lawman said calmly. "But we both know you hated him. And with good reason. Now, are you coming with me willingly, or do I need to handcuff you?"

Matt's face blanched at the idea, and tears pressed against Ivy's eyelids.

Tension stretched taut between the men. "No, I'll come," Matt barked. "But someone needs to watch out for Ivy. She received another threatening phone call tonight."

The sheriff slanted her an odd look. "I'll have my deputy ride out here."

Ivy stroked Matt's back. "Matt, what can I do?"

"Stay put and keep the doors locked until I return." He angled his head toward her, and the pain in his eyes nearly made her knees buckle. "And call Abram Willis for me." He reached inside his pocket and pulled out the number. "Explain what happened."

She nodded. "I will, and Matt—" she gave him an imploring look, willing him to trust her "—it'll be okay this time. I promise."

But the desolation in his eyes indicated he didn't believe her. Ivy realized then just how truly damaged his soul had become over the years. Heartache engulfed her, but she vowed to prevent history from repeating itself.

This time she'd do everything she could to keep Matt from going to prison.

And then she'd prove to him that he had a life to look forward to, that she wanted to build that life with him.

That she cared about him and that they couldn't allow their pasts to ruin their future.

CHAPTER THIRTEEN

KILLING TRASH'S MOTHER turned out to be as sweet as eating apple pie.

Tommy and Trash had laid the trap perfectly. First, pretend they were asleep. Sack out in Trash's room, Trash on the bottom bunk, Tommy on the top. Tommy had lain perfectly still, feigning a light snore when she had tiptoed in and checked on Trash. Trash had sprawled on his stomach, while the stereo blared heavy metal rock in the background. She had turned down the volume, clicked on her heels back to her own room and gone to bed. The two of them had dissolved in laughter, muffling the sounds with their pillows for a good half hour, giving her time to fall asleep.

Then they'd smoked another joint, Trash had taken the butcher knife, slipped into her room by her big four-poster bed with the fancy white satin comforter, and driven the point into her heart. Tommy smothered her scream with the pillow, while Trash twisted the knife deeper and deeper. Blood spurted and spewed, running like a red river down her white gown and soaking the sheets until they turned a crimson color.

"That serves her right for trying to ruin my life," Trash said as they dragged her lifeless body onto the Oriental rug, rolled her in it, then carried it to Trash's new pickup truck.

"Free at last, free at last," Tommy sang, reliving the euphoria he'd felt when he'd finally rid himself of his own old hag.

They tossed the body in the back, climbed in the truck and drove toward the woods.

"I've got an idea," Trash said, wired. "Why don't we leave her on that crazy old Lady Bella Rue's doorstep?"

Tommy laughed. "Good idea. The old witch will freak out when she wakes up and finds a dead body waiting for her."

"Then we have to go back and clean up the blood," Trash said.

"Bleach will do the trick." Tommy's chest puffed up with confidence. He'd read all about destroying evidence on the Internet. But they'd party first, clean up later.

The truck bounced over the ruts in the road, fresh rain falling and soaking Trash's mother's body in the back. Tommy squinted through the fog as Trash slammed over a stick in the road. A stray animal darted out in front of them, and Trash swerved. Tommy yelled and gripped the dashboard. Trash's mother's body in back bounced, flying across the truck bed and slamming against the side.

"Whoopee!" Trash yelled, barely missing a row of trees as he rounded the curve. "Mama's going for her last ride." He screeched to a stop when they reached the overhang where they parked to hike into the woods by the river, and they both climbed out, laughing.

"Shit, she's heavy," Trash said as they dragged the body from the back of the truck.

"Yeah, but she's one weight off your neck now." Tommy grabbed her feet while Trash braced her head and torso in his arms, then they stomped through the muddy woods toward Lady Bella Rue's.

Tommy wished he'd brought his camera so they could take a picture of the witch's face when she found her present in the morning. Then again, by then, they'd be sleeping like babies.

MATT'S STOMACH HAD cramped into a permanent knot. This couldn't be happening—not *again*. To be arrested by his former best friend only carved the knife deeper into the open wounds he'd lived with all these years. A.J. didn't really believe he'd killed his father, did he?

And who had?

All these years Matt had thought his dad had simply run off and deserted his family. Although the truth be told, he'd been relieved when his father hadn't come home. It had meant no more beatings for his mother. No more abuse for him or his brothers. Hope had even seeped through that he and his brothers might have a chance at life.

But that had fallen apart for Matt a few years later. And after he'd been imprisoned, his brothers had had their own troubles. He wondered where they were now.

Still, he couldn't pretend he regretted that his old man was dead.

"Matt, have a seat." A.J. gestured toward the battered wooden chair by his desk, and Matt settled into it, reminding himself to be grateful A.J. hadn't handcuffed him. Although Matt already felt the weight of metal cutting into his wrists, his ankles, felt the hard thin mattress in the cell, saw the endless nights of nothingness stretching ahead. Sweat exploded on his forehead and trickled down his neck.

Dammit, he wouldn't lose control in front of A.J.

"We both know you hated your old man," the sheriff began.

Matt shrugged. "I don't remember you being all that close with yours."

A.J. flinched slightly, then chewed his lip. "Look, Matt, I don't want to do this any more than you do, so why don't you explain what happened and let's get it over with?"

"How can I tell you something I don't know?" Matt glared at him. "You don't really believe I killed my father, A.J. I was eleven years old when he left. You and I were shooting the bull, learning to play pool, cutting school. I wasn't out killing people."

"You'd already taken a bat to him a couple of times."

"To defend my goddamn mother."

A.J. leaned forward, fists on his knees. "I didn't say I blamed you. Hell, maybe this time you can plead self-defense, get a suspended sentence."

Another court case. More jail. Locked in a box.

His record tainted again. The air froze in his wind-pipe. He'd die first.

"How was my father killed?" Matt finally asked, curious.

A.J. closed his eyes briefly as if he was grappling for control, then opened them, his gaze steady and level. "You tell me."

"I don't know," Matt said between gritted teeth. "I'm sure the medical examiner informed you of the cause of death."

The telephone rang, slicing into the moment, and A.J. picked it up. "Sheriff Boles here." A hesitation. "Listen, Lady Bella Rue, if this is another—" He paused, then dropped his head into his hands. "Shit. I'll be right there."

Matt held his breath while he waited, praying the call didn't have anything to do with Ivy. Surely she wouldn't have ventured out to that old woman's house.

"I need to go." A.J. stood, then gestured for Matt to do the same. "I have to hold you. We'll finish this later."

Matt breathed through clenched teeth. "You don't have to do anything, A.J. You were my friend. And you know that if you release me, I'll stick around."

A.J. hesitated, but shook his head. "I'm the sheriff now, sworn to uphold the law, and I have another murder on my hands to deal with." He gestured toward the back door and Matt's stomach heaved. He knew what was behind that door. Bars. A cell. Prison all over again.

He contemplated running.

Only pride locked his legs in place. And the fact that hiding out years ago had cemented the seal on his conviction.

"Go on inside, Matt. I'll be back as soon as I can."

Matt held his head high and walked toward the cell, the familiar clank of the metal door slamming shut ringing in his ears.

IVY QUICKLY DIALED Abram Willis's number and left a message explaining Matt's situation. Hopefully, he could keep Matt from spending any more time in jail.

She hung up and twisted her hands together, feeling only marginally better. What should she do now? The sun was barely rising in the sky, but there was no way on earth she could sleep. Not until she did something more to help Matt. The injustice of him sitting behind bars turned her stomach. How would he handle being locked up again after finally tasting freedom?

Furious at the circumstances, she started at the sound of a car motor outside, then jumped up and peered out the window. Another squad car. So Sheriff Boles had sent his deputy out to check on her as he'd said. Small consolation for carting Matt off to jail.

Rage heated her bloodstream again. She felt so helpless. She had to do something.

The sheriff had said he'd stopped by Mrs. Mahoney's house to tell her about her husband before coming to question Matt. Surely she knew her son was innocent. His mother had to stand up for him this time. Just as Ivy did.

And she had to find a way to remember the truth about what had happened that night her parents had died. Only finding the real killer could end this horror.

Fueled by her emotions for Matt, she tugged on boots and her jacket, grabbed her keys and headed out the door. The deputy had circled the cabin and was already leaving. She ran to her Jetta, then drove toward the trailer park, hoping she would recognize Matt's mother's trailer.

Mud and leaves spewed on the black asphalt as she rounded the curvy road, and fresh rain drizzled onto the windshield. A sliver of sun fought to break through the clouds, but failed and disappeared quickly. Just as her fleeting peace with Matt had when A.J. had hauled him away.

She wanted more moments in bed with Matt, evenings where they lay enveloped in nothing but the warmth of each other's bodies. Where nothing could touch them except their feelings for one another. Where she could finally feel his body pulsing inside her.

She would no longer run from life or her past, or the fear that someone would rob her of happiness. Without Matt, nothing else mattered.

The trailer park looked old and even more dismal in the thick gray light. Too early for children to play outside, the silence of morning seemed ominous and dreary, reminiscent of the lifestyles of the people who lived in the rusted trailers.

Ivy vowed that she and Matt would end the vicious cycle that had kept oppressed women and men trapped in the town, tied to poverty and abuse, without hope for a brighter future.

Surprisingly, she found Matt's homestead quickly. The years fell away, as if it had been only yesterday when she'd seen Matt outside, tinkering with that old junker. He hadn't asked for much in life, had been willing to accept the scraps from the junkyard and build a ride for himself with the brittle leftovers of the junkers people had discarded.

He deserved more than leftovers.

She stopped, slipped the car into Park and let her mind carry her back in time. She saw him as a young boy, angry but with the promise of life ahead of him. She had to convince his mother that the boy still lived inside Matt, and that he deserved the life he'd been robbed of because of Ivy's memory loss.

Inhaling to control her emotions, she climbed out and picked her way through the overgrown, rocky path, then mounted the steps. Praying the woman didn't slam the door in her face, Ivy knocked softly at first, then more forcefully. Footsteps clattered inside, and finally a small, gray-haired woman peered through the opening, clutching the robe around her.

"Mrs. Mahoney, please, I need to talk to you."

"Who are you?"

"My name is Ivy Stanton."

"Stanton?" the woman screeched. "I heard you were back in town. What do you want with me, girl?"

"I need to talk to you about Matt. Please open up, it's important."

"I lost my son a long time ago," she said, her voice breaking. "Now go away and leave me alone."

"But you shouldn't have lost Matt, Mrs. Mahoney, and if you don't talk to me now, you might lose him again." Ivy waited, whispering a silent prayer and finally the door screeched open.

She could see the wariness and anguish in the woman's tight expression. Matt's mother looked so frail and beaten by life. She had suffered greatly because of Ivy, just as Matt had.

"I'm so sorry, Mrs. Mahoney, for all the pain I've caused your family," Ivy murmured, assaulted by guilt.

The woman's eyes widened in shock. "Pain you've caused us? Girl, are you crazy? My boy killed your parents. Have mercy, but you should *hate* us."

Ivy moved past her, and the woman tottered behind her into the small cramped den. She faced Mrs. Mahoney, her heart in her throat. "That's just it—Matt was innocent. Didn't you see the exoneration papers?"

Mrs. Mahoney cut her gaze toward the back room, her chin wobbling. "I…didn't believe them." She flapped her bony arms around in circles. "You can't trust the government these days. They're always letting murderers and thieves go free. Can't afford to keep the criminals in jail so they turn 'em loose."

"And sometimes they make mistakes and put

innocent people in jail," Ivy said firmly. "That's what happened with Matt, Mrs. Mahoney. I repressed memories of my parents' murder that night, or I could have helped him." She paused for a breath. "I know that he isn't a killer. He *saved* me the night my parents were killed. He found me in the junkyard, running for my life. Someone, whoever killed my parents, was chasing me, and I fell in the mud. Matt picked me up and carried me to safety." She took the old woman's frail hands in her own. "Don't you see? Matt is not a killer, he's a hero."

"But…"

"It's true," Ivy said, squeezing her hands. "I'm sorry about your husband. I heard they found his body, but Matt didn't kill him, and I'm sure you don't believe that, either. Not really."

The woman paled even more and collapsed into a faded, overstuffed chair.

"The sheriff has taken him into custody again," Ivy said. "We have to do something, Mrs. Mahoney. We can't let Matt go to prison again, not for another crime he didn't commit. It will kill him."

EILEEN MAHONEY ROCKED BACK and forth in her rocking chair, clickety-clacking against the linoleum. Knotting the afghan in her lap, she studied the faded threads and broken stitches, trying to weave a thread that had come loose back through the knitted pattern. The blanket was old and frayed now, just as she was, all these stitches coming unraveled just as her life had.

Fifteen years ago she had spoken the truth at her

son's trial. Had believed that he had killed those Stantons. Heaven help her, she'd known he had meanness in him, just like his daddy.

But now...now that little Stanton girl was saying he really was innocent. And Matt was sitting in the sheriff's office being questioned for killing his daddy.

Her hands began to shake, and she dropped the thread, knowing her fingers were too gnarled, weak and unsteady to weave it back through the pattern. Was it too late for her son, as well?

Too late for her?

A knock sounded at the door, and she jerked her head up, unable to stop her hands from trembling as Larry Lumbar walked in. He'd been a good friend all these years. Land sakes alive, she didn't know why. She'd never encouraged him. Oh, he'd wanted more and he'd been patient, but after living with Jerry Mahoney, she'd never have married again. But she'd finally learned to trust Larry. He would know what to do.

His face looked tired as he entered, his thinning hair worn, his scalp red where he'd run his hand over his bald spot. "You sounded upset, Eileen," he said as he stepped toward her.

He smelled like coffee and rain as he knelt to press a kiss to her cheek.

"I can't believe this nightmare," she cried, her voice so shrill it didn't even sound like hers.

"I know, I heard they found Jerry's body." His expression was grave as he slumped onto the sofa beside her chair. Splaying his beefy legs, he leaned forward. "But it'll be all right, Eileen. You didn't want that boy bothering you. Now A.J. will lock him up, and you won't have to worry about him again. You can put him out of your mind just like you have for the past few years, and you'll be safe."

Tears pushed against her eyelids. "That's just it, Larry. I can't let them lock Matt up for killing Jerry."

Larry steepled his hands and rested his chin on them. "Yes, you can, Eileen. That boy inherited a violent streak from his daddy. We both know it." He paused and wheezed a breath. "And when his father run off, I was glad to see it. I always thought your Matthew killed him, but I let it go and didn't look too hard for him because I was glad he was dead." His voice turned gravelly. "I thought once he was gone, that you…that I…might have a chance."

The tears broke free and rained down Eileen's face. "Oh, my word, Larry, what have we done?"

He grabbed her hands and pressed them to his chest. "Don't cry, Eileen, it's all right. Why do you think I tried so hard to make sure Matt was convicted of the Stanton slayings? I knew the violence had to stop. I was afraid he'd hurt you one day."

"No…oh, God." Her voice broke. "You did that because you thought he'd killed Jerry?"

"Hell, yes. I was afraid he might hurt you next, so I had to stop him some way."

"But he didn't kill his daddy," Eileen sobbed. "And if that was the reason you arrested Matt, then maybe you were wrong. Maybe he didn't kill the Stantons, either."

"What are you saying, Eileen? That you don't think he was guilty?"

"Remember what I told you back then—"

"I thought you were trying to protect him," Larry argued.

She shook her head. That Stanton girl had been so convincing. She believed Matt was innocent of her parents' murders. And Eileen knew the truth about her husband. "All I know for sure is that Matt didn't kill his daddy."

Larry sucked in a sharp breath. "Don't…Eileen, don't try to defend that boy now because you're his mother."

"It's not that," she argued. "I'm speaking the truth." For the first time in fifteen years, Eileen believed in her son again. But he would never forgive her for being too late.

"Eileen?"

She stood, her arthritic knees popping and cracking as she forced strength into her voice. She was going to need it. "I have to help my son now, Larry. I have to tell the truth."

Larry gripped her arms. "Tell the truth about what?"

"That Matt didn't kill Jerry." Her legs wobbled but she pushed forward and grabbed her raincoat. "I know he didn't, because I killed him myself."

IVY HAD MADE MRS. MAHONEY face some harsh truths, and only prayed she'd persuaded her that Matt was innocent. Now, Ivy had to face some harsh truths herself.

Finding out what had happened fifteen years ago was the only way to really save Matt. Maybe if she could convince A.J. of Matt's innocence, the sheriff would be more apt to believe him about his father.

The familiar stirring of a panic attack seized her chest as she neared her childhood home. Her breathing grew erratic, her heart pumped, her face felt flushed and her hands trembled. She fought her way through the attack with deep breathing, refusing to run back to the safe patterns and routines that had trapped her all these years.

Rain drizzled onto the already saturated ground, turning the blanket of brown leaves into a murky, ankle-deep marsh. She waded through it, kicking the worst of it from her boots as she climbed the three rickety steps to the trailer. The windows had been boarded up, and she jiggled the door and found it locked. She had to get inside.

Suddenly the years fell away, and she was eight years old. Voices echoed from the crack in the door, the sound of her mother's cry like a siren warning.

Ivy fumbled inside her purse until she found the tiny nail file on her key ring, then used it to jimmy the lock. The knob was so old and fragile, the door popped open in seconds. Cobwebs hung like Halloween decorations above the doorway, and fifteen years of dust and mold nearly caused her to gag. Exhaling sharply and battling the urge to run, she forced her protesting feet to carry her forward.

A cockroach skittered across the floor, and somewhere mice scratched in the cabinets, searching for food. The faded, brown plaid sofa she'd grown up with hugged the moldy wall: a recliner in another dark shade faced the battered TV, which probably hadn't worked in a decade. A shattered lamp still lay on the floor, a testament to the fact that no one had been inside the trailer since her parents had been murdered.

Outside, the wind howled, and light clawed through the thin cracks in the plywood boarding up the windows. She paused, picturing her mother sitting at the kitchen table, cutting out paper doll clothes. Her throat burned. They had sewn little clothes for her Skipper doll, made a snow castle out of sugar cubes and stenciled teddy bears on T-shirts. The memory of the chocolate chip cookies they'd baked scented the air as if it had been yesterday, and she suddenly saw the scrawny Christmas tree she and her mother had cut down on a hike into the mountains. The pine had smelled fresh, the limbs slightly sticky with sap, but they had laughed and strung popcorn and hung it on the tree along with homemade ornaments and red and silver balls they'd bought at Wal-Mart. Then her mother had brought out the Santas—big ones, little ones, cloth, ceramic, plastic …she had loved them all.

"What are you doing, wasting money on all those goddamn Santa Clauses?" her father had bellowed.

"I like them," her mother had said. "They remind me of childhood, when anything was possible."

Ivy's heart swelled, aching for her mother.

Dragging her feet through the trailer, Ivy paused to glance into her room. A faded comforter that she remembered being yellow lay haphazardly across a single oak bed. A Raggedy Ann doll and an old chalkboard were the only toys in sight, leaning against a battered dresser.

Knowing the answers she needed were in her parents' room, she pivoted and crossed the hall. A floral bedspread covered a double maple bed, a dark brown stain streaking the fabric.

Blood. The stain had once been red.

But then Ivy had stopped seeing red.

She'd watched in horror as it had spilled from her mother's body that day, thick, pungent. So much blood.

Who had stabbed her?

Ivy closed her eyes, willing back the memories. She'd been in her room, just like in the nightmare. She'd heard a man's voice. Not her father's. She'd been curious, so she'd tiptoed to the hall and listened. The man and her mother had been laughing. Then arguing. When Ivy looked inside, the man had been naked, climbing on top of her mommy. Ivy had screamed at him not to hurt her, and he'd turned....

She clutched her stomach, shaking as the memory bombarded her.

Run, Ivy. Run like the wind or the monster will get you.

No, she couldn't run. She had to go back. Save her mommy. See the man's face.

She turned, screeched to a halt. Hid under the table in the kitchen. Her mother screamed and ran into the room. She knelt to pull at Ivy.

"Shh, honey, it's not what you think, Mommy's okay. Mommy was just…playing with the man."

Ivy frowned and hugged her mother tight. "Playing? But, Mommy, he was..."

"You'll understand when you get older, Ivy. Now, come on, go back to bed. The man won't hurt us."

Ivy buried her head in her mother's arms. She had to trust her. Tears trickled down her cheeks as her mommy tucked her back in bed, and Ivy closed her eyes, shutting out the memory. But still the man's presence haunted her. There was something familiar about him....

Ivy jerked herself back to the present and covered her hand with her mouth. Her mother had had a lover. But who was it? She couldn't see his face....

Had he killed her mother after Ivy had fallen asleep?

Or had she gotten up and witnessed the murder? And when had her father come in?

A creaking sound startled her, and she spun around, but something hard slammed into the back of her head. Ivy staggered and hit the wall, clutched her head and felt blood spurting. Blinking through the haze, she grabbed for something to steady herself, but dizziness overcame her and she slumped to the floor, the room spinning. Two rough hands jerked her sideways and threw her facedown, then another whack on her head, and pain exploded in her skull. She fought for consciousness, struggled to scream, but the room went black.

Just before she passed out, the scent of her father's cigarette smoke filled her nostrils.

He had to do it. Get rid of Ivy.

His heart pounded, the need to finish her off warring with his instinctive desire to take her and make her his lover first. Just as he had her mother.

But he couldn't take the chance of getting caught.

Ivy being here was dangerous enough. She was going to remember; he knew it without a doubt. And then his life would be ruined. Over.

He stuffed her into the closet, closed the door and melted into the darkness outside the old trailer. His mind spinning, he crouched on the muddy ground and contemplated just how to end it.

Mahoney was back in jail.

The others…they were just as frantic as him, afraid the truth would come out.

Killing Ivy was the only answer.

He reached inside his pocket, removed the matches, then rose. Lily Stanton's screams echoed in his ears as he grabbed the gasoline can, went back inside and doused the inside of the trailer.

CHAPTER FOURTEEN

LADY BELLA RUE FOLDED her hands and prayed over Terri Lynn McClinton's body as the sheriff approached. The work of Satan had killed her boy years ago and continued taking the people in Kudzu Hollow. Her black magic and mojos didn't seem strong enough to ward it off. Determined to keep up her efforts, she spread incense around Terri Lynn's body, sprinkled holy water on her head and chanted a spell to ease the woman's transition to the other side.

Sheriff Boles zoomed to a stop, spewing gravel and mud from the squad car tires, and the chickens Bella kept in the pen went crazy, clucking and flapping wildly. Blood and death hung heavy in the air, the stench stronger than the odors she'd grown accustomed to from the chickens.

She waved the sheriff toward her, and tugged her shawl around her shoulders, warding off another chill. Folks thought death didn't bother her, but she was only a footstep away from her own grave, her time nearing. She'd made peace with herself and her maker long ago and would welcome the trip into glory. Then she could be with her little boy and hold him in her arms once again. And maybe from heaven she could look down on this town and help people find the good within.

"Good G-God almighty," Sheriff Boles stammered as he removed his hat and swiped his arm across his forehead. "When did you find her?"

"About an hour ago," Lady Bella Rue said. "I thought I heard a noise out here, and looked outside, then came to the door and there she was on the porch, all bloody and...dead."

"The medical examiner is on his way. Looks like she hasn't been dead long." He jammed his hat back on his head, bending under the stoop to escape the rain and examine the body. "Did you see who left her?"

"No. Heard a car, but it was a ways off. They must have parked in the woods and carried her up here."

The sheriff sniffed. "I smell dope on her clothing."

Lady Bella Rue clacked her teeth. "The opiates they burn by the river. The evil comes from the earth."

He touched Terri Lynn's torn gown, examining the jagged knife marks in her torso, pushed at her eyelids to check her pupils, then shook his head. "Whoever did this was angry. They wanted to hurt her."

"They are possessed and had no mercy," Lady Bella Rue said.

"I'll have the M.E. check for drugs in her system. This black paint...it looks like the same stuff Ivy described those kids wearing at the river."

"Whoever killed her was doing drugs," Lady

Bella Rue said with conviction. "That's part of their sickness, part of what gives them the strength to carry through on their twisted desires."

The sheriff cut his eyes toward her. "More of your insights, Lady Bella Rue?"

She nodded solemnly. "It is related to the cult you found near my house. To the land, the river, the ground beneath us, the air we breathe. The evil is all around us."

"It's the teenagers," Sheriff Boles said. "First Dora Leigh Werth, now Terri Lynn. Their boys are friends." He stood and glanced down toward the river. The sound of water rushing over rocks filled the momentary silence. "As soon as the medical examiner arrives, I'll pay those boys a visit."

"Bring them to the body," Lady Bella Rue said, falling back on the old hoodoo beliefs. "If you make them touch the corpse, it will respond to the murderer's hand. Even if the body is cold and rigor mortis has set in, blood will spurt from her mouth or her heart in response to the guilty party."

MATT LOWERED HIS HEAD INTO his hands as he sat on the hard prison cot, emotions twisting his lungs with such a viselike grip that the breath could no longer flow through his throat. He felt himself falling into an endless pit of darkness. The painful memories sucked him into the vortex of despair like quicksand pulling at his feet. Deeper, deeper he sank, the thick hands of ugliness yanking at him, the shadows in the corners trapping his mind. He clawed for a limb, a hand, anything to keep him from slipping beneath the murky surface, but his fingers became mired in the thick mud, sliding downward until they touched the cold bars of the prison cell. If he didn't escape now, he would suffocate, drown, die. And never again see the light.

Or Ivy.

Ivy—God, he had to drag himself up through the abyss to find Ivy. She was waiting somewhere beyond the murk, where light shone and flowers grew and sunshine breathed warmth into his body. Where for a fleeting second, when he'd held her in his arms, hope had splintered through the darkness and sprung to life. Where he'd started to dream…

He latched onto that memory and replayed it in his mind. The feel of her in his arms. The sight of her naked body wet from his kisses and trembling from his touch.

Forcing renewed strength into his flailing spirit, he stood and walked to the edge of the cell and stared at the clock. The seconds ticked by as slowly as sand slipping through an hourglass, signaling the end of that dream. But Ivy was alone and she might be in trouble. He had to get out of here.

When the hell would A.J. get back? And how could Matt make him listen?

Cold steel met his fingers as he wrapped his hands around the bars. Finally, after an eternity, it seemed, the front door of the jail opened. Boots pounded on the hard flooring, and the scent of sweat permeated the room. The deputy's face appeared.

"The sheriff's on his way."

Matt nodded. He hoped to hell Abram Willis was, too.

Seconds later, the door opened again, and another man's voice echoed from the outer room. The former sheriff, Lumbar. What the hell was he doing here?

"I don't think you should do this, Eileen."

Matt froze. Eileen? Had his mother come to see him? Christ, he didn't want her to see him behind bars again.

Or had she shown up to make sure he was locked up so he couldn't hurt her? Maybe to gloat?

"I have to do this," her voice trilled. "Where is the sheriff?"

"I'm right here, ma'am."

Matt peered through the bars, wishing like hell he was in the front room. Although the door between the jail cells and the front office was ajar, he couldn't see what was going on.

"What do you need to talk to me about?" A.J. asked.

"My boy," Matt's mother said. "I want you to let him out of that cell right now."

Shock hit Matt square in the gut.

"Why should I do that?" A.J. asked.

"Because he didn't kill his father."

His mother's voice sounded strong and firm, more assured than he'd ever heard her.

"I appreciate you coming in, Mrs. Mahoney, and I can understand you wanting to take up for your son—"

"You're damn right I do. I don't intend for him to go to prison for something I did."

Matt's fingers tightened around the bars. What the hell was she doing?

"Mrs. Mahoney," A.J. said in a steely voice. "You don't need to confess to a crime you didn't commit just to protect your son —"

"I'm not," she said. "I killed my husband."

"It was self-defense." Larry Lumbar's voice sounded urgent, panicked. "A.J., you remember what kind of man Jerry was. He used to beat Eileen, and her boys, and one night he threatened to kill her, so she killed him instead."

"That's not entirely true," his mother said. "Actually, I wasn't afraid of him for me, but he told me Matt and the other boys were trouble, that he was going to get rid of them."

"Get rid of them?" A.J. asked. "How?"

"He…" Her voice broke. "He planned to tie 'em up that night, lock 'em in the car and drive it into the river." A strangled cry escaped her. "Lord forgive me, but I can't believe I was married to a man who'd threaten to kill his own kids like some heathen. I…knew then, Sheriff, that I had to do something. I had to stop him, and I did."

Matt swallowed hard, his head reeling. Was it possible that his mother's confession was true? If so, had she really killed his father to protect him?

And all this time, he thought she hadn't loved him….

WELL, WASN'T THIS JUST the picture of the perfect little family, A.J. thought sourly. How the hell was he supposed to lock up a seventy-year-old woman who'd been fighting for her kids' lives when he knew good and well what a bastard Jerry Mahoney had been? He had no doubt in his mind that she spoke the truth, at least about the fact that the old man would have killed his boys. He'd witnessed the evidence of Jerry Mahoney's wrath himself, and he'd been scared shitless when the man was around.

But letting Matt go meant freeing him to continue probing into the past. Opening doors that had been glued shut long ago.

What else could he do, though?

He grabbed the cell keys with a vicious yank, stalked to the back and stared at Matt. Shock rode all over Mahoney's face. "You didn't know?" A.J. asked.

"No."

"Hell, I figured if she had done it, you would have covered for her."

"You can't put her in jail, A.J. She's too old. It was self-defense."

A.J. stared at him, sweat pouring down his back. "I know."

Relief whooshed through Matt's chest, and A.J. gestured for Matt to precede him to the front office.

"Mother?"

Mrs. Mahoney's wrinkled, aged face quivered with tears as she looked up at her son. For a minute, A.J. felt choked up. He couldn't remember when his own mother had been alive.

"I'm sorry, Matt," she said in a shaky voice. "I…should have had more faith."

Matt cleared his throat, his shoulders still rigid from years of anguish and hurt. "You didn't have to come here today."

"Yes, I did," she said with earnest. "I should have stood up for you a long time ago."

Another hesitation, and A.J. watched Matt warring with his own need for absolution.

"Then you believe that I didn't kill the Stantons now?"

She nodded and pressed a gnarled hand to her trembling lips. "That girl of yours, Ivy, she can be very persuasive."

"Ivy visited you?" Matt asked.

"Yes. She told me about you saving her that night." Tears trickled down her cheeks. "My son was a hero, not a killer," she whispered. "And all along no one knew it, not even me."

"It doesn't matter, Mother," Matt said.

"Yes, it does. I'm s…so sorry, Matt." She reached out her arms and Matt went into them.

A.J. frowned, moved in spite of himself. Matt's family had been dysfunctional, but so had his own. And so had Ivy's.

Then all their lives and families had intersected, gotten tangled together.

But in the end, blood had been thicker than water, alliances had had to be made, and the friendships had had to end. There was no turning back time and changing things now.

If Ivy remembered that Matt had saved her, A.J. had to find out what else she remembered. Then he still had to arrest those teenage boys….

MATT WASN'T SURE IF THE moisture trickling down his cheek belonged to his mother or him. Finally, after all these years, she had accepted him back into her life. And she had faith in him.

He couldn't believe it. But dawn was cracking the sky on a new day, and maybe the sun would finally shine.

All thanks to Ivy. Dear God, Ivy. Where was she?

He pulled back from his mother's embrace. "Mother, where is Ivy now?"

She searched his face, then smiled. "I think she went to her old trailer. I saw her car parked there when Larry and I drove by."

A.J.'s phone bleeped, and he yanked it up with a frown. "Sheriff Boles here." A pause. "Okay, I'll be right there." He slammed down the phone and reached for his jacket. "That was my deputy. There's a fire out at the trailer park. I gotta go."

Matt grabbed his arm. "Which trailer?"

A.J.'s sudden silence answered his question.

"It's Ivy's, isn't it?"

"Yes." A.J. headed toward the door.

"Let me go with you, A.J.," Matt said.

"No, Matt—"

Larry Lumber cleared his throat. "We'll give you a ride, Matt. That's the least I can do to make up for the past."

Matt nodded, trying to ignore the possessive hand the former sheriff pressed to his mother's back as they hurried outside to his car.

TALULAH COULDN'T BELIEVE Arthur Boles had come to her again. He looked almost desperate and smelled of sweat and nerves and...gasoline.

He told her he'd spilled some on his hands at the gas station when he was filling up that pricey Mercedes, but his eyes had twitched the way they always did when he lied.

Her mind took a blast back to the past to another night he'd visited her with that same desperate look in his eyes. Another night he'd smelled like trouble.

The night the Stantons had died.

She still wondered....

"Talulah, honey, you gonna get in this tub with me?"

She smiled and poured two glasses of champagne, curled her fingers along the stem of the goblets and sashayed back into the bathroom. The bubbles oozed near the edge of the tub, threatening to spill over, and Arthur, big man that he was, looked ridiculous submerged to his neck in the froth. But he tolerated the bubble baths for her.

And she always made the indulgence to his male pride worthwhile later.

The bubble baths were her little gift to herself. Sometimes Talulah wanted to lie back and pretend that the man in her bed was her husband, a devoted man who loved her, a man who brought her wine and roses and chocolates. A man who enjoyed pleasuring her, one who would promise her forever.

At least Arthur kept choosing her, even after all these years. He didn't seem to mind that she'd aged or that her body had gone softer.

"Talulah, you are a sight for sore eyes tonight, you know that." He reached up and tweaked her nipple, twisting the tight bud until she threw her head back and laughed.

"Arthur, you haven't lost your touch."

His eyes looked glassy as he sipped his drink. "I like being with you, Talulah. I...always have."

She slid the sheer teddy down her body and kicked it onto the padded makeup chair. "Lordy, you get sexier and sexier. I...can't imagine why you returned tonight, but I'm sure glad you did."

His eyes, full of lust and male appreciation, skated over her, and Talulah's heart fluttered like a schoolgirl's. "Maybe the first time wasn't enough."

She batted her lashes, enjoying the flirtatious foreplay. So many of her customers in the past didn't bother with the hunt, they just cut straight to the chase. So boring. They hadn't learned the manners of the older generation. "You're pretty potent for a man your age, too," she said, placing her glass beside the tub.

"What do you mean, a man my age?" He growled, yanking her hand so she slid down into the water with him. Her breasts swayed, tingling as the hot soapy froth floated over her naked body and sloshed over the edge of the tub.

"Why didn't you ever remarry?" she asked, vying for lighthearted but curious.

A hooded look guarded his eyes. "Because the woman I wanted was...unavailable."

He slid his hand down between her legs, and her thighs tingled with anticipation. She lifted her glass and sipped her champagne, intending to probe for details about the woman, but his fingers moved inside her and she forgot words. Instead, she allowed his lovemaking to take her for a joyride. After all, the essence of Talulah meant loving. Feeling. Not thinking or answering questions.

Especially ones she didn't want the answers to.

Like where Arthur had been during the time he'd left her earlier and the time he'd returned. If she knew she might have to lie about it later.

And Talulah would rather not know than have to lie....

A SEA OF BLACK HAD swallowed Ivy. Her head swirled, images bombarding her as she faded in and out of consciousness. Dust, mildew and smoke filled her nostrils, and she coughed, fighting to stay awake, but losing the battle.

Years slid away. She was back in the trailer. She'd seen the man in her mother's bedroom. He was chasing her.

No. Her mother had sent her back to bed. She was safe. Nothing was going to happen.

But she'd awakened again later. Heard shouting. A man's voice—was it the same man? She didn't know....

"Please," her mother begged. "Don't hurt me. I just want to take my baby and leave."

Her mother's sob wrenched at Ivy, and she'd flung the door open and run toward the man shaking her mommy. But she couldn't see his face. Could only feel his strength as he jerked her up by one arm and threw her against the wall. She flew backward, her head slamming into the wood, and pain exploded behind her eyes. The black emptiness swallowed her.

Sometime later, white dots twinkled in the darkness. She opened her eyes, felt something sticky on her hands. Looked down and saw the blood flowing onto the floor in a puddle around her mother like a muddy river.

Ivy screamed and squinted through the shadows. Her stomach lurched as she spotted her mother's body. She was so pale. Lying so still. Her chest gaped open. Skin had been slashed. Layers of muscle and tissue spilled over.

Ivy opened her mouth to scream again, but no sound came out. Suddenly her father loomed above her. He yanked her up by her already sore arm. A sickening odor swirled around her. Her mother's blood. Her father's sweat. Cigarette smoke. Death.

"It's all your fault your mama is dead, Ivy! Just look, I want you to see what you've done."

But she'd closed her eyes. She didn't want to look. Her mommy couldn't be dead. No, if she just kissed her, she'd wake up and hug her and hold her again.

A shadow moved behind her. A sound...a footstep. The wooden board squeaked. Someone was in the room with her and her daddy. He heard it, too. He cursed and jerked around to see the intruder. Ivy took that split second to escape.

Run, Ivy. Run like the wind. Run from the monster.

But there was more than one. Her father. And the other man. They were both chasing her....

Ivy opened her eyes, dizzy, nauseated. Pain pounded her temples. Darkness engulfed her. She struggled to sit up, but swayed, then clutched for something to steady herself. Her hands were tied behind her back, she discovered. Her feet were bound, too. She rolled sideways and slammed into the wall. The space was tiny. Cramped. Dank.

Where was she?

She blinked to clear the fog from her head. She'd been having the nightmare again. But she was awake now, and *this* nightmare was real. Fragments of disjointed memories flashed back. She was inside the trailer, locked in the closet. She twisted to her side, panic seizing her. She had to get out. See Matt. Save him from going to jail again. Find the other man…

Adrenaline surging through her, she kicked at the door with both feet. Pounded it over and over. Her head throbbed with the effort. Blood trickled down her forehead.

How long had she been here? She'd lost all sense of time.

Smoke curled and seeped through the crack below the door. A splinter of light broke the dark, and the sound of wood crackling mingled with her choppy breathing.

Dear God, the trailer was on fire. And she was trapped inside. She was going to die. And she hadn't even told Matt she loved him.

Or that in her nightmare, she thought she'd seen the face of the man in the bedroom with her mother.

MAYBE IVY HADN'T STAYED at the trailer park. Maybe she'd returned to the cabin and she was safe.

Even as Matt tried to reassure himself, his body and mind weren't listening. He knew Ivy was in trouble. He sensed that she needed him, and feared he might be too late.

He quickly dialed her cell number as he climbed in the car with Lumbar and his mother, tension tightening his insides when Ivy didn't answer. Lumbar followed A.J., while Matt phoned Abram Willis and explained the situation, then alerted him to remain on standby in case A.J. decided to press charges against his mother.

Matt's heart pounded as they neared the trailer park. Smoke spiraled into the gray sky, but the rain had let up. For once, Matt wished the damn sky would pour rain.

"Where's the fire truck?" Matt asked, surprised he hadn't heard a siren.

"We only have a volunteer service around here," his mother said. "Some of the guys have to come from the other side of the mountain."

A volunteer service? They might not make it in time.

Lumbar turned the corner and sped down the street, and Matt's stomach churned at the sight of Ivy's Jetta parked in front of her old home. She'd received threats, a warning…someone wanted her out of the picture. And now this fire at the mobile home where her mother had died…

She must be inside. Fire spewed from the cracks of one of the boarded-up windows, and smoke hissed through the edges, growing thicker. His lungs tightened with panic.

What if he was too late? What if the killer had gotten to her this time?

CHAPTER FIFTEEN

MATT FOUGHT TO STAY afloat through the blinding sea of panic. Maybe Ivy had escaped when the fire started.

He quickly scanned the perimeter of the trailer park and searched the growing crowd on the lawn, but didn't see her anywhere.

What if she was trapped inside?

He threw open the car door as soon as Lumbar screeched to a stop, and his feet hit the ground running. He yelled Ivy's name as he crossed the distance, shouting, hoping she might be outside, not in the blazing trailer.

A.J. grabbed his arm as he reached for the front door.

"Matt, you can't go in there!" the sheriff yelled. "Let the firemen handle it."

"I can't wait," Matt shouted. "Ivy might be inside."

A.J. swallowed hard. "You don't know that. And it's too dangerous."

Dangerous? Christ, Ivy might not even be alive. Every second counted.

He felt the door and found it hot. Flames shot

through the cracks and smoke spewed from below the doorway.

Was there a back entrance?

"Matt, come on, back up." A.J. yanked on his arm, but Matt jerked free.

"I can't just stand back and watch her die."

A.J.'s face hardened at the implication that he would do just that, but Matt didn't care. He'd lost his friend years ago. All that mattered now was Ivy.

He jogged around the side of the trailer and found another door. Pulse racing, he ripped away one of the boards from the window and peered inside. The fire was spreading fast, rippling along the walls of the living room area toward the kitchen. So far the bedrooms weren't ablaze, but considering the small space and old wood, the entire space would be completely engulfed in seconds.

He jiggled the door, but it was locked. Frantic, he raced back to A.J. Several trailer park residents had congregated, watching the disaster, and A.J. worked to control the crowd. Matt's mother looked pale and shaken as she huddled beside Lumbar.

"Do you have any tools in that squad car?" Matt asked.

A.J. nodded and opened the trunk. Matt found a hatchet, ran back to the rear entrance and slammed it into the thin wood, splintering it in seconds. Heaving for air, he shoved open the door, inhaled sharply, then darted inside.

"Ivy!" He quickly swept through the bedrooms, but they were empty. Sweat poured down his face, the scalding heat from the flames growing more intense as he ran to the living room. Patches of flames crawled along the front door, eating the faded sofa and carpet, rippling toward the kitchen cabinets.

"Ivy!"

Suddenly a pounding noise cut through the sound of the crackling fire. He jerked around, searching for the source, then heard it again. A noise coming from the closet.

Ivy. She must be trapped inside.

Pulse racing, he darted through the blaze and yanked at the door. The heat scalded his hands, and fire clawed at his feet. He ignored it and yanked harder. The door finally gave way, wood splintering.

The air froze in his lungs at the sight of Ivy bound and tied, curled on the floor, bruised and bleeding. He scooped her up and raced back the way he'd come, dodging a wall of flames, barely keeping one step ahead of the fire as it chewed at his heels. Ivy was half-unconscious, gasping for air, her cheeks pale but hot from the flames.

But she was alive.

Flames caught the hallway flooring and he leaped outside, then ran around the trailer, carrying her to safety just as the dilapidated structure erupted into a full blaze. Orange, red and yellow flames shot into the heavens, flaring against the murky sky.

A.J. met them in front, keeping the spectators back as Matt dropped to the ground to check Ivy. Anger poured through him as he untied her hands and feet. The fire truck finally squealed up, and three men jumped out, unrolling hoses and dousing water on the flames to keep them from spreading to the other mobile homes.

Matt pressed a hand to Ivy's cheek. Soot and sweat soaked her clothing and face. Her fingers were bleeding from trying to claw her way out, and blood matted her hair. He felt the back of her head, angled it slightly and saw a contusion. Fury surged through him.

"Ivy, honey, can you hear me?"

Matt's mother and Lumbar scooted closer, looking concerned, and A.J. yelled for one of the rescue workers to check Ivy. Seconds later, an EMT pressed an oxygen mask over her face. Matt cradled her against him as the rescue worker checked her vitals.

"An ambulance should be here any minute. If they don't arrive by the time the fire's out, we'll take her to the hospital," the fireman said.

Ivy stirred and clutched at Matt's hand, then gasped, struggling for oxygen.

"Shh, just rest, baby. You'll be fine," he murmured.

Across the lawn, Talulah and Arthur Boles appeared in the crowd, standing out because they appeared to be together. Matt was shocked to see the two of them in public.

Had Arthur been visiting Talulah's again?

Eyes wide with terror, Ivy pulled at the oxygen mask, sliding it down. "Matt, someone was…in the trailer with me."

His blood ran cold. "I know. He hit you over the head, tied you up and left you there to die." His breath hissed out. "Did you see his face?"

"No, but I...I remembered something. I think it's important."

He stroked her cheek, urging her to put the mask back on. "What?"

"Arthur Boles...he was at the trailer the night my mother died. He...I'm not sure, but I—I think he might have been in bed...with my mother."

ARTHUR BOLES PRESSED A sweating hand over his heart, a sharp pain shooting through his chest. He'd forgotten his blood pressure pills earlier and needed one now. The stress was more than he could handle.

Last night, he'd almost set fire to the cabin where Ivy Stanton had been staying, but his son's phone call had stopped him just before he'd lit the damn match. He'd had gasoline on him when he'd arrived at Talulah's. And now Ivy's cabin would smell like gas.

What if Talulah got suspicious? What if someone had seen him and connected him with *this* fire?

And dammit, why hadn't Ivy Stanton died inside? What was she, some kind of cat with nine lives? And what the hell was Mahoney doing here, free and clear, running in to save her. He was supposed to be in jail.

"Let me go talk to my boy," he said. "See what I can do to help with this situation." Yes, that was good. Salvage himself by offering help. Turn this disaster around so he could look like a good guy.

Talulah's bottled-blond eyebrow rose in response. She was smart as shit under that ton of makeup. How much would her silence cost him this time?

Whatever the price, he'd pay it.

"What's going on?" he asked as he approached A.J. "I thought Mahoney was in jail."

A.J. rubbed a handkerchief across his own sweat-streaked face. "I had to release him."

"How come?"

"His mother copped to killing her husband." A.J.'s cold eyes met his father's. "She claims she did it to protect him."

Arthur hadn't seen that one coming. He should have. He'd spent half his life doing things to protect his own son.

And that deal with the devil would probably land him in hell for eternity.

A.J. TENSED AS MATT approached him. "We're going to take Ivy to the hospital. You saw she was bound. This wasn't an accidental fire, A.J. You need to investigate thoroughly."

A.J.'s temper flared. "I know how to do my job."

"Then do it. This guy is cold-blooded, A.J. You'd better find him before I do, because when I do, I'll kill him."

A smile almost erupted from A.J. Matt might just hang himself, after all. At least ten people nearby had heard his threats. Of course, they had seen the ropes binding Ivy's hands and feet, too. Fear-filled whispers rippled through the crowd. People would ask questions.

He cut his gaze back toward his father. What if he didn't like the information he gleaned when he finally confronted him?

Lumbar sidled over, holding the ropes the man had used to tie Ivy. "Have these checked out, A.J. You might find some fingerprints on them." Lumbar arched his bushy brows. "You're calling an arson team to investigate the fire, too, aren't you?"

A.J. agreed through gritted teeth. There were too many witnesses for him not to. But damn, bringing in other cops would complicate things.

Matt and Lumbar strode back toward Ivy, and A.J. felt his father move up beside him again. But his cell phone shrilled before his father could start in on him again. "Sheriff Boles."

"It's Lady Bella Rue. That cult is back down at the river."

"Damn." A.J.'s fingers tightened around the tiny mobile unit. He glanced at his deputy. "Get out there and set up a watch, but don't move in until I arrive. Maybe we can kill two birds with one stone and those boys will be there."

As soon as he ended the call, his cell phone rang again. "Sheriff Boles."

"It's Roger Umbry from the crime scene unit. We have the results from Dora Leigh Werth's body."

"And?"

"We found traces of skin underneath her fingernails that belonged to a family member. She probably scratched her attacker when she fought to escape."

Dora Leigh's only surviving family member was her son, Tommy.

"Anything else?"

"Yeah, we found three different DNA types on

Terri Lynn McClinton. Her own. A family member's. And a third one. The third DNA sample matches the skin samples from Dora Leigh's body."

Meaning they were probably Tommy's. "Good work. I'll get an arrest warrant." A.J. phoned the judge and relayed the facts, then hung up, weary. Those boys had murdered their mothers, and he had the evidence to prove it.

The ambulance squealed down the road and barreled to a stop beside the fire truck. The firemen were finishing up, the blaze had dwindled, and charred ashes, soot and the metal frame lay in heaping piles of rubbish. A.J. decided to take a look around before the crime unit arrived. By then he'd have his warrant for the boys' arrest.

He just hoped this fire turned out to be their work, too. But he cut his gaze back to his daddy, nerves knotting his stomach.

A.J. AND HIS FATHER were holding out, stalking near the fire like two men trying to guard their secrets. Matt didn't trust either one of them worth a damn. Especially now that Ivy remembered seeing Arthur at her mother's house.

The fact that Arthur Boles was here, watching, his gaze occasionally jumping back to Ivy, heightened Matt's suspicions. Had he been in the trailer? Had he knocked Ivy out and left her to die, then driven to Talulah's to give himself an alibi? Or had he decided to visit Talulah's so he would be close by, allowing him to be present at the scene so he could make sure Ivy didn't escape alive?

Matt had to stay with her to protect her. Lumbar and his mother hovered nearby while the EMTs who'd just arrived treated Ivy. She was lying on a stretcher by the fire truck, covered with a blanket, the oxygen mask in place.

Matt knelt and cradled her icy hand in his. "We're taking you to the hospital now. How are you feeling, Ivy?"

She moved the mask to whisper, "Better."

She still looked shaken, her face and hands covered in soot and dirt, and blood darkened her silky blond hair. Cold fury swept over Matt again. He sure as hell didn't trust Lumbar, but trusted A.J. and Arthur Boles less.

"Go with her," the ex-sheriff said. "I'll stay here and wait for the crime unit."

Why? So he could cover evidence? Or was he sincere about finding the truth this time?

"I…know you don't trust me, Matt," Lumbar said in a grave voice, "but I am sorry about what happened years ago. I…honestly thought you were bad news, and I wanted to protect your mother."

Matt nodded, but the scars and distrust from his prison days couldn't be alleviated so easily. Still, another pair of eyes watching A.J. would offer some small semblance of comfort.

"I don't want them blowing this over," Matt said harshly. "Someone tried to kill Ivy and I want that person found."

"You think it was the same man who murdered her folks, don't you?"

He nodded. "You're damn right."

"That happened during my term," Lumbar said. "I put the wrong man in jail. Now let me set things right."

Matt stared at him for a long time, then glanced at his mother who leaned against Lumbar, looking old and frail, her friendship toward the former sheriff evident.

The EMTs loaded Ivy into the back of the ambulance. Matt nodded to Lumbar, then climbed inside to accompany her. As much as he wanted to stay and push for answers, he didn't trust that Ivy was safe anywhere now. He had to remain by her side to ensure her protection.

And when she was safe and feeling better, he'd find the man who'd left her to die, and kill him.

IVY FOUGHT THE EXHAUSTION and haze of dizziness that engulfed her, desperately wanting to stay awake as she lay in the hospital bed. Sleep resurrected the nightmares in full force. The dark, closed-in spaces. The smoke. The scents of gasoline, sweat and cigarettes. The blood.

The day her world went black.

The day the monsters attacked.

She shuddered, burrowing under the covers. Matt had held her hand in the ambulance, had sounded so worried and anxious that she'd wanted to comfort him. But her arms ached, and she barely had the energy to squeeze his hand. The last few hours she'd drifted in a tunnel of darkness, where reality became blurred and fuzzy. Being admitted to the hospital. Having X-rays. She thought she had stitches, but wasn't sure. Her breathing hadn't been normal, someone had said. They'd treated her for smoke inhalation.

And Matt…sitting beside her bed.

She roused and tried to call his name, but her throat was so dry her voice sounded like sandpaper crinkling. Matt scooted near her bed and stroked her hand, hugging it between his own.

"You're awake now?" He kissed her palm. "I…I've been so worried about you."

"How long have I been here?"

"An hour."

His husky voice washed over her, eliciting emotions already raw from her close call with death. "Matt…you didn't have to stay."

"Yes, I did. I needed to make sure you were safe." He leaned forward, his voice tortured. "God, Ivy, I…almost lost you back there."

A shudder rippled through her, but she blocked out the memory of the attack and the fire. "What happened at the jail? You're free?"

He nodded and hugged her hand to his chest. His heart pounded against her palm, his heat warming her. "My mother came to see me. You…made quite an impression on her."

Ivy forced a smile, although her head throbbed with the effort. "She loves you."

Matt closed his eyes as if her words pained him. Finally he cleared his throat, but his voice reverberated with emotions. "She killed my father, Ivy. She did it to protect me and my brothers."

Shock mushroomed inside Ivy, but faded quickly. "A mother's instinct is to protect her children, Matt."

"But I thought…all these years…that she didn't care. She was so disappointed in me…."

"Maybe she thought that she'd taken her husband's life for nothing."

His breath hissed out, and she wanted to retract the words. "Matt, I didn't mean it like that."

"I know what you meant, and you're right." Regret thickened his voice. "We were hellions and troublemakers. I wish I could change the past."

"You're doing what you can now." She stroked his palm with her fingers. "Thank you for saving my life. Again."

He tucked a strand of hair behind her ear, then kissed her cheek gently. "I don't want to lose you, Ivy. We'll figure this mess out together." He hesitated, wanting to say more, to declare that he loved her, but he refused to make promises he couldn't keep. "Did…you remember anything else?"

Arthur Boles's face flashed like lightning against the black sky that had clouded her memories. The Arthur Boles from her dream had been younger, trimmer, and he had been in bed with her mother.

Tears trickled from her eyes and rolled down her cheeks. She didn't want to think about her mother in bed with that man. She'd been terrified of him when she was little. Had hated the grunting sounds they'd made, night after night. And when her father had caught them once, he'd hit her mother and called her all kinds of vulgar names.

Had her father found her mother in bed with
Arthur a second time, then flown into a jealous rage
and killed her?

No, her father hadn't murdered her mother. The
man who'd threatened Ivy on the phone had admitted his guilt.

Arthur had been powerful back then, a wealthy
real estate agent. He wouldn't want his affair with a
woman from the trailer trash crowd divulged.

Would he murder both her parents to keep that
affair a secret?

CHAPTER SIXTEEN

"Burn up the old witch
With her own spell.
Devil come and take her
Straight to hell."

LADY BELLA RUE'S CATS snarled and hissed, clawing at the windows as the chanting outside continued. She spread salt around the inside of the cabin, lit several candles and murmured a prayer of protection.

The teenagers with black painted faces circled her shanty in their black hooded sweatshirts, some carrying torches, others throwing eggs and rocks at her house. She peered through the haze of the clouds and saw two of them open the latch to her chicken pen. The chickens flapped and squawked as the boys chased them through the mud, trying to catch them. They'd stolen chickens from her before, slaughtered them and left the bloody remains and feathers on her doorstep, as if they thought they could run her off. She still didn't understand the madness that erupted in the town during the rains, but she continued to fight it with her potions and spells.

But the kids had never gathered in such a large group before, never encircled her house as if they meant to burn it down. The violence seemed to be escalating, the devil's followers growing in numbers as if the kids had actually gone through the seven devils' rooms to become voodoo practitioners themselves. A rock hit the window, smashing glass and sending a shower of broken shards over the floor.

Maybe there was another explanation. Another witch in town. One who'd cast an insanity spell on the children. Any minute Lady Bella Rue expected worms or snakes to slither out of their bodies and crawl across the ground.

> "Witch in the hollow
> Die tonight.
> Burn at the stake
> On a Saturday night."

She shivered even though she stood by the fire, twisting the knotted cloth at her neck as the chanting voices echoed through the window. She'd already planted mustard seed under her steps to keep the evil at bay, but the spell didn't seem to be warding off the devil.

A siren wailed in the distance, and she moved even closer to the fireplace, warming herself as she waited on the sheriff to arrive. He had to put a stop to this. It was getting out of control.

But then, he was no saint himself.

Outside, shouts and jeers magnified by the sound of the howling wind rocked the walls. The police car squealed to a stop, and the sheriff's voice bellowed through a bullhorn, ordering the kids to freeze.

Black-hooded figures raced into the woods, scattering in a dozen directions, disappearing into the dark forest like black bats and crows. But their evil chants hung thick in the air with the promise of more evil.

And Lady Bella Rue knew they'd be back.

A.J. RAN TOWARD A black hooded sweatshirt and tried to snag the sleeve, but the kid threw his torch down on the marshy ground, and he had to jump to miss the fire. His heart raced as his deputy chased two more kids, but they disappeared into the dense woods and the darkness swallowed them, creating a perfect hiding place.

A.J. heaved a breath, wondering if he should call in reinforcements from the city. He and Pritchard weren't going to be able to manage the mess. Not with two women's murders on their plate, a fire and an attempted murder tonight, and now this river cult threatening the old witch.

Head pounding from strain, he stalked to the shanty door and knocked. He'd make sure the old woman was safe, then he might have to post someone at her door. Pritchard wouldn't be happy, but A.J. didn't know what else to do. They had to catch these brats and end their streak of violence.

Lady Bella Rue opened the door, her wrinkled face shielded by a black scarf, the age lines sagging on her face with worry. "You couldn't catch any of them, could you?"

He shook his head. "Are you all right?"

She nodded, her gaze shooting to the woods. In the distance, he saw the occasional flicker of a torch, but most of them had been extinguished.

"I thought they were going to burn the house down," she said in a strained, low-pitched voice.

A.J. frowned and ran his hand through his hair. "My deputy and I will check out the woods. Why don't you stay in town tonight?"

"I'm not letting those young'uns run me out of my home."

"Did you recognize anyone?"

"No, it's dark as Hades with these clouds." She gestured toward the yard. "They tried to steal my chickens again, though. I reckon I'll have to conjure another spell."

"Your black magic can't stop them," A.J. snapped. "So use some common sense, Lady Bella Rue. You're just inviting trouble by staying out here alone."

"I know they'll be back," she said, clutching the knots at her neck. "But someone has to take a stand against the evil in this town and not give these kids so much power."

A.J. flinched. "I'm doing the best I can. For God's sake, old woman, there's been two women murdered, and tonight someone tried to kill Ivy Stanton. Whoever assaulted her burned down her trailer." The minute he muttered the admission, regret set in.

"That poor girl. She's been through so much." She swayed as if the wind had whistled through her bones. "The danger will only get worse. Her parents' killers must be found if she is to live at all."

His jaw tightened at her accusatory look.

He angled his head toward Lady Bella Rue. "I'll have my deputy watch your place in case they return and threaten you again tonight."

And maybe once he arrested Tommy Werth and Clete McClinton, they'd lead him to the rest of the gang.

At least stopping this cult would be a start.

But he still had to deal with the Stanton murders, the threats to Ivy, and Matt's questions….

MATT HAD THOUGHT THE HOURS in jail dragged, but sitting beside Ivy in the hospital room seemed like an eternity. Every time he looked at her, the realization that she might have died assaulted him. He'd gladly lock himself back in jail if doing so meant sparing her life.

She was weak, floating in and out of consciousness, tormented by nightmares of the fire and her past. He didn't know how to help her except to sit with her and pray that she finally rested.

Frustration ate at him, urging him to go out and hunt down the man who'd attacked her. He needed to question Arthur Boles. If Boles had had an affair with Lily Stanton, and had killed her, Matt would beat him until he confessed.

He leaned back in the chair beside Ivy's bed and closed his eyes, trying to make sense of things. Could he really trust Lumbar now? And how would Matt and his mother recover from years of distrust to have a decent relationship?

Finally, exhaustion claimed him, and he drifted to sleep. But snatches of prison life haunted his troubled slumber, along with remnants of seeing Ivy's trailer burning down, and he jerked awake every few minutes.

As the gray light of morning filtered through the thin hospital curtain, more rain pinged off the roof. Ivy stirred and opened her eyes just as a knock sounded at the door. Lady Bella Rue poked her head inside.

"Can I come in, dear?"

Ivy tried to sit up but winced, and Matt quickly situated another pillow behind her back to make her comfortable. Her color looked more normal now, although deep purple shadows darkened the ivory skin beneath her eyes.

"Yes, come in." Her voice was still hoarse from the smoke and tinged with terror.

"I heard you were attacked yesterday, child." Lady Bella Rue hobbled over, and Matt offered her the chair beside Ivy's bed. He stood on the other side as if to act as guard, but not because he feared the old woman. He simply couldn't drag himself more than a few feet from Ivy for fear of losing her. What would he do when this mess ended? Could he really walk away from her?

"The sheriff told me about the fire."

"He did?" Ivy asked.

She nodded. "That river cult of kids visited my house last night. They had torches and were circling my place like they intended to set me on fire."

"Oh, my gosh, Lady Bella Rue, are you okay?"

She nodded. "The sheriff run 'em off. But something has to be done to put a stop to their wickedness once and for all."

"I don't understand," Ivy whispered. "Why do those teenagers want to hurt you?"

"It's the meanness in them," Lady Bella Rue said. "It's been happening the last ten years. Kids turning on their families. And I'm just an easy target for their hatred."

"All we want is to find out who killed Ivy's parents," Matt said. "Then we're leaving town." His gaze met Ivy's, determined. Emotions flickered in her eyes, ones that confused him. Would she want to be with him afterward? Could they possibly have a future together?

His heart stumbled to a stop. Was he really contemplating the idea?

"It's all connected somehow," Lady Bella Rue said mysteriously. "The evil started the night your parents died, and has grown worse the past ten years. It's as out of control as the kudzu."

"How can everything possibly be related?" Matt asked. "Except for Ivy's attack, the other crimes have involved teenagers. None of those kids knew Ivy or her parents. Some weren't even born when the Stantons died."

"All of 'em live out there near the junkyard. Most in that new subdivision with its fancy woodwork and flooring. The parents have money, but they have no time for their children, so they spoil them, and the kids get bored and rebellious," Lady Bella Rue said. "I believe whoever killed your parents started a chain of events that must be stopped. They stirred up the devil from the ground in that area. The land must be haunted, that's all I can figure out. Needs an exorcism of some kind."

Matt quirked his brow at Ivy, wondering if Lady Bella Rue was really crazy or if she might have latched onto some semblance of the truth, albeit a supernatural one. No, the theory that the kids were spoiled made sense. The rest of it…impossible.

But her comment about the land nagged at the far recesses of his mind. Fifteen years ago, Ivy's mother was supposedly selling property to an out-of-town developer. Who was that developer?

Maybe he'd better find out.

Lady Bella Rue lifted a mojo from her purse and pressed it into Ivy's hands. "Please, dear, wear this at all times. It's stronger than the last one I gave you, and you need it." She paused, her expression grave. "The worst is not over for you. There is more pain and suffering to come, more loss."

Ivy's face paled, and Matt cleared his throat, anxious now for the old woman to leave. He didn't like her spooking Ivy.

"And you, Mr. Mahoney," the old woman said, "you should let go of your hatred and secrets. They will destroy you in the end."

Matt stared at her, his jaw tight.

Revealing his secrets meant trusting. Possibly hurting Ivy more.

No, it was better she didn't know, not about the ugly things that had happened to him in prison. And especially about Red Row…

A.J. CRAWLED FROM THE COUCH and gripped the arm for support, then staggered to the bathroom, downed three painkillers and splashed cold water on his face. The bourbon he'd had at dinner still heated his blood, but his mouth felt as if cotton balls had been jammed all the way down his throat, clear up to the top of his head.

He'd done it again. Blocked out hours.

But the events of the previous twenty-four hours rolled past. Matt's mother's confession. Ivy being attacked. The fire. The river cult circling Lady Bella Rue's house.

Hunting for Tommy Werth and Trash McClinton. But the boys had hidden out somewhere, had escaped for the night, and he'd had to wait on a warrant for their houses.

So he'd stopped for a drink.

And then what had happened?

He'd found enough balls to visit his father.

Shit…their fight had tipped him right off the ledge, and he'd driven straight to the Ole Peculiar for another round.

What then? He thought he'd driven home after the bar, but maybe he'd taken a side trip to Red Row.

A fog glazed his mind, as if a plastic bag had been yanked over his head and suffocated him. How many brain cells had he lost?

He flipped on the shower, dove beneath the spray, reminding himself that he had to find and arrest those boys. The warrant should be ready by now. Damned ironic. Tommy and Clete were the same age as he and Matt had been when the Stantons were slaughtered.

A.J. had been cocky and full of himself; Matt had been angry and looking for trouble. He'd found it big time.

Guilt threatened to shatter A.J., but he shoved it back down. He and his father had done whatever necessary in order to protect themselves back then. Otherwise A.J. might have been locked up instead of Matt. A.J.'s life ruined.

He would never have survived prison.

Oh, who the hell was he kidding? His life had been ruined, anyway. He'd been stuck in this town, paying penance, indebted to his old man ever since.

And they still didn't talk about that night.

He dragged himself from the hot water, toweled off, dressed, then drove by the diner and picked up coffee. Maybe he'd find Tommy or Clete home. First, he stopped by the Werths', but the door was locked and there weren't any cars in the drive or garage. He walked around the outside, but the rooms were dark, and no one appeared to be inside. He jiggled the doorknob and entered cautiously, then checked the house that appeared just as it had the last time he'd visited, as if the boy had had a party. He climbed back in his squad car and drove the short distance to the McClinton house.

Just like the Werths', the log house was dark, but a muddy Jeep and a new pickup were parked outside, the pickup's wheels caked thick with red mud from the river. Clete's.

Pay dirt.

A.J. pounded on the door and hit the doorbell at the same time. Tapping his foot as he waited, he circled the house and noticed a small garden area near the woods, past Terri Lynn's roses. He'd check it out later, but suspected the boys might be growing

their own stash of dope. He walked back, pounded
on the door again, then pushed on the doorknob.

"Clete, Tommy, it's the sheriff. Let me in."

The door jiggled, then squeaked open. They
hadn't bothered to lock it. Pretty stupid for criminals. Then again, they were *boys*.

His boots screeched on the parquet flooring as
he inched through the den. He kept one hand on his
gun just in case. The perps who'd killed Dora Leigh
and Terri Lynn were damn dangerous, and he did
not want to die at the hand of a couple of vicious teenagers.

The scents of weed and booze stifled the air.
Empty pizza boxes littered the mahogany coffee
table in the den. Cigarette stubs and Cheetos bags
added to the mess, at odds with the plush furnish-
ings. Terri Lynn had taken pride in her home, had
hired a decorator to give the house a formal, sophis-
ticated look. Her son's lack of respect was obvious.

A.J. worked his way upstairs, and checked the
bedrooms but found them empty. Blood stained the
bedsheets and white satin comforter in the mother's
room, and a trail of it dotted the gray carpet leading
to the door. He sniffed and leaned closer to check it
out. It was pretty fresh. He'd get the crime unit out
here right away.

Frowning, he strode back down the steps when
he noticed the basement door ajar. Placing his hand
over his gun, he eased down the steps. Pitch-black
silence greeted him, until he flipped on a switch and
light flooded the basement. Tommy and Clete both
groaned and rolled over, shading their eyes with

their hands. Still wearing the black hooded sweat-shirts, black paint covering their faces, they looked like two hooligans.

Clete threw his shoe across the room. "What the hell? Get out!"

"Turn off that light!" Tommy bellowed. "You're blinding us!"

A.J. braced himself. "It's the sheriff, boys. You're under arrest for murder."

Tommy suddenly shot up, but staggered and crashed into the wall. Cursing like a sailor, he toppled over, rubbing his foot, obviously still half-stoned. Clete reached for a baseball bat on the floor beside him, but A.J. removed his gun from its holster.

"I have a weapon and it's aimed right at you," he snarled, letting them know he meant business. "Now, put your hands up above your heads where I can see them. And don't make any sudden moves or I'll shoot."

IVY HAD ALMOST DIED the day before. The thought reverberated over and over in her head like a video that had been stuck on Rewind. As Matt helped her into his SUV, she breathed the fresh damp after-noon air, grateful to be free of the hospital room and on her way back to the cabin. The majestic Appala-chians rose around her, the sweeping canyons and mountain ridges reminding her of the daunting beauty of the area, and the breathless exuberance of simply being alive. Yes, there was beauty here, as she'd first thought; she simply had to look hard enough beneath the evil to find it.

Although her body still struggled with exhaustion, her heart fluttered at the protective way Matt had been treating her. He hadn't strayed more than a few feet from her side since the attack and the fire. She didn't want him more than an arm's length away, either.

She had never felt this close to another person. Especially a man.

Tension throbbed relentlessly in the air between them as he checked behind him to make sure no one followed.

"Should we talk to Arthur Boles tonight?" Ivy asked.

Matt's fingers tightened in a death grip around the steering wheel. "No, rest one more day. We'll confront him first thing in the morning. I want to do a little more homework before I approach him."

"Homework?"

"Research," Matt answered, although he didn't elaborate.

Ivy accepted his silence, anxious that he might be keeping information from her. But fatigue lines crisscrossed his face, and she realized he hadn't slept the night before because he'd stayed alert guarding her, so she didn't push him.

He stopped long enough at the diner to pick up two dinner trays again, and the scent of turkey and dressing filled the car as they drove on to the cabins. Inside, they ate in virtual silence, then Matt excused himself to shower.

Ivy stared at his back as he retreated into the bathroom, worry knotting her insides. Matt had withdrawn from her. But why? What had happened?

Two nights ago, they'd almost made love. The beautiful memory still taunted her with what-ifs. And when Matt had pulled her from the burning trailer, she'd felt his body trembling with fear. When he'd held her…she'd sensed that he wanted her.

Why did he keep resisting, continually holding her at a distance? Did he think if he made love to her she'd demand a commitment?

Granted, she thought she loved him, but she didn't expect him to return the sentiment.

Shadows from her nightmares threatened to steal into the cabin, but Ivy mentally blocked them. For one night, she simply wanted to forget that her traumatic past had brought her here. That her father hadn't loved her. That everyone deserted her.

That if she hadn't repressed her memories, then Matt wouldn't have suffered.

Tonight she wanted to feel alive again, and she wanted Matt to know that she loved him.

Even if she couldn't speak the words out loud, she could show him.

Summoning her courage, she tiptoed toward the bathroom and eased the door open. The hot spray of water clouded the room. Matt's clothes lay on the floor in a heap, the outline of his naked form silhouetted through the frosted shower door. Her heart stuttered.

But the need to touch Matt and hold him overwhelmed her, and she moved forward. He had his back toward her, his head turned upward, water sluicing down his throat and body. He looked tormented. Troubled. She eased the shower door open, her breath catching at the sight of his taut muscles and lean, strong body. So male. So perfect.

But anguish dug at her throat at the sight of the long gashes and jagged scars on his back. Dear heavens, what had happened to him in prison?

Matt suddenly jerked around, his eyes feral, his expression tortured as he grabbed her arms. It was almost as if he couldn't see her.

"Matt?"

He gripped her wrists so hard she thought her bones would snap.

"Matt, you're hurting me."

He suddenly blinked and stared at her in horror. "God, Ivy… I'm sorry," he said in a gruff whisper. "I…can't stand for anyone to sneak up behind me."

The truth dawned on her, and her stomach roiled. Then his eyes met hers and raw misery darkened the depths.

The need to take away his pain overrode her own feelings.

"I want to be with you," she said.

He dropped his head forward, rubbing his eyes as if to clear them, but mumbled no.

She gripped his wrists this time, and forced his hands away from his face. "Look at me, Matt."

He groaned. "Please, Ivy, go back in the den."

"No, I told you, I want to be with you." She released his hands, then slowly began to remove her clothes. Her shirt fell to the floor, and his eyes darted to the garment. Her bra went next, then her jeans and socks and underwear.

"Ivy…"

A second of shyness assaulted her. She'd never felt so vulnerable. Never thrown herself at a man. What if he didn't want her?

HE KNOCKED ON TALULAH'S door, his body jumpy with tension that needed to be released. Ivy had survived and Mahoney was hovering over her at that cabin. He should just finish them both off tonight. But he'd already taken enough chances the last two days. He needed to lie low for a few hours. Regroup. Rest. Figure out his next move.

Tomorrow he'd find a way to kill Mahoney and get Ivy.

Tonight, he'd satisfy his cravings with whatever choice Talulah had for him. Hell, Red Row was every man's fantasy come true. Beautiful, available women. Always ready when a man wanted. Great sex. No ties. And the girls would do anything he ordered.

Just like Lily Stanton years ago. Until she'd gotten greedy...

He knocked again, and lights flickered inside, the soft glow of a red light bathing the interior as the door opened.

Piles of blond hair topped her head in some kind of glittery comb concoction, but wispy tendrils escaped, feathering around her perfectly made-up face. She dotted perfume between her breasts as he entered.

"Come on in, sexy stranger. Talulah has just what you need."

"I hope so," he said in a low voice. "Because I'm feeling pretty needy."

Her light laughter floated through the air like music, and a sea of candles flickered on every piece of furniture in her bedroom. Talulah had been one of his first. He wondered if she remembered. Half hoped she didn't. That would be dangerous. Then again, he wanted her to remember. He had been good; she'd said so. One of her best pupils.

But he'd first had Lily Stanton, and she was pure heaven.

Talulah sprawled on top of the sheets, her skin glistening from bath oils, the flutter of the candlelight painting her in soft golden shadows. The red satin robe she wore parted, revealing luscious, plump breasts, and tight, red-tipped nipples. For a woman her age, she looked athletic and fit. Only the softening of her thighs told him that she was not the same young girl she'd been when he'd last seen her. Some things just got more beautiful with age, better with experience.

But those thighs had seen a lot of men over the years, and those bad times had carved tiny lines along her mouth. With a throaty sigh, she murmured, "Tell me your name."

He smiled and shook his head. "No names, just bodies touching."

She wiggled her eyebrows, picked up a long red feather, rose onto her knees and drew it along his cheek. Excitement stirred within him, pumping his blood through his body in a hot stream. She nipped at his shirt with her teeth, and his breath hissed out, ragged, uneven, sweat already beading on his lip, come already rising to the tip of his erection. He stripped off his clothes and tossed them to the floor, desire and pure lust rippling through him. Her gaze traveled down his chest, across his stomach to his cock. An appreciative smile tipped her ruby-red lips.

Her gaze rose to meet his while she circled one hand around his length.

"You know how I like it, Talulah."

Suddenly an odd look flashed into those age-old eyes. He grabbed her wrists, threw her facedown on the bed and tied her wrists to the bedposts. She made a small protest, then angled her head to search his face.

"Lily wouldn't let me take her this way," he said, the memory clear in his head of the last time he'd been with her.

Those blond eyebrows rose, the blue mascara above her eyes climbing upward as she twisted toward him. "Oh, my goodness, sugar…it can't be." She hesitated, recognition dawning as she licked her lips. "It is you, isn't it?"

He swallowed, his body as hard as a rock, his mind ticking away the inevitable.

"I can't believe you're here," Talulah whispered. "Your mama said you were dead…."

A rumble of laughter escaped him as he lowered himself onto the bed beside her and nudged her thigh with his dick. "Do I look dead, Talulah?"

Her appreciative gaze flew to his sex, then back to his face, but her smile disappeared. "I don't understand. You…where have you been all these years?"

"You shouldn't ask questions, Talulah."

Too late, awareness flooded her. Talulah knew she had made a mistake in recognizing him. He couldn't let her go now, not and take the chance she'd reveal his identity.

No, once he had his fill of her, it was bye-bye, Talulah.

CHAPTER SEVENTEEN

IVY DESERVED BETTER, but Matt's resistance shattered. He wanted her with a need so strong it defied logic. Watching her offering herself to him so unselfishly only stoked the fire burning in his body.

But she had seen his scars. Had seen his reaction...

He had to make her understand that sometimes the inner beast inside him snapped, that someday he might hurt her. Not that he'd intentionally do so, but if she came up behind him and the dark trapped him...well, sometimes he simply reacted.

"Ivy—"

"Shh." She licked her lips, the vulnerability of her innocence glowing softly in her sparkling eyes. And some other emotion—tenderness? Affection? Love?

No, he couldn't allow himself to believe in love. Not for a man like him.

But one night of touching, holding, intimacy...

How could he possibly turn away from her offering? After all, he had almost lost her once.

And he would lose her when this whole mess ended.

But tonight they could be together. Create a

beautiful memory for him to carry with him during the lonely nights ahead.

She gripped the edge of the shower door, and he drank his fill of her naked body as she climbed in the shower with him. Hot water sluiced off his back, running down his torso. Without speaking, she took the soft bath sponge, dotted it with soap and began to rub it over his chest. A shudder rippled through him, but he smiled and savored her gentle ministrations. Slowly, she swirled the soapy bubbles through his thick, coarse chest hair, over his nipples, then to his stomach. His muscles clenched as she trailed the sponge over his erection. Then she gently turned him around.

He swallowed hard, feeling raw and exposed, but she simply leaned up and kissed the soft, puckered scars on his back, trailing the soapy bubbles, then her fingers, then her lips over each wound that had been so deeply and violently embedded in his skin. He closed his eyes, willing her loving touches to heal him. Then something miraculous happened. His shame and pain slowly faded. Somehow Ivy magically made them float into the distance.

Her arms lowered, the sponge dropping to the floor as she spread her hands across his buttocks and massaged his cheeks. Pure hunger speared through him, and he whipped around, knowing he would never last if she tortured him further. He desperately wanted to touch her now. To feel her quiver in his arms before he finally made her his.

With a wicked smile, he retrieved the sponge and resoaped it. "Your turn, sugar."

She threw her head back to give him access, the moment of abandon unlocking yet another closed door to his emotions, and his heart opened. In all his life, he'd never seen anything as beautiful as Ivy with her long blond hair damp with water, soap dribbling over her puckered nipples, her pale throat glistening with moisture as he bent to kiss it. His hands trailed over her breasts, circling each nipple until she groaned and arched into him. He suckled them next, discarding the sponge to slide his soapy hands over her flat stomach, then lower into the curls at the juncture of her thighs. She clung to his arms, moaning as he parted her legs and slid first one finger, then a second inside her. Wet and panting, he finally kissed her mouth, catching her sighs of rising euphoria into his own throat as he moved his fingers deep inside her, then withdrew to tease the rosebud of her desire. She stiffened and deepened the kiss, pressing herself into his hand as she cupped his sex and began to stroke his length. His cock was engorged to the point of exploding. But sanity emerged a second before she guided him inside her.

"Condom," he whispered.

She hesitated, clenching back her orgasm, as he jerked open the door and reached inside his jeans pocket. Seconds later, sheathed and anxious, he lifted her hips, thrust inside and felt her splinter into a thousand quivering pieces as pleasure rippled through her. Her cry of ecstasy heated his raw desire, but he hesitated. She was so tight.... She was a virgin. The realization humbled him. He didn't deserve her. Why had she chosen him as her first? "Ivy?"

"Shh, it's okay. Don't stop now, Matt. I love you."

His heart twisted. Emotions pummeled him. He didn't deserve her, but Ivy's whisper of love filled his soul with hope, longing, and he pumped inside her harder, thrusting in and out, deeper, deeper, pulling her hips closer until he could go no deeper, until she collapsed against his chest in a ragged heap, whispering his name and her love as he poured himself inside her.

THE WATER HAD CHILLED, yet Ivy's body still burned from Matt's touch as they rinsed off, climbed from the shower, and he wrapped a big towel around her. His dark eyes looked hooded as he gazed down at her, but a smile curved his lips, and she dropped a kiss on his neck, catching a water droplet.

She hadn't meant to confess her love out loud, and wondered what he was thinking.

"Ivy—"

"Shh, you don't have to say anything," she whispered, reaching up to thumb through his dark hair. "I can't help the way I feel, Matt." She kissed him tenderly. "And I can't help but want you again."

His body went rock hard, and he quickly ran a towel over his damp body. With another deep growl, he scooped her into his arms and carried her to the bed. When he'd eased her onto the mattress, his eyes skated over her, his look of male hunger triggering need within her again.

I can't help wanting you, too," he said. His fingers

felt like feathers as he gently trailed them along her cheek. "But I don't want to hurt you, Ivy. God knows you don't deserve having another man do that."

She kissed his palm. "You couldn't hurt me, Matt. Not ever."

His jaw tightened, but his hands remained gentle as he peeled back the covers, discarded his towel and climbed in bed beside her. Ivy turned into his arms, traced her fingers along his jaw, then lower to the thick dark hair on his chest, over a jagged scar, then down to his stomach. His muscles clenched, his sex pulsing harder as she explored him.

He flipped her to her back and rose above her, pausing long enough to sheath himself and stare into her eyes before he thrust into her. She groaned and gripped his arms, clinging to him as he lowered his mouth and kissed her again. The kisses were tender, but quickly turned urgent as the heat between them built to a raging inferno. His hands roamed everywhere, teasing, torturing, and his body filled hers to the core, joining them so deeply that she knew Matt had become a part of her forever. She would always remember his touch, his scent, the feel of his hard body firmly embedded inside her. Love soared in her heart as the first tremors of her release rocked through her and her muscles clenched around him. And when he cried out her name in a gruff whisper, she vowed that nothing would tear them apart, that Matt would be hers forever.

MATT CRADLED IVY IN his arms, closing his eyes as he listened to her breathing relax into the slow rhythm of sleep. She had said she loved him.

Emotions choked him even as he warned himself it didn't matter. Ivy deserved more than he had to offer. Besides, he couldn't even think of a future until they found her parents' killer. Keeping Ivy safe was his first priority.

Then he had to make something of his life so he would be worthy of her.

But he couldn't do anything until morning. So he twined his legs with hers and allowed himself to fall asleep with her in his arms. If he only had a night or two with Ivy, he intended to savor every minute.

A.J. RESTED HIS BOOTED feet on his desk and rubbed at his weary eyes, every minute that passed bringing more tension to his already aching body. From the cell block in the back room they'd had built to hold juveniles, Tommy Werth and Clete McClinton howled, bawled and cussed. One of them sounded like a damn baby, completely freaked out from coming off his high. A.J. had been forced to call a paramedic to check on the stupid kid, and had been warned not to leave the boys alone. One or both might be suicidal.

It would serve the little pricks right if he threw a rope in the cell and left 'em with it. He sure as hell wouldn't miss their scrawny asses. They'd cussed and beaten the walls for the first hour, then taken to moaning and screeching promises vile enough to blister the paint on the scarred concrete walls.

A.J. massaged his neck, checking the time. Pritchard was supposed to come back and relieve him in an hour. A.J. had to have a few hours of sleep before morning. All hell had broken loose after he'd brought in the boys. Word of their arrest and the river cult had somehow spread to the county commissioner. The governor had heard about it, and the feds were sending over agents to investigate the town. Apparently they had had their eyes on Kudzu Hollow and the mysterious crime sprees over the last few years, and thought A.J. needed help.

He needed help, all right. He needed a way out of this town, away from the madness.

But there seemed to be no relief in sight.

In the morning the place would be covered with feds and reporters.

And he still had to worry about Mahoney and Ivy Stanton.

The telephone rang, and he shook his head, praying it wasn't another problem. But as soon as he picked up the line, a shrill cry pierced the silence.

"Sheriff…" the woman hiccuped, "this is Chantel. I…just got to Talulah's and…she's dead, Sheriff. *Dead.* Someone killed her!"

A.J. cursed and dropped his booted feet onto the floor with a thud. "You're there now?"

"Yes, at her trailer," she sobbed. "And—and she's all bloody…."

Hell. First the boys' mothers, now a hooker. They couldn't be connected, could they?

"I'll get out there right away," A.J. said. "Chantel, you need to stick around and answer some questions."

But the line had already died, indicating Chantel had decided not to wait.

Probably best for her. For all A.J. knew, the killer might still be in the trailer park, primed for another victim.

A SHORT FEW HOURS later, Matt woke up, more rested and energized than he'd felt in ages. Having Ivy next to him had given him a peace he'd never thought he'd experience again. With that peace and elation also came arousal, and anticipation.

Along with hope, which he tried not to dwell on.

But the fact that she'd chosen him as her first made his pride swell, replacing some of the bitterness in his soul. He had felt connected with Ivy years ago, and now that connection had grown stronger. But would it breach when she learned the truth about him and her mother? No, she didn't have to know.

But he had to find the killer before he attacked Ivy again. Adrenaline kicked in, and he rose and headed to the kitchen nook. He made a pot of coffee, then sat down and reread the transcripts of his trial. Next, he jotted down notes on what he'd learned so far, drawing lines to the suspects he had in mind.

Ivy's mother had entertained men from Red Row. From what Ivy remembered, Matt thought it likely

Arthur had been one of her clients. And he'd seen Arthur at Red Row recently. He'd also been at the trailer fire.

Larry Lumbar? Matt scribbled his name, but had no real information on the man. Unless he'd fingered Matt to cover his own crime?

Who else?

Maybe a person who had something to do with the real estate deal. Matt needed to stop by the county courthouse and explore the possibility, find out how much property the Stantons had owned. If they still held the deed to the junkyard, that property rightfully belonged to Ivy. She could sell it if she wanted.

But if they'd owned other property that had been sold, then who had profited?

When Ivy awakened, he'd ask her about the land. Maybe the profits from a sale had gone into an account or trust fund for her. Or perhaps the woman who'd raised her had used the money to take care of her.

He checked his watch. Damn. He couldn't talk to anyone at the courthouse for at least a couple of hours. Restless, he opened the front door of the cabin to check the perimeter, searching the dense woods and shadows for signs that someone might be lurking nearby. The morning paper lay on the stoop, so he picked it up, his eyes narrowing on the lead story.

Two local boys arrested for murdering their mothers. Both are thought to belong to a river cult in Kudzu Hollow. Drugs have been confiscated and are thought to have been a precipitator of the crimes. Sheriff Boles stated that he will be working with county and state officials to put an end to the violence in Kudzu Hollow, as well as destroy the cult and disband the drug operations.

Matt glanced at the neighboring headline and groaned. Kudzu Hollow's Own Resident Mistress Strangled. Talulah. Dead?

What was going on around here?

He frowned, something about the murders nagging at him as he walked back inside. Arthur Boles had to be the connection. Matt would question him today, push him for information. And maybe even a confession.

The bed squeaked, and Ivy roused, looking sleepy and tousled, well loved and at least partially rested. But the bruises on her neck stood out stark and purple in the morning light, renewing Matt's anger.

His gut twisted, and he started toward her. But if he touched her again, they'd end up back in bed, and he had to focus on this case. Find out the truth.

Then make something of himself.

It was the only way he and Ivy had any kind of future. A future that he suddenly wanted with every fiber of his being.

IVY HAD FELT EMPTY and alone without Matt in the bed beside her. She offered him a tentative smile, and heat flared in his eyes, setting her heart aflutter. But the darkness flashed back a second later.

Matt gestured toward the paper. "A.J. arrested two boys in that cult for killing their mothers. One of them might be the boy who attacked you."

A chill rippled through Ivy. She hoped A.J. had caught the youth.

Matt poured a cup of coffee and handed it to her. "I want to talk to Arthur Boles this morning," he said. "Then do some research at the courthouse."

"I'll get dressed and go with you. I want to hear what Arthur Boles has to say about my mother."

An odd look twitched in Matt's face, but he nodded.

A few minutes later, Ivy hugged a second cup of coffee to her as Matt drove into Kudzu Hollow. A gray haze had settled over the sky, the onset of a winter storm evident in the cold mist hanging in the air. Her cell phone rang and she checked it, frowning when George's name appeared. She didn't want to deal with him now, so she let the recording take a message.

"Who was that?" he asked, wondering if the caller was the man who'd threatened her.

"George Riddon," she said quietly, "a man I work with. I'll phone him back later."

He let the comment slide, although her clipped response and refusal to answer the call spiked his curiosity. What if the two of them had a personal relationship he'd stepped into the middle of? He didn't want to pursue that now. Couldn't think of Ivy with another man.

"Ivy, do you know anything about the property your parents owned?"

She shrugged. "No. Why?"

"The woman who raised you never mentioned monies collected from a real estate sale? Maybe she used the funds to raise you. Or maybe she put them in a trust fund for you."

"Miss Nellie never mentioned it. And the lawyer who handled her affairs said there was nothing but her house when she died." Ivy sipped her coffee. "What's this about, Matt?"

"Just a theory." His lips thinned to a grim line. "I'm looking for a motive that might explain your parents' deaths."

She grew quiet for a minute, obviously contemplating the possibilities. "Arthur Boles worked in real estate, didn't he?"

Matt nodded, sped around the curve past the new subdivision, and drove to the more affluent side of Kudzu Hollow. They passed a large white building at the top of one of the ridges that looked as if it had once been a business, but was shut down. She wondered what it had been.

"I don't remember this part of town," Ivy said.

"Boles owns an estate on the river."

She swallowed, studying her surroundings as she spotted the black wrought-iron gate surrounding the estate. Boles's antebellum house was reminiscent of a picture from *Southern Living* magazine. Set off from the main road, the two-mile drive was flanked by dogwood trees and live oaks.

Ivy frowned, surprised to see A.J.'s squad car in

front of the house. Facing Arthur was daunting, but having his son present unsettled her even more.

A few minutes later, a butler with white hair and a curt expression answered the door. Loud, heated voices echoed through the hallway as they approached the study. The voices quieted immediately when the butler knocked, and they entered the massive paneled study. A.J. and his father stood on opposite sides of the room, staring at each other warily.

"We need to talk," Matt said without preamble.

"Look, Mahoney," A.J. began, "I've gotta go. I have two boys who need to be arraigned, a dead hooker, and the feds are on their way here today to ask questions."

"I think you should stick around," Matt said. "Hear what your father has to say."

Momentary panic flickered in A.J.'s eyes, and Ivy stiffened. What did he know that he wasn't telling?

Then Ivy glanced from A.J. to his father, and the air caught in her lungs as another distant memory surfaced. Arthur Boles had been at her mother's house the night she died.

But so had A.J.

ARTHUR BOLES SHOT Matt an intimidating look, but Matt didn't waver.

"What's this about?" Boles asked.

"The night the Stantons died," Matt said in a cold voice. "Ivy remembered that you were at the house. I think you were working a land deal back then, and that you had an affair with Lily with the intentions of swaying her to sell for less money than the property's value. Either she caught on to your scam, or she wanted more money. Maybe she even threatened to expose your affair—"

"What Lily Stanton and I had was not an affair," the older man snarled.

Matt's heart hammered in his chest. He knew what Boles was going to say, but the truth would hurt Ivy.

Hoping to protect her, he hurriedly cut off Boles before he could continue. "Did she threaten to expose you—is that what happened?"

Boles shook his head, a bead of sweat trickling down his jaw.

"My father didn't kill anyone," A.J. snapped. "You're way out of line, Matt."

"Am I?" he asked. "Ivy saw him in her house with her mother that night. And I've seen him with Talulah a couple of times since I've been back, and now Talulah's dead. Maybe Talulah knew the truth and threatened to expose him, too."

"Don't be crazy," Arthur shouted.

"He was standing beside her outside Ivy's trailer at the fire." Matt's voice rose a decibel. "I think he was afraid Ivy would remember, and he tried to kill her to keep her quiet."

"That's ridiculous," A.J. hissed.

"Is it?" Matt asked.

Ivy cleared her throat. "Then if you didn't kill my mother, Mr. Boles, maybe your son did, and you covered for him."

Matt jerked his head toward her, confused.

A.J. pounced toward Ivy. "Shut up, that's not true."

"You were there, too," Ivy said, her voice low, distant. "I remember now. I saw you. You were in bed with my mother…."

A.J. shook his head, but Matt read the blind panic in his eyes. He'd suspected Arthur Boles Sr. but not his son. Dear God, had his own best friend killed the Stantons and left Ivy without a family—then let Matt take the fall?

CHAPTER EIGHTEEN

BITS AND PIECES OF THAT night flashed back like fire-flies flickering in the darkness. Ivy had woken up and seen A.J. in the bedroom with her mother. She'd heard the noises, the ugly sounds of the two of them grunting like rutting animals. Then A.J. had chased Ivy away.

Later, she'd awakened again, and when her father came in, she'd seen Arthur Boles helping A.J. out the back door. Panicked and frightened, she'd turned away from the men, then had spotted her mother lying on the floor in a pool of blood.

She dropped onto the floor and sobbed, pulling at her mother's arm, trying to wake her. She couldn't be dead. No, her mother wouldn't leave her.

Her father had grabbed her and forced her to look at the blood…. "It's all your fault, Ivy. You're poison…."

"Ivy?" Matt slid a hand to her arm. "Are you okay?"

She nodded, the image of A.J. and his father running away from her mother's dead body haunting her. "You killed her, then you left her there to die," she whispered. "How could you just leave her that way?"

"It wasn't like that," Arthur Boles argued.

"Dad's right," A.J. said in a hoarse voice. "I...did sleep with your mother, but I was drunk, and then I passed out. After that, I don't know exactly what happened."

Ivy shuddered and backed away, her stomach twisting into a knot.

"My son did nothing wrong," Arthur said. "Your mama was a whore. Half the men in this town slept with her."

Shock immobilized Ivy. "No...no, my mother wasn't—"

"Yes, she was," A.J. said sharply. "She made money on her back while you went to school, Ivy. And sometimes at night, she'd sneak in more customers. She liked the money, she liked men and she was damn good at seducing them."

Ivy swung toward Matt. He had to deny it. Tell her it wasn't true. Her mother was a good person. She'd loved Ivy. She'd baked cookies with her, collected Santa Clauses and told her stories about the Ivy League universities. "Matt, no, they're wrong—"

"Ivy..." Matt's own voice broke, the denial failing to materialize.

"You knew?" she rasped.

His eyes flickered with guilt as he reached for her, but she yanked her arm away.

"Of course he knew," A.J. hissed. "The two of us went to Red Row together for our first time. Who do you think broke us both in, Ivy?"

Ivy gasped.

Regret and guilt filled Matt's eyes. "Listen to me, Ivy—"

"No." She shook her head and took another step backward, disgust pouring through her in waves of nausea. The three of them were repulsive. "I can't believe you, Matt. God, I trusted you."

She had fallen in love with him. She'd even thrown herself at him.

And he had slept with her mother.

Pain, raw and fiery, rippled through her, and she clutched her abdomen and doubled over. A sob welled in her throat, the image of Matt in bed with her mother racing in her mind like a horror show.

She had to get out of there. Away from all three of them. Away from the sight of Matt reaching for her, trying to placate her when he'd denied her the truth about her mother.

And that he had taken her mother to bed before Ivy had jumped in the sack with him.

A cry wrenched from her as she turned and fled, fighting the bile rising to her throat. Outside, rain splattered her hair and clothes as she threw herself into Matt's SUV and groped for the key. Thunder roared above, and lightning shot its jagged line across the hood. Matt raced outside and grabbed the car door. "Stop, Ivy, listen—"

"Don't, Matt. I…if you lied about that, maybe you've lied about everything. Maybe you did kill my parents."

PAIN STABBED AT MATT as Ivy sped away. He had to go after her. Explain. Make her forgive him.

But her accusations stung so deeply that his feet remained rooted to the concrete. It would always be this way for him—people would never fully trust him. Why had he thought Ivy was different?

Rain drenched his face and ran into his eyes, and he finally latched onto the anger and bitterness that had driven him for so long, spun around and headed back inside. The Boleses had some explaining to do. If his former buddy and A.J.'s father had killed the Stantons, they had to pay.

Their booming voices pierced the hall as he strode back into the study.

"I hope you're proud of yourself, you asshole," Matt shouted.

A.J. jammed his hands into the pockets of his uniform. "She had to know the truth before she attacked me. Her mother was a slut and you know it."

"Did you kill Lily Stanton?" Matt asked between clenched teeth.

For a second, A.J.'s face paled to a deathly white. "I don't remember what happened. I got drunk and blacked out."

"Shut up," Arthur barked. "Don't say another word, A.J."

"Why? So you can cover his ass?" Matt asked. "Is that what happened that night? A.J. got drunk and killed Lily, then you had to step in and protect him by setting me up?"

Red stained Boles's cheeks. "He's my son. I had to protect him."

"So why did you do it, A.J.?" Matt asked. "It wasn't about the land deal, and Lily Stanton couldn't have blackmailed you. You were just a kid. Did you kill her just for kicks?"

"He told you, he had sex with her, then blacked out," Arthur interjected. "When he woke up, Lily Stanton was dead. He panicked and called me, so I drove over and got him. End of story."

"If that's the truth, then why didn't you speak up fifteen years ago?" Matt asked.

A.J. looked at him deadpan. "When they arrested you, I...thought maybe you had done it."

The blood roared in Matt's ears. "That's a lie." He glanced from father to son. "But I get it now—you actually thought your dad might have killed her."

A.J. refused to look at his father.

Boles's voice thundered across the study. "Is that true, A.J.? You thought that I killed the woman?" Arthur dropped his head into his hands. "Hell, son, I almost set fire to those cabins to protect you, and you were innocent. I could have killed Ivy."

A.J. shrugged, a helpless look on his face. "I'm sorry, Dad. But I didn't call you that night. You were already there when I woke up, and Lily was dead."

Caught in a lie, Boles scrubbed a hand through his thinning hair. "I knew you were drinking, and that you might be in trouble. Dammit, it wasn't the first time. You never knew how to hold your liquor."

He wheezed a breath. "Anyway, I went driving around looking for you, then I saw your car at the Stantons'. I was trying to arrange this land deal with her and didn't want you to screw it up by getting involved with her. When I went in, I smelled whiskey and saw all that goddamn blood. You were passed out cold, so I dragged your butt out of there."

"And you thought I'd killed her?" A.J. asked.

Arthur stared down at his fisted hands but refused to answer.

Matt's head spun. He wasn't sure who to believe. All these years, both men thought they'd been protecting the other, yet each had suspected the other was guilty.

So which one of them was lying now? Which one had killed the Stantons?

And if neither of them had killed Lily and her husband, who had?

IVY FELT AS IF SOMEONE had driven a stake into her heart. Her chest throbbed with the effort to breathe, the sobs racking her body consuming her remaining energy. Blinded by tears, she hit a rut in the road, nearly lost control and swerved, barely missing an oncoming truck. It blared its horn, and she jumped and overcorrected, skidding near the rail where the mountain ridge dropped off hundreds of feet below. Ivy screamed, then slammed into it with such force that fiery sparks spewed from the car hood, and the metal rail buckled. She held her breath at the sound of tires screeching and gears grinding, and heaved in relief when the SUV finally lurched to a stop.

Hands trembling, she dropped her head forward, closed her eyes, shuddering. She should have listened to Miss Nellie and stayed away. A car zoomed past, and she jerked upright, praying Matt hadn't followed her. She had to pull herself together, go back to the cabin and pack, then leave town right away. She couldn't stay one more minute in a town where people thought her mother was a hooker, where men like Arthur and A.J. Boles lived.

And she couldn't bear to stay another second in the cabin she had shared with Matt. Not and smell the lingering scent of his body, or sleep in the bed where she'd proclaimed her love to the man. She felt dirty all over, sick and aching. She'd have to shower, wash off the stench of his hands and his lies.

But the mere idea of a shower only reminded her of the night before when she'd climbed inside with him and nearly begged him to take her. Her misery tripled, running so deep she thought that surely his betrayal had sliced open an artery. A horn blasted the air, and Ivy jerked her head up to see a pickup truck approaching. She was well off the road, but didn't feel like dealing with anyone now, even a kind stranger, if one actually existed in this town.

Shaking all over, she inhaled several deep breaths, determined to make it back to the cabin and pack before Matt could catch her. Then again, he might not. He had his answers now—Arthur Boles and his son had killed her parents, then framed Matt.

She had just been a pawn to him, used to find out

the truth. And she'd thrown in a night of hot sex for free, volunteered it on her own. How could she really blame Matt?

She had been the fool. She had proclaimed her love. Matt had never made any promises.

No, he'd simply lied and taken what she'd offered without bothering to fill her in on the— No, she couldn't think about it again or she would be too ill to drive back to the cabin.

And she would survive, dammit.

She flipped the key again, and the engine caught. Thank God. Shifting into gear, she hit the accelerator, swerved onto the road and blinked away tears. In an hour, she'd be out of Kudzu Hollow. She couldn't leave this godforsaken place fast enough.

Then somehow, she had to figure out a way to forget Matt Mahoney.

MATT DESPERATELY WANTED to make Ivy believe him, but she hadn't had enough faith in him to listen to an explanation. Just as his mother hadn't years ago, and others hadn't when he'd returned to Kudzu Hollow. And now that he suspected both A.J. and his father had had something to do with the Stantons' deaths, he wasn't about to leave them alone. Ivy needed time to calm down, then maybe she'd listen to the truth about him and Red Row.

At least if Arthur or A.J. turned out to be the killer, Ivy was safe.

A.J.'s phone buzzed, and he cursed as he glanced at the caller ID. "It's the damn feds. They're at my office. I have to go now."

"We're all going," Matt said. "Then we can sort out the past."

Arthur and A.J. exchanged furtive looks. "I'm calling my lawyer to meet us there," Arthur said.

Lumbar's offer to help Matt right the wrong from years ago echoed in his head. Maybe his own lawyer had evidence that he hadn't pursued, evidence that would pinpoint the killer's identity. "I'm calling Lumbar, as well," Matt stated.

A.J. grunted and headed to his car, and Matt and his father followed. Arthur grabbed his cell phone, punched in his lawyer's number and arranged for him to meet them at the station.

The ride to the station was strained. A.J. worked his mouth as he drove, the rain drilling into the ground.

Matt remembered the other arrests. "Do you know for sure that those boys killed their mothers?"

"We've got pretty solid evidence. DNA from both boys on their mother's bodies. They were also both part of that river cult. One of the boys' sweatshirts was ripped. He might have been the one who attacked Ivy."

Matt clenched his jaw. "I'd like a minute alone with him."

"I can't allow that, Matt," A.J. said. "The law will take care of him."

He made a sarcastic sound. "I don't have much faith in the law, A.J., especially with you as sheriff."

A.J. shot him a hurt look. "I…I'm sorry, Matt."

"It's too late for apologies," he snapped. "But

if you're any kind of man, you could at least speak up now and tell the truth."

He cut his eyes to the back at Arthur Boles, but he remained tight-lipped, his hands fisted.

A.J. looked at the road and clammed up tight. Matt grimaced and said a silent prayer that Lumbar had some concrete evidence to uncover the real killer's identity.

Then Matt had to find Ivy and make things right with her.

He just hoped to hell she could forgive him for that night at Red Row....

THE SUV BOUNCED over the ruts in the road, the windows rattling with the wind. Ivy swiped at her tears, barreled down the graveled drive and careened to a stop a few feet away from her Jetta. Desperate to escape, she bolted to the cabin, then frantically began throwing her clothes into it, not bothering to fold or arrange the articles neatly as she normally did. When she'd filled the suitcase, she stuffed her notes into her briefcase, threw her camera bag over her shoulder and turned toward the door. A knock sounded, and she started, yelping at the unexpected pounding. Was it Matt?

She didn't want to see him now. Not ever again.

"Ivy? It's me, George, let me in."

Hissing out a breath of relief, she vaulted forward. She might have avoided him before but if Matt showed up, George would be a good buffer. And he could help expedite her escape.

Striving for an emotionless expression, she threw open the door. "George, what are you doing here?"

He looked frantic, his short blond hair shoved haphazardly in different directions as if he'd been running his hands through it. "I've been worried sick about you," he said, his voice strained. "The news reported that the feds have come here to investigate all the crimes. They said a woman was attacked by some teenage cult. When you didn't answer your phone earlier, I panicked and called the hospital. A nurse told me you were admitted yesterday but that you were released." He gripped her arms, his eyes wild. "I drove here as fast as I could, Ivy. Are you all right?"

She nodded, the concern in his voice triggering her emotions. A tear escaped, but she swallowed hard to hold back another round.

"I need to get out of here," she said in an anguished voice. "I have to leave Kudzu Hollow, George. It was a m-mistake for me to come here. I should have listened to Miss Nellie."

"I told you that." He bent down and grabbed her suitcase. "Come on, I don't want you here a minute longer, either."

She carried her camera case and briefcase, while he followed with her suitcase. Reaching her car, she screeched to a halt. "Someone slashed my tires, George!" A deep trembling started within her, vibrating through every cell in her body. "Someone wanted me to be stranded." She turned and peered around the cabin, then toward the thick woods and shadows. "He must be here watching me. He was waiting for me to come back alone."

George grabbed her arm. "Come on, get in my car, Ivy. I'll drive you back to Chattanooga. We can send for your car later."

Ivy nodded, unable to escape the eerie feeling that the killer was nearby, watching her. That another second and he would have had her exactly where he'd wanted her.

Alone and vulnerable with nowhere to run.

HE HAD HER NOW.

A slow smile of satisfaction curled his mouth as Ivy climbed in the car. He inhaled her scent, her breath, eyed the tears still visible on her cheek. Something had happened to upset her. Something he guessed had to do with that Mahoney guy.

Something that had torn down her defenses and left her vulnerable.

And he had pounced.

She still had no idea what had happened that night with her parents. Still didn't remember that he'd been there.

But she would.

He knew it without a doubt.

And he couldn't keep pretending otherwise, worrying when the thin dam that held her memories at bay would crack and crumble, destroying him

She settled inside his car, and the rattle of her shaky breathing filled the quiet. He would ask her what had happened, but doubted she'd confide in him yet. But he'd comfort her, anyway. Take the moment to soothe her worries until she trusted him again.

And then he'd have his way with her. Show her exactly how he felt. How much he'd wanted her all these months and years. How much he wanted her now.

Then the silence would be broken.

She would be his, just like Lily.

Then she would have to die.

CHAPTER NINETEEN

MATT GRIMACED AT the sight of the two federal agents waiting inside A.J.'s office. He half expected them to throw the cuffs on him and arrest him, although he certainly wasn't the criminal here. But old habits were hard to break, and years of being abused by the system bred distrust. He had to make them understand what was going on. And he had to make sure Ivy was safe. Even if she wanted nothing more to do with him.

A.J. glared at the suited men, obviously angry at their interference. Introductions were stilted and cautious.

"Special Agent Lucas Gentry and Special Agent Karl Blackberry."

"Sheriff Boles." He gestured toward his father and introduced him. Arthur's lawyer arrived, and Arthur pulled him aside to fill him in.

Matt squared his shoulders and introduced himself.

"What are you doing here, Mahoney?" Agent Blackberry asked.

Matt braced himself for the inquisition, then explained his reasons for coming to Kudzu Hollow, and the threats to Ivy. "I think everything going on here might be related. The Stantons' murders. The recent crimes. But I haven't figured out the connection yet." He hesitated, waiting for A.J. to explain his relationship to Lily Stanton. But the man said nothing.

"Mr. Boles and the sheriff both admit being at Lily Stanton's house the night she died," Matt said.

Agents Gentry and Blackberry exchanged interested looks. "Go on."

"Lily Stanton was a hooker," Arthur said. "My son simply paid for services rendered."

"Then I got drunk and passed out," A.J. said, nearly stuttering. "I—didn't kill the Stantons."

"What about the land deal?" Matt asked, still unclear about the details.

"Land deal?" Agent Gentry asked.

Arthur shrugged but cast his eyes downward toward his fisted hands, then strode to the window. "I work in real estate. I connected Lily with this developer from Nashville who wanted to buy property around here. She intended to sell the junkyard and take the money and leave town."

So she could move Ivy to a better place, Matt realized.

"What happened?" Agent Gentry asked.

"She died," Boles said quietly. "The developer bought her property and the land next to the junkyard. He didn't build on it, though, just held on to it for a few years."

"Why didn't he build?" Agent Blackberry asked.

Arthur hesitated, until his lawyer nodded for him to answer.

Agent Gentry cut in. "Tell the truth, Mr. Boles. We've been watching this town for a while. And when your son arrested these last two boys, we took a look at the drugs he confiscated."

Boles's eyebrows shot up in surprise.

"The lab faxed us results of the analysis of the drugs, and we've discovered some interesting properties in the mixture," Agent Blackberry continued. "Reason for us to take a deeper look into the town here. Especially the property where the marijuana was grown."

"What are you looking for?" A.J. asked in a wary voice.

"We're not certain yet," Agent Blackberry said. "But we have a team ready to interrogate the residents. And we intend to take soil samples where the boys grew this weed."

Matt suddenly remembered seeing that empty scientific research building on his way to Arthur's. He'd read articles in prison about chemicals being dumped illegally in rural areas, and how the dangerous toxins had been absorbed into the water and soil, causing birth defects. Erratic, violent behavior in children who'd ingested or inhaled the chemicals over long periods of time had also been cited. Was it possible...

"The original developer who bought the property didn't build because a chemical company was dumping toxic wastes on the land?" Matt asked.

The agents perked up with interest, but Arthur dropped his head forward, sighing in defeat. "That's correct."

"You knew about this illegal dumping and didn't report it?" Matt pressed.

The older man nodded. "But after a few years, the research company folded."

"And no one was harmed, so what's the big deal?" A.J. said, defending his father.

Matt let the comment slide. "So you bought the property and built a subdivision on it?"

Arthur rubbed an invisible spot on his tie. "Yes. The developer who bought the property sold it to me. I thought any effects of the chemicals would have long since disintegrated."

Matt frowned, realization dawning as he recalled Lady Bella Rue's comments. "Both those boys lived in the new subdivision built on the property near the junkyard, and so did most of the other kids who attacked their families the past few years." He turned back to the federal agents. "You should check the land. Those chemicals might be responsible for the erratic behavior of the kids who live there. If the dangerous substances were absorbed into the water or soil, or even the trees used to build the log houses, then they could still be harmful." He continued, speculating out loud. "All the reports show that the crimes occur during heavy bouts of rain. What if the wood used to build the log houses is diseased? Maybe there's some kind of dangerous mold or bacteria growing inside it, and the rain accentuates it and brings out the spores."

Agent Gentry muttered in agreement, and Arthur Boles shifted uncomfortably.

"You know something about this, don't you?" Matt asked, turning to the real estate agent.

"I…no, but I was afraid it might be connected," he admitted. "I just didn't understand how."

Agent Gentry unpocketed his cell phone and began to punch in numbers. "I'm ordering an environmental team out here right away to check the land, water and those houses. If you're right, Mahoney, you might have just discovered the connection to all these crimes and saved lives."

Matt hoped he was right, but a bad premonition tugged at his gut. The developer… Boles hadn't mentioned who he was. What if he was the person who'd killed Ivy's parents? No, it was more likely that some muscle man from the chemical company was responsible, someone who'd wanted to protect the business even though it had gone belly-up.

Then Ivy might still be in danger, and she was alone, upset and vulnerable.

Matt called the cabin on his cell, and got no answer, so he punched in her cell number, but she didn't answer that, either. Panic hit him. "Who owned the chemical company?"

Boles cleared his throat. "A man named Russ Kintrell. The company was a small start-up research operation, but like I said, it folded years ago."

Agent Blackberry handed him a pen and paper. "Write down Kintrell's contact information."

Boles scribbled a phone number, and Blackberry snapped it up. "I'm going to pick him up and bring him in for questioning."

Matt stood. "I'm going with you."

IVY'S NERVES ZINGED with apprehension when George veered off the main road leading out of town, onto a dirt one that led down to the river. At first she thought they were going to Lady Bella Rue's, but he passed the old woman's shanty and turned onto yet another even more isolated road that seemingly went nowhere but deeper into the bowels of the woods. The gray clouds roiled above, warning of another storm, and wind whipped through the bare trees, swirling leaves and debris across the marshy ground.

"Where are you going?" she asked, suddenly nervous. He'd been acting odd ever since they'd gotten in the car. Checking over his back. Looking at his watch. Acting unusually quiet and sullen.

"I did some research on this town myself, and heard about a place off this road that we might want to use in the magazine."

"What kind of place?" Ivy asked.

"A haunted cabin," he said, an odd tinge to his voice. "According to the legend, a young boy died here. After that, his brother went crazy."

Ivy glanced through the shadowy woods. The tall trees and mountain ridges suddenly seemed ominous, the idea of visiting a haunted house sent a shudder through her. "We have enough for the article, George. Let's just leave town and go back to Chattanooga."

"Oh, but we're so close to it, Ivy. They say if you stand in the cabin, you can hear tormented cries at night. Cries of him losing his mind, cries of the brother dying."

Ivy hugged her arms around her middle. "Does anyone live there now?"

He shook his head. "The cabin has been deserted for years. But I thought you should see it and take some photographs."

His tone sent alarm bells ringing through her. "Why, George? I told you, we have enough material for the magazine spread."

He reached across the console and pressed his hand over hers. "Because the cabin belonged to Miss Nellie."

Ivy gaped at him in shock. "Miss Nellie? She never told me..." Her voice trailed off as faint snatches of conversations with the older woman speared through the black holes of her memory. "Miss Nellie did say that she'd lost a son when he was young."

"But she never mentioned the second son?" he asked, one eyebrow lifted.

Ivy swallowed hard, sorting through other conversations. "No, never."

A bitter laugh escaped him, echoing off the inside of the car. "No, she never talked about her other child. She was too ashamed of him. She decided he was crazy, so she sent him away."

Ivy's stomach tightened. "Where did she send him?"

"A mental facility where they locked him up, tied him down and beat him. And sometimes they gave him drugs that made his mind spin out of control."

Ivy gasped. "Oh, my heavens, that's horrible."

Tension vibrated between them as the first stirrings of fear gripped her. "Who told you this, George? I didn't realize you knew Miss Nellie."

"Oh, I knew her very well." He angled his head toward her just as he bounced over a rut in the road and broke through a clearing to a dilapidated old cabin set on the edge of the mountain. "You see, Ivy, I'm the forgotten son."

MATT TRIED AGAIN TO PHONE Ivy, but still she didn't answer. Tension tightened every muscle in his body as he closed his phone. She probably wasn't answering because she didn't want to talk to him, he reminded himself, but still worry clawed at him.

Agent Blackberry maneuvered his sedan over the mountain to another small town called Ridgeview, noted for its scenic views of the valley and river. "What's wrong?" he asked.

Matt explained his concern for Ivy. "We have to find her parents' killer or she'll never be safe."

Blackberry nodded, then turned onto a long drive flanked by massive trees, which ended at a huge, two-story Georgian mansion. "Apparently Kintrell has done well for himself financially," the agent stated as they climbed out. Seconds later, he rang the doorbell, while Matt tapped his foot impatiently.

He was antsy to complete this interview and find Ivy. Finally, a maid clad in a uniform greeted them at the door. "Special Agent Blackberry from the FBI," the agent said, then gestured toward Matt. "And this is Matt Mahoney. I need to speak to Mr. Kintrell."

The maid looked them both up and down, her

nervous gaze shifting as if she might argue, but then she obviously decided she couldn't stop the FBI, so gestured for them to enter. "He's in his study. Please follow me."

As soon as they entered the stately room and introduced themselves, Agent Blackberry explained the situation, including their suspicions about the chemical dumping and its hazardous effects.

Kintrell was a portly man in his fifties, with pocked skin and a tick in his shoulder. He slumped at his cherry desk and rolled his shoulders. "I'm going to call my attorney."

Matt exploded. "Do you realize what your silence has already cost? Lives, Mr. Kintrell—a lot of *lives*." He grabbed the man by his shirt collar and jerked him out of his seat. "Ivy Stanton's parents were murdered because of that land. People adversely affected by the chemicals have turned on their own loved ones. And someone has been trying to kill Ivy because she's returned to town asking questions."

Agent Blackberry reached for Matt, but Matt glared at him and shook Kintrell until his eyes bulged.

"How many more murders do you want on your conscience?"

Kintrell turned a sickly shade of green. "I was afraid there might be fallout," he admitted in a grave voice. "When Daly became ill, I...I was worried."

"Daly?" Agent Blackberry interjected.

"The head chemist who was working on the research," Kintrell muttered. "He was trying to develop a cure for cancer, and we thought we had something that would work, but the clinical studies failed."

Matt released him so abruptly the man fell into his chair. "Was Daly taking the drug himself?" Matt asked.

Kintrell nodded. "He volunteered to be a control subject. But the drug reacted with the normal body in a different way, eating away brain cells, which adversely affected his behavior. So Daly dumped the chemicals into the soil to get rid of them."

"And he never disclosed the dumping?" Matt asked.

"No, he had other projects he wanted the company to pursue. Unfortunately, he became ill." Kintrell dropped his head in his hands in defeat. "He died five years after the study began, and the company folded."

Agent Blackberry leaned forward on the desk. "And when it did, the land was sold again?"

"Yes, to Arthur Boles." Kintrell's shoulder jerked faster. "He knew about the dumping, but we were all certain any aftereffects would be long gone."

Matt cursed, and Agent Blackberry ordered the man to stand. "We need you to come with us and make a statement. There are some other folks who will want to talk to you, the environmental team I have coming for one."

"The people who bought houses on that property deserve the truth," Matt added. "You have no idea the damage your cover-up operation has created in Kudzu Hollow."

"We also need more details on the land deal and

the chemical company's work," Agent Blackberry said as he escorted him to the car.

Matt frantically punched in Ivy's number while the federal agent drove back to the station, but once again, she didn't respond. Nervous tension gripped his muscles. Where the hell was she?

Was she simply not answering because she hated him, or was she in trouble again?

Frantic, he drove to the cabin. He had to see if Ivy was there, if she was safe.

But a bad premonition clutched at his gut....

AFTER ALL THESE YEARS, it was liberating to finally reveal himself to Ivy. He'd wanted her ever since he'd made contact with her, two years before.

No, that was a lie. He'd wanted her over the years as he'd watched her grow into a woman. He'd fantasized and dreamed about having her the same way he'd had her mother, Lily Stanton. Naked. Vulnerable. Opening her legs to take him into her body.

Then begging for mercy and her life.

The fact that his own mother had raised Ivy after she'd thrown him out had infuriated him. He'd made her pay the last few years by showing up at odd hours when she was alone. He'd sworn that if she told Ivy about him, he'd kill them both, just as he had her parents.

Terrified out of her mind, she had reported to him weekly, reassuring him that Ivy didn't remember.

"George, you're scaring me," Ivy said now.

He almost laughed at her doe-eyed, innocent

look. And he could feel the fear radiating from her. That fear stirred his cock.

"You still don't understand, do you, Ivy?"

Her hand trembled as she brushed her hair from her cheek. "No, I...I'm sorry Miss Nellie sent you away. Why didn't you ever tell me? Why didn't she?"

His harsh laughter rumbled through the car as he careened to a stop in front of his old homestead. Memories of the dark days inside those walls rose to haunt him. The cries of his mother when his brother had died.

His own when she had thrown him out.

He recalled the elation he'd felt when he'd returned as an adult to make that land deal. Granted, he'd stolen the property deed from the Stantons after he killed them and forged their signatures, but he'd wanted his mother to be proud of him, had thought that she might finally acknowledge him. Instead she'd turned her back. What kind of mother abandoned her child? Why, he'd almost felt sorry for Mahoney when *his* old lady had done the same thing at his trial.

But not sorry enough to confess...

He never should have gotten tangled up with Lily Stanton. It was all her fault. She was too much temptation for any man.

But at least he'd made enough money off the first land deal to invest. He had a good eye for investment.

The sound of Ivy punching in her cell phone jerked him back to the present, and he reached out and grabbed it, then flung it out the door.

Ivy cowered against the cold leather seat. "What are you doing, George?"

He latched onto her wrist and dragged her toward him. "You're finally mine, Ivy. I'm going to take care of you just like I did your mother."

Terror registered in her eyes as she realized his words were the same ones from the threatening phone call.

"You…oh, God, no, George, don't do this," Ivy whispered. "You have to let me go."

"Not until you love me the way your mother did, Ivy." He jerked her to him, pressed his mouth over hers and kissed her hard. She struggled against him, then bit his lip. He bellowed, jerking back, any tenderness for her disintegrating.

"You'll be sorry you did that, Ivy."

"I'm sorry I ever trusted you," she said raggedly.

She reached for the car door, but he slapped her across the face. Her head flew forward and hit the dash, then he lunged toward her, grabbed her by the wrists and dragged her from the car. She screamed and shoved her foot into his groin, fighting wildly. He cursed, but she jerked free and ran toward the woods. Spurred by fury and adrenaline, he chased her, dodging tree limbs as he closed the distance.

Run, Ivy. Run like the wind or the monsters will get you.

Oblivious to where she was going, but desperate to escape, she raced through the briars and thick brush, scraping her legs and hands and arms as she struggled to escape. If she could make it to the river, maybe she could dive in and swim to safety. Rain peppered her face, its icy chill slapping her cheeks, and fear tore at her. If she did make it to the river and dove in, she'd probably die of hypothermia.

Maybe she could make it back to Lady Bella Rue's.

But then George would follow and kill the old woman. Ivy couldn't put her in danger.

Panting for air, she pumped her legs harder, fighting the darkness and pushing vines and brush out of her way. But the briars and tree limbs stabbed at her, slowing her down, and George bellowed behind her like a madman.

How could she have not seen the truth about him?

Twigs and branches snapped as he closed the distance, and she reached for a broken limb to use as a weapon, but just as she turned, he snagged her by the hair. She thrust the limb at him, but he yanked it from her, swung it down until it connected with her knees. Raw pain sliced through her kneecaps, and she fell to the ground, screaming. Still she pushed at his hands and face, trying to scratch his eyes and throat, but he slammed his fist into the side of her face, and the world spun.

He took advantage of the moment, throwing her over his shoulder and hauling her back toward the cabin. Nausea rose in her throat and she sobbed, pulling at his hair and pounding his back with her fists.

Seconds later, he swung open the door to the cabin and tossed her against the brick fireplace. She scrambled to her knees and tried to stand, but the room swayed, and it was so dark she had to blink to orient herself. He slapped her one more time, and her body bounced backward. Her head hit the jagged edge of a brick, pain sliced her skull and blood trickled down her forehead as she sank into unconsciousness.

CHAPTER TWENTY

PANIC SEIZED MATT AS HE stared at the empty cabin. Ivy's things were gone. And her tires had been slashed. So where was she?

He phoned A.J. and he sent out his deputy. They searched the woods surrounding the cabin, but found no signs Ivy had gone on foot into the woods. Besides, she had her suitcase.

Frantic, he and Pritchard returned to the police station. He hoped Ivy had gotten a ride, but fear gnawed at him.

Matt paced the sheriff's office while the agents began the interrogation again, this time with Kintrell included.

"What's the name of the developer who originally purchased the Stanton property?" Agent Gentry asked Boles.

"The head of the company was a man named Allan Parkins, but a young guy named George Smith actually brokered the deal with the Stantons. He was the only one I ever spoke with."

"Where can we find this Smith?" Agent Blackberry asked.

"He lives in Chattanooga now," Boles admitted.

"He's funded several smaller companies, some real-estate based, others not so."

The hair on the back of Matt's neck prickled. George Smith—the name didn't ring a bell, but hadn't Ivy received a phone call from a coworker named George? Could it possibly be the same man?

The door opened and Lady Bella Rue teetered in, her black veiled hat angled sideways, her long black cloak wrapped around her. When she saw the two suited federal agents, her eyes flickered perceptibly.

"Lady Bella Rue," A.J. stared. "We're in the middle of something here."

"I'm sorry to interrupt," she said, waddling on in, "but I had another bad premonition this morning."

The agents narrowed their eyes.

"Lady Bella Rue is our resident witch," A.J. said sarcastically.

"You're the lady those boys targeted, aren't you?" Agent Gentry asked.

Lady Bella Rue nodded and offered her outstretched, gnarled hand. The suits shook it, introducing themselves.

Lady Bella Rue turned to Matt, her expression grave. "Mr. Mahoney, you have to do something. Ivy Stanton is in trouble."

Matt's heart accelerated. "What makes you think that?"

"I…went by the cabin to see her and found the car there, but the tires were slashed, and she wasn't anywhere around." She worried the knots tied at her neck. "Besides, I've had this feeling all day that someone else would die tonight. That the killing wasn't over."

Matt's body went cold. He had the same feeling. He hurriedly tried Ivy's number again, but no one answered. What if this George Smith was the one who'd tried to kill Ivy? What if he'd wanted the land deal enough to cheat Lily and her husband out of the money? If Ivy had witnessed the murder, she might be able to identify him. And if he was here in Kudzu Hollow, she might have accepted a ride from him without knowing who he really was.

"Boles, tell us more about George Smith," Matt ordered. "Where is he?"

Arthur shrugged, looking haggard and weary. "I told you all I know."

"George Smith," Lady Bella Rue said, clapping one hand over her cheek. "Oh, my word, is that boy back?"

"What do you mean, *back?*" Matt asked.

She clucked her tongue. "His mama, Nellie, sent him away when he was younger. After his brother died, the boy went crazy." She leaned closer. "Some folks thought that he was possessed by the devil, that he was insane, that he even killed his brother."

Nellie? The name sounded familiar. *Miss Nellie raised me after my parents died,* Ivy had said. Dammit, could it be the same Nellie? "Who was his mother?" Matt asked.

"Nellie Smith," Lady Bella Rue said in a screechy voice. "She was so lonely she took Ivy in after her parents died. Poor little Ivy didn't have anyone else in the world, so the authorities finally agreed."

Miss Nellie was George's mother?

Miss Nellie always seemed to hold something back, Ivy had said. They'd never been close. And Miss Nellie hadn't wanted Ivy to come to Kudzu Hollow to look into her past.

Christ. What if George had killed the Stantons, and Miss Nellie had known? Maybe she hadn't taken Ivy in to atone for her son's sins, but to make sure Ivy never remembered him and revealed his identity.

RAIN POUNDED THE METAL roof, rousing Ivy from unconsciousness. Her head throbbed and the room spun in dizzying circles, white dots popping before her eyes. She blinked several times and finally managed to bring the room into focus. But when she tried to move, panic shot through her.

Her arms were tied to the rickety iron bedposts, and heavy ropes bound her ankles to the footboard. The room was dark, the old curtains faded and closed, the scent of dust and mildew swirling around her. George's familiar cologne turned her stomach.

"So you're awake now, my pretty Ivy."

At the sound of his grating voice, Ivy yanked at the ropes, but the heavy cord chewed at the skin around her wrists. George moved to the edge of the bed beside her, slid a finger along her cheek, down her throat and to the top of the flimsy white gown he'd put on her.

Tears pricked her eyelids as she noticed her clothes on the floor and realized that he had undressed her. She felt bare, naked in the garment, especially with his eyes trailing over her.

How long had she been here? Hours. Hours in which he'd touched her...

"This gown is like the one your mother wore for me," George said. "You know she was so beautiful. She taught me how to thoroughly love a woman." His fingers dipped lower to graze Ivy's nipple through the lacy weave.

"Please don't...."

"Yes, Ivy. She liked entertaining men." He smiled and moved his fingers to her other nipple. "She liked it when I did that. Liked for me to tease her. And she liked the money."

"She wanted to take me away from Kudzu Hollow," Ivy whispered. "That's what she planned to do with the money."

"Yes, and when I offered to buy the junkyard, she jumped at the chance."

"So why did you kill her?" Ivy asked.

He had a crazed look in his eyes as he paused, contemplating how to answer.

"When I came to see her that night, she had another lover in her bed."

"A.J.?"

He nodded, a muscle twitching in his jaw. "He was drunk, passed out in her bed, the asshole. I thought I was special. That she would leave your father and come with me."

"You wanted my mother to marry you?" Ivy asked, shocked. "But she was older than you—"

"Not that much older." He shrugged. "But she said I was too young. That she had plans for you. That she was leaving us all behind." He reached up and flicked the lacy top of the gown open with one finger. "Then she said she didn't want me, just wanted the money for the land."

"And that's why you killed her?" Ivy asked in horror.

"I tried to convince her she was wrong, that we were meant to be together, but she refused to listen. Then she laughed and told me to sign the papers for the deal and leave."

Ivy's head swam as the memories bombarded her. George and her mother had fought, bitterly.

"I'm taking my little girl away from this hell-hole," *her mother shouted.*

George grabbed her and they struggled. The kitchen knife lay on the table, and George picked it up and stabbed Lily in the back. Her mother's cry of terror pierced the air. Ivy ran into the room and tried to wrestle the knife from him, but he knocked her down. She saw the blood, the beet-red color, and screamed, unable to move. Her mother was dead. Then George lurched at her with the knife.

She thought she was going to die, and she froze.

"You tried to kill me that night?" Ivy said in a haunted whisper.

"But I couldn't." His self-deprecating tone rumbled out, low and husky. "I looked at you, that little girl with the big green eyes, and I couldn't do it. If I had…all these years I would have slept so much better."

"You can't kill me now, either, George. Don't you see, the violence has to stop."

"You're not a little girl now, Ivy." He twirled a

strand of her hair around his finger. "And you know everything, so I can't let you live. Just like I couldn't let Nellie."

"You…killed your own mother?" Cold terror trapped the air in Ivy's lungs. "How could you?"

"She threw me away like I was nothing," he wheezed. "And then in the end, she threatened to tell you everything. I warned her, just like I did you that night I killed Lily, that if you ever told anyone, I'd come back and finish you off."

No wonder she'd suppressed the memory, Ivy realized. She'd been terrified he would make good on his threat.

"Then I left to hunt for your father at the junkyard so he would sign the papers," he said in a rant. "But I couldn't find him."

Ivy put the pieces together in her mind. Her father had come home after George left, and found her mother dead. He'd blamed Ivy and chased her into the junkyard. She'd fallen and Matt had saved her.

Then George had seen her father in the graveyard and had killed him.

"That bastard refused to sign the papers for the land deal," George continued bitterly. "He said the junkyard was his home, and he wouldn't give it up. But he had to. Lily promised it to me. I earned the commission for the sale."

"I don't understand," Ivy said, in an attempt to stall. She had to sway George from this madness. "The junkyard is still there."

"I forged the papers," he explained. "But the deed proved that there was more property than I'd originally thought. The developer I worked for only needed half the land, so he left the junkyard intact."

George slowly turned back to her, a sadness and desperation flickering in the depths of his cold eyes that rocked Ivy to her core.

"All I wanted was for Lily to love me. And then...when my mother took you in, when I watched you grow up and saw that you looked like Lily, I wanted you, Ivy." He finished untying the lacy top of the gown and trailed his fingers over the soft swell of her breasts. "You were just as beautiful as your mother, but you were innocent. So innocent."

Ivy shuddered at his demented tone.

"I knew every date you had," he continued. "And when you never got close to anyone, I knew you weren't like your mother, that you would be faithful. I just had to convince you that we belonged together." He flicked the edges of the gown open to reveal her breasts, then bent and licked a path down her ear, her neck, to her cleavage.

"We could have built a good life together," he said in a low, heated voice. "If only you hadn't insisted on coming back to Kudzu Hollow. If only you hadn't started asking questions."

"We can still have that life," Ivy whispered. "Please just release me, George."

His sharp laughter echoed through the dim room. "It's too late, Ivy. You're no better than Lily was in the end. You crawled into bed with Mahoney." Anger hardened his voice. "And now I'm going to erase his touch, then finish what should have been done in that trailer fire." He leaned closer, so close his rancid breath bathed her cheek. Slowly and deliberately, he pressed his lips over hers and whispered, "When you die, my face will be the one you see, the last man you'll remember sliding inside of you."

Then he began to sing in a whisper:

> "One kiss, two kisses, three kisses,
> Sigh.
> Four kisses, five kisses, six kisses,
> Cry.
> Seven kisses, eight kisses, nine kisses,
> Die.
> One last kiss
> and then goodbye."

MATT'S BODY THROBBED with tension. "Let me borrow your computer for a second."

A.J. frowned but gave him a clipped nod. Matt frantically logged on to the Internet and located the Web site for Ivy's magazine, *Southern Scrapbooks.* When he'd first searched for her after being released from prison, he'd found the magazine and a photo of her online, as well as the cofounder of the magazine, George Riddon. The minutes ticked by now, every second adding to his frayed nerves as he waited for the picture to download. What if the man had Ivy? What if Matt was too late?

God, he'd never forgive himself if anything happened to her.

"Lady Bella Rue, look at this picture."

The older woman leaned over his shoulder. "What am I looking for?"

"Could this man, George Riddon, be George Smith, Nellie Smith's son?"

The bones in her cheeks protruded, leathery skin stretching over them as she frowned. "It's been a long time, but…yes, I think it could be."

"Christ."

"What is it?" she rasped.

"That man works with Ivy. He…he invested in her magazine."

A.J. peered at the screen. "Shit. I saw him in town a couple of nights ago at Red Row."

Matt swallowed, his stomach churning. He glanced up at Boles, A.J. and Lady Bella Rue. "Where would he take her?"

"His mother used to have a cabin out past mine," Lady Bella Rue said. "It's pretty deserted."

"Could you tell us how to get there?" Matt asked.

She nodded, and offered directions. A.J. jangled his keys. "Come on, Matt, I'll drive."

Matt stood and faced the federal agents. "We'll take care of Boles," Gentry said.

Agent Blackberry gestured to Kintrell. "And I'm going to question him further. He might know more than he's told us."

Right. Maybe they were wrong about George, and Matt was on a wild-goose chase. Maybe there had been a muscle man and he'd come after Ivy.

Matt and A.J. rushed out the door, tension thick as A.J. started the engine and raced toward the river. If he'd come forward sooner, and if his daddy hadn't tried to cover up for him and had confessed about the illegal chemical dumping, lives might have been saved.

Dusk approached as they raced around the mountain. Matt clung desperately to the hope that Ivy was all right, but fear trapped him in its clutches. He could still see her tormented face when she'd run from him. The pain in her eyes, which he had caused.

Even if he did save her, she might not listen to him.

The shrill sound of the siren cut into the howling wind as they closed the distance to the cabin.

IVY STRUGGLED AND FOUGHT against the bindings, but there was no way she could rip them from the posts. Finally she closed her eyes, forcing herself to focus on something other than George's vile touch as he moved his lips across her body and chanted the crude words about kissing her goodbye. Maybe if she tried hard enough she could block it all out. Just as she had years ago.

But pain and reality intruded, her body convulsing in horror at the thought of him touching her the way Matt had.

No, this was different. Matt's touch had been gentle. Loving. Meant to give her pleasure.

George's was harsh. Rough. Meant to take, not give. Meant to make her feel ugly.

Tears trailed down her cheeks, and she spat at him in disgust. Furious, he slapped her across the face. She screamed, but he smothered her mouth with his hand, and she gagged.

Matt…

Still, Matt had been with her mother, just like George.

The thought nauseated Ivy, and she sobbed, but renewed strength surged through her, and she bit her captor's hand. Salt and sweat singed her tongue, and George bellowed in fury. His eyes went wild as he hit her again, then he ripped the gown completely open and ran his hands over her naked body.

She nearly lost consciousness, but a siren split the air, and she heaved a breath, praying help was on its way.

"No!" George yelled. "They can't find us now."

Frantically, he jerked the bindings from her arms and legs free, then grabbed her. Ivy yelled out and pounded him, but he slammed his fist into her face, and stars swam in front of her eyes.

Maybe he'd go ahead and kill her, she thought just before she blacked out. Anything would be better than having to endure his touch again.

Minutes, hours later—she had no idea how long it was—she roused from unconsciousness and panic tightened every nerve in her body. The heavy scent of wet earth and kudzu nearly choked her. She tried to move, but George had tied her up again. "I can't get caught with you, Ivy." He opened the trunk of a car, tossed her inside, then slammed it shut. Ivy cried out, panting for air. She was buried beneath the kudzu. Seconds later, she smelled smoke. Tears rained down her cheeks as it seeped through the cracks of the trunk. Dear Lord.

George had set the field of weeds on fire. Even

with the light rain, if the gas tank had gas, the car might explode.

She was going to die here where her father had lost his life, and no one would ever find her.

CHAPTER TWENTY-ONE

MATT'S HEART RACED as they approached the old cabin. A.J. had flipped off the sirens and lights so they wouldn't announce their arrival. A black sedan sat in the drive, offering hope that they had at least located the man, although technically the car might belong to someone else. But the house was boarded up in front, and so far off the main road no one would know about it who hadn't visited before.

"Let's circle around back, see if there's an open door or window," A.J. said.

Matt nodded and climbed out, taking the right side while A.J. went left. Knee-high weeds and scraggly bushes surrounded the rotting wooden structure, and the torn screens on the back porch quivered in the wind. Rain had collected on the sagging porch, and fresh mud splattered the steps near the door. Someone was here or recently had been. Matt eased toward the opening, then nodded when A.J. approached with his weapon drawn, and gestured for Matt to let him enter first. The wooden planks squeaked as he stepped inside.

The eerie silence felt daunting, the smells of sweat and dust permeated the air. Matt followed close behind A.J. as they checked the kitchen, the living room, then the bedroom.

The sight of the unmade bed and Ivy's clothes discarded in a heap beside it stopped Matt cold. Blood dotted the sheets and he saw drag marks across it. What had Smith done to Ivy?

A.J. checked the tiny bath. "They're not here."

Matt spun around and raced back through the house. The car was still in the drive, which meant they had to be on foot.

"He carried her to the woods," Matt yelled, studying the heavy boot prints in the wet ground. He frantically searched for signs of Ivy's footprints, but didn't see any.

"I'll get a couple of flashlights!"

Matt didn't wait. The rain died as he darted into the woods. He listened for sounds, but heard only the whine of an animal in the distance. A.J. caught up with him and handed him a flashlight. "Ivy?" Matt yelled. "Ivy, are you out here?"

"Smith, stop!" A.J. shouted. "You won't get away."

Only the howling wind answered.

Blind fear drove Matt forward at a dead run. He had to find Ivy and save her. A minute later, he broke through the clearing, but halted when he saw the trail leading to the junkyard. George must have taken her to where he'd killed her father.

"He's going to the junkyard," Matt shouted. "Come on, we have to hurry."

Up ahead, smoke curled into the sky, and fury gripped him. "He set the kudzu on fire, A.J." Hopefully, the wet leaves wouldn't catch too quickly.

"I'll call the firemen." A.J. quickly phoned for assistance, then followed on Matt's heels, running along the river. After a while they veered onto a shortcut they both remembered from their youth. A.J.'s labored breathing cut through the air, but Matt pumped his legs harder, grateful he'd maintained a rigid exercise program in prison.

When he finally reached the junkyard, his legs ached, but the acrid smell of smoke made him quicken his pace. He spotted a man running from the small blaze toward the trailer park.

"A.J., there he is!" Matt shouted.

The sheriff darted across the property, and Matt halted. He wanted to kill the man with his bare hands, but what if Ivy was trapped somewhere in the kudzu and it burned in spite of the earlier rain?

"Ivy!" He yelled her name over and over as he plunged into the thick viny weeds, bypassing old broken-down car parts, tire rims and vehicles. Once, he'd saved Ivy's life here.

Would he be able to do so this time?

The blood roared in his ears. What if he was wrong? What if she wasn't here?

"Ivy!"

A gunshot pinged through the air, and Matt pivoted to see the man who'd been escaping drop to the ground. A.J. had shot him.

"Ivy!" Matt plowed on through the vines, flashing

the light beam ahead of him. Heat singed him as a few of the leaves caught fire. Smoke filled his nostrils but he covered his mouth and forged on, looking for any sign of movement.

"Ivy! Please tell me where you are, baby!"

A low sob caught in the howling wind. Was it the spirits the locals said roamed the junkyard or Ivy?

"Ivy?"

Matt paused and listened. And when another cry erupted to his right, he removed his pocketknife and whacked away at the choking vines as he rushed forward. He kept calling her name, then listening, letting the sound of her terrified cries lead him to her.

A heartbeat later, he whacked away a thick layer of kudzu, then wrenched at the door of a '67 Chevy, pulling it open. But Ivy wasn't inside. "Ivy!"

Banging came from the trunk, and he raced to it, then yanked it up. Ivy, dressed in a long white gown, coughed and struggled toward him. Matt's heart tripped in his chest as he untied her restraints, and she wrapped her arms around his neck.

He lifted her and ran, the fire nipping at his heels as he carried her to safety.

IVY CLUNG TO MATT as he lowered her to the gurney in the ambulance and wrapped a blanket around her. "Where is George?"

"A.J.'s taking care of him."

Through the haze of smoke, she spotted the sheriff leaning over a body. A paramedic knelt beside them, blocking her view.

"He shot him?" Ivy asked. "Is George alive?"

Matt fingered her torn gown, a muscle ticking in his jaw. "I hope so. I want to kill him myself."

Ivy shuddered and accepted another blanket the paramedic wrapped around her. While one of the EMTs took her vitals and checked her over, Matt walked toward A.J.

Ivy's heart broke all over again. In spite of the fact that Matt had slept with her mother, she was still grateful he'd been freed from jail and that George had been caught.

But things could never work out between them. Even though her heart did an odd tap dance as Matt turned back to look at her, and she knew that she would always love him.

Forgetting about him and her mother was impossible, however. She would always wonder… No, she couldn't allow her mind to travel to that disgusting place where she saw the two of them together.

But she had survived, and Matt was free now to pursue his own life. She could go back to hers.

Alone. The way she'd felt most of her life.

Back to the routines, the patterns, the rituals that had helped her overcome adversity.

Tears threatened, the horror of the past few hours and weeks too daunting to stifle, and she trembled all over.

The paramedic placed ice on the bruise on her forehead. "Are you all right now, ma'am?"

She nodded, although it was a lie. George, a man who'd pretended to be her friend, had killed her parents and almost raped her. He would have if he'd had time and hadn't heard those sirens.

And Matt…

She was heartbroken and would miss Matt terribly. But it was time she said goodbye and left Kudzu Hollow forever. There was nothing here for her but sorrow and painful memories.

MATT FELT WALLS BEING erected between him and Ivy, separating them both physically and emotionally. Guilt and regret weighed down his shoulders, but hurt still dug at his throat at the fact that she hadn't trusted him. Still, he had to talk to her in private and explain.

"Smith is dead," A.J. stated.

Matt frowned. "He didn't deserve to live, but the punishment wasn't harsh enough." In fact, he felt robbed that he hadn't been the one to kill George.

"I know you're bitter," A.J. said. "But maybe it's time to let it go, Matt."

Matt glared at his former friend, the cold rage he'd felt since he'd returned fading slightly, replaced by pity. A.J. had been a coward years ago, but today he'd helped save Ivy, and catch the man who'd tried to kill her. Matt owed him for that.

But letting go of his bitterness would take time. Anger had been his friend, his constant companion, for so long that he didn't know how to exist without it.

He stalked back to the ambulance, fury mounting at the sight of the bruises on Ivy's face and cheeks.

He gripped his hands into fists, aching to hold her and comfort her. But her wary gaze warned him not to bother, that his touch was as unwelcome as her attacker's.

The realization sickened him, reminding him of his prison days and the ugliness that had blackened his soul. He wanted the Stantons' real murderer to experience that pain, but suddenly his need for vengeance took second stage to his need for Ivy.

"She's stable, but we'll take her to the hospital for rest and observation," the paramedic said.

Matt wiped sweat from his brow. "Can I talk to her for a minute?"

The EMT cut his eyes between them, then nodded, stood and walked to the end of the ambulance.

Ivy bit down on her bottom lip. "Matt—"

"Are you all right, Ivy?" He gently touched her bruised cheek. "Did he…"

She shook her head, but shuddered, and Matt swallowed hard. She had barely missed being sexually assaulted and murdered, and it was all his fault.

"I…thank you for finding me, Matt. You were just in time."

"Don't thank me," he growled. She never would have run off alone if he hadn't hurt her. "I almost went out of my mind when I realized he had you."

"Matt, don't—"

"Don't tell you how I feel about you?" Emotions thickened his voice. "I have to, Ivy. I love you. I almost went crazy thinking that he might hurt you. That I might not see you again."

"Matt, it doesn't matter now. It's over."

His heart shattered. She was talking about more than the mystery surrounding her parents' death. "Don't say that, Ivy. I know I don't deserve you, but I love you more than I ever thought I could love anyone. I'm just sorry that you didn't trust me, that you ever thought I killed your parents."

She averted her eyes, glanced down at her knotted hands. "It won't work, Matt—"

He pressed his fingers over her lips. "Shh, you have to listen for just a minute. About what A.J. told you—"

Ivy gave him a sharp look. "I don't want to talk about my mother."

"Well, that's too bad because we're going to." Matt's voice hardened, the need to hold her driving him insane. She'd almost died, and he ached to touch her.

"Matt, please, I don't want to hear this." She covered her ears with her hands. "I had to listen to George tell me about sleeping with my mother." Her voice caught. "I understand that she was a hooker, I do, but still, I can't bear to hear the details, especially not about her and you…."

Guilt slammed into him, but he pried her hands from her ears.

"I'm sorry for all the turmoil you've been through, Ivy. But you have to hear this. Then, if you still can't forgive me or trust me, I'll walk away and never bother you again." He tipped her chin up and forced her to look at him. "I didn't sleep with your mother."

Confusion filled her beautiful green eyes. Disbelief followed, driving a knife into his already throbbing chest. "Then why did A.J. claim that you did?"

Matt shoved a hand through his hair. "Because I let him believe that I did." This was the tricky part, the part she'd have to forgive. "I did go to Red Row," he admitted in a low voice. "A.J. and I went the same night, it was a boys' thing. A stupid rite of passage into manhood, or so we thought back then."

"And my mother was a part of that passage," Ivy said in a tortured voice.

He hesitated, hated that he was hurting her, but she had to hear him out and know the truth.

"Anyway, we drove over," he said again. "A.J. went into a trailer with one hooker. Then…then I went inside with your mother."

Ivy's chin quivered, tears sparkling on her eyelashes. "Why are you doing this? I told you I don't want to hear about you and her—"

"You have to listen, Ivy." Matt's voice cracked. "When I saw your mother, all I could do was think about you and your family. I'd seen you out in the yard playing with her, in town with her buying ice cream, then outside your trailer, putting up Christmas decorations, and I…couldn't go through with it. She was a mom and you didn't deserve to have a hooker for a mother." He reached for her hand, hesitated. "I'm not proud of going there, but nothing happened, Ivy. I…swear I never touched her."

"But what about A.J.?"

Matt muttered a sound of disgust. "I didn't want to lose face, have him think I chickened out, so I never told him the truth. I just let him believe I went through with it." He cleared his throat, took her hands in his. "There's something else you should know. Your mother...she told me she was getting out, that she was taking you away so you would have a better life."

Ivy bit her lip, but tears streaked her face. "Oh, Matt, I'm sorry I didn't trust you, I was just hurt—"

"Shh." He wiped the tears from her cheeks with his thumb. "Don't cry, Ivy. I don't want to make you cry again. I never want you to hurt." He cleared his throat, bracing himself for a rejection. "And I'll understand if you don't want me now, but if you'd give me a chance, I swear I'll make something of myself. I studied law the last few years in prison, and I'm going to take the bar exam, become a lawyer, become a man you can be proud of—"

Ivy reached for his hand, gently kissed his fingers, hating that she had hurt him, too. "Oh, God, Matt, I *am* proud of you. I love you with all my heart. And you've been so wonderful to forgive me for not remembering—"

"I don't want your thanks, Ivy, just your love—"

"But I do love you. I have for a long time. Maybe forever."

He couldn't believe his ears. He gazed into her eyes, expecting to see wariness there, or regrets, but she smiled and cupped his jaw in her hands, then leaned forward and kissed him.

The tenderness and love in her touch finally dissolved the bitterness from his heart. The anger faded, once and for all.

Instead of hatred, love filled his soul as he kissed her, a love he knew would last forever.

EPILOGUE

Christmas

OUTSIDE THE CHAPEL WINDOW, a rainbow glistened over the mountain ridges, painting the sky with a myriad of bright colors, vivid greens and yellows, rich purples and blues, vibrant reds and oranges, a perfect ending to the dismal rain and gray of fall.

The colors had returned slowly to Ivy, as had other memories. Over the past few weeks, she had healed, allowing them to drift back into her mind of their own accord, accepting the unpleasant ones along with the more pleasant. Some were as fuzzy as the sky had been in Kudzu Hollow, others were as sharp and vivid as the red of the Christmas decorations, the Santas her mother had loved so much.

Life, after all, was not all black and white, and neither had Lily been. She had loved Ivy and wanted to give her a better life. Granted, Ivy didn't agree with her methods, but she had come to terms with what had happened, and had finally visited her parents' graves. She remembered seeing George kill her mother. And Matt had discovered that the state had appointed an attorney to take care of her parents' estate and the money they received from the land deal. George had taken a commission but Miss Nellie had made certain Ivy's money was put in a savings bond.

Now she intended to concentrate on the future.

Her future with Matt.

She positioned her veil on her head, cradled the bouquet of red roses in her hands, smiling at the sound of the wedding march. She and Matt had decided to marry in the Chapel of Forever that Daisy had described, then return to Chattanooga. Matt had passed his bar exam and Abram Willis had been thrilled to hire him. A.J. had resigned as sheriff, and Arthur was looking at charges for spreading gasoline around Cliff's Cabins, and negligence regarding keeping silent about the chemical dumping. Civil and criminal charges were also being filed against the owner of the defunct chemical company. And the two teenagers were facing murder charges, although the tainted drugs would play into their defense.

Music chimed and echoed around her, and she hurried to the chapel entrance. Matt's mother met her with a smile and hugged her, and Ivy's heart warmed. Mrs. Mahoney looked ten years younger since she'd reunited with her son.

"Thank you for bringing my oldest boy back to me," Eileen whispered.

Ivy pressed a gentle hand to the woman's arm, knowing she still missed her other two sons, as did

Matt. He'd even talked about searching for them. "I love Matt, Mrs. Mahoney. I want him to be happy."

"Thank you, hon. I feel like I'm gaining a daughter now, too." Eileen dabbed at her eyes, and tears pricked at Ivy's. "I…I'd like for us to be close, so if there's anything you need, just let me know."

"Thank you, Mrs. Mahoney, but all I need is Matt." Ivy glanced down the aisle, and her heart fluttered as he winked at her.

His mother rushed to the front pew to join Larry Lumbar. Daisy and Lady Bella Rue sat beside them. The church was full of Kudzu Hollow's citizens, who considered Matt a hero now that he'd exposed the land deal and chemical problems. The residents in the new subdivision had filed lawsuits, and Matt and Abram Willis were overflowing with legal work. Abram was still working on his book *Saving the Innocents*. Environmental services had jumped in to clean up the chemicals, and a special team of medical experts were evaluating each of the residents and homes in the subdivision, especially the children, to see if they could treat the symptoms and disorders caused by the long-term chemical exposure. The bluish-green glow from the kudzu was actually an afterglow of the chemical, not the spirits of ghosts or Lady Bella Rue's tears.

Although Ivy still thought Lady Bella Rue might be a seer.

But hopefully, the evil in the town had been extinguished, and the gray skies and stormy days had come to an end.

Seconds later, Ivy stood in front of Matt and

accepted his hand in marriage, a union made more precious by the years that had separated them.

Ivy's heart squeezed, the need to cry almost overwhelming her, but these were tears of joy. "Matt, you saved me when I was a little girl, then again a few weeks ago. Through all the years where darkness filled my mind, somehow you were there, hidden among the shadows. Protecting me. Leading me back here. Driving me home so I could make everything right." She swallowed hard and kissed his hand, then slid a simple gold band on his finger. "You brought the colors back into my life. You are my rainbow of reds and greens and golds. I love you with all my heart, and am yours forever."

Matt smiled, emotions shimmering in his eyes. "I first remember you as a little girl, Ivy. With bundles of long blond hair and big green eyes. As a kid, you haunted me with your goodness. As a woman, you stole my heart." He kissed her hand, then slid a diamond-studded gold band on her finger. "I once thought that my life was over. That bitter vengeance and anger were all I had to live for. But you made me whole again and gave me a future." His voice cracked. "You may think that I saved you, but, honey, you really saved me." He paused, kissed her hand again. "I promise to love, honor and cherish you all the days of our lives."

The preacher pronounced them husband and wife, and Matt took her in his arms and kissed his bride.

LATER THAT NIGHT, AS they lay in their honeymoon bed, sated from loving each other all over again, Ivy closed her eyes, a fireworks show of colors exploding in her mind.

"Ivy," Matt whispered against her neck. "I...have a gift for you."

She gazed into his eyes and her throat swelled. "You've already given me my heart's desire, Matt."

He licked the sensitive skin of her neck, then reached under the bed and brought out a package. She smiled and tore into the paper, anxious to see the gift Matt had chosen.

Her heart soared at the sight of the glittering ceramic Santa. The details were so intricately carved the figure almost looked real.

"It's beautiful, Matt." She kissed him tenderly. "I love it."

He grinned, then placed it on the nightstand by their bed. "I wanted you to have a new one for your collection."

Emotions crowded her chest. She'd finally unpacked the box of her mother's Santas and placed them on the mantel above the fireplace in her and Matt's home. The Santas were symbolic both of a painful past and of the love and hope her mother had shared with Ivy.

Matt nuzzled her neck. "I want this one to remind you that miracles really happen."

"I know they do," she whispered as she cupped his face in her hands. "Because I'm holding you in my arms."

He rolled her to her back and slid inside her, telling her with his body what they no longer needed words to say.

* * * * *

Look for Rita Herron's upcoming book
from Harlequin Intrigue,
LOOK-ALIKE,
on sale in September 2006.

And for more titles from
HQN Books and Rita Herron,
SAY YOU LOVE ME
will be out in February 2007!

*Turn the page for a short interview
with award-winning author Rita Herron,
as well as discussion questions you can use
in your book club....*

Last Kiss Goodbye
Reader and Book Club Guide

A short interview with Rita Herron

1) When did you first start writing and what inspired you to write?

I was an avid reader when I was a child, and loved the Trixie Belden mystery series. But I grew up in a rural area and didn't think writing was a career option, so I earned an early childhood education degree and taught kindergarten. There, I rediscovered my love of storytelling, began to write stories for the children, encouraged them to write and first pursued publication in the children's book market. I wrote nine books for Francine Pascal's Sweet Valley Kids series as well as articles for a children's magazine.

Then a friend turned me on to romance, and I fell in love with the genre. I've written thirty books so far!

2) Do you keep a writing schedule?

Yes, although I'm flexible, and *not* a morning person. I usually get to the computer around ten and work

most of the day, with breaks for exercise and also for
sanity purposes! But writing is a full-time career for
me, so I usually write about eight hours a day. Some
of that time may also be used for editing my own
work, researching, or "thinking" about the story—
planning is vital to producing smooth work and being
prolific.

3) What do you read?

I love a variety of types of books, from comedies to
suspense to paranormal to women's fiction. I also
enjoy folklore, local legends and weird stories about
places or people, and read nonfiction books to get
that. You'll find some of these interesting tidbits and
folklore cropping up in my books!

4) What inspired you to write Last Kiss Goodbye?

I had written a young adult book (that never sold)
awhile back and built the story around an old abandoned junkyard. I've seen so many of them in the
rural South that I began to look at them symboli-
cally. I knew I wanted to include that in my story. I
also wanted to use Southern ghost stories, and the
idea of the town being called Kudzu Hollow seemed
to fit. I had also heard an interview about a man who
had researched "the innocents"—people who had
been falsely imprisoned and later released due to
new evidence. He not only focused on the person's
lost years but on the difficulty of transitioning back

into normal life. It really made me think about those innocents, and sparked the idea for my own hero.

From there, the other characters emerged, then the title and the rest of the story.

I hope you enjoy it!

Discussion Questions

1) How would you describe this book to a friend? What drove each character to return to his/her hometown? How had the characters changed since leaving Kudzu Hollow?

2) Why couldn't the hero and heroine be together in the beginning?

3) How did the hero's and heroine's personalities/conflicts/emotions help bring them together in the end? What would you say is the climactic turning point for each character?

4) What important theme or themes run throughout the book?

5) This book has a lot of symbolism. Name at least four metaphors and describe.

6) What interesting visual elements (either object or place) have significance in the book?

7) What is the significance of the title? Is it literal or metaphorical or both?

8) In the town of Kudzu Hollow, the kudzu chokes the life out of the town and land just as the evil and lost loved ones trap the people into staying. Do you believe that evil exists? Do you think spirits are trapped so that they can't move on? Do you believe people's spirits try to communicate once the people are dead?

9) Lady Bella Rue is very superstitious and thinks she can control/change/protect the town with her potions and spells. Do you believe in the supernatural or paranormal? Witchcraft or voodoo? Do you have any superstitions? Why do you think the people are afraid of her? Because they think she's evil or because they're afraid she's right? Or because they believe she really has powers?

10) The bad weather and rains are used both literally and metaphorically. Discuss the significance of weather and setting in the story.

11) Ivy owns a magazine called *Southern Scrapbooks*. Do you make scrapbooks yourself? What kinds of things do you include? How did her job parallel her life?

12) Have you, a friend or loved one ever been wrongfully accused of something? How did you feel? Do you know someone who was falsely imprisoned for a crime he/she didn't commit? How did his/her life change?

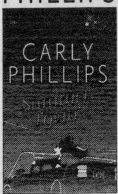

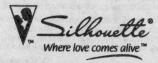

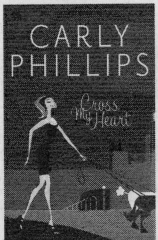

RITA HERRON

77030	A BREATH AWAY	__	$5.99 U.S.	__	$6.99 CAN.
77105	IN A HEARTBEAT	__	$5.99 U.S.	__	$6.99 CAN.

(limited quantities available)

TOTAL AMOUNT .... $ _____
POSTAGE & HANDLING .... $ _____
($1.00 FOR 1 BOOK, 50¢ for each additional)
APPLICABLE TAXES* .... $ _____
TOTAL PAYABLE .... $ _____

(check or money order—please do not send cash)

To order, complete this form and send it, along with a check or money order for the total above, payable to HQN Books, to: **In the U.S.:** 3010 Walden Avenue, P.O. Box 9077, Buffalo, NY 14269-9077; **In Canada:** P.O. Box 636, Fort Erie, Ontario, L2A 5X3.

Name: _____
Address: _____ City: _____
State/Prov.: _____ Zip/Postal Code: _____
Account Number (if applicable): _____

075 CSAS

*New York residents remit applicable sales taxes.
*Canadian residents remit applicable GST and provincial taxes.

HQN™

We *are* romance™

www.HQNBooks.com

PHRH0806BL